AGENCY AT WAR

BOOKS BY DONY JAY

<u>WARRIOR SPY THRILLER SERIES</u>
The Warrior Spy
Artifacts of Conspiracy
Agency at War

<u>NATHAN PRESS THRILLER SERIES</u>
Murder by Half

FOR *AGENCY AT WAR*

"Dony Jay proves, once again, that he is a master storyteller who—just like his protagonist Reagan Rainey—is clearly at the top of his game. In *Agency at War*, Jay brings a pulse-pounding thriller ripped right from the headlines with a brutal pace that will keep you reading well into the night. Rainey comes to life on the page in a way only a writer who has been there, done that can achieve. Bravo Zulu!"

—Andrews & Wilson, *New York Times* bestselling authors of the Tier One, Shepherds, and Tom Clancy Jack Ryan Series

"Dony Jay delivers a high-octane thriller packed with faith, firepower, and unshakable conviction. Reagan Rainey isn't just a warrior, he's a righteous force, standing in the gap between good and evil. *Agency at War* grips your soul from page one and doesn't let go until the final, pulse-pounding moment. Brace yourself for a battle where justice is more than a mission—it's a calling."

—Jack Stewart, bestselling author of *Unknown Rider*

"Dynamic action and an explosive start kick off an incendiary plot that takes us for a high-stakes romp around the globe. Reagan Rainey in *Agency at War* is a hero for the ages."

—Steve Urszenyi, bestselling author of *Perfect Shot* and *Out in the Cold*

"*Agency at War* is an outstanding high-stakes thriller that kept me on the edge of my seat until the last page. Written with rich detail and superb characterization, the author's law enforcement background shone through every scene. This is my first book by this author, but it won't be my last. Highly recommended!"

—**Colleen Coble**, *Publishers Weekly* **and**
USA Today **bestselling author**

"*Agency at War* pulls you in from the explosive first chapter and never lets go. Dony Jay crafts an espionage thriller that stands alongside the works of Vince Flynn, Brad Thor, and Nelson DeMille—yet with a distinctive worldview and a perspective shaped by his law enforcement background. His realism and attention to detail bring every mission to life. I was hooked from the start, and you will be too."

—**Bob Hamer, veteran undercover FBI agent and
the author of** *The Last Undercover*

"Dony Jay is back with another high-octane thriller that fires on all cylinders. Packed with explosive action, sharp intrigue, and a hero pushed to the edge, Jay delivers an absolute masterclass in tension and pacing. If you love non-stop action and jaw-dropping twists, *Agency At War* is your next must-read."
—**Ryan Steck, The Real Book Spy and author of Ted Bell's** *Monarch*

FOR *MURDER BY HALF*

"Razor sharp, thoroughly captivating, and just one-more-chapter addictive. A perfect reason for thriller and crime fiction fans to stay up way too late. Give me more Nathan Press, please!"
—**Tosca Lee,** *New York Times* **bestselling author of** *The Line Between*

"With *Murder by Half*, Dony Jay launches a bold and brash detective series featuring Nathan Press—a brilliant yet unconventional hero who is a heart attack for criminals but also for his bosses in Major Crimes. High stakes and action-packed, *Murder by Half* will thrill fans of Marc Cameron's Arliss Cutter series and leave readers clamoring for the next installment!"

—Andrews & Wilson, *New York Times* bestselling authors of the Tier One, Shepherds, and Tom Clancy Jack Ryan Series

"Entering a world where reality blurs and secrets lie just beneath the surface, Dony Jay's gripping and unpredictable new novel, *Murder by Half*, is a masterfully crafted thriller that will leave you breathless and reading well into the night."

—Ryan Steck, The Real Book Spy and author of *Out for Blood*

"Meticulous and masterful! With a level of precision and detail born only from real-world experience, Dony Jay has brought to life a police procedural that stands tall against the best out there! *Murder by Half* has tight, compelling action and riveting suspense. Do not miss this one!"

—Ronie Kendig, bestselling author of The Tox Files series and *Havoc*

FOR *ARTIFACTS OF CONSPIRACY*

"A smart, fast-paced thriller...fans of Joel C. Rosenberg will devour this book!"

—The Real Book Spy

"*Artifacts of Conspiracy* is all thriller, no filler. Guaranteed to satisfy the most discerning literary palate."

—Joshua Hood, author of *Burn Out* & Robert Ludlum's *The Treadstone Rendition*

"Special Forces operator Reagan Rainey is back in *Artifacts of Conspiracy*, the exciting second installment of Dony Jay's Warrior Spy thriller series. Like Joel C. Rosenberg, Jay has found the perfect balance of well-crafted military and covert operations thriller and faith-based fiction. In Rainey we see an operator true to his faith, but with the frailties and weaknesses of all of us, making a realistic character we are eager to root for. Jay has masterfully crafted a non-stop thrill ride that will keep you turning the pages well into the night. This second book in the series proves that Dony Jay is a rising star in the genre."

—**Andrews & Wilson, *New York Times* bestselling authors of the Tier One, Shepherds, and Tom Clancy Jack Ryan Series**

FOR *THE WARRIOR SPY*

"A fast-paced story, full of action and adventure."

—**Luana Ehrlich, *USA Today* bestselling author of the Titus Ray thrillers and Mylas Grey mysteries**

AGENCY AT WAR

A WARRIOR SPY THRILLER

DONY JAY

MERRY HILL
PUBLISHING

MERRY HILL
PUBLISHING

Agency at War

Published in the United States of America by Merry Hill Publishing
Cover design by Dony Jay

Scripture taken from the New King James Version®. Copyright © 1982 by Thomas Nelson. Used by permission. All rights reserved.

For more information visit the author's website at DonyJayBooks.com.

ISBN 979-8-9924645-0-4 (hardcover)
ISBN 979-8-9924645-1-1 (softcover)
ISBN 979-8-9924645-2-8 (ebook)

For President Donald J. Trump and family.
And all those bold and courageous souls
who fearlessly and honorably stand and fight for America,
for truth and justice even in the face of despicable evil.

And for God and country.

I pursued my enemies and overtook them;
I did not turn back till they were destroyed.
— Psalm 18:37

Let your plans be dark and impenetrable as night,
and when you move, fall like a thunderbolt.
— Sun Tzu

1

There they are again. Those same vans.

From behind the frosted windowpane of the Café Basil, Reagan Rainey craned his neck as a throng of pedestrians stampeded through his field of view. The two minivans had already circled the block twice within the last eight minutes and now here they were again. The vans were plain, ordinary, base-model types, likely rentals, but it was their behavior that made them stand out. And Rainey was a man who noticed such things.

Both vehicles sat idling at the intersection of East 47th and 3rd Avenues, their right turn indicators pulsing with competing rhythms. The driver of the first minivan—his eyes were dark and manic—was tapping the steering wheel with his fingertips as he waited for the traffic signal to change. The man in the front seat next to him was talking in an animated way, his clean-shaven, olive-skinned face turning back and forth from the street to the occupants seated behind him.

Rainey squinted. He counted at least three men in the back seat. The van's darkly tinted rear windows prevented him from making out their features, only their silhouettes.

A tug on the sleeve of his coat. "Earth to Reagan. What would you like? The lady's waiting."

He leaned in the direction of the voice while keeping his eyes fixed on the minivans. Was this the hypervigilance, paranoia even, they speak of? The kind that so many combat vets like him suffer from? Indeed, war can do crazy things to a person's mind. How could it be though that every instinct he had was telling him the men in those vehicles were up to something and it wasn't anything good?

"Hang on a sec, honey, okay? I'll be right back."

"What? Where are you going?" said Kayla Chapman, confusion and disbelief on her face.

He left her standing there in front of the Asian woman waiting to take their order, pushed through the door, and stepped outside into the bright and bustling New York City morning. The crisp, mid-December air instantly transformed his even breaths into small, nickel-colored clouds that drifted upward and away from his bearded face. A swarm of yellow taxis buzzed past him from right to left. He pushed his hands into his pockets as he scanned the sidewalk with a seemingly casual glance, something he had mastered long ago.

He took in every face and posture, every passing vehicle, but in large part Rainey's attention remained on the minivans. Just like the two previous times, the minivans turned north onto 3rd Avenue. As the first vehicle made the turn, the front passenger stared down a pair of NYPD beat cops who were ambling down the sidewalk in the opposite direction. The man twisted in his seat and continued watching them as the van drifted past. It was then that Rainey saw it: the muzzle of an AK-47, its familiar front sight, barrel, and gas tube jutting upward against the dash. With so much time downrange, Rainey would recognize it anywhere.

In the next instant, the man suddenly turned back toward the windshield, and the rifle was gone. Was this really happening? Was he just seeing things? No. This was real. The front passenger was armed with an AK. And that could only mean bad things were about to happen.

For a fraction of a second, Rainey considered poking his head back into the café and telling Kayla to stay put and stay down, but there was no time for that.

He sprinted into the street just as the second minivan completed its turn onto 48th Avenue. Tires screeched in protest. Horns honked with the rhythm of a fibrillating heart. He ignored them all. Rainey called out to the two police officers as he ran. "Hey! You got trouble! C'mon!"

The cops whipped their heads around and stopped, gave him a strange look—there were lots of kooks in the Big Apple—then, seeing he wasn't sticking around to explain himself, took off after him.

Rainey raced around the corner onto East 48th Avenue. He expected the minivans to be about twenty yards ahead of him, but they must have sped up in the meantime. They were already halfway down the block. He charged forward with even greater urgency, yelling for people on the sidewalk in front of him to get out of the way. The second minivan disappeared around the corner onto 2nd Avenue as he reached midblock.

He pumped his arms and legs as hard as he could, already feeling the heat of his exertions on his forehead and back.

———

Salim Hariri peered back at the two policemen, praying that Allah would keep the infidels oblivious to their presence. Somehow, despite their careful planning, they had gotten to the target several minutes too soon, so he'd told Ali to drive them around the block until the proper time. His orders were clear. He was to commence the attack at precisely 8:30 a.m. If he and his men were early or late, even just by a minute, their families would not receive a penny of the promised martyr's reward. *A good soldier of Allah is always punctual,*" his handler recited often.

Hariri glared at the policemen for a few more seconds. Finally satisfied his men had not drawn their suspicion, he turned back toward the dash. He gripped his AK-47, flipped the safety catch up and down several times with his right index finger, finally making sure it was in the down position. His body was alive with nervous energy. This was not Lebanon or the training camps in Iran, after all. This was America—New York City, the very heart of the Great Satan.

Hariri checked his watch as they turned onto East 48th Avenue. "Okay, Ali. We have twenty seconds. Pick up the speed."

Rainey didn't know if the cops were on his heels or not. He prayed they were at least on the radio by now. As he ran, he considered the fact that he had no gun. With all the museums and tourist hotspots he and Kayla had planned to visit, carrying a pistol—and setting off countless metal detectors—would have just been a humongous hassle. Consequently, the only weapon he had on him was his Fox Knives OD green folding karambit. A weapon, yes, but far easier to explain than a firearm.

He took the corner onto 2nd Avenue so fast that his momentum nearly carried him into a slow-moving group of senior citizens on a walking tour. As Rainey wove around and through them, he caught a second pair of police officers in his peripheral vision. The two uniformed men—one Black, one of Asian descent—were trotting beneath the sidewalk scaffolding on the east side of the street. The first pair of cops must have put out a radio broadcast.

Rainey hollered to them, pointed down the street. "The two Dodge minivans about a block up! The guys inside are armed with AKs!" Again, he didn't stick around to elaborate. Instead, he blazed forward through the small crowd of people gathering on the street corner, waiting en masse for traffic to clear so they could cross to the other side. Some faces exhibited fear and confusion at his sudden exclamation. A heavyset lady with a chubby, overgrown toddler clinging to her leg swung her handbag at him and spouted off a string of vulgarities as he shot past.

Rainey hopped a few times between strides, searching for the minivans in earnest. He caught sight of them as they sped across East 47th Avenue. A chorus of horns erupted ahead of him as the first van came to a sudden stop in the middle of the street directly in front of a tall, black building bearing the label *2 Hammarskjold Plaza*. At the same time, the second minivan swerved to the left, plowing into a man on a bicycle before skidding to a stop on the wide, brick walkway adjacent to the building. The sliding doors on both vans whipped open and heavily armed men spilled out of them. People were already screaming when the opening salvo of automatic gunfire came, its riotous jackhammering drowning out the din of the morning bustle.

Terror had returned to America's shores.

2

Hariri and the seven other men from his vehicle burst onto the pavement. After weeks of rehearsals, they knew their assignments well. Two of them would remain outside while the rest, including Hariri, hopped the sidewalk and ran toward the front entrance of the target building.

A security guard in a black blazer appeared on the opposite side of the wall of glass that fronted the street. Recognizing the immediate threat, the guard swept the side of his blazer back and reached for the pistol on his hip when in a blink the left side of his head exploded. But this was no surprise to Hariri. In fact, this was part of the intricate and well-choreographed plan to storm the building.

As Hariri and his men charged through the revolving door, a well-groomed man of Middle Eastern descent in a wool overcoat, dress slacks, and expensive loafers, who to this point had been standing just inside the door fumbling with his gloves and scarf on this side of the body scanners, moved swiftly toward the receptionist at the lobby's front desk. He pointed his SIG Sauer SP 2009—the gun he had just used to put down the security guard—and fired repeatedly into her. She fell behind the counter with a thud.

The dapper man—Farooq was his name—spirited behind the desk and made sure the receptionist had not activated any alarms. He then pressed a series of buttons that effectively locked down the elevators in the lobby. Now no one could go up or, more importantly, down the elevators. Other teams of men at this very moment were already securing the levels below the street and the lesser-known entry and exit points of the building. There was no escape now for their target.

Farooq looked up at Hariri and uttered in rapid Arabic, "You are good to go. May the blessings of Allah be upon you!"

Hariri had already relieved the dead security guard of his secure-access proximity card, which would permit him and his team entry to every floor in the building. But the only floor Hariri really cared about was the fifth. He and his men were now standing by a door that would take them to a secure set of stairs and onward to their target. He nodded while waving the card in front of the sensor for the electronic lock. "May they be upon us all, my brother."

Then Hariri and his team disappeared through the door.

———

Rainey ducked while sprinting for cover behind the right rear wheel of a city bus. The large vehicle was boxed in by the chaos created by wrecked and stranded vehicles and people fleeing in desperation. When no rounds came his way, he stepped onto the bus tire and hoisted himself upward, so he could see through the bus windows to the plaza on the other side of the street. Armed men had taken up various positions. They were shooting at anything that moved. The piercing cracks of gunfire echoed back and forth against buildings that reached up to the heavens.

One of the AK-toting men turned, walked toward the bus. Rainey recognized the look in his eyes. It was that of pure hatred. The man shouted something in Arabic then ripped off a volley of 7.62mm rounds, sweeping his muzzle back and forth down the length of the bus. Rainey dropped to the sidewalk behind the bus wheel and made himself as small as he could. Men, women, and children, who were already screaming at the top of their lungs, fell silent for all eternity as hot lead from the man's rifle shredded their bodies. A mixture of high-velocity blood spatter and glass particles wafted from the blown-out windows above him. Blood and chunks of bone and flesh and brain matter dotted the pavement and adjacent sidewalk all around.

Rainey took a deep breath and swallowed hard as he considered the innocent lives that these terrorists had so brutally just taken. These men, whoever they were, would certainly take many more unless they were stopped. Unless *he* stopped them. Righteous fury consumed his every fiber. He wanted to kill every last one of them.

He peered through the now glassless window frames and caught sight of the terrorist who had just killed those inside the bus. The man paced toward the front of the vehicle. It was apparent that he was headed around it on his way to the sidewalk. If the gunman continued on this course, he would easily see Rainey crouched beside the bus.

Rainey slipped out of his coat, dropped it beside the bus wheel. He needed to be able to move freely. Keeping his eyes on the terrorist, Rainey poked his right index finger through the black metal loop protruding from his right front pants pocket. He pulled up on it swiftly causing the karambit to snap open. The curved blade extended out and away from the bottom of his fist such that he could still deliver a punch while gripping the knife. Rainey looked right, checking for windows on the street in which the man might see his reflection. None were intact, however; they had already been shot out.

Darting forward, Rainey paused beside the bus's front wheel until the man's muzzle protruded around the corner of the vehicle. Then he was on him. With his left hand, Rainey latched onto and pushed the business end of the rifle down and away, so that even if a round went off, he would be out of the line of fire. The surprise attack caused the terrorist to stumble forward. At the same time, while maintaining control of the rifle's muzzle, Rainey delivered three lightning-quick punches to the man's face followed by a fourth that was not a punch at all. With this last blow, Rainey drove the razor-sharp karambit through the right side of the man's neck, shredding tissue and vessels alike. Rainey kept the blade moving, sweeping it next across the inside of the man's bicep, the purpose being to sever the man's brachial artery. Blood already pulsing from the gaping wound in the man's neck, painted long arches down the side of the bus.

Rainey twisted the gun from the doomed man's withering grasp. With the knife still looped around his index finger, he gripped the rifle with both hands and delivered a vicious butt-strike to the side of the man's head that rendered him unconscious but still pumping blood onto the street.

Rainey knelt, scanned for immediate threats then secured his knife. He removed the magazine from the gun and found it almost empty. Staying low, he rolled the terrorist over and pulled four fresh magazines from the pouches of the man's tactical vest, snapped one into the rifle, and shoved the other three into his back pants pockets. It was then that he realized something terrifying. Below the tactical vest, the man was wearing an explosive-laden suicide belt. Rainey quickly located the bomb's trigger mechanism: a small plunger that was threaded through the webbing of the vest and taped to one of the black Nylon straps at the center of his chest probably so he could reach it with either hand. *Thank God they're not using dead-man switches.*

Rainey again scanned for threats. The two NYPD guys he had initially hailed over on 3rd Avenue were farther down the sidewalk. Both were crouched down behind a white work van that had been turned into Swiss cheese. Rainey waved to get the cops' attention then signaled for them to stay put before turning back toward the first minivan. Another terrorist walked into the street, approached a Honda Camry. The driver was hunched behind the steering wheel, panic-stricken and frozen in place. The terrorist stepped closer and raised his weapon. He fired a burst of rounds into her then moved farther into the intersection as if he were just out for a nice stroll.

Rainey shouldered the rifle, aimed at the man's right ear, and squeezed the trigger. The terrorist's head jerked to the side, and he collapsed to the ground.

Rainey immediately swept his muzzle to the left and engaged another terrorist. He pulled the trigger in two rapid but smooth motions. The first burst of rounds hit the man in the center of the chest, the second tore into his throat and lower jaw. Rainey dropped into a combat crouch, scrambled to a different position of cover then reassessed his field of fire for new targets.

3

Ryan Killian and his wife Lacey had been sitting in the back of a cab on East 47th just east of 2nd Avenue when the shooting began. Their driver was killed instantly in the first hail of gunfire during which time they had managed to scramble out the back of the vehicle. They couldn't go far without the risk of being hit themselves, so they had taken refuge here on the side of the car opposite the shooter.

An automatic rifle crackled from somewhere nearby. Killian instinctively covered his wife with his own body. When the shooting stopped, he opened his eyes and immediately spied two of NYPD's finest behind a tiny SUV that was directly in front of their cab. One of the officers had been shot in the face. His partner was screaming and trying to pull him back behind cover, but the man was clearly already dead.

The terrorist who had done the shooting stepped into the street from the plaza and fired again on full auto. Rounds decimated the little vehicle this time finding the second officer. His lifeless body rolled backward and away from the SUV. The terrorist continued around the vehicle, where he paused to fire another round into each of the officers then turned his attention down the sidewalk to the north. He seemed to be unaware that Killian and his wife were hunkered down no more than thirty feet behind him.

Killian held his index finger to his lips then steadied his wife's trembling hands. Tears tumbling from her eyes, she mouthed the word *no* and offered a silent plea for him to stay with her. Killian cupped her face in his hands, leaned forward, and kissed her forehead. He held her there for a few seconds then whispered into her ear, "I love you." At last, he managed to pull away from her, still unnoticed by the terrorist. This was no time to cower in fear. It was time to act. And do so decisively.

Killian quietly crawled to the first officer who lay dead in the street. He retrieved the Glock that the man still partially held in his hand then without hesitation, using a two-handed grip, aimed for the back of the terrorist's head. He squeezed the trigger, and the weapon responded. The heavily armed terrorist fell forward onto the sidewalk and didn't move.

The pop of a pistol drew Rainey's attention. Its sound was distinct from that of an AK. His eyes darted to a man—one of the terrorists—just in time to see him fall out of sight on the far side of a row of vehicles. *One of the cops must have drilled him. Way to go, guys!*

Tucked behind cover, Rainey scanned the street, the plaza, the front of the building into which the men from the first minivan had run. There was a well-dressed man drifting around the lobby. He didn't seem to fit. Number one, he was still alive after gunmen had just stormed the building. Number two, he was far too composed in the chaos to not be working with the terrorists. And three, Rainey could now plainly see, he was holding a pistol in his right hand.

Hedging around the front end of a Chevy sedan, Rainey shifted the front sight post of the AK about thirty degrees to the left and fired. All at once, his rounds carved a large hole in the glass and ripped into the man's chest, turning his white dress shirt into a bloody mess. The man tumbled backward over a burgundy velvet queue line which caused several connected stanchions to fall to the shiny marble floor already slick with spilled blood.

The commotion caused several of the terrorists out of view to snap their heads toward Rainey's position. One of them spotted him and started shooting immediately. Rainey withdrew behind the Chevy's small engine block as rounds hammered all around him, blowing out tires and throwing off sparks and bits of the vehicle. His nostrils were suddenly filled with a mixture of gunsmoke and the sweet odor of engine coolant. Rainey waited for a break in the man's fire. When it came, he leaned out and ripped off a quick burst of his own then ducked back behind cover. Immediately, Rainey spun and speed-crawled to the back of the vehicle, paused, then sprinted behind a black pickup truck where he performed a speed reload. A second terrorist let loose this time but was still focused on Rainey's prior location—a classic mistake in a gunfight. Rainey popped out and lit up the right side of the man, who twisted and fell to the ground in a lifeless heap.

Rainey flattened himself to the pavement and watched for movement beneath the truck he was using for cover. Soon the lower legs of two of the gunmen came into view. Rainey fired into them then quickly rolled up to his feet. Both men were writhing around on the ground as he raced over to them. He delivered headshots in rapid succession before either one could activate his suicide vest. As Rainey ran back to cover, he caught sight of another gunman, who immediately leveled his carbine and fired. Rounds chipped the sidewalk, slammed into a light standard while others snapped past him. Rainey changed direction and dove over a low-slung wall at the corner of the building just as bullets chewed into a tan marble barrier.

―――――

Ryan Killian couldn't believe his eyes. Some crazy civilian armed with an AK-47 had just taken out two of the terrorists by shooting them in the legs, then, as they were down, ran up to them and shot them in the head. The guy was like a machine.

A killing machine.

It suddenly occurred to him that this crazy dude wasn't just some crazy dude. No way. He moved and shot like no one Killian had ever seen before except for maybe in the movies. He was a mixture of speed, violence of action, and decisiveness. His movements and tactics demonstrated highly specialized training. The man could be a soldier—a soldier of *good* fortune—who like him had been in the right place at the right time and had decided to fight back.

Killian jolted as one of the terrorists began shooting at the soldier. Then in another flash of comprehension, he noticed the man was wearing something around his waist. He'd seen pictures of suicide belts in training schools, in books, and on the internet.

His eyes shot right. Two uniformed cops were advancing toward the terrorist who was still firing at the tan-colored wall and the good guy behind it. The cops were using a GMC Yukon for cover in their approach. Killian waved to get their attention. When he had it, he motioned as if to say, "They're wearing suicide belts! Head shots!" The officer closer to him nodded then turned and relayed the message to his partner. Still, they were too far away, their pistols well out of effective range. Unless they got off lucky shots, the terrorist could easily turn and cut them down. Or detonate his belt.

Killian quickly scanned the plaza. He had no idea how many gunmen there were, but it appeared that a good number of them were down. People screamed in the distance amidst an occasional burst of gunfire, but the only terrorist that was moving within his field of view was the man shooting at the soldier trapped behind the wall.

Now's my chance.

Rainey scrambled about twenty yards along the wall, scuffing his hands and knees as he went. A fist-size object suddenly dropped ten yards in front of him, causing him to stop in his tracks. It was too far away to pick up and toss back before it detonated, so he chose the only viable option he had. He dove back over the wall, landing in a small patch of shrubbery and mulch just as the grenade went boom.

The explosion left a high-pitched tone coupled with the droning sound of static in his ears. He shook his head, trying to make the white noise stop. Bullets nipped at the leaves and thin branches all around him. The terrorist's gun chatter was now muted pops, like fireworks in the distance. The concussed air from the explosion had also disoriented him. He smacked the ground around him, searching for the AK, but couldn't find it. As the fuzziness in his mind began to abate, he reasoned that he must have left it on the other side of the wall. With no gun, no cover, and the only possibility of concealment being the leaves and twigs of a few lousy shrubs, he knew he was toast. Then came a moment of unexplained silence. Rainey whipped his head to the right, his fierce, brown eyes quickly landing on his adversary.

Well, this is it.

The terrorist must have reloaded the rifle with a fresh magazine. He was just now bringing the stock back up to the pocket of his shoulder. There was nowhere for Rainey to go. Nothing to use for cover.

Rainey rolled onto his knee, slowly stood with his chin raised in defiance. He would not run. He would not be shot in the back. With eyes brimming with intensity and unstoppable resolve, he fixed his gaze on the face of evil, flicked out his knife, and prepared to charge. At least he would have the honor of dying a soldier's death.

Killian scanned left and right then regained his feet. He took a few quiet steps toward the terrorist, who was still facing away from him. The gunmen now plucked a grenade from his vest and tossed it behind the wall. The blast wave was largely deflected, but Killian still felt a punch to his sternum. The terrorist pivoted to the left toward the man who had just dove back over the wall and into his field of fire, took aim, and pulled the trigger. After two loud cracks, the gun fell silent. The terrorist jerked his head downward, performed a well-rehearsed magazine change. With a fresh 30-round mag, the terrorist charged the rifle and leveled it once more at the man in the bushes, who by now surely must have understood his perilous situation. Killian watched the soldier stand and fearlessly, defiantly stare back at his would-be killer. The terrorist smiled and pulled the stock of his rifle tighter into his shoulder.

No!!!

Killian broke into a furious sprint. He was twenty-five yards from the armed man when he raised the pistol and began firing. His first round grazed the terrorist in the back of the head, his second the shoulder. The third, fourth, and fifth rounds connected with the terrorist's upper left arm and chest. His eyes wide and face a mask of wild determination, Killian continued to fire as the vest-clad man turned toward him, the AK-47 still held firmly in his grasp.

At first, he felt nothing then all at once his chest was on fire. Despite the adrenaline still flowing through him, he knew he'd been hit and hit badly. He staggered, fell forward. Killian now lay face down on the ground beside the terrorist. Both were still breathing but in a labored way. Killian gritted his teeth and tried to will away the agonizing pain charging through his body. His vision grew blurry. And yet he was still able to register the movements of his dying foe. The man's face shivered with hate, with resolve. He was reaching for something. A trigger mechanism.

The suicide belt.

With the last bit of strength he could muster, Killian lifted the pistol an inch off the sidewalk, steadied it for a second then fired a single round into the terrorist's left temple. His hand lurched backward with the kick of the gun. A hot breath of gunsmoke curled upward from the muzzle into the cold winter air. He held the gun there for another moment until the weight of it exhausted his muscles. His fingers still wrapped around its grip, he let his hand fall to the rough surface of the plaza. Killian stared at the terrorist he had just killed. He had never felt such animus for another human being.

One of the cops nearby bellowed out a string of exclamations, which just so happened to be the same coarse word several times over. The other was yelling into the lapel mic of his radio.

Next, Killian sensed a pair of hands tugging at him, yet he felt nothing. At last, Lacey's voice registered in his brain.

Lacey. My beautiful Lacey.

"Ryan! Ryaaaan! No! Don't you die! Please! *Please!* Ryaaaaaaaan!" She was sprawled over him, clinging to him, shaking him. She screamed again, this time even louder.

But he was already gone.

4

C ar alarms and sirens from responding emergency vehicles wailed without ceasing. Rainey rushed over to the man who had just saved his life. A pretty woman who looked to be in her mid-thirties was already weeping at his side. Meanwhile, several paces away, two of New York City's finest, pistols drawn and scanning for threats, directed personnel into the area.

It was bedlam.

A loud boom emanated from somewhere east of their location. Screws and hex nuts—tiny instruments of death—came skittering across the veneer of the plaza. A terrorist unseen had just detonated his suicide belt. There were victims everywhere—in the street and in the plaza, in vehicles, on vehicles, even under vehicles. Some of the wounded were screaming, some crying, while others walked around in circles with a look of confusion on their blood- and grime-smeared faces. Suddenly, the fifth-floor windows of the building looming overhead blew out.

"Take cover!" Rainey scooped up the sobbing woman over her emotional protestations and ran back toward the knee-high wall. He paused just long enough to step over it, then, tramping over bits of broken window glass, rushed into the safety of the building's lobby thankful that the exploded grenade had created a readymade escape route. The cops scrambled inside, too, just as a torrent of glass and metal rained down all around them.

He gently laid the woman down. "Are you okay?"

The woman's disheveled hair partially covered her face. Her makeup was smeared, her eyes filled with desperation. "He might be alive! Please! Ryaaaan!" She attempted to get up and run back out into the debris that continued to fall.

But Rainey refused to let her go. He pulled her into his chest and held her there firmly. "No. No, no. He's gone. There's nothing you can do for him now." Her body went limp in his arms and she wept uncontrollably. Rainey gazed out at the carnage. He pressed his cheek against her head and spoke in a low, deliberate voice. "He saved my life. I won't forget it. I'm going to get the people who did this. I promise you."

The chaos continued to grow as emergency personnel began flooding into the area. Rainey eased the woman back, held her by the shoulders, and looked deep into her eyes. "Be strong." He then allowed a police officer to wrap her in his coat and usher her deeper into the room away from the commotion.

Rainey pivoted and examined the lobby. He kept his head tilted down in order to avoid the surveillance cameras that were doubtless mounted about the large room. The well-dressed man he'd killed moments ago lay sprawled on the floor in a tangle of velvet rope, one leg extended across the thin burgundy carpet runner that shot toward the entranceway. Rainey paced over to him and knelt, rummaged through the man's pockets. Save for a single hand grenade, he found nothing. With the chaos still swirling around him, he rolled the man over. Using the camera on his mobile phone, he snapped several photos of the man's face at various angles. Finally, Rainey glanced up just enough so he could take a good look around. He was about to stand when suddenly there was an enormous blast that shook the earth beneath him.

That was no suicide belt.

Rainey tucked his chin into his collarbone and slipped outside. He trotted past the Turkish restaurant next door, turned the corner onto 46th Avenue, and at that moment glimpsed an ominous gray-white cloud of dust and detonated explosives drifting upward against a backdrop of brilliant blue sky. The slight December breeze was already pushing it out over the East River. Soon, the entire sun was eclipsed sending a lightning bolt of grief, fear, and loss charging through him. He didn't know exactly what had happened, only that America had been struck again. For a moment, thoughts of 9/11 flooded his mind and the only thing he could feel was a fresh surge of adrenaline releasing into his system. Then white-hot rage.

Whoever did this, you had better run. Because I'm coming for you.

5

Rainey stepped out of David's Cleaners on 46th Street wearing a navy-blue suit jacket and sandstone slacks that were about two inches too short. He had stuffed his bloody clothing—including his discarded coat, which he had managed to scoop up from the street—into a plastic garment bag that was now tightly rolled up and tucked under his arm. He trotted over to a bicycle that lay abandoned in the street. After tying the knotted end of the garment bag to his belt, he mounted the bike and set off toward the East River.

When he reached United Nations Plaza, he turned south and really put his legs into the pedals. He had to get away from the swarm of emergency responders—police, state, and federal investigators—who were doubtless already flocking to the area to begin the tedious job of sifting through the detritus to make sense of what had happened and why. He had no qualms about what he had done to the terrorists, but if he were stopped, it would invariably lead to questions and likely an official request from police to produce identification. Sure, he had a few business cards on him for his cover job here in the States, but he carried no forged documents, no false ID, or passport as he would if he were operating overseas. And while he had nothing to fear as far as arrest was concerned, if he were identified by police, or worse yet, by the media, his career as America's best secret weapon would be over. And his life would forever be in danger. The same could be said for his family.

He had to get out of the area. And fast.

His cell phone vibrated against his chest. He allowed himself to coast as he fished it out of the borrowed jacket's inner breast pocket and examined the screen. It was then that he noticed several unanswered text messages from Kayla.

Where r u?

Reagan?

Hellooooo?

Whats wrong?

Omg. Whats going on? R u okay?

Reagan???

He swiped his finger across the screen, allowing the call to connect. "Hi, Kay."

"Reagan! Where are you!? What's happening? I heard machine guns and what sounded like bombs going off! There are people running all over the place! There are cops every—"

"Kayla."

"Why did you run off like that? Where, what—"

"Kayla! Listen to me!" His voice carried more force than he had intended. When she fell silent, he softened his tone. "Are you okay? You're all right?"

"Yes. I'm fine. But—"

"Where are you?"

"I'm at the hotel. I got scared when I heard all the shooting, so I ran back here."

"Okay. Good. Sit tight for now."

"What happened? Where are you?"

"I'll explain when I see you. Right now, I have to go."

"Reagan, I—"

"I'm sorry, hon, but I really have to go. I'll call you back as soon as I can." He paused then said, "Kay... I love you."

"I love you, too, Reagan."

The fear in Kayla's voice only compounded his anger. He had never heard her sound so frightened.

He next dialed a number from memory. The call connected after two rings.

"Yes?" The man on the other end seemed hurried.

"It's me. I take it you've seen what's happened in New York."

"New York, Chicago, and Los Angeles. We've been hit in three cities, Ray."

Rainey tried to process this. *Three cities.* Finally, he said, "Well, I'm here. Now. In New York, I mean. I was there when everything went down. On Second Avenue."

There was dead silence then, "Are you okay?"

"Yes, I'm fine. I'm sending you some photos of one of the men involved. See what you can do with them. I have to get Kay then I'm heading home."

"All right, call me as soon as you get back."

Rainey leaned into a right turn and coasted. "Will do." He ended the call, dropped the phone into his jacket pocket then resumed his furious peddling in a somewhat circuitous route back toward Kayla through streets knotted with people, vehicles, and the expanding turmoil of another terrorist attack perpetrated on American soil.

Three cities.

Unreal.

———

Rainey had a good sweat going when he arrived at the 58th Street entrance of his hotel. On any other day and under any other conditions, his mismatched attire in a place like the Park Lane Hotel would have drawn a bevy of puzzled looks, but like most people in New York City and the rest of the country right now—the world even—all eyes were on the closest television screen. It was for that reason that he made it to his hotel room on the 42nd floor with nary a passing glance from fellow guests or the dutiful hotel staff.

Keying into his room, he quickly pushed inside and stripped out of his clothing. He walked to the bathroom, dropped his karambit in the vanity, and turned on the faucet, letting the hot water wash over it. The polished white sink ran red with blood. Rainey recalled the man he had killed with it as he twisted it back and forth under the water. He felt nothing for the man. Nothing but rage, that is. Even now, he could see the terrorist's murderous eyes staring up at him from the sidewalk, blood gushing from his wounds. Rainey's thoughts were replaced by the man who had sacrificed his life to save his. He thought of the woman he presumed to be his wife, her face, racked with agony and grief. It would come to haunt his dreams in the ensuing weeks and months.

Rainey carried on efficiently, his face a mask of concentration. Steam rose against the mirror, clouding his reflection. He opened and closed the blade several times, loosening the stickiness from the hinge mechanism. With his toothbrush, he scrubbed the last of the blood from its nooks and crannies, ran scalding hot water over it once more then quickly dried it with a hotel hand towel before leveling his eyes on his shed clothes, which lay in a small pile on the floor. He scooped them up and shoved them into an extra garbage bag he had pulled from the bottom of the bathroom trash can. Before stepping into the shower, he washed his hands then quickly padded back to the bedroom and tapped out a brief text message to Kayla, letting her know he was back in his room and that they would be checking out in less than an hour. In brief, he told her to get packed. Two minutes later, as he was toweling off, he heard knocking on his door. He threw on a fresh set of pants and leaned into the peephole. Kayla stood there expectantly, kneading the backs of her hands. The anxiety in her eyes was obvious.

As soon as he pulled the door open, Kayla burst inside. Before he could utter a word, she latched onto him. Rainey held her tightly against his bare chest, swept a strand of her lustrous brown hair from her face when she'd finally leaned back and looked up at him.

"What's going on, Ray? What happened? People on the news are saying there's been a terrorist attack."

Rainey closed the door and ushered her farther into the room.

"They're right, aren't they? There *has* been an attack. That's why you ran out of the café? You saw it coming, didn't you? You saw them, the men who did it?"

Letting her questions hang in the air, Rainey pushed his damp head through the collar of a plain white T-shirt, yanked it down, and smoothed it against his lean, powerful frame. The look on his face was businesslike and all the confirmation he would offer. "I need to get home, Kay."

"I don't understand. Why? What's going on?"

"I just need to get home. I'll explain later."

Kayla relented with a crestfallen nod. "Okay, but... The trains are probably a nightmare. That's assuming they're even still running. And flights around the city are probably grounded."

"Yes, I know." With his thumb, Ray wiped a droplet of water from her forehead and forced a smile. For better or worse, Reagan Rainey hid his emotions well. He always could. Rather than conveying a sense of alarm or revealing the anger that still coursed through him, he was calm and unflappable. For the most part, his face was an empty page.

"Are you packed?"

"Yes."

"Good." Rainey leaned into her and gently kissed her lips.

"What are we going to do?"

"We'll drive home."

"How? Rent a car?"

Rainey nodded. "In a manner of speaking."

He sat on the bed and reclaimed his phone from the nightstand. There was a new text message waiting to be read. He unlocked the device and tapped open the messaging app.

Car will be out front in 20 min. Black Jeep GC.

Rainey fired off a quick response. *Ok. Thx.*

"Who's that?" said Kayla, trying to steal a glimpse of the screen.

Rainey darkened the device and shoved it into his pants pocket. He reached for a pair of athletic socks on his closed suitcase. "A friend."

He didn't bother to mention—nor could he—that that friend was Job Jackson. He also refrained from telling her that Job had phoned the local DX office, which was tucked away in a rather large building on Fifth Avenue a few blocks south of Rockefeller Center, and arranged for a car to be delivered to the hotel for Rainey's use.

"Don't worry, Kay. You're safe with me."

If she was curious about Ray's mysterious *friend*, she didn't mention it.

Using the hotel room phone on the nightstand, he dialed the front desk. As he waited for the call to connect, Rainey zipped up the pockets of the suitcase beside him on the bed, which Kayla then pushed aside so she could sit next to him. She tilted her head to the left and rested her cheek on his shoulder, took his free hand in hers and interlaced their fingers.

Without preface, Rainey alerted the hotel staff that he and Miss Chapman would be checking out of their rooms early and asked that any outstanding charges be promptly charged to his credit card. After a few moments of silence, he doled out a polite thank you and returned the receiver to its cradle. It was then that he glanced up at the muted television on the credenza.

Kayla traced his fingers with her own, stroked the rough sinews of his palm, then drew his hand against her chest. She held it there with an unfocused gaze in the direction of a framed black-and-white print on the wall at the far side of the room. In the reflection of the mirror on an adjacent wall, Rainey studied her face as though she were a priceless work of art. A rendering of absolute perfection. She may have been a tomboy at heart, but Kayla Chapman was a bombshell and Rainey thanked God to finally have her back in his life. He also detected something else. It was subtle, but he could sense it. Kayla was off somewhere in another world. His attempt at reading her thoughts was quickly interrupted by a breaking news alert that flashed in a bright red banner on the TV. Rainey pressed a button on the remote and sound from the broadcast filled the room. A warning appeared at the bottom of the screen. *Graphic footage of terror attack in NYC. Viewer discretion strongly advised.* A moment later, the view of the anchor desk in the newsroom was replaced by a video clip that someone had obviously captured with their phone. A small citation in the lower left corner indicated that the video had been submitted by a viewer—a viewer who had to have been standing at a window several floors up in one of the buildings across the street from 866 Second Avenue when the first crackle of gunfire transformed the otherwise typical New York City morning into a battlefield.

Rainey's eyes narrowed. His breath caught in his lungs. It was at this same moment that Kayla broke from her reverie and turned toward the screen. Rainey would later remember this instant as being one of the most pivotal in his life. And one of the few times he had ever experienced a sense of complete helplessness.

They both sat in silence as the shocking events of the morning unfolded in high definition, some of them hastily blurred out because they were just too horrific for the networks to broadcast. Nevertheless, the video revealed people being gunned down in the street in cold blood, a hail of bullets shredding a bus and everyone inside it. Next came the scene of Rainey—though his face was too out of focus to be identifiable—encountering one of the terrorists with his knife—a menacing claw of a blade that the video footage made look plain evil. Rainey cringed at the sight of himself going to work on the man, relieving him of his rifle, and dispatching him with a skull-caving butt-strike.

Not because he regretted his efficient and entirely justified lethal actions, but because his brutal violence was right there on display for Kayla to behold.

He reached for the remote to stop the madness, but she beat him to it, seemingly transfixed by events unfolding on the screen.

Kayla flinched when the grenade went off. If what she had witnessed on the screen to that point wasn't traumatic enough, the next part would be.

The face-off with his would-be killer. The intercession by the stranger who had saved his life by sacrificing his own.

When the camera focused on the woman shaking and weeping over her dead husband, Rainey could no longer watch. He turned away, the muscles in his jaw taut with emotion.

Kayla clutched his hand to her chest even tighter. Her heart was pounding. *She knew.*

Knew it was him on the screen—the one who had come this close to being blown up and shot to death. She also now knew he had done his own share of killing. And did so in brutal, expert fashion.

Rainey slipped his hand from her grasp and wrapped it around her, pulled her closer. The video played again. It would be replayed thousands of times on countless networks, garner tens of millions of views on social media. Thankfully, the features of his face were never clearly captured in the footage. Even if it were to be enhanced, the video would be of no use for identification purposes. He was certain that even those who knew him intimately—his fellow operators, his family even—would be hard-pressed to recognize him. His identity was safe but for one person.

Kayla.

6

They drove north to the Tappan Zee Bridge, Rainey at the wheel of the Jeep Grand Cherokee, Kayla seated next to him icup holdern contemplative silence. He had seen this type of thing before in combat. People react in any number of ways when they experience a sudden traumatic event. Some people become talky—as in you can't get them to shut up. Others grow as quiet as a shadow.

Even though Kayla had never been in any real danger, her perception in hindsight was that she could have very easily been killed. Maybe equally traumatic in her mind was that Rainey had *left* her in that moment. Never mind the fact that he had run into the storm in an attempt to stop the terrorists from effecting their plan. To top it off, Kayla had witnessed Rainey in action. War was no easy thing to experience even for hardened men. For someone not accustomed, or at least prepared, to bear witness to such brutal violence, an unfiltered peek at the realities of armed conflict can savage one's sensibilities. It can and will shock the conscience. Rainey would never know it, but seeing him dispatching other human beings with artful precision, speed, and overwhelming violence of action frightened Kayla to the core.

They were just outside Trenton when Kayla uttered her first words since the hotel.

"Who are you?"

The question hit him like an open hand across the face. "What do you mean?"

"I mean who *are* you?"

"Who *am* I? Kay... You know who I am."

"No, I don't. I knew the boy I met in college. Who are you now, Reagan Rainey?"

He fidgeted in his seat. "Listen, I know what happened this morning was scary. I think it's best if we just get home and get some rest."

"Stop it." She paused, seeming to fight back tears. "That was you on TV, killing..." she trailed off. "Is that what you do for a living, Reagan? Do you kill people?"

"Dear, you know what I do. I work for the Green—"

"—briar Foundation. Yes, so I've been told. But is that what you *really* do? Is that the truth? I know what I saw today, Reagan. I saw a trained killer. And I also saw you almost get shot to death. Ray, I can't—" Tears tumbled down her cheeks. When her voice returned, she posed the question again this time with much more conviction, "Is that the *truth*?"

Rainey looked at her. He wanted to tell her everything, wanted to tell her that he was *not* a guy who simply pushed paper around a desk at the nebulous Greenbriar Foundation—the quasi-governmental think tank based in Arlington, Virginia. An organization that had its hands in all kinds of things from building water wells in Third World nations and funding museums and institutions of higher learning to conducting important scientific and medical research all around the world. He wanted to tell her that the Greenbriar Foundation *did* all of those things, but in truth it did so much more. He wanted to tell her that it was the umbrella organization, a great big front, for the CIA's Directorate X and all its black operations and programs—a veritable CIA within the CIA.

Something so secret that few outside its hallowed halls even knew existed. He wanted to tell her that he was an operations officer—a sometime spy, sometime assassin—and that he was very good at his job. If he were permitted by statute, or his conscience, he would tell her all of it and more. Instead, he turned back toward the windshield and focused on the ribbon of road in front of them.

"I see." Two words. Two simple words, so innocent, so naïve, yet they pierced his heart like a rusty dagger.

The steering wheel bore most of his anxiety in the hours that followed. His muscled hands flexed and massaged the leather until they became cramped from exertion. When he finally looked back at Kayla, he found she had curled up in the seat with her back to him and, best he could tell, was fast asleep.

What on earth is happening?

He thought a weekend trip to New York City would allow them some time to catch up, become better acquainted. They had been college sweethearts and had only recently rekindled their relationship. Despite what he desperately wanted to believe, he knew in his bones that they were not the same people they had once been.

His mind drifted back. At first, it was as if they had picked up right where they'd left off all those years ago. But after what had just happened, he sensed that something had shifted in their relationship, something over which he had no control. He didn't want to face it, especially now. Not with all that was going on as well as what he knew was sure to be coming down the pike.

Needing some caffeine and a chance to stretch his back and legs, Rainey stopped at a Dunkin Donuts along the interstate near Newark, Delaware. Kayla was still asleep or at least was acting the part when he climbed back into the Jeep. He set the coffee he had purchased for her in the cup holder and was soon back up to speed and sifting through the events of the morning that now played in slow motion in his head. *What was their target? Was it New York City in general? Why then the apparent assault on the building at 866 Second Avenue? And what about the other cities?*

Rainey clicked on the radio and learned that the enormous explosion he'd heard while still inside the lobby of the building was now being reported as a truck bomb. It had detonated directly in front of the United States Mission to the UN. Over one hundred people were confirmed dead so far with the death toll sure to keep growing. The hospitals were flooded with countless casualties.

Rainey eased down on the accelerator as his thoughts once again faded to the woman in the plaza. He could feel her overwhelming grief in his soul. It pressed in on him, against his chest as if some great, big weight were lodged there, refusing to allow his lungs to expand and fill with air. He had been there, in her shoes more times than he wanted to remember. He knew well the staggering pain of losing someone close. His best friend—a fellow special operator and teammate—was killed just one year ago on a daring mission in Qatar. Thus, he understood exactly what she was going through. He would never forget her face. He would also never forget the promise he'd made to her.

There *would* be justice.

And he would be its deliverer.

7

The sun cut a harsh angle through the tangled, bare neighborhood trees as Rainey pulled to the curb outside Kayla's house on Fort Sumner Drive. Opening his car door, he heard the sharp, urgent barking of a large dog in a backyard somewhere nearby. It paused briefly, probably to sniff the air, then let loose with another ominous warning to the unseen interlopers.

A man firmly in his sixties, wearing a colorful rendition of a running suit, labored past with an equally eye-catching stride—something akin to a forward moonwalk. Water sloshed in small canisters holstered on his belt. A thick white goatee framed his mouth, which incidentally hung open as if he were laughing from way down deep in his belly.

Rainey stepped out and subtly scanned the street, the parked cars, the windows of nearby houses. All of it was done out of habit. Again, his eyes found the running man, just before he disappeared around the corner. Several more seconds would pass until the sound of shoes scuffing the pavement faded away.

Rainey opened the back door, leaned into the Jeep, and grabbed Kayla's bags off the seat then circled around to her side of the vehicle. She was already on her feet by the time he drew alongside her. Kayla twisted back and forth at the waist and finally let out a long, tired sigh. She stuffed her hands in the pockets of her jacket, tilted her head back, and peered toward the lambent sky. Rainey waited patiently beside her. He said nothing, revealed nothing. He was still reading her, trying to figure out what she was thinking. He'd hoped the long drive would give them time to talk, but Kayla had not been in the talking mood. In fact, she had spent nearly the entire time sleeping. He didn't hold it against her. What happened in New York was a very big deal. He considered what she must have felt when she realized *he* was the man in the plaza. What must she think of him now? Was she frightened of him? Was she frightened *for* him? After all, he could very well have been killed. In any case, the morning had taken an emotional toll on her. And now he feared their recently rekindled relationship would never be the same.

Kayla pulled a set of keys from her purse and set off toward the house. Rainey followed dutifully without comment. He studied her from behind and only slightly felt guilty about it. She was breathtaking from every angle. Even after their time apart, or maybe because of it, he was madly in love with her. After all that had happened, he hoped she still felt the same way about him. By anyone's standard, he was a warrior's warrior, yet Kayla Chapman could still make him feel like a wide-eyed teenager, young and innocent and free. With her, he was once again the shaggy-haired college kid with dreams of practicing law, living in a big house, and having lots of kids to fill it. Kayla made him forget all the terrible things he had seen and experienced during his time in the military. If only he could go back in time. Before New York. Before he'd dropped out of school and run off to enlist. Back to when they were discussing marriage. There was no doubt in his mind. He still wanted to marry her, have lots of kids, and grow old together. Have a shot at a normal life and be called husband, father, lover, friend.

Kayla mounted the brick steps to the small, concrete-slab porch. She inserted her key into the lock then pivoted toward him. Rays from the setting sun shimmered against her hair, giving her a diadem of angelic light.

"Well?" she said.

"Well... I'm sorry the trip didn't turn out the way I had planned."

"Not your fault."

"Kayla, I—"

"Don't, Reagan. Not now." Her eyes averted to something in the distance as if she were searching for something or was making a valiant effort not to say something she might later regret. Then they landed on his. "I think I just need some time to digest everything. You know?"

Rainey studied the features of her flawless face then offered a conciliatory nod.

She unlocked the door and pushed it open. Rainey stepped inside and set her bags down in the foyer. He let his eyes move about the room, the pictures on the wall, the doorway to the kitchen at the back of the house. It didn't take long for them to return to Kayla. He was desperate to say something that would matter, something that would put things back in their proper place. Instead, he remained silent, torn in more ways than one. Kayla drew close to him, rose up on her toes, and put her lips to his. She cupped his face with both her hands, and he was lost, set free on an ocean current.

She slid her hands around his muscled shoulders, pulled him closer. Rainey closed his eyes. Her scent was magical, the warmth of her body against his beyond words. He wanted to stay here forever.

"I love you, Reagan."

"I love you, too, Kay."

Rainey was convinced as he paced back to the Jeep that a bullet to the heart could not have felt any worse than what he was experiencing right now. He knew she still loved him, but was that enough to overcome the other thoughts and feelings that were surely assaulting her sensibilities? He wasn't so sure. He was a conflicted man. And yet outwardly, he remained his usual stoic self, ever the one in complete control of his emotions. Till he rounded the corner that is, and the knot that had lodged deep in his throat pushed up into his chin like a dull blade. He fought back tears, quickly smearing the wetness from his cheek. In that moment, when he was once again alone with his thoughts and his God, he whispered aloud, "I don't know what You are doing, Lord, what Your plan is for my life. But whatever Your will, let it be done."

8

ALDIE, VIRGINIA

A platoon of dead leaves marched across the driveway and beyond the reach of the Jeep's headlights. Rainey pulled near the flagstone path leading to the house and switched off the engine. What had been a modest breeze when he'd left Kayla's nearly an hour ago, was now a churning wind. He felt the Jeep rocking on its axles.

A storm is coming.

A strong gust assailed him, tugged at his beard and jacket as he exited the vehicle and took in the large, white-brick Adam Federal before him. But for the riotous wind, all was quiet. Rainey squinted against it, grabbed his things from the back seat, and followed the curved path to the door. When he got there, he turned back toward the driveway, which was a small parking lot really. The wooded landscape that surrounded him was awash in blackness, save for a few soft burning lights: those on the porch behind him; one in the lamppost at the end of the footpath; and another over by the garage. A few snowflakes streaked by his face. If not for the glow from the lamppost, they would have been unseen. He drew in a deep breath of cold air rich with the pleasing scent of woodsmoke, let it out slowly. It was good to be home.

Rainey entered through the heavy, wooden front door, dropped his bags in the foyer, and trod into the kitchen, where he found two men seated at the breakfast table behind plates of food.

Saul Baker plunged his fork into a hunk of charred chicken. "Hiya, bud."

"Hey, Pappy."

Saul "Pappy" Baker was a CIA legend if ever there was one. In the bygone era of spy versus spy, he was the Soviet Union's most formidable and most ruthless opponent. He was Moscow station chief when the Berlin Wall—and the entire Evil Empire—came crumbling down. Soon after that, he was put in charge of the Agency's Near East Division and his remit officially became battling the growing threat of Islamic fundamentalism, state-sponsored terrorism, and everything in between. To help accomplish that mission, he had brought over a talented, young case officer by the name of Job Jackson, who up until then had been working in various capacities within the busy Agency stations of Southeast Asia. Saul Baker had been the very first in the Intelligence Community to propose a small, nimble, and lethal force made up of highly skilled, highly trained, and highly motivated Agency personnel to combat terror. A group of individuals that could operate quietly and efficiently—with lethal consequence if necessary—and leave zero footprint, much in the manner of say, the American OSS in years past, or the Israeli Mossad. A specialized kind of task force built to carry out the most sensitive of assignments and fight America's new enemies on terms they would understand.

It had been an uphill battle from the start. As is often the case in the annals of American history, politics carried the day, and so for years Saul's visionary concept was ignored. Sadly, it took the embassy bombings in Kenya and Nairobi in 1998 for the Clinton administration to finally sit up and take notice of what he had been telling them. Even then, the response had been to give him a paltry little office and a paltry budget, which amounted to nothing much at all. And yet, with a hand-picked staff of nine men and three women, his covert and very off-the-books working group, initially dubbed Directorate Twelve, was born.

Slowly, Saul's task force of a dozen warrior spies began to find its footing notwithstanding the shoestring budget and the gross lack of manpower.

Then 9/11 happened. And everything changed.

Directorate Twelve was finally given a budget worthy of its mission. Recently rebranded Directorate X, the mission remained the same even if Saul was no longer running the show: covert action, intelligence-gathering, cyber warfare, and everything in between.

Now a retired widower, Saul lived with Rainey here, on a farm that had belonged to his family for generations until a few short years ago, when he'd sold it to the talented up-and-comer for a song.

Job's bodyguard, Zane Davis, collected his plate and glass of apple juice from the table and headed off for the living room.

At the sound of a rebroadcast hockey game coming from the large TV in the living room, Rainey returned his focus to Saul and quickly filled him in on what had happened in New York.

"How's Kayla?"

"Frightened."

"Poor kid."

"She knows it was me in the plaza."

"You think she'll keep it to herself?"

"Yeah, but..." Rainey sighed.

"You think this may have changed her feelings toward you in some way?" It was more statement than question.

Rainey didn't respond. For better or worse, he was a man who preferred to keep his feelings buried deep down inside.

Saul Baker clearly understood the heavy price of a life spent in the shadows. Despite its glamorous veneer, the dark world of intelligence was a cruel master. Even now his children wanted nothing to do with him. "Well, let me fix you something to eat."

"I'm not hungry."

Saul shrugged, scooped up a forkful of steamed broccoli. "Job's in the study. Been on the phone ever since he walked in the door."

Rainey registered the clock on the microwave. It was almost quarter till six. He had called Job just after leaving Kayla's place. The spymaster had said he wanted to meet with him privately, which was why Job was here and not in his office at DX headquarters.

Rainey paced down the short corridor of tongue-and-groove floorboards and stopped at a partially open sliding door of polished rosewood. He gently rolled back the door to his study and stepped across the threshold. The room was well-appointed yet cozy with a mixture of modern and antique wooden furniture, floor-to-ceiling bookcases, and an elegant walnut desk in the center of the wall on the right. Job sat behind the desk, his face partially obscured by the green glow of a banker's lamp. The wall-mounted flat-screen TV directly across from the desk was switched on but muted. From it came a flourish of light that every few seconds or so grew so bright that even the deep corners of the room were stripped of their cloak of darkness.

At the sight of him, Job immediately waved him inside as if it were his own private fiefdom and not Rainey's. He held a mobile phone against his left ear, papers and files cluttering the desk before him in no discernible pattern. Job bore the weary visage of a novelist beset by an impossible deadline.

Rainey took a seat in a captain's chair along the wall to his left. His eyes drifted up to the framed painting that hung above his desk—a reproduction of Arnold Friberg's *The Prayer at Valley Forge.* As it did with many Americans, the imagery of George Washington kneeling before God in a private moment of prayer and submission resonated deep within him. He studied it now as the sound of Job issuing orders to someone over the phone faded into the background. Suddenly, the undulating television light that flashed against the painting was streaks of lighting. Then came the booming report of a cannon or perhaps it was a crack of thunder. The horse at Washington's side neighed and anxiously stomped its hooves. And though the storm raged all around him, Washington himself was a picture of calm as he continued his petitioning of Almighty God.

The television flashed again, this time snapping him from his reverie. Job held up the forefinger of his right hand then switched the phone to his right cheek and continued his conversation. Though fit for his 57 years, Job Emory Jackson was not a physically imposing man by any stretch of the imagination. His was a taut, but modest physique, one that belied an agile and cunning mind—the mind of a spymaster. He was a man of few peers in the intelligence business. What he lacked in physical size, he more than made up for with his ability to process information quickly and develop cunning strategies to defeat an enemy, rescue an agent, or aid a friendly intelligence service. Aside from Saul Baker, Rainey knew of no other human being alive who could navigate the murky waters of espionage like Job Jackson.

Rainey placed both hands on the arms of the chair and eased his head backward until it rested against the wall. If he closed his eyes, he would doubtless be asleep in a matter of seconds. What happened in New York followed by six hours of driving had sapped his strength.

The sliding door beside him yielded a low growl. Saul slipped into the room and handed him a stainless-steel mug of jet-black coffee. Stamped into the side was the emblem of the United States Army's 3rd Special Forces Group, the unit in which Rainey had proudly served in the years leading up to his time in what was now colloquially referred to as Delta Force.

He took a careful sip while Saul deposited a second mug on the desk for Job then retreated to the brown leather sofa along the far wall.

"*Now* who's he talking to?" Saul whispered.

Rainey shrugged.

Job scribbled something onto the pad in front of him and a few seconds later disconnected the call. He set the phone down on the desk, pinched the bridge of his nose then reached for the mug that Saul had placed in front of him.

"Any news?" queried Rainey.

"Not much. It's still early." Job leaned back in the chair while cradling his coffee with both hands. "We've identified the man in the photos you sent me. His name is Farooq Khalil. Born in Lyon. Father's French, mother's Lebanese. Came to the States about ten years ago on a student visa. Graduated from Michigan with a degree in communications. After school, he became a naturalized citizen. Been out of the country twelve times since then. Always on direct flights to Paris. For the past few years, he worked as a sales associate for a company in New York that sells office products.

"The Bureau has identified two more of the attackers." He leaned forward and handed him three jacketed files. "They were among the shooters in the plaza. Both of them entered the country on the same day—a few hours apart, just eleven days ago—on French passports. One via Baltimore, the other Atlanta. I've got our people, including those at Langley and Paris Station digging into their backgrounds."

Rainey studied the faces of the men, read the names printed inside the jackets. After thumbing through the files, he handed them back to Job, extended his legs, and stared up at the stilled blades of the ceiling fan. "Do we know what their target was?"

"New York is unique compared to the other cities that were hit."

"What do you mean?"

"The Chicago and LA attacks were similar to the one in New York as far as the Mumbai-style tactics, but unlike New York, there were no truck bombs in those cities. Gunmen with suicide vests only."

"So, New York was their *primary* target? Why?"

"We believe our mission to the UN was hit largely because of what it represents: America. It was a symbolic target. The building's blast-resistant construction helped minimize the damage to the facility and thus the number of fatalities inside. I'm afraid the building next door wasn't as fortunate.

You've seen the footage. It's an utter mess. The cause of the explosion was a VBIED—a truck bomb. And it was *massive*."

Saul slowly nodded his head.

"What about the building on Second Avenue?" said Rainey.

"Well, it seems the terrorists' primary focus there was on a block of offices on the fifth floor."

"What's on the fifth floor?" pressed Rainey.

Job's face remained grim. "The Saudi consulate."

9

A small, though highly significant, meeting had been scheduled to occur
there at 8:15 a.m., Job explained. Among those expected to attend
were a special envoy from the Kingdom and an Israeli delegation that included their foreign minister as well as Nahum Ben-Amit, deputy director
of Mossad. According to his sources, Job went on, Ben-Amit was the one
who'd masterminded the famous Hezbollah pager operation. Valetta Ivory,
the current national security advisor, and the number two from State were
also to have been in attendance. Due to the sensitive nature of the talks, all
plans of the meeting had been shrouded in secrecy.

"The attackers were methodical and resourceful. Once they breached the
fifth floor, they took the small security element with overwhelming force.
They were obviously well-trained and proficient in their use of weapons and
tactics. The staff had no chance of survival. Each of them was summarily
executed. It took the attackers several minutes, but they eventually located
the Saudi consul general and his deputy holed up in the consulate's safe
room, which they accessed by blowing a hole in the wall with explosives.

"The fact that the meeting had been postponed at the very last minute
appears to have been our only bit of good fortune today aside from the
obvious heroics in the plaza," said Job. "As such, with the exception of the

Saudi CG and his staff, none of the parties scheduled to meet were anywhere near the consulate when the attack occurred."

Saul leaned forward. "What are the Saudis saying?"

"So far, their response to the entire affair—their *public* response, that is—has been to suggest that the consul general and he alone had been the intended target all along. They are dredging up the attempted assassination of their ambassador in DC in 2011 perpetrated by the Iranians as evidence."

"And what about our friends in Tel Aviv?" said Saul.

Job shook his head. "They have extended their sympathies to us and the Saudis, and have, of course, offered whatever help we may need, but otherwise haven't made a peep."

"I wonder why they didn't use a truck bomb at the Second Avenue location, too? Why send in an assault team?" said Rainey.

Saul's forehead suggested he was in deep thought. "They definitely had a reason. Maybe there was uncertainty about whether a truck bomb could reach those in attendance at the meeting. The use of a direct-action team in a building assault would be much more complicated to deploy, but it *would* mean a greater probability of success. This was clearly no circus act. It was a well-planned and well-executed attack. Another possibility is they wanted to take Ben-Amit alive."

Rainey nodded in agreement. "Do we know what the central purpose of the meeting was?"

Job set his empty mug down on the desk. "My sources say that they'd planned to discuss several things: the rapidly changing situation in Syria (the Assad regime had fallen a week ago), the fallout from Israel's recent campaign against Hezbollah, ongoing operations against Hamas in Gaza, and the likelihood of responsive attacks from Iran. We've known for a while now that Israel and the House of Saud have been considering the formation of some sort of strategic, and very *covert*, alliance to contend with the expanding Iranian influence in the region.

"One thing is certain. No one is saying anything about the meeting and that includes our people in Foggy Bottom. And I don't expect them to anytime soon, at least not publicly."

"Any idea on how word about the meeting leaked out?" said Rainey.

"No, but that's one of the things being looked at."

"What about the actual attack? Do we know who is behind it?" said Rainey.

"Every jihadist group in existence is claiming responsibility, but some of our senior analysts believe it to be the work of Hezbollah."

The eldest of the trio placed his elbows on his thighs, tented his thick hands beneath his chin. "I concur with that assessment. Hezbollah makes the most sense. Aside from the obvious with respect to the targets, the attack—especially the use of a truck bomb—bears all of their hallmarks, save for one. They've never hit us like this at home before. This could be a game-changer."

"Indeed," said Job. "I've cabled all our stations with the explicit message to turn up the heat on our sources. The Israelis and the Saudis have both quietly offered to do the same with their people.

"Kendall has made it abundantly clear to the director that he wants to hit the ground running the moment he is sworn into office. To that end, he has expressed his desire for Valetta and the director to continue serving in their current capacities at least for the time being." Valetta Ivory was the national security advisor while Ken Thompson was the director of the CIA. "Word is that Kendall is going to nominate Ivory to be the new DNI, but I'm getting ahead of myself. Bottom line for us: I don't expect any bureaucratic haggling from anyone in the incoming administration over our involvement in the investigation or any of our recommendations for a prospective course of action. The director said that Kendall wants the FBI to conduct the criminal investigation just as they normally would, while at the same time, he wants us to carry out a parallel, very quiet inquiry of our own. The kind that we're good at. Do you understand what I'm saying?"

Rainey nodded. "I wouldn't have it any other way."

When Job's phone vibrated against the desktop, Rainey and Saul headed off for another round of coffee. Rainey downed his rather quickly, placed his empty cup in the sink then stepped outside into the chill night air. The wind had calmed in the past two hours. It was now a playful breeze that carried with it a freshness, which seemed to charge his every fiber with renewed vigor. Standing with his back to the house, Rainey plunged his hands into his pants pockets. The restored blacksmith shop in the near distance was a mere charcoal drawing on a thick curtain of velvet. The trees that framed the landscape were indistinguishable from the severe darkness but for their uppermost limbs, which stretched like hands high into the glittery sky. Straight ahead, past the large barn and nestled within a thick wood of oak and pine, was a rolling horse pasture, though it, too, was currently veiled in impenetrable darkness.

Rainey frowned as the morning's events played yet again in his mind. He looked up and took in the whole sky at once. Indeed, he was grateful to be alive, but at the same time, the heavy hammer of guilt bludgeoned his conscience without ceasing. Only God knew why he had survived the attack, while so many others had not. People like Ryan Killian. Back in the study, Job had supplied a rough sketch of the man's life.

Ryan Killian was the second youngest of four brothers and a highly respected veteran of the Upper Darby Township Police Department in southeast Pennsylvania. The woman who had wept over his lifeless body in the plaza was his wife, Lacey. The couple had two sons, eleven and three, both of whom had thankfully been left with their grandparents in Malvern during the couple's getaway weekend in the Big Apple. Killian and his wife had apparently been in the city for much the same reason that he and Kayla had been there: to enjoy each other's exclusive company in the quintessential romantic setting of New York City at Christmastime, with all its storied pomp and pageantry.

Ryan Killian.

It was a name that would be forever etched in his memory. So, too, would the image of his wife as she clung to his bullet-riddled body. Rainey was staring into her tear-streaked face by way of his mind's eye when the door behind him softly clicked open. Job pulled on his black wool overcoat and drew next to him. They stood shoulder to shoulder with nary a word spoken between them for nearly a minute, two warrior spies looking long and hard into the darkness.

Finally, Job flipped up the collar of his coat. The sound of an engine humming softly on the opposite side of the house meant that Zane, his bodyguard, was waiting to carry him home. Rainey guessed that it would not be home to Annapolis tonight but to the townhouse Job kept in George-town. Job often made use of it when he wanted to stay close to headquarters, which was usually in times of intense op-tempo or during a particularly worrisome operation.

"You all right?"

Rainey was silent for several seconds then posed a question of his own. "Who did this, Job?"

The spymaster twisted at the torso and looked up at him. "That's exactly what I want you to find out. And when you do, I want you to find, fix, and finish them."

The muscles in Rainey's jaw flexed.

"We'll talk more in the morning. For now, get some sleep. You're going to be busy. We all are. Count on it."

10

It was shortly after 10:30 p.m. when Saul fetched him from his bedroom and informed him that President-elect Kendall was about to address the nation. Incidentally, this was also the precise time that the news media outlets, particularly the ones of the more disreputable persuasion, would later point to as the genesis of the Kendall Doctrine, something they would characterize as a "ruefully nationalistic response to another dreadful demonstration of extremism." Rainey would never understand how for most of the quote/unquote smart people in the mainstream media, having pride in America, and the flag for which it stands, was something to be downplayed or even ridiculed. *Let* them *sacrifice life and limb for their freedom.*

With Saul in his robe and slippers and Rainey wearing only a plain white T-shirt and a pair of blue mesh athletic shorts with "Duke Soccer" on the right thigh, they returned to the study and inclined their heads toward the glow of the large flat-screen television on the wall.

"He needs to be forceful and direct," said Saul. "This right here will set the stage for his entire term. Our enemies will be watching. Our allies, too."

President-elect Martin Kendall was by all accounts a new breed of politician. A strong and articulate conservative, he was set to assume the Oval Office in a few weeks' time. Despite his vast support among the electorate, Marty Kendall had no shortage of detractors within the elites of both political parties, which extended to their incestuous partnership with myriad news media outlets and their faceless sycophants in the blogosphere. Notwithstanding the fact that Kendall had yet to be sworn into office, their machinery was already operating at full capacity with the express purpose of ruining him, politically, socially, and, as was evident in some dark and disturbed corners of various social media platforms, physically. For them, a Kendall presidency meant death to America. In reality, it meant the end to a runaway anti-liberty agenda and the rebirth and celebration of everything that had made America great in the first place: love of country; peace through strength; the pursuit of justice for all and a commensurate adherence to the rule of law; the recognition of the burning desire in every human heart to be free; and most importantly, humble submission to the will of Almighty God.

Saul spoke as they waited in the flickering TV light. "The press are calling you and Killian the 'Angels of Second Avenue.' Every media outlet—large and small—is talking about you two. They've already identified Killian. They would love to know who you are, too, bud. Are you sure Kayla can keep a secret?"

"I'm sure."

The camera feed switched from a small gathering of political commentators at a news desk to America's next commander in chief. President-elect Martin Kendall was seated behind an elegant wooden desk at his home just outside Fort Worth, Texas. The American flag and that of the Lone Star State stood over his right shoulder, a tall bookcase with family photos and odd mementos, his left. He wore a charcoal-colored suit, a white, pinpoint oxford dress shirt with a yellow and blue striped necktie that exuded optimism and an abundance of energy for which he was well known. The businessman-turned-senator from Texas was a photogenic man, a handsome man in fact, which seemed to play equally well to both sides of the electorate. The lighting against Kendall's neatly combed gray hair revealed remnants of the dirty blond of his youth. Those among the media outlets concerned with optics would later point out that Kendall's visage was a perfect depiction of a seasoned statesman and confident executive. The more partisan commentators, however, the knavish political hacks who had little use for objective truth, referred to Kendall as a foreign agent, an evil outsider, anything to diminish his successes and his America-centric platform. The fact that the billionaire Republican senator regularly challenged the status quo and rebuffed elites in *both* parties, coupled with his independent wealth—Marty Kendall was beholden to no one inside or outside the Beltway—gulled them to no end.

Kendall was a man of the people in the truest sense, not just because he'd built his business empire from scratch, but because his proposed policies promised to wrench power away from the entrenched political class and their globalist puppet masters and return it to its rightful owner: the American people. Kendall's landslide election victory proved that the man and his message resonated with voters.

With his hands folded atop the desk, Kendall began. "Good evening, America. I come to you tonight with a heavy heart. As you well know, this morning our beloved nation suffered another dastardly attack from cruel, weak-minded savages. First, to the families and friends of those who perished, Dottie and I offer our deepest condolences. We also offer our heartfelt sympathy to the countless injured and all those otherwise affected by these acts of horror and depravity. We are praying for you all.

"My fellow Americans, this morning's attack demonstrated the very worst of humanity, but it also revealed the exact opposite. It revealed the very essence of America and the nature of what it means to be a citizen of this great nation. What I—the whole world—saw today was people helping people, men and women responding to their fellow citizens' most urgent needs in their darkest of hours with little to no regard for their own safety.

"To our emergency responders—our police, fire, and EMS heroes, I cannot express with words the amount of sheer gratitude I have for you. Thank you for running *toward* the storm. Thank you for doing what you do each and every day. Like millions of my fellow Americans across this great land of ours, I continue to be in awe of your heroic acts of bravery, your commitment to duty, and humble service. Thank you to our wonderful doctors and nurses and all those who are working long and hard to care for the wounded. In addition, I would like to thank the selfless individuals who have and are continuing to donate blood and render aid in countless other ways. You are amazing. From the bottom of my heart, I thank you."

Kendall hesitated. His lower lip stiffened as though he were caught off guard by an unexpected wave of emotion. No one would know until much later that from the moment he first sat down, he was speaking the words that he himself had penned. He was speaking from the heart.

"Though we too often bicker over politics and trivial matters, the events of this morning exposed to the world the strong bonds we share for one another. This morning, we demonstrated that when the chips are down, we really are one nation. *United* under God. You see, the cowards that perpetrated this morning's attack did not target man or woman, Republican or Democrat. They did not aim to kill White, Black, or Hispanic. Christian or Muslim. They targeted *Americans*. And it is *as* Americans that we will respond going forward.

"For the past few weeks, President Beasley and his people have been graciously and diligently working with me and my transition team in order to make the transfer of power a smooth and peaceful one, and for that I am eternally grateful. I can gladly say that this morning was no different. The president and I have been and continue to be in close communication with those in our nation's security, intelligence, and law enforcement communities. We want to assure you that the federal government is diligently working with our local, state, and international partners to determine exactly who is responsible for these heinous acts of terrorism and to hold them fully accountable.

"To the nations of the world, I say to you, you can either stand with us or you can stand against us. There is no middle ground in this enduring battle for peace and security, this battle between good and evil. There is a cancer in our midst. It must be rooted out and destroyed for good. To our allies, those already dug into the trenches alongside us and doing the tough, dirty work: Thank you. Thank you for choosing peace, humanity, and freedom over extremism, darkness, and despair."

It was then that Kendall's mood turned convincingly resolute, dark even. His voice was firm, his words clear and deliberate.

"Now... To the cowards who perpetrated this attack, know that we will never surrender to you. We will never surrender to your agenda of terror and destruction, never submit to your sinister attempts to bring a hegemony of hate, conflict, and desolation to our shores. You see, we Americans proudly celebrate our freedoms and liberties, and we are willing to fight to the death to protect them. We have done it throughout our history. We have fought and prevailed against tyrants and evil regimes, despots and Islamists before, and we will continue to do so for as long as we must. Even to the end of the age. We are Americans after all. It's in our DNA.

"To those responsible for this attack, hear me when I say that your days are numbered. We are united, and we are coming for you. May God bless America and all who faithfully stand for truth and liberty, virtue and honor.

"Thank you and good night."

11

Rainey was still thinking about Kendall's speech as he guided the DX loaner vehicle from Lee Highway onto Fort Myer Drive in the bustling urban community of Rosslyn. He slowed at the traffic light to let a tandem of men clad in dark suits and colorful neckties trot across the pavement, then turned left onto 19th Street North. After two blocks, he clicked on his left-turn indicator and nosed the vehicle onto the ramp of a restricted-access underground parking facility. Once clear of the security gate, he descended into a cavernous, multi-level garage. The three contiguous buildings above? Hiding in plain sight amidst the numerous skyscrapers lining the western bank of the Potomac? None other than the headquarters of Directorate X—the CIA's invisible directorate.

The largest of the three buildings, referred to as Main for obvious reason, bore on its face a small rectangle of granite into which the words *Greenbriar Foundation* were chiseled in simple block letters. The Hotel, the one in the middle, was a thinner version of Main but every bit as tall. The Annex, meanwhile, stood on the complex's eastern flank and was easily the shortest of the DX headquarters buildings. With sharp, angular features, broad shoulders, and an outer shell that resembled alligator skin, it had a noticeably different feel than that of its sleek, glass-and-steel siblings. A powerful little brother with something to prove.

It was said that if Langley ever went down for any reason, the CIA could temporarily shift all its functions to this facility on Lynn Street without skipping a beat.

Using his keycard and numeric PIN, Rainey forged through two sets of doors and followed a secure underground corridor that bore him into a small lobby on the first sublevel of Main, where he swiped his badge against a keycard reader under the watchful eyes of armed guards. Once past the security checkpoint, he headed for a bank of elevators. He boarded the car and pressed the button for the twenty-fourth floor. When the doors opened, he turned right and strode down a long hall at the end of which was a vestibule. Swiping his way inside, he found himself in a reception area outside the director's executive office suite, where he presented himself to Job's loyal administrative assistant.

"Hi, Eleanor."

"Good morning, Mr. Rainey. Go right in."

Rainey slipped into the office and found Job standing by the window, arms crossed, peering over America's capital like a dutiful sentinel. He knew Job. In many ways, he knew him better than his own father. The spymaster was deep in thought.

As he eased into one of the chairs in front of Job's desk, the spymaster turned and began without prelude. "There's been a claim of responsibility. One we believe is legitimate."

"From whom?"

"They call themselves *Jaysh al-Naar al-Muqadasa*."

"The Army of Holy Fire."

Job nodded.

"Never heard of them."

"No one has. Not our people, not the Saudis or the Brits, not even the Israelis." He pursed his lips as if carefully weighing his words. "Remember what Saul and I said last night about Hezbollah?"

"Yeah."

"Well, it's only a theory, but I think we could be seeing some kind of new iteration or splinter cell of the organization. If I'm right, I'd say it has something to do with the way Israel decimated Hezbollah's leadership structure. Perhaps this is an asymmetric response by some faction or still-living sector of their organizational chart. But that's just conjecture on my part. Could be some new group entirely." Job walked to his desk, picked up a remote, and pointed it at one of the screens on the wall. Soon they were watching a video clip of a figure, cloaked in black from head to toe. The dark eyes and heavy gray brow were the only visible features. The voice was disguised electronically, but the man's words were clear and foreboding and dripping with the usual anti-America, anti-Israel, and anti-humanity bile. But it was the ending that was most ominous and the thing that would drive the operation to come: *The Army of Holy Fire has struck a fearsome blow to the harlots and infidels assembled in New York City, Chicago, and Los Angeles. And we are only getting started. Allahu Akbar.*

"Where did it come from?" said Rainey.

Job sat down. "We're still working on its origin, but the video file was on a computer disc delivered to the Paris offices of *Le Monde* a little before ten hundred this morning local time. Upon the discovery of its contents, one of the editors notified French authorities who in turn notified us. In the hours since, the video has been popping up all over social media and YouTube faster than it can be taken down."

"How was the disc delivered?"

"By courier. This is him in the lobby." Job spun a laptop computer around on his desk. On the screen were several still images from the *Le Monde* building's CCTV footage.

"Looks like he's wearing some kind of disguise," said Rainey scrutinizing the man in the photos.

"I agree. All we know at this point is that he arrived on foot and left the same way. We're working with our local assets as well as the French government to track his likely routes of ingress and egress through the city. Hopefully, we'll find him, but I'm not holding my breath.

"Our analysts and linguistics experts are still combing through the disc. So far, all they can tell me with any amount of certainty is that the man speaking was probably raised in Lebanon."

"More evidence that points to Hezbollah."

Job nodded. "In the meantime, there is something that I would like you to do."

"Name it."

Job rolled back in his chair and stood. "I want you to go to Greece."

"Why? What's in Greece?"

The spymaster smiled as he resumed his place by the window, crossed his arms, and peered eastward over the Potomac. "A source has come forward. He says he has an important piece of information. Pappy is going to meet with him. I want you there, too."

———

As Rainey emerged from the elevator, his cell phone vibrated against his chest. He pulled it from his jacket pocket and stared at the screen. It was Kayla. With everything going on he had nearly forgotten about how they had parted ways last evening. Suddenly, the emotions of that moment slammed into the anxieties of his latest assignment.

"Reagan, it's me."

"Hi, Kay. How are you holding up?"

"I'm okay, I guess. Listen, I want to apologize for the way that I behaved yesterday. I wasn't being fair to you. I don't know what you really do, but I'm sure whatever it is is probably very important."

"It's fine, hon. Really. No need to apologize. We're good."

"I was hoping you would say that. I love you, Reagan." He could sense her smile on the other end of the line.

"I love you, too, Kay."

"So... How about dinner tonight? I'm thinking someplace quiet and then maybe we can go for a stroll along the river, check out the Christmas lights."

Rainey now sat in the Jeep with his left elbow propped along the window, phone pressed against his ear. He grimaced. "I can't, Kay."

"Okay, well, what if we meet for lunch instead? I need to see you, Reagan."

He closed his eyes. "I want to see you, too, babe, but today's not a good day. I have to work."

"What about after work? Can we get together then?"

She seemed to be trying to hide the rising emotion in her voice. He knew she was fragile right now, so he spoke gently. "Kay, I have to go out of town."

The pause was interminable.

"Kay? You still there?" He looked at the screen to be sure he hadn't lost the connection.

"When will you be back?"

"Tell you the truth, I'm not sure, but—" The click might as well have been a door slamming in his face. He sat there staring at the wall of the parking garage for several long minutes, phone still in his hand. It was moments like these when he wished he were just an ordinary guy with an ordinary job and an ordinary life.

12

The high-pitched whine of a motorbike echoed down the narrow pedestrian thoroughfare. Rainey assessed the raven-haired woman astride it, his eyes hidden behind dark wraparound sunglasses as he sipped coffee beneath the yellow awning of an outdoor café in Thessaloniki's Ladadika District.

The old port city had a long and storied history. It was also a place that bore a great deal of biblical significance, especially with respect to the spread of the Gospel. It was here, during his second missionary journey through Macedonia, that the Apostle Paul preached about Christ's death and resurrection and how Jesus of Nazareth was, in fact, the Messiah as promised in the Old Testament Scriptures. Rainey was hopeful that nothing would result in him or his colleagues being chased out of the old city like Paul had been centuries ago.

He swirled the remnants of his coffee around the bottom of his cup. When Saul Baker trod past, Rainey casually set it down, dabbed his mouth with a napkin, and dropped a five-euro note on the table. He waited until Saul turned the corner before setting off after him.

The assignment was simple Job had said: Watch Pappy's back as he endeavored to make contact with an old friend from his operational days—a friend who was now the head of the Russian SVR's *rezidentura* in Athens, and also just so happened to be a long-serving CIA source.

Over the course of his long and storied career with Russian foreign intelligence, Grigory Kapustin had been posted to such notable terrorist hotbeds as Sudan, Syria, Lebanon, and Iran. It was because of Kapustin's considerable experience and past assignments, particularly his familiarity with Hezbollah that Job had given his unsolicited contact particular attention. The Russian wanted to meet. And refused to do so with anyone other than Saul Baker, retired or not.

In a fleeting thought that he quickly dismissed, Rainey wondered if it was safe to be linking up with someone with such deep ties to the Russian Federation so soon after what he and his team had done on Russian soil. That operation had centered on a secret that had been held for decades, a secret involving his father and various members of the Russian intelligence apparatus. The DX had already heard rumblings about elements within Russia's intelligence and security agencies that were white hot for revenge and that extended to the Tsar himself.

Saul turned right and headed into a narrow pathway of worn stone. It was dark along the edges and strewn with trash. From twenty paces behind, Rainey watched him pass beneath the glow of a lamp and continue around a bend to the right. Here, the short pathway emptied into a small square of sorts with a dormant fountain at its center. The unusually warm December evening had the streets flooded with people. It wouldn't be difficult to lose Saul in the crowds.

Rainey tilted his head to the right and found Saul standing outside a restaurant on the southeast corner of the square. He was pretending to read the menu posted outside while tapping his hand on his thigh in rhythm to the music emanating from the restaurant's speakers. Because of the unseasonably warm air, the outdoor tables had been reassembled and were full of patrons.

Playing the part of a tourist, Rainey fumbled with the straps of his backpack as he maintained a constant vigil for anyone who seemed to be paying

Saul too much attention. Countersurveillance in such a busy setting was no easy feat, but the crowds did afford him some amount of camouflage.

The local CIA station had been tasked with keeping tabs on Kapustin ever since he'd been posted here. Kapustin had dutifully obliged by passing along regular bits of intelligence involving Russian activities in Greece as well as intel he picked up concerning things like human trafficking and the drug and arms trades in the broader Mediterranean region.

Kapustin was currently planted at a table in front of Palati, a restaurant popular with locals and tourists alike. The sexagenarian had a head of short gray hair and a rather boring face, half of which was currently illuminated by the light cast from the streetlamps in the square, the other veiled in heavy shadow. His collared dress shirt was open at the neck. A slash of blazing red where the handkerchief peeked out of his gray suit jacket hinted at a sense of refinement and style.

"He's finishing up now," came a voice over the encrypted radio channel via his earbud. As if trying to get his bearings, Rainey consulted the map feature on his phone and peered to his left. The woman who had passed by on the scooter only moments ago was standing on the far side of the square, a cell phone pressed to her cheek so as to disguise her radio traffic. She was among the local support staff working out of Athens Station and would remain in the vicinity to assist as needed.

Grigory Kapustin pulled the cloth napkin from his lap and dropped it on his plate. After paying his bill, he pushed back from the table and stood. His knees and back were stiff, thus he took a few seconds to stretch them. A grimace formed on his face as he pressed his palms into his lower back and straightened his torso. Kapustin finally gathered himself, waved to the waitress a few tables over, and began toward the square. As he stepped into the swirl of humanity, he glimpsed someone standing in a dim light, a cigarette between his lips: Saul Baker, though Kapustin made no outward show of recognition. Saul pinched the cigarette with his thumb and index finger, took one final drag causing the ash end to turn brilliant red then dropped it to the smooth stone pavers before smashing it with the toe of his shoe. Kapustin assessed the other faces in the square with a casual turn of the head. He noticed the athletically proportioned man hovering over his phone almost immediately; he was likely conducting surveillance or countersurveillance as it were.

Kapustin turned back toward Saul, who was now lighting up another cigarette. They held each other's gaze for only a moment then Saul casually headed off.

Kapustin followed him.

13

It was a rather impressive display and Rainey was thankful for a chance to witness the fieldwork of a legendary artisan of espionage. He imagined what Saul Baker must have been like during his operational days, the turmoil he surely created for hostile intelligence services. The man's instincts, his feel for the street were without blemish, his movements flawless.

Rainey looked on as Saul dropped the cigarette butt to the street, ground it to oblivion with his shoe, and brought a fresh one to his lips. The old man pulled a lighter from his pants pocket, set fire to the cigarette, and took several puffs from it in a practiced flourish. His eyes narrowed and something akin to a grin formed at the corners of his mouth. Whether this was because of the secondhand smoke settling over him or it was an honest show of bemusement with the warm weather and the Greeks flooding the square, Rainey did not know. Regardless, it was during this time that Saul made eye contact with Kapustin as though by mere coincidence. Rainey watched Saul pocket the lighter and continue on, a man and his cigarette out for a stroll. In a matter of seconds, the Russian in a similar demonstration of apparent aloofness, paid his bill and followed in Saul's wake.

Rainey hung behind, scanning the cobbled street, the windows, and the benches that encircled the fountain for anyone showing the slightest interest in Kapustin's actions. Finally satisfied the Russian agent was clean, Rainey, in turn, dropped in behind him and the woman on the scooter disappeared.

———

Saul worked his way down the narrow street in such a manner that Kapustin was sure to keep up. He rounded the corner onto Tsimiski and acted as though he were contemplating whether to take a cab. When Kapustin emerged, Saul turned on his heel and pressed on. At almost midblock, he stopped outside a coffee bar, dropped his cigarette to the sidewalk, and stepped on it. Out of the corner of his eye, he watched Kapustin approach, pull the door of the establishment open, and enter. Saul gave it a second then stepped in after him.

The phalanx of waiting patrons was long but seemed to move with relative quickness. The back of the line consisted of a young couple holding hands and a man in his forties in a faded blue PAOK FC jersey.

Saul and Kapustin shuffled along in concert with the rest of the line. Both of their heads were tilted backward, their eyes on the menu board above the cashier.

Saul was the first one to speak, his words just above a whisper so as not to draw unwanted attention. "It's been a long time, Grisha," he said, using the shortened form of the man's name.

"Yes. It has." Kapustin's eyes remained on the menu board.

Hands in his pockets, Saul stepped forward in unison with Kapustin as the line ahead of them advanced again.

Kapustin tilted his head ever so slightly to the left. "Something's come up, old friend. Something important."

Saul glanced toward the small hallway that led to the restrooms and a rear exit. "So I've heard."

They remained silent from that point on until the cashier handed Kapustin his cup, foam nearly spilling over the top. Kapustin set it down and reached for one of the plastic lids that were stacked like skyscrapers farther down the counter. In doing so, some of the hot liquid ran over the lip of the cup and splashed onto the countertop. At that moment, Saul stepped forward and handed him several napkins he'd pulled from the dispenser, one old-timer helping another.

Kapustin, feigning embarrassment, accepted the napkins and immediately dabbed up the spilled coffee. The fact that Kapustin pocketed one of the unused crumpled napkins had gone unseen by all. Even Rainey had not noticed it and he'd been watching the whole thing unfold with a sharp eye. Had he not known beforehand how Saul was going to pass the message to Kapustin, he would have thought nothing of their brief interaction.

After paying for his own coffee, Saul exited to the street. He headed south on Tsimiski Avenue, crossed the street in front of an apothecary, and hooked a left onto Ionos Dragoumi. He walked for half a block more then veered left onto the one-lane Agiou Mina, where he fell into the back seat of a waiting Suzuki SUV. The driver, another support staffer from Athens Station, made no comment and asked no questions before pulling away.

Kapustin didn't open the balled-up napkin until he had closed and locked the door of his flat. He walked into the kitchen, poured himself three thumbs of vodka, and looked at his reflection in the microwave oven above the stove. He stood over the napkin, which lay unfurled on the counter, and stared down once more at the message written in black ink.

The Statue. 2000.

Kapustin struck a match and touched it to the bottom corner of the napkin. He let the flame climb halfway up the white paper then dropped it into the kitchen sink, where it writhed about. When there was nothing left but a few blackened ashes, he turned on the faucet and washed them down the drain.

14

There were many monuments in Thessaloniki, but only one had served as a previous meeting location in Saul and Grigory Kapustin's storied past, though it was long ago, well before Kapustin had been named Athens *rezident*. Situated along the seaside promenade, the Alexander the Great Statue was a well-known city landmark and therefore a favorite attraction for tourists. Sword in hand, cape stretched out behind him, Alexander astride his mighty bronco, Bucephalus, cut quite a profile on the waterfront. The bright spotlights aimed at the magnificently carved image made the statue a focal point for everyone milling about the promenade and that included Reagan Rainey. He wondered if Alexander and his rearing horse had been purposefully positioned to face east or if that was merely a product of serendipity.

A gray fog thick as stone had begun to settle over the city, blurring the lights on the cargo ships out in the Thermaic Gulf into a scene right out of a Monet painting. The temperature had dipped since the coffee-shop encounter. Rainey could feel a chill, like thin, bony fingers, probing along the edges of his jacket.

"Any sign of him?" said Rainey. The tiny earbud in his left ear, a marvel of modern technology, was connected to the phone he carried in his jacket. The phone looked like the latest iteration of a Samsung Galaxy smartphone even down to the branding but also had an additional secure radio comms capability designed specifically for DX operatives. The device was also linked to a specially modified key fob he carried in his left front pants pocket. This, so he could click a response, if need be, instead of talking. He could also use it to change channels on the secure radio network or send an emergency alert to someone monitoring the comms traffic from say, a local tactical operations center or even DX headquarters back home.

Saul eased into one of the empty benches that framed the large, rectangular piazza, rubbed his hands together for warmth. "Not yet. But don't worry. He'll show."

It was a few minutes past eight when Rainey spied Kapustin strolling down the promenade, collar up, hands pushed deep inside the pockets of his wool overcoat.

"I got him," said Rainey beneath the curled bill of a weathered Greece national football club ball cap. "Walking southbound, just north of the Statue. He sees you."

Now wearing a thick mustache as a disguise, eyeglasses, and a gray wool driving cap, Saul uncrossed his legs and murmured into his own lapel mic, "Very good."

Rainey looked up and down the promenade then turned toward the sea. Best he could tell, the Russian was not being followed, though the gauzy fog made it difficult to be certain. The hard-and-fast rules of the game dictated that the Russian would have taken great care in his pre-meeting run to flush out any surveillance before ever setting foot in the area. But nothing was guaranteed in this business. The best pavement artists were ghosts.

"Looks clean," Rainey said.

Saul stood up and greeted Kapustin with a handshake then the two old spies set off, side by side, toward a black Land Rover parked along the tree-lined street. Kapustin climbed into the back seat and slid over to the far side. Saul ducked in after him while Rainey took the front seat beside the driver.

Before long, after a series of surveillance-detection maneuvers of their own, they were barreling up the rising slope into Asvestochori—a small hamlet within the wooded hill country due east of Thessaloniki. They eventually came to a stop in front of a white-washed villa, which was nestled atop a quiet hillock on the outskirts of town. The safe house was one of many that a small but punctilious support unit at DX headquarters maintained for operations the world over.

Rainey hopped out and opened the front door. After doing a quick walk-through of the place, he waved Saul and Kapustin inside. He held the front door open till the Land Rover's taillights were well out of sight then headed into the kitchen to search out a coffeemaker. Saul and Kapustin shed their coats and each took a seat in the living room at the front of the villa while Rainey continued his assault on the kitchen cabinets. In a matter of minutes, he had the tea kettle on the stove working toward a boil, coffee brewing in the machine on the countertop, and had procured a plate of unsalted crackers and feta cheese, which he now set on the low table in front of his elders. He then took a seat on the sofa at the end opposite the Russian in time to hear Saul's rather truncated monologue about his credentials and how the Russian need not worry about speaking freely before him.

After formal introductions, Kapustin leaned back and said, "So, how are you, my friend? How is Grace?"

"She passed. It will be three years this spring. Cancer, I'm afraid."

"I'm sorry. I hadn't heard."

"Thank you." Saul picked up a cracker, turned it over in his hands. "I trust Yulia is well."

The Russian smiled. "The grandchildren keep her busy. In fact, she is back home visiting them right now."

"And Viktor and Darya?"

"Viktor's company is growing fast. He is swamped, in fact. He's been forced to travel more than he'd like. So, it's nice when Yulia can go back to Moscow and help his dear wife with the children.

"And Darya." The Russian shrugged. "Well, she's Darya."

"Where is she this time?"

Kapustin chuckled. "London. Last I knew she was working for some green energy upstart. I give her six months then something else will catch her eye. How are yours?"

"The same, I suppose." There was more than a hint of melancholy in Saul's voice.

After a brief pause, the conversation naturally switched gears.

"I apologize for the breach in protocol, but what I have to say is...well, too important to be entrusted to just anyone." Kapustin clasped his hands together. "The reason I needed to speak with you is..." He swallowed. "I have information concerning what happened in your country. The terrorist attack, I mean. I know who is responsible."

Saul was instantly serious. "Go on."

"It's Hezbollah. But I'm sure you've already considered this." Kapustin did not wait for affirmation from Saul. "Allow me to explain. The contacts I have developed over the years in Iran, in Lebanon, in Syria, and elsewhere, I still have regular communication with them despite my current posting. A man I knew in Damascus came to see me last night. He's fled the country on account of recent events." Kapustin rotated the cracker in his hand several times. He did not have to elaborate on the fact that just a week ago Bashar al-Assad's government had been overrun by rebels. Syria had fallen. "My friend literally showed up on my doorstep, hat in hand. Apparently, he'd missed the last plane out of the country before the rebels shut down the airport. How he managed to make it to Athens, I haven't the foggiest."

"What did he want?"

70

"My help. Like many of his fellow government officials, he is seeking asylum in my country. He wants a new identity, Russian citizenship. But first and most importantly to him, he wants my assistance—or rather Moscow's assistance—in getting his family out of Syria. They are still there, I'm afraid.

"In any case, based on my suspicions, I took the liberty of asking him what he knew about what happened in the US, the attack there."

"And?"

"He quite plainly said that Hezbollah was responsible for carrying out the attack."

"This source," said Saul. "Who is he? Is he credible?"

"He's credible. His name is Ziad Suleiman, now *former* deputy to General Muhammad Habib."

"Syria's liaison to Hezbollah?"

"*Former* liaison. Yes."

"Do you think he is worth approaching?"

"By *your* service?"

Saul nodded.

Kapustin shook his head vehemently. "No. In fact, if he or my service had any idea that I was speaking with you, they would both want me dead. Let me be clear. Suleiman is a hardened extremist. He did not tell me this out of the goodness of his heart. Frankly, he only answered my questions because of what he thinks I can do for him."

"What else did he say?"

"He alluded to the fact that the attack was born out of information the group had acquired from a Saudi source. He said he didn't know who that person was. The Saudi spy's identity is highly compartmented. Likely only known to a few individuals.

"Suleiman said the *reason* for the attack was twofold: one) because of Israel's pager operation, and two) the assassination of Nasrallah in the headquarters bombing. He said both the organization and Tehran were utterly humiliated over the pager op and had vowed to get even. But the killing of the Hezbollah leader sent them into a furious rage."

Saul considered this. "Have you seen the video with the claim of responsibility?"

Rainey focused his attention on Kapustin's bland face.

"I have," said the Russian. "The Army of Holy Fire."

"What do you make of it?"

Kapustin wrinkled his nose. "Clearly another front, so that Hezbollah and their Iranian backers can deny involvement. I'm sure you've come to the same conclusion. What I don't get is why target the US. Especially if Hezbollah is intent on evening the score with *Israel*. It doesn't track. Maybe I'm just missing a piece of the puzzle."

Without letting on about the canceled meeting at the Saudi consulate, Saul said, "So, who is it? Who planned and coordinated the attack? Most, if not all, of Hezbollah's command structure is dead or buried under mountains of rubble. Who's the mystery man?"

The Russian closed his eyes for a few seconds, apparently in deep thought.

"Grisha? Are you okay? What is it?"

"I am retiring, Saul."

"And?"

"I believe I can help you get who you are looking for, but it will come at a heavy cost to me. If the information I give you is ever traced back to me, I will be a marked man. I will have to look over my shoulder for the rest of my life."

"I'm not sure I follow. You've been spying for us for years. Why would this be any more dangerous for you than before?"

Rainey excused himself and slipped out of the room to calm the shrieking teapot. He delivered a cup to each man then returned to his post at the end of the sofa, gripping a mug that he had filled to the brim with strong, black coffee.

"Maybe there is another way," Kapustin said thoughtfully. "What do you know so far? About the attack, I mean."

Rainey watched Saul's face. He could see the chess game unfolding. This would have to be a careful dance. A give and take. For whatever reason, Kapustin was legitimately fearful.

Saul explained the sequence of events in a brief but concise monologue. He spoke of the gunmen in the plaza, the assaulters who took the Saudi consulate, the VBIED that detonated in front of the US Mission to the United Nations and carved a rather large crater into 1st Avenue. Aside from the secret meeting at the Saudi consulate, the only information he bothered to withhold was the fact that one of the angels of Second Avenue was sitting in their midst. "We're still developing the situation, but early signs are pointing us to France. Of the men we've identified thus far, all three held French passports. Also, the video file containing the claim of responsibility was delivered to the Paris offices of *Le Monde*."

Rainey detected a slight movement in the tiny muscles around Kapustin's eyes, one that suggested Saul's words had triggered a memory.

As if on cue, the Russian looked at Rainey. "Did you know it was your father who recruited me? It happened in Paris. And to believe I had actually gone there to take a shot at recruiting *him*."

Rainey sipped his coffee. Up to this point, he'd been unsure about trusting a Russian intelligence officer especially so soon after his operation on Russian soil, but the comment about his father forced him to recalculate. "If you know something Mr. Kapustin, we would appreciate it if you'd tell us."

Kapustin grinned and tilted his head in Saul's direction. "He looks just like him, doesn't he?"

"Grisha, please," said Saul.

Kapustin uttered a name then quickly added, "This according to Suleiman."

"Abu Ghazi. As in Qais al-Nourani? That Abu Ghazi?" Saul held his gaze. "He's been MIA ever since we took out Mughniyeh. You're sure?"

"I double- and triple-checked with Suleiman. Said that about four months ago Nourani reappeared in southern Lebanon. Just out of the blue."

"Reappeared? From where, Iran?"

Kapustin nodded. "Word has it he fled across the border into Syria just before Israel let loose on Hezbollah's headquarters, tunnel networks, and weapons depots. Got out by the skin of his teeth, I'm told."

"Where is he now, Grisha?"

"Suleiman said that as the rebels took control of Homs and moved on toward Damascus, Nourani and his inner circle disappeared. Whereabouts unknown."

Rainey registered the concerned look on Kapustin's face. Saul apparently noticed it, too.

"What is it?" said the old spy.

"Suleiman said that Nourani and the remnants of Hezbollah are regroup-ing, refortifying, and have promised to make Israel and the West pay a heavy price. He said they are planning more attacks. Bigger, more elaborate. His words, not mine."

"Where? When?"

"I'm sorry. Suleiman didn't know specifics."

"And you believe him?"

"I hold his life and the lives of his family members in my hands. I believe him."

Saul pondered this. "What's the Paris connection? Does Nourani have people there or what?"

The Russian lowered his voice as if he were concerned about eavesdrop-pers. "There is a man. He works out of the office for the permanent repre-sentative of France to the European Union in Brussels. Based on what you and Suleiman have told me, it would stand to reason that he may have played a role in the preoperational phase of the attack. It's only a hunch mind you. In any case, tread carefully, my friend. He belongs to Moscow Center."

"He's a Russian agent," said Rainey matter-of-factly.

Kapustin nodded. "Code name *Luchnik*. ARCHER. He has been a good source of intelligence on the EU and NATO. He's also provided our intelligence services from time to time access to French passports, visas, that type of thing via sub-sources he has developed. There have been recent grumblings in Yasenevo about ARCHER. We've known about his involvement with Hezbollah for some time, but recently it seems his activities with the organization are becoming increasingly *inconvenient*."

"How so?"

Kapustin shrugged. "He has been giving their operatives new identities. Turning them into legitimate French passport holders, so they can travel abroad without complication."

"What else?"

"I'm afraid that's all I know."

"Why didn't you report this to your case officer?" snapped Saul.

"I am retiring soon. I want a life beyond this miserable business. The most recent case officer your service assigned to me is just a young kid, Saul. He is green and awkward. Maybe his intentions are pure, I don't know, but to be perfectly frank, I don't trust him. That's why I wanted to speak with you directly. This is too important."

Saul leaned forward and lowered his chin. "I need a name, Grisha."

15

In less than twenty-four hours, the full-court press was on. Alban Clement, France's deputy ambassador to the European Union, had become the centerpiece of an intense DX surveillance operation. With information provided by Kapustin and a little help from the National Security Agency, the CIA's Directorate X soon had unfettered access to Clement's mobile devices, which meant they were privy to his incoming and outgoing calls, text messages, emails, stored contacts, account logins. They had it all. Cameras were set up to monitor his Woluwe-Saint-Pierre apartment and a team of watchers was dispatched to keep track of his movements at all times. For now, the DX would not bother to notify the French about their rogue diplomat or inform the Belgians of the clandestine undertaking on their soil. Operational security dictated such.

It would be another twenty-four hours until one of the young up-and-comers in the DX's Technical Operations Group unearthed a batch of deleted files on the hard drive of Clement's personal notebook computer. This came after a TOG team had burgled the apartment while the diplomat and his wife were out for dinner. Once inside, the team made mirror images of every device they could find—laptops, phones, flash drives, SSDs, PDAs, MP3 players, everything.

The subsequent discovery of the deleted files on Clement's machine confirmed that Alban Clement was indeed a spy. The files included photographs of Middle Eastern-looking men along with corresponding biographical information—false names, dates of birth, addresses, and more. The TOG techs had no idea how the files wound up in Clement's possession—but the prevailing theory was that they had been delivered via an undiscovered USB drive. In any case, the Frenchman had at some point deleted the files on his computer hard drive in a futile attempt to cover his tracks.

Two of the names in the deleted files jumped out. Rainey had seen them beneath the photos Job had given him in his study. These were the same names that the FBI had already tied to two of the gunmen in New York City.

Rainey was now hunched over his secure laptop computer, scrolling through Clement's email correspondence from the last several months trying to find a thread to pull.

"Anything?" said Saul.

"Not yet. Just a lot of EU bureaucratic junk. I'll tell you what I'd like to do."

Saul nodded. "I know, but we need more." He circled behind Rainey in thoughtful repose. "Is he going back to France for the holidays? Maybe we can have a chat with him there."

He remembered seeing mention of it in one of the emails from the month previous. "Here it is. Yeah, he and his wife are traveling back home for Christmas. They are planning to return to Brussels after the New Year."

"When is he scheduled to leave Belgium?"

Rainey clicked the mouse a few times until he found the right email. "In three days."

"So, unless you want to wait for his return to Brussels, it's France then."

Rainey peered into the computer screen, willing time to stand still. This would be the first Christmas since his father had been discovered alive and repatriated to American soil. For the last twenty years, Ben Rainey had been held at a Russian black site. Rainey wanted to be home with his family this Christmas more than anything. It would surely be special. But the likelihood of that happening was evaporating fast. It was one of the things he hated most about his job. But someone had to do it. Someone had to be on the front lines of the shadow wars going on around the globe. He glared at the screen, suppressing the anger that had welled up inside him. He needed to set aside his emotions and focus.

As much as Rainey wanted to go to Brussels right now and mug Clement off the street, he knew Pappy was right. They needed to proceed carefully. Clement was a French citizen, a diplomat. Abducting him in Brussels could very well create an international row between the United States and its critical foreign partner in France. There were too many variables. It was just too risky. Rainey considered the possibility of bringing in the French but dismissed the notion immediately. There weren't enough compelling reasons yet to do so. Plus, control over the operation could quickly get out of hand. It was about this time that he remembered reading something about a Christmas party in one of Clement's emails. He opened it anew and read it this time more carefully. A smile soon formed on his face. There were some more details to work out, but he knew it was likely their best chance at developing the situation. Now he just needed to convince Job.

Rainey picked up his secure mobile phone and dialed Lynn Street.

16

They touched down at Charles de Gaulle Airport a few hours apart. Saul boarded the Métro and headed for Bougival. Rainey, meanwhile, stopped off for a ham and cheese sandwich and a bottle of water then hired a cab to take him to the city center. After being dropped off outside the Paris Opera House, he walked north for a block and into the Galeries Lafayette, a large department store in the Ninth Arrondissement. He moved swiftly through the crowds careful not to appear like a hurried man until he emerged onto the rue de la Chaussée d'Antin. There, he hailed another cab to the Louvre. But a few blocks shy, Rainey alerted the driver—a small man with large ears and a flat cap—that he had changed his mind. After paying the driver, he paced toward the aquamarine-colored canopy of the brasserie across the street. He waited in its shade until the cab was out of sight then studied the faces swirling about. He had no sense of being followed, but for a man in his business, it was just prudent to be sure.

Rainey walked several more blocks then crossed the rue de Rivoli before turning right onto the footpath that skirted the Jardin des Tuileries. He assumed the sporadic pace of a tourist, stopping every so often to take photos with his smartphone: the December trees of the park; now the azure sky alive with brilliant white clouds; and of course, the selfie as he held the phone high in the sky pointed back on himself smiling and making happy faces.

He drifted farther down the footpath, snapping away with his phone in like manner until he reached a pre-determined spot. Here, he turned toward the street and stared between the rungs of the wrought-iron fence. He noticed the elegant façade of Le Meurice, which was the object of his little jaunt in the first place. The French and European Union flags were dancing in the breeze as he lowered his phone and continued his visual inspection of the grand hotel's exterior and the street stretching in either direction before it. He pictured in his mind how it might all go down. Finally, he raised the phone and took another selfie for good measure, then set off again.

By the time Rainey reached the safe house in Bougival, the sky had grown dark and the streets quiet. He slipped through the gate at the edge of the property, which led him down a short concrete driveway. A pad, really. The small garage attached to the right flank of the home had been painted white but showed obvious signs of its age. The home itself was perfect as safe houses go. The property on which it was situated was a corner lot surrounded by a tall, thick hedge. A cemetery lay to its rear and the surrounding neighborhood was altogether just as dead as those who were buried beneath it. He approached the front door and knocked twice in quick succession then twice more. Saul ushered him inside then pointed him to the pot of soup on the stove.

"How did it go?" said Rainey, filling a chipped enamel bowl with thick beef vegetable stew.

"Fine. His place is perfect. The streets around it are free of cameras, too. I think it'll work, bud."

Rainey eased a spoon into the bowl and stirred in a slow, clockwise motion. "Good deal."

Saul yawned then trotted to the sofa in the sitting room where he collapsed.

"You think Job will go for it?" Rainey said.

"He may need some convincing, but in the end, I think he'll come around. He won't be here for at least another couple of hours. Why don't you get some sleep when you're finished there."

Eyes burning, Rainey nodded. "I think I might. It feels like I'm running on fumes."

———

When Rainey awoke, he sat up on the bed and stared at the wall for several long minutes, the details of his planned pitch once again running through his mind. The glorious aroma of strong coffee brewing in the kitchen interrupted his thoughts. It was still dark outside, so in keeping with the neighborhood, he kept the light in the bedroom doused as he stood and slipped on his shoes.

He found Saul and Zane Davis, Job's bodyguard, in the sitting room with the TV on. They were watching France 24's coverage of the ongoing search-and-rescue efforts in New York City. A graphic with various statistical facts of the injured and dead appeared. According to the current figures, 113 people were still missing, most of them presumed buried in the partially collapsed hotel at One United Nations Plaza. Others had doubtless been blown to bits by the powerful blast or lay somewhere below street level in the crater that stretched down into the 1st Avenue Tunnel. For most of America, it was difficult *not* to compare the attack in New York to 9/11. Emergency workers dotted the landscape amidst all manner of carnage, while encampments of camera crews and dolled-up newsmen and women jockeyed for position on the periphery.

Rainey heard the toilet flush in the bathroom down the hall followed by the sound of water in the sink. His eyes remained on the TV footage as his focus sharpened to the impending brief with Job.

After another minute, the DX spymaster entered the room behind him. Job patted Rainey on the shoulder on his way to the chair next to the sofa. "Saul says the meeting in Greece went well."

"It did," said Rainey. "Anything new on the home front?"

"The Bureau believes it has identified the man who rented the trucks and the warehouses in which the New York City bombs were likely built. Juan Lopez-Diaz."

"Alias?"

Job nodded. "It's the name on the fake Pennsylvania driver's license he presented at the truck rental company in Stamford, Connecticut."

"After coming up dry on our end, we forwarded his photo to the Israelis. They sent this back about an hour ago." Job leaned forward and opened his secure laptop computer on the coffee table, spun it around so Rainey could see it. On the screen was the photo of a young man in his mid-thirties along with his known biographical information. "He has some rather strong ties to Foz do Iguaçu in the TBA." Foz do Iguaçu was a city located at the confluence of the borders of Brazil, Paraguay, and Argentina, a place otherwise referred to as the Tri-Border Area, or TBA. It was a known hotbed of Hezbollah terrorist activity.

"He's Lebanese," added Job. "Born in Majdaloun, according to our Israeli friends."

"The very heart of the Bekaa," said Saul.

Rainey stared at the man on the screen. "How did he get into the country?"

"We don't know. Could be he came across the border with the flood of illegals that the Winslow administration, in its infinite wisdom, has let in over the past four years."

"Any idea where he might be now?" Rainey said.

"Assuming he is not one of the attackers who blew himself to bits, we have none." Job leaned back in the chair and crossed his legs. "So... You said on the phone that you have a plan with respect to the Frenchman. Let's hear it."

Rainey took a seat and began his monologue. To his credit, Job allowed him to speak for a solid twenty minutes without interruption. After Rainey had finished his opening salvo, the real battle began. The battle of ideas. It was one of the reasons why Directorate X was so formidable. Groupthink did not exist in the DX. There was no room for it. Ideas were challenged, put to the test. No aspect of a plan was off limits. It was within this crucible of discussion that the best operations were forged. Operations for which the DX was well known and supremely well suited. This was nothing new to Rainey. In fact, it was something to which he was rather accustomed. It was how his former unit in Fort Bragg was run. Sometimes tempers flared, but everyone intrinsically knew they were working toward one goal and as one team. After everything had been hashed out and the final decision had been made by the man in charge, everyone fell in line and did their best to see that every aspect of the plan would work to the fullest, so the operation would result in success. But sometimes getting there took some time.

Job shook his head. "Not gonna work, Ray."

"Why not?"

"First of all, we don't even know if those files *came* from Hezbollah. It could have been the Russians or the man in the moon for Pete's sake. There are too many unknowns right now."

Rainey inched forward in his chair. "It's Hezbollah, Job."

"How do you know?"

"Kapustin. According to him, the Russians contact Clement in person, never through electronic communications. They consider it too risky."

"Do we know the identity of his handler?"

"No. Kapustin has access to the raw intelligence reports but doesn't know who is actually running Clement."

Job got up, began to pace the room. Finally, he stopped, put his hands on his hips. "I still don't like it. Whatever we do, he's sure to run and tell the Russians."

Rainey shook his head. "He won't. I promise you."

"And what makes you so sure?"

"I can be very persuasive. Clement won't think twice about screwing us over, because he'll know I can get to him any time, any place." It was time to close the deal. "Listen, Job. We know Clement is selling French and EU secrets to the Russians. Based on what Kapustin told us, he's got something heavy going with Hezbollah, too. And that, as we all know, certainly loops in the Iranians. The guy's prostituting himself all over the place. Worst case, as I see it, is that we blow him out of the water, expose him. We turn off the freaking spigot. But maybe, just *maybe*, after we're through with him, we, the French, or both of us, can run him back against the Russians or the Iranians. I don't know. In the meantime, if he knows something about the attack, I think he's worth the effort. We have nothing to lose, Job. He's cooked any way you like it."

"You make an interesting argument, Ray, I must admit." Job returned to his chair. "And the apartment house?"

"Sits in the middle of the rue Daubigny. No cameras," added Saul.

"What about the daughter? What was her name?"

"Vivienne. She's away at school—Stanford. She isn't coming home for the holidays this year due to an internship she's got with an outfit in San Fran. It's perfect, Job."

"I hear what you're saying, Ray, but this is something that I cannot authorize on my own. I need to run this by the director. And he'll need to get approval from POTUS."

"Whatever. Just make it soon. We have a narrow window in which to make this work," said Rainey. "While you work on getting the authority, let's at least start moving pieces into place."

"What do you need?"

He handed Job two sheets of paper. On the first was a list of names. "I'll also need someone here to monitor the radio traffic, camera feeds, et cetera. You know, act as a hub. On the second page there, you'll find a list of things we're going to need in order to pull this off."

Job examined the papers. "You seem to have thought of everything."

Rainey smiled. "That's what you pay me to do."

"All right, I'll be in touch."

17

C IA Director Ken Thompson watched the president-elect enter the room and assume his place at the conference table. Marty Kendall had an air of easy optimism about him and a quiet confidence that seemed to infect everyone with whom he came in contact, at least most everyone. Holding court at the head of the table was Acting President Beasley. Sitting just to his left was Valetta Ivory, the national security advisor. Word from the incoming administration was that Kendall intended to keep her on after being sworn into office. Ivory's aversion to politics was common knowledge but this was only part of the reason Thompson loved working with her. Like him, Valetta Ivory was a patriot first. And a fierce one at that. He suspected Kendall liked her for the very same reason.

"Good afternoon, all. I appreciate everyone coming on such short notice." Beasley folded his hands on the table. "Let's get right to it, shall we? Ken? You want to begin?"

"Thank you, Mr. President. Yes. As you all know, we are working with our international partners and sources to find out who perpetrated the attack on our soil. We believe we may have identified someone with information that could propel the investigation forward, however..." Thompson looked around the room.

"Yes?" said Beasley impatiently.

"He's a French national. A high-ranking diplomat, sir."

"Who is he?"

"His name is Alban Clement and he is currently serving as France's deputy ambassador to the European Union."

"I don't understand. What could he possibly know about the attack?" said Beasley.

"Well, sir, that's one of the things we'd like to ask him. You see, we have a source who has informed us that Clement provides intelligence as well as support in the form of procurement of travel documents—passports, et cetera—to a hostile intelligence service. We've been able to substantiate some of this with our technical surveillance efforts. According to the source, Clement is involved in creating new identities specifically for members of Hezbollah. Members who are then sent abroad to carry out terrorist operations. Whether he actually knows they are blooded Hezbollah operatives is unclear."

"So, what are you proposing here, Ken?"

"Mr. President, sir, we are requesting authority to approach Clement so that we can ask him some questions directly. It would be in contravention to his will, I should add."

"In contravention to his will?" blurted Karen Griggs. "And about three dozen laws."

Beasley swiveled his head toward the secretary of state. "Let's at least hear him out, Karen. What do you say?"

Griggs shrugged while shaking her head.

Beasley turned his attention back to Thompson. "You wish to secure him for interrogation? Is that right, Ken?"

"Yes, sir. That's exactly right."

"But why not go to the French? I'm sure if I made a direct plea to their president, we could get the same result, no?"

"Sir, we think that would be too risky at this point. It could tip off our targets, inadvertently or otherwise." Thompson saw Ivory nodding in agreement out of the corner of his eye.

"And these targets? Who might they be exactly?"

"At this point, sir, the evidence points to Hezbollah."

"And that means Iran."

"Very probable. Yes, sir."

"I thought we had a claim of responsibility already. This Army of Holy Fire whozeewhatsit," said Marvin Inman. The acting director of national intelligence was a normally quiet man with large eyes, the thin, colorless lips of a smallmouth bass, and white eyebrows that shot out from his forehead in a manner that suggested they might have been glued on. Thompson thought he was nice enough but grossly out of his depth. Inman was a placeholder, nothing more.

"Well, sir, we assess with a high degree of probability that the Army of Holy Fire is another one of Hezbollah's aliases. A *front* if you will."

"A high degree... But not conclusive."

"No, sir. Which is why we need to question Clement."

Beasley leaned back in his chair. "Marty, what are *your* thoughts?"

Kendall regarded the expectant faces with a thoughtful gaze. "Well, if I understand Director Thompson correctly, and I think that I do, approaching Clement in any other way than that stated could jeopardize potential follow-on operations. And thus the need to do so clandestinely."

"Correct, sir," said Thompson. "We will likely only have one crack at him. Our assessment is that it needs to be done on *our* terms. I would also like to state that Clement will not be roughed up. In fact, our intention is that the whole thing be executed in such a way as to appear to have never happened, so he will be—he *must* be—treated accordingly for this to work."

Griggs huffed. "This is outrageous." All eyes turned on her again. "To be blunt, sir, I don't like it. What Director Thompson is suggesting is abducting a *French citizen*—and a government official, at that—on *French soil*. It's illegal and just plain wrong. We have no business meddling in the affairs of the French."

This time it was Ivory who spoke. She was not one to be bullied. "Karen, do you even know what the Agency does? Their charter permits them to break laws on foreign soil. It's what they do. It's what they do for the good of our national security interests. Above all, let's not forget that a patch of ground in New York City is still smoldering with the remains of our countrymen. Bodies are still being collected from the streets of *three* of our cities. If Alban Clement was somehow involved in this terrorist attack then he has *made* himself our business."

"My feeling precisely," added Kendall.

"Oh, please!" said Griggs. "Listen, I get it. What happened in New York and those other cities is unfortunate. Acts of despicable extremism. They are tragic and horrific and I'm sorry for the families, but they do not give us the right to go kidnap a French citizen, an am*bass*ador for crying out loud, off the streets of Paris."

Thompson studied Griggs from across the table. In large part, he regarded her as the most dangerous of anyone in the room, mainly because he didn't trust her. She had a reputation for only looking out for herself. He had it on good authority that she would do *anything* to prevail over her rivals, no matter how unseemly, unethical, or even illegal. Rumors were already flying in some quarters of DC that she was contemplating challenging Kendall in the next presidential election. It was no secret that she and her party were seething with rage after the utterly disgraceful episode involving the ousted President Winslow. Even now, the whole affair was still steeped in mystery and political intrigue.

It seemed apparent that Karen Griggs was ready to pick up the mantle and fight the incoming president at every turn. Even at the detriment of the very nation she was sworn to serve.

Thompson, considered by most to be the quintessential gentlemen spy, was stone-faced. From his outward demeanor, nary a person at the table could know that a storm of anger churned within his belly. He folded his hands on the table, offered a mild grin, the kind that people like Griggs usually considered a provocation, and added a simple rejoinder. "Notwithstanding Karen's advocacy for the devil, I believe we are well within our purview to hold a quiet conversation with Clement, Mr. President, sir. As I alluded before… The premise is that this be devoid of our sponsorship."

Beasley raised his eyebrows. "Zero footprint?"

"Zero footprint, sir."

The acting president drummed his fingers on the polished wood surface of the table. "Marty?"

Kendall nodded. "My position is that we grab him." No one could accuse Kendall of using lawyer speak. He was direct and unapologetic in his manner.

"Very well."

Griggs exploded. "But Richard! *Mr. President*, sir—"

Beasley held up his hand commanding her to be silent. He was clearly not a fan of the secretary of state. He evaluated each of the faces angled toward him, saving Kendall for last. "This is going to be Marty's ship in a few weeks. I think it incumbent upon me to defer to his wishes in this matter. However, it's still my name on the desk so to speak. That said, Director Thompson, I want you to hear me loud and clear. I am *not* telling you to do this. I am *not* telling you to abduct Alban Clement for the purpose of interrogation. I will stress that if this thing were to blow up it would be very embarrassing for the country. It would also harm relations with our French friends likely for years to come. Do you understand me?"

"Yes, Mr. President. I do."

Once back in his seventh-floor office suite at Langley, Thompson picked up the secure phone on his desk and dialed Paris Station. In a matter of seconds, the call was routed to the house in Bougival.

"Yes?" said Job on his secure mobile.

"You have your authority. Don't let me down. Don't let America down."

"Thank you, sir. We won't."

18

They arrived over the course of the next two days, some of them coming from as far away as Montana. The first to pass through the door was Maddie, Rainey's kid sister. She was younger than him by three years, but every bit as motivated, intelligent, and lethal. Still considered new to the game, Maddie's contributions to the last operation—a dangerous romp through South America and other points abroad—helped lead Rainey and his team to their CIA-officer father, who had been long considered dead after a plane crash in the Venezuelan jungle in 1996. It had been her first operation and offered unequivocal proof that she belonged in the DX.

Next came Evelina Krantz, a blond-haired, green-eyed intelligence veteran, who was as gifted an operations officer as she was beautiful. Evie had a unique background though it was still plenty opaque to her DX colleagues. She was, in fact, the only soul in the entire directorate who had officially served in a foreign military service, that being the Israel Defense Forces. One thing was abundantly clear, she was positively fearless.

The others soon followed. Mouse and Tonka were two of America's best special operators and among Rainey's closest friends. The three of them had served in an assault troop in the Army's special missions unit, still commonly referred to as Delta Force, prior to making their way to the DX.

"Hey, Shep," said Rainey. "Good to see you, brother."

"I gotta tell ya, Bronc, it feels like nine-eleven all over again. I wouldn't miss this for anything." Mark "Shepherd" Alcott was an AFO—Advanced Force Operations—specialist from the Field Support Unit, one of the important component pieces that made up the DX's Support Services Group. A veteran of the Army's 3rd Special Forces Group and the Defense Intelligence Agency, he was now a permanent fixture in the DX with his remit being difficult surveillance operations and other complicated tasks in line with supporting DX personnel in the field. Nevertheless, he was not opposed to getting his hands dirty and joining in on the fun stuff. He had always been the type of man to lead from the front and that extended back to his days as detachment commander of Rainey's Special Forces A-team.

"No doubt," said Rainey with a smack on the former Army captain's shoulder.

"Where are the JSG guys? It's awfully quiet in here." JSG, pronounced *Jay-Sig*, was the DX's Joint Services Group. It housed the special operators—the shooters. Its members almost exclusively came from the special missions units of the US military's Joint Special Operations Command.

"Jazz is downstairs going over the satellite imagery. The others are out getting a feel for the streets. Job's going to brief everyone here at twenty-three hundred."

"Roger that."

When they had all finally arrived and settled into the house, Job corralled them into the large unfinished basement, which by now had been converted into a makeshift tactical operations center. A large folding table had been erected. Around it sat Rainey, Evelina, Maddie, Alcott, Mouse, and Tonka. The JSG shooters filled a hodgepodge of mismatched couches and armchairs on the perimeter. Saul stood off by himself near the stairs. All eyes were on Job at the front of the room, a large, wall-mounted chalkboard relic his backdrop.

"Okay, folks, we have two days to prepare for this little jaunt. Some folks from FSU out of Paris Station are going to pitch in." Job related how the Field Support Unit staff would contribute to the operation by renting the cars necessary for their plan to work. They would also procure items detailed on the list Rainey had given to him previously. Clothes, shoes, radios, firearms, and other gear.

"Maddie, tomorrow you will pay a visit to Le Meurice." He handed her a slim leather case and watched as she opened it. Inside were several business cards that had already been printed up by FSU staff from Paris Station.

With her thumb and index finger, she pulled out one of the cards and read her alias aloud, adding a Russian accent for good measure. "Vanya Konstantinovna Primakova."

"It's last minute but not complicated," said Job. "As your NOC, you will be the personal assistant of a Russian oligarch. Your cover story is that you're doing advance planning for an event he is considering for the spring. You meet with the hotel's director of events tomorrow morning at nine. In reality, you'll be gathering intel for us on the layout of the hotel to include the room in which the Christmas bash is to be held."

"*Ya ponimayu*." I understand.

"Swan! You speak Russian?" blurted Mouse, surprise still spreading across his rugged features.

Maddie replied with a coy smile.

"Swan has many talents," added Tonka, referring to the call sign she had earned during their last operation together. The comment evoked chuckles mostly because of the serious manner in which he had said it. Operator humor was all dry, all the time.

Maddie looked at Fig, who had just nudged Rainey in the shoulder from behind. When the Hispanic man realized she was staring at him, he held up his hands as if to block her incoming blows. "Don't hit me."

Like Fig, Maddie was a gifted martial artist. She just shook her head. "Are you guys ever serious?"

"She's right. Let's focus shall we?" added Saul from the shadows.

The briefing lasted a total of two hours during which time each person was given their assignment. Questions were asked and answered. There were even a handful of objections raised. Some were overruled, some sustained. Nothing involving the operation was off limits. After each detail had been addressed and ironed out, everyone retired for the night.

Rainey was still awake after an hour and a half of staring at the ceiling. Eventually, he slipped down to the kitchen, opened a bottle of Perrier then sat down in the dining room, the slight wooden chair creaking under his bulk.

She entered the kitchen a few minutes later, apparently unaware of his presence in the darkened room. Rainey watched her reach for the refrigerator door but pause before opening it. Did she suspect he was there?

"Couldn't sleep either, huh?" Her jolt answered his question.

Evelina turned back toward the fridge, pulled it open. The glow cast from within revealed a silhouette of athletic feminine lines that Rainey couldn't help noticing. Her mussed golden locks shimmered in the refrigerator light. "Guess not." She pulled a container of milk from the door and poured half a glass. She was barefoot with toenails painted lavender. The white tank top and gray pajama leggings only accentuated her killer figure.

Evelina took a sip of milk then leaned against the counter. "What are you looking at?"

"What do you mean?"

"I mean you were staring at me."

"I was?"

"Mmm hmm."

"Just tired, I guess."

She maneuvered to a chair across from him and sat down, crossed her legs. Finally breaking a lull of silence, she said, "Maddie has told me a lot about you, you know. Mouse and Tonka, too. The good, the bad, and the *ugly*." Her face was filled with mischief.

"Is that right?" He took some amount of pleasure in the current shape of her hair and—though he would never outwardly admit it—the dangerous curves of her body. Yes, he thought, they were indeed *dangerous*.

The two of them facing one another bore the illusion of a soft interrogation. There was a moment of awkward silence, neither one looking away from the other.

Rainey finally yawned and Evelina did likewise.

"You know, I never personally thanked you for saving my life last year."

"Not necessary. You know how this job works."

"Yes, but it's still proper manners to thank someone when they save your life." She studied his face. "So, what made you include *me* in this operation anyway?"

"Job says you're one of the best. And based on the reports I've read from this past year, I don't disagree. Mouse and Tonka likewise speak very highly of you. I've worked with both of them a long time. If they say you're good, you're good."

"You're very good yourself. Trust me, I've seen you in action. In fact, the whole world has if I'm not mistaken."

The comment caught him off guard. When he tried changing the subject, she would have none of it.

"I know what happened, Ray. I've seen the footage. That was you in New York—the angel of Second Avenue."

He remained quiet, his dark, chocolate eyes weary for sleep.

Evelina leaned forward, placed her hand on his. "We're going to get whoever is responsible. Everything will be fine. Believe me."

He felt a surge of adrenaline. "I have no doubt."

"Then what is it? Something seems to be bothering you. Why were you sitting here in the dark and not racked out in bed like everyone else?" With an index finger, she looped several strands of hair behind her ear. The dim light caused her normally bright, peridot eyes to take on the darkened hue of a Christmas fern. They stared up at him, probing for answers.

"Nothing. Just thinking about the operation is all. Listen, we should get some sleep."

"I will if you will."

After an awkward pause, they both smiled.

"That didn't sound good, did it?"

"Goodnight, Evie." With that, he stood and trod off to bed already feeling guilty for the electric sensation now charging through his body.

Dangerous.

19

Le Meurice was a storybook hotel, perhaps the most luxurious in all of Paris. And it was now in full Christmas mode. Garland and wreaths and red ribbons were everywhere. Tiny white lights set about the hotel's marvelous façade sparkled against the wet pavement. A light snow had fallen earlier in the afternoon, the kind that dusted the grass but immediately melted upon contact with the roads and sidewalks.

Rainey's breath clouded the air around him as he walked. If everything went smoothly this would be the hardest part of the evening—crashing the party. But according to the head of the DX's Technical Operations Group, which housed, in part, a dedicated unit of sophisticated hackers, there was no need to worry; Rainey's name—his cover name—would indeed be on the guest list. Maddie had done a fabulous job with her assignment. Because of her thorough reconnaissance of the facilities for her fictitious employer's fictitious spring gala, the team had been able to map out the entire first floor of the hotel to include points of ingress and egress, the lobby, kitchen, and, most importantly, the Salons Pompadour, Tuileries, and Jeu de Paume. With a Christmas bash the size of this one, all three adjacent event rooms had been booked to accommodate the 374-strong guest list. The host, it turned out, was Julien Battier, a French billionaire who had made his fortune

98

on perfume, lotions, and personal hygiene products. How he knew Alban Clement was still something of a mystery.

Rainey entered the hotel, crossed the marble-floored lobby. Opulence oozed from every nook and cranny. On the left, a towering Christmas tree. Adorned with shiny red and silver ornaments and strands of white lights, packages carefully placed beneath, it was quite the spectacle even in a place referred to as *Hotel des Rois* (Hotel of Kings).

He continued farther into the hotel, to the grand Salon Pompadour. An attendant stood behind a brass-lighted podium just outside the room's entrance. He smiled stiffly and said, "*Nom monsieur?*"

"Fabron."

The attendant ran his finger down a computer tablet housed in a supple leather case. He reached the bottom of the list and looked up as if there had been some mistake.

Rainey offered a natural smile.

"The name again, monsieur?"

"Fabron. Gustave Fabron." Rainey counted several security men milling around in suits. To the regular guests, they might have easily blended in. But Rainey knew what to look for. The security men all wore the same tiny gold pin in the shape of a Christmas tree on their jacket lapels. None of their suit coats were buttoned because to do so would cause unnecessary delay in accessing the firearms doubtless on their hips. They mingled near doorways, kept their backs to the walls, and remained within eyesight of each other. And speaking of their eyes, they were constantly moving, scanning for threats, for problems before they arose.

The attendant repeated his routine. This time his finger stopped a quarter of the way down the screen. "Ah, yes. *Fabron.* Here you are. Enjoy the party, monsieur."

"*Je vous remercie.*"

The room was packed. Chamber music, calm and resonant, offered a distinct counterpoint to the din of competing conversations and frequent ebullitions of laughter. He made his way through the flood of wealthy patrons and nonpareils of high society and in so doing caught a glimpse of the foursome earnestly working their stringed instruments in the corner of the grand room nearest the bar. In perfect French, he petitioned the bartender for an Armorik Dervenn, neat. As he waited, Rainey pivoted toward the musicians now playing "Pastorale" from Bach's *Christmas Oratorio*. Behind them, a gilded wall stretched nearly twenty feet high. He might well have been standing in the ballroom at the Palace of Versailles. The intricate woodwork and marvelous stately furnishings were right out of the late 1700s.

Rainey accepted his drink from the bartender and for several minutes stood there enjoying the splendid piece. His left hand in his pants pocket, he raised his glass when the cellist glanced up at him. The thin-boned musician returned a sentiment of profound appreciation.

Rainey soon found himself in conversation with a man he had seen on television while he'd been waiting for the team to arrive at the safe house in Bougival. Thankfully, the French actor was less interested in asking him questions than he was in shameless self-promotion. Rainey urged him on with every prompt. Curiously, the man was under the distinct impression that they'd met at the Cannes Film Festival a few years back. Not surprising though, since Rainey was the one who had suggested it in the first place.

Rainey continued working the room, making sure he was seen by plenty of people with a drink in his hand. Over the course of the next several hours, he began to smile a little too easily. His words became slurred, his gate unsteady. When he stood still, he swayed, noticeably so.

At the first sight of Evelina early in the evening, he'd nearly spilled his drink, and not on purpose. Her chiffon and satin evening gown was a strapless number the color of Roman silver with a slit on the right side that went all the way up, revealing a smooth, tan leg when she walked. She wore her hair up, the purpose being to draw attention to the bejeweled necklace that hung from her flawless neck. The necklace's rectangular emerald pendant—a marvelous fake according to the support staff who'd procured it—plunged dangerously low into her winsome décolletage. If the women in the room were looking at the necklace, the men most certainly were not. Evelina Krantz was a paragon of elegance, sophistication, and unattainable allure.

During their deliberations at the safe house, Rainey had expressed to Job that Evelina need not expose this amount of skin for his plan to work, but Job had overruled him. This was Paris, he'd said, the epicenter of glamour and fashion. If you want to draw the room's attention, you need to be bold. Rainey still didn't think it was necessary, but now, seeing Evelina such as she was, he wasn't complaining. She was positively stunning.

Evelina and Mark Alcott had taken up a position behind a standing table. They'd arrived thirty minutes prior to Rainey and had so far—like him—done well to blend into the swell of guests in tuxedos and evening gowns.

They danced, they mingled, they sipped Champagne, all the while marking their targets and waiting for the right moment. Currently, Alban Clement and his wife were engaged with a local politician a few tables over. When their conversation finally ended, Evelina and Alcott made their move.

They waded into a current of people trickling by Clement and stopped on the other side of him midstream as if they had somehow by pure chance wound up there. It was at this time that Alcott held up his empty flute and said—loud enough for Clement to hear—that he would return with more Champagne for himself and his darling. Now left alone, Evelina casually rotated toward Clement and his wife. Evelina offered a polite if not awkward smile as if she were embarrassed to find herself suddenly alone. The reports later filed by Rainey and his team members would make no overt mention of it, but this was the precise moment in which the hook had been set.

Rainey watched it all from the far side of the room. If the bartender were to be later questioned, he would firmly testify that the monsieur—Gustave Fabron—was now working on his fifth scotch whisky. Rainey lifted the caramel-colored drink to his mouth, took in its cinnamon and nutmeg bouquet, and held it there just long enough to whisper into his lapel mic. "Cinderella has made contact. Everyone stand by."

"I don't believe we've met. I am Alban Clement and this is my wife, Noelle." The diplomat extended his hand, palm down, his face a beacon of avidity. "And who might you be?"

"I'm Reneé... Reneé Appell." She put forth an attitude of forced pleasantness.

Clement grinned with amusement. "Wonderful party, isn't it?"

"*Mais oui,*" said Evelina. "My husband... Ah, here he comes now."

Alcott appeared with two glasses of Champagne and a doting smile on his face. He handed one to Evelina.

"Darling, this is Monsieur and Madame..." She let the diplomat remind her. "Yes. Clement. They are...*Je suis désolée*. How do you know Julien?"

"We are friends and business acquaintances. And you?"

Evelina flashed a look of earnest gaiety. "I'm one of the girls in Julien's latest ad campaign." She spouted off the name of a Battier brand perfume. "The ads are everywhere. Surely, you've seen them."

Clement seemed to be searching his memory. "I'm sorry. No."

"*Mais oui!* You're simply beautiful in them, my dear," fawned Madame Clement. Either she was confusing Evelina for one of the real models in the commercials or she was simply being polite by pretending to have recognized her.

"Thank you. You're very kind. And now you must excuse me." She added a giggle of feigned embarrassment. "Too much Champagne, I suppose." She turned to Alcott and patted him on the bicep. When he leaned his head closer to her, she spoke in a voice loud enough for the Clements to hear. "I'm off to the ladies' room, darling. Be right back."

The three of them watched Evelina retreat from the table and disappear through a huddle of guests. Alcott was particularly attentive at this moment, but not to the ravishing Reneé Appell. Though his eyes may have been on her, his focus was entirely on the glass of Champagne in front of the beautiful and rather stately figure of Madame Clement.

They had three *plays*, Rainey had called them, options by which to carry out the plan. Each play was dependent upon any one of three different scenarios. Each play also had its own vulnerabilities, its own complications, which is why Rainey had insisted Evelina and Alcott rehearse them all by rote at the house in Bougival until each one could be performed by muscle memory even under duress. Fortunately for them, they had, because when the crucial moment finally came that evening, Madame Clement did *not* accompany Evelina to the restroom as every team member believed she would. Instead, she chose to stay at her husband's side, basking in the glory of his understated fame.

And so it was that the team wordlessly, seamlessly audibled to the third option.

20

PARIS – BOUGIVAL, FRANCE

Evelina waded through the crowd toward the ladies' room, Rainey ahead on her right. She could feel the eyes of well over 300 people on her as she walked, which was entirely the idea, of course. According to Rainey's third option, her remit was simple. Be a siren. Everything else would take care of itself.

She stepped past him and tried to focus on anyone, anything other than him. The bump in her heart rate, she knew, was merely her body's sympathetic nervous system engaging because of what was about to occur. When she finally felt his hand on her backside, she immediately spun and smacked him hard across the face. "*Porc!*" She then launched into a loud rebuke over his offensive behavior. She was still in the middle of her rant when Rainey, lazy-eyed, smiled and made Pepé Le Pew-like attempts to kiss her. Evelina recoiled at each one, which only seemed to urge him on all the more. In the next instant, he grabbed her by the shoulders and pulled her hard against his frame. Her forearms trapped against his chest, Evelina squirmed with desperation. She twisted her face this way and that as his searching lips mirrored her movements. At last, she shrieked, sending half of the room into near pandemonium.

This persisted for several seconds more until all at once she mustered her strength and, arms flailing, drove him backward into a round table, which flipped over, launching everything on it into the air. Curses were shouted, drink glasses shattered against the polished floor.

———

Alcott stepped closer to the table and prepared to make his move. At first, he sensed a minor commotion then it sounded like an all-out bar brawl had erupted. All heads turned toward the epicenter of the mayhem. All but one.

The distraction was one of perfection. Not one person bore witness to the man with the forgettable face and the form-fitting tuxedo maneuver forward ever so slightly and switch his glass of Champagne for the one inches away from the bejeweled hand of Madame Clement. It took a mere a second in real-time and was performed with a magician's sleight of hand.

———

Two large hands gripped him under the arms and hoisted him up. Rainey turned to face one of the security men at which time he noticed the coiled acoustic tubing of an earpiece. His French slurred and haphazard, Rainey listed forward and barked into the man's ear as if the Salon Pompadour were a noisy discotheque, "Hey! That's not very nice! Come now. Come now, see... Père Noël... Père Noël knows you've been bad... Bad boy, you! Yes, you've been naughty. Very, very naughty, now... No gifts for you!"

Not amused in the slightest, the serious-looking men frog-marched him through the double doors and into the lobby where the host suddenly appeared, his face crimson with anger. "What is the meaning of this outrage, monsieur? Who are you?!"

Rainey straightened his tuxedo jacket. "*Hé regarde tout le monde! C'est Rudolph le renne au nez rouge !*" Hey, look everyone. It's Rudolph the red-nosed reindeer!

"You, sir, are drunk! You will leave at once! Or I will have these gentlemen escort you out to the street and summon the police."

"Okay. Okaaaay. I'm...going." As the men on either side of him released their grip, Rainey smiled glassy-eyed, then promptly attempted to walk back into the party at which point they latched on to him again, this time using considerably more force.

"That's it! Gentlemen, please see that our drunken friend does not cause any more unpleasantness this evening."

The larger of the two security men smiled as if he took great pleasure in his handiwork. "Yes, sir."

As they carried him through the lobby, Rainey jerked his head to the right, toward a flock of gawking partygoers and bellowed, *"Joyeux Noël à tous! Et bonne nuit à tous!"* Merry Christmas to all! And to all a good night!"

They shoved him to the sidewalk and one of them, seeing a cab approaching, whistled. The vehicle chirped to a stop and one of the security men leaned into the open passenger-side window. Rainey heard the security man spout off an address in Barbès, one of the most dangerous neighborhoods in all of Paris, especially at this time of night.

They yanked him to his feet, opened the cab door. Before heaving him inside, one of them punched him in the stomach. Rainey heard them laughing as the door slammed against the soles of his shoes and the cab lurched forward.

———

His part complete, Alcott bid the Clements a gracious but hasty goodnight and hurried toward his *wife*, whom he found in a circle of Good Samaritans repeatedly asking if she were all right. Some were still hurling insults at the drunken interloper for intruding on their merriment.

At the first glimmer of recognition, Evelina clung to him as though he were a life raft in a stormy sea. Alcott thanked the do-gooders for coming to her aid then beseeched them for privacy to save his wife further embarrassment. All but one of them obliged. A man in gleaming black wingtips, pressed black slacks, and a trim suit jacket with a shiny gold Le Meurice pin on his lapel shuffled forward, a small handheld radio in his right fist. He promptly introduced himself as the hotel manager, the ends of his pencil-thin mustache fluttering as he spoke.

He was still heaping apologies on them—on behalf of the hotel, on behalf of the party's host, and on behalf of all the decent men of France—as Evenlina and Alcott, still locked together as one, turned toward the doors leading to the lobby.

"I'm sure Monsieur Battier would like to personally apologize for what happened here tonight. If you would be so kind to wait here, I will summon him at once." The man lifted the radio to his small, rose-colored lips, and his mustache danced.

"That will not be necessary," said Evelina, her tone conveying the fact that she was well accustomed to getting her way.

"But—"

"But nothing. I am fine. Just a little embarrassed is all."

"*Très bien, madame.* If there is anything that I or the hotel can do for either of you…"

Evelina offered a bleak smile. "You can send for our car, *s'il vous plaît.*"

The mood within the hotel salons resumed to its prior cheerfulness after the host of the party issued a grand, albeit brief, apology for the ugliness that had befallen them during the evening's festivities. In contrast, Evelina and Alcott made a quiet exit through the front entrance after the valet had retrieved their black Mercedes SUV from the car park.

At the same time Evelina and Alcott were departing the hotel, Saul Baker was holding a keen vigil on Madame Clement. Like the others, he had crashed the party under an assumed name. Wearing a smart pair of European spectacles and an ordinary black tuxedo, he kept his own counsel in a corner of the room nearest the musicians who were now playing a festive rendition of Handel's "Messiah."

Upon seeing Madame Clement lift her glass to her lips for the third time, Saul slipped into a corridor normally reserved for hotel staff. He soon turned a corner and headed for a dormant conference room through which was a door that issued into yet another hallway. He strode to its terminus, where he pushed through a door, which ultimately bore him down a short flight of steps and onto the rue du Mont Thabor.

He veered eastward, ambling at a normal pace to a BMW sedan, which was parked in the dim glow of a Japanese restaurant. Saul sunk into the back seat and calmly proclaimed to the driver—one of the JSG shooters, in this case, a sniper known as Wizard, "We're in business."

Wizard immediately repeated the phrase into his lapel mic.

Job Jackson paced the sitting room, eyes trained on the four open notebook computers before him. On one screen, a digital map showed the precise geolocation of each member of the DX team in France, a solitary green dot for each beating heart. On another was a grid of windows that represented the audio feeds from each of the party crashers' mobile phones, which were currently acting as remote listening devices. With the click of a mouse, the man seated at the table—an operator named Jazz—could tap into any audio feed of his choosing. The third screen showed live video feeds streaming from the stationary posts held by the JSG special operators who were strategically positioned around Clement's apartment house in the rue Daubigny in the event of trouble.

The final notebook computer was used to maintain a secure communications link with the XOC—Directorate X's Operations Center—which lay six stories below ground at DX headquarters in Arlington, Virginia. At this very minute, CIA Director Ken Thompson was standing by there, patiently reading the incoming watch reports and observing the live audio and video feeds.

"Can you turn that up, please?" said Job.

Jazz increased the volume for the audio feed coming from Rainey's phone. He smiled hearing the last bit.

"That's it! Gentlemen, please see that our drunken friend does not cause any more unpleasantness this evening."

"Yes, sir."

"Merry Christmas to all! And to all a good night!"

"And the Academy Award goes to Reagan 'Bronco' Rainey," joked Jazz from the glow of the computer screens.

But Job, having never been a special operator, had no use for the man's dry humor, especially at a time like this. He was all business. "Give me Evie."

What came across the speakers next was a mix of male voices, certainly several Frenchmen, a German, and a Russian making a rather clumsy attempt at the French language. All of them were singing the same song but in different meter. And all of them were focused on the star of the ball. Was she hurt? Was she okay? How dare that scoundrel do what he did?

Job had his right hand tucked under his left arm and his left hand over his mouth, his index and middle fingers extended and pressed firmly against his jawbone. He remained like this, hovering over Jazz's right shoulder until the voice of the sniper-turned-chauffer came over the secure radio. "We're in business."

It was a message that was received with great anticipation. Job nodded once and issued an order for Jazz to update the director via the secure link.

A good first step, but their night was just getting started.

21

The engine of the taxi purred as the cobbled street gently rocked him in the back seat. Rainey quickly shed his tux for a pair of gray work trousers, a navy-blue fleece pullover, and a black-and-gray ski jacket. He tied his hikers then bundled his party attire into a trash bag and set it on the seat beside him. His mind was already churning as the glazed storefronts swept past his window.

"You good?" The cab driver's eyes bore down on him in the rearview mirror.

"What?"

"Are you all right?"

He had been thinking of what Kapustin had said about Clement belonging to the Russians. What if they were watching Clement? What if they had someone on him at the party?

"Yeah, Mouse. I'm good. He didn't hit me that hard."

"Whatever you say, Bronc."

They nosed into a parking garage a few blocks away and headed for a dimly lit corner on the second level. Rainey exited the back seat of the cab and slid into the driver's seat of a black Renault Megane. The leather was cold against his butt and thighs. He reached over and opened the glovebox. A Sig Sauer P365-XMacro Comp 9mm pistol lay secure in a T.Rex Arms IWB holster.

He made sure the magazine was full and a round was in the pipe before clipping the pistol inside the front of his trousers and covering it with his fleece.

Rainey sat in silence as he waited for Mouse to return from the fourth level, where he would leave the cab parked in a vacant stall. A support staff member from Paris Station would arrive in twenty minutes to dispose of it properly. Soon Mouse joined him in the front passenger seat and together they headed for an address on the Quai Henri Pourchassé in Ivry-sur-Seine.

"Give me Clement," said Job as he circled the room.

Jazz clicked the mouse and the audio feed from the French diplomat's phone came alive on the speakers. The sound was a bit muffled, probably because the phone was currently tucked inside the Frenchman's coat pocket. Still, the conversation was easy to understand but only to Job since Jazz did not speak the language of the French.

Job closed his eyes and stood stock still as if he were listening to some moving piece of music.

"C'mon, Alban. I can barely keep my eyes open. Let's go."

"Very well, my dear."

He listened as the couple bid their farewells to politicians and other favored government officials, to CEOs and bankers, celebrities and robber barons. Finally, they thanked the host of the Christmas bash, Julien Battier, and took their leave.

As the couple waited for the valet to bring their car around, it seemed that Madame Clement was having a bit of trouble keeping herself upright. The diplomat questioned her a number of times about just how much she had had to drink.

Inside the couple's car, the conversation was minimal and predictable. The male gushed over meeting this person and that, while Madame Clement yawned repeatedly. For one short moment in time, Job thought he heard snoring. There was even a brief mention of the lovely perfume model, Reneé Appell, and her husband—what was his name?—to which Madame Clement responded with slurred speech some incoherent babble that Job interpreted as unbridled jealousy.

After several minutes, Job opened his eyes. The red dot on the screen, which currently corresponded to the location of Clement's mobile phone, was traveling a route just as they had expected: northwest along the boulevard Malesherbes. As Clement crossed over the avenue de Villiers, Job lifted the secure radio to his mouth and said, "All units, this is TOC. The Grinch is two blocks out."

Each of the units positioned around Clement's apartment building responded in succession by stating their operational call sign followed by "Copy."

"Charlie One. Copy." The man behind the wheel raised his seatback and extended his right arm toward her, his hand forming a loose fist. "Go get 'em, Swan."

Maddie knocked her fist against Tonka's then slipped out of the Opel sedan. The air was cold. The street was wet and dark but for the few streetlamps that jutted from the building façades like outstretched fingers. The light each of them cast was gathered into fuzzy cotton balls by the settling fog. Traffic moving along the nearby rue Jouffroy d'Abbans and the boulevard Malesherbes had died down considerably over the past few hours giving way to an eerie quiet.

She cinched the belt of her khaki-colored, woolen trench coat and withdrew into the shadowy, unmarked doorway of Number 19. There, she waited until Clement's shiny black BMW M3 sedan swept around the corner. She watched as he pulled the vehicle to the same side of the street, a few spaces down from his building at Number 15. The brake lights glowed for several long seconds then finally went dark. After a handful of beats, the diplomat rose into view and circled around to his front passenger's door. It was then that Maddie, chin down and hands in her pockets, stepped from the shadows and set off toward him.

Tonka was already in her ear. "All is well, Swan. You're clear."

It was also at this time that a white work van, which up until now had been parked at the corner of the rue Jouffroy d'Abbans and rue Daubigny, pulled casually across the entrance of the street and engaged its flashers. Its lone occupant promptly exited the van and propped open the hood.

As Maddie drew near, the Frenchman's efforts became more frenzied. Alban Clement held his wife, one arm around her waist, the other fumbling with her unwilling right arm, which he labored to keep draped around his neck. Bent forward, the diplomat tugged on her firmly and hefted her to her feet. The woman appeared to be grossly inebriated, one moment talking in incoherent sentences, the next retreating with recalcitrant eyes to incipient slumber. Clement spat a curse word and for a moment it looked as though both he and his wife were going to tumble to the damp, gray sidewalk.

Perfect.

The muscles in his lower back were screaming and his left shoulder was threatening to pull free from its socket. He clung to her though not wanting her or the both of them to go spilling to the ground. Clement stopped for a moment and drew several cold breaths of oxygen into his lungs, wiped a film of sweat from his forehead with the back of his gloved hand. What on earth was going on? Noelle hadn't had *that* much Champagne, had she?

It was then that he registered the sharp clip-clop of heels against the sidewalk. He twisted toward the sound, while at the same time, his wife's legs buckled, the weight of her body forcing him to hinge awkwardly at the waist.

"Monsieur, allow me to help you," said the approaching woman.

"Thank you," he breathed, attempting to disguise the urgency of his predicament.

The mystery woman shuffled to the other side of his wife. The first thing he noticed was her black knee-high boots then the tan, woolen trench coat pulled tightly over her athletic lines. A shiny, brown ponytail bobbed beneath the wheat-colored ear warmer wrapped around her head.

"Your apartment is in Number Fifteen, yes?" Her French was flawless, her manner and bearing dripping with sophistication.

"Yes," he said with a grunt. "Top floor."

"Very well."

Together they walked Madame Clement to the giant double wooden door of Number 15, each of them with an arm around her waist and a hand clasping the wrist that dangled from their outside shoulder. The diplomat briefly fumbled with a key ring, which his wife in her stupor must have confused for sleigh bells because it was then that she instantly began singing a popular French Christmas tune.

They giggled conspiratorially at his wife's expense and finally crossed the threshold into the stately foyer. It took them every bit of fifteen minutes to ascend the staircase. Clement huffed and puffed the entire way.

Once inside the apartment, Clement tossed his keys for a tabletop but shorted his throw and they clattered across the wooden planks of the floor.

"Let's just get her to the couch," suggested the diplomat.

They set her down gently on the soft, woven fabric. Clement pulled off her gloves and stripped her of her heavy coat and heels then reached for a thick afghan throw that was folded up on a nearby chair. Kneeling, he swiped her hair from her face and made sure she appeared comfortable, which wasn't difficult, for Madame Clement was already fast asleep.

"There," he said, standing. He was about to offer the beautiful stranger a warm sentiment of gratitude, but instead, his body froze at the recognition of the stubby snout of a silenced pistol that was now pointed directly at his face.

22

PARIS

It had been a key element of Rainey's plan and, for that matter, the methodology of any good intelligence operation: the studious use of psychology. In this case, playing on the diplomat's predilections and biases had gotten them dangerously close to him and thereby had set into motion a series of events that would allow them to accomplish their central objective: abducting a French dignitary on French soil with zero footprint. To Clement, a man not trained in the calculating arts of espionage, a woman, especially one with Maddie's physical characteristics, would be deemed far less of a threat than a man. Though Rainey and his DX team didn't know it at the time, they would soon learn that they had not been the first to mount an operation against the Frenchman via the exploits of a beautiful woman.

"What is the meaning of this?!" implored Clement.

"Take off your coat," Maddie said icily. "Do it now."

"You are robbing me? But—"

She jabbed the gun into the air. "Do it *now!*"

He obeyed, unsheathing himself from the heavy topcoat and letting it fall to the floor.

"Now, remove the phone from the breast pocket of your suit coat and place it on the floor. Slowly! Any sudden movements and you and your wife will be shot." Once he complied, she continued. "Lift up your shirt and turn around."

He did as instructed.

She then had him turn each of his pockets inside out and lift up each pant leg. Finally, she had him loosen his belt and lower his trousers to the knees. If he had any weapons on him at this point, they would have to be secreted in a bodily orifice.

"Pull up your pants and sit down in that chair."

Clement eyed the wing-back chair to his right as he sheepishly drew up his pants and buckled his belt. He shuffled sideways until he was standing beside it then eased himself down onto the woven fabric, his forehead glistening with sweat.

"Good." Maddie tilted her chin toward the lapel of her coat and murmured something in Russian into the unseen mic then touched the fingertips of her left hand against her ear warmer as if to make abundantly clear to her quarry that she was wearing an earpiece and thus was not operating alone. With the gun still pointed at the diplomat, she removed a cell phone from her coat pocket, waited a few seconds until it began to ring, then tossed it to Clement.

"Answer it."

Confused and frightened, Clement stared at her.

"Alban, answer the phone."

He blinked his eyes and focused his attention on the device, which was buzzing softly in his grasp. He swallowed hard then swiped a finger across the screen.

———

Reagan Rainey sat at a metal table in the center of a vast, austere room. In front of him were two things: a large Styrofoam cup of hot, black coffee and a notebook computer, which currently displayed a live video feed of the front door of Clement's building via a tiny camera mounted on the "disabled" work van blocking the street.

Moments ago, he had watched Maddie pull off a simple, but effective, penetration of the man's apartment by way of a ruse. A ruse made possible by some careful choreography and the strong sedative Madame Clement had unknowingly imbibed at the Christmas party.

He waited until he heard Maddie's voice on the radio telling him in Russian that she was all set. Adding a little Russian intrigue into the mix was one more thing Rainey had decided to throw at Clement. It would keep him off balance. And that's just where Rainey wanted him.

Rainey lifted the phone from the table and dialed.

"Hello?"

"Listen very carefully, Monsieur Clement. Your life depends on it. Your wife's, too."

"I'm listening," said Clement, his voice trembling.

"Now, do exactly as I say. Go down to the street. Take the phone with you. And don't bother trying to use it to contact anyone for help. It can only receive calls. All other features have been disabled. Do you understand?"

"I understand. But why are you doing this?"

Rainey ignored the man's question. "When you reach the street, a car will pull to the curb. Get into the back seat. Do not speak to the driver. This is your first and only warning."

Clement was silent save for his exaggerated breathing.

"You have thirty seconds."

Clement glanced at the screen to be sure that the call had ended then looked up at the woman holding the gun before settling his eyes finally on his slumbering wife. She was lying on her right side, peacefully unaware of the danger that had befallen them.

The armed woman glared at him. "Tick tock. Tick tock," she hissed.

He was immediately jolted back to the fact that he was on the clock. *Thirty seconds. How many had already slipped by?*

Clement plucked his coat off the floor and hurried to the door. He glanced back quickly then pulled it shut and headed for the stairs. Just as the man had said, when he reached the sidewalk, a car approached—a dark Opel sedan. It stopped in front of him, its engine purring softly against the quiet of the night. A faint, gray plume of exhaust spilled from its tailpipe and rose with an odd serenity into the gauzy fog.

He leaned forward and squinted at the vehicle's darkly tinted windows then swept his eyes up and down the street. Chillingly, he found himself alone in the middle of Paris.

Tick tock.

Clement tugged open the back door and eased his sleight frame into the vehicle.

"Close the door," said the driver. The words were French but the accent foreign. German? Hungarian? He pulled it shut with a thud and instantly the phone, still in his hand, buzzed again. He answered it.

"There's a hood on the seat next to you. Put it on."

Clement searched the dark cabin, patting the seat with his hands until he found it. Not a hood but a ski mask. It was cold and scratchy to the touch. His fingers revealed that pieces of thick cloth had been snitched over the eyeholes. Cautiously, he pulled it over his head.

At that, the car jerked forward and they were off.

Even without the hood, the likelihood was remote that Clement would have noticed the silver Peugeot pulling in behind them. They drove in what seemed like circles for close to twenty minutes. He had tried to memorize the route but eventually got confused and lost track of where he was. Finally, the car stopped with a frightening abruptness and the cell phone cried out once more. He blindly swept his shaking finger across the screen and held it against the fabric now stretched over his left ear.

"Hello," he stammered.

"Get out of the car. Keep the hood on."

After doing so, Clement said, "Okay, I am out."

"Now, get in the trunk. The driver will help you."

His breath caught in his throat. "But—"

In the next instant, the phone was snatched from his hand and he was ushered to the back of the car. Arms outstretched, he felt for the rim of the trunk, sat down then rolled inside. He lay there for no more than a second before the lid snapped shut with morbid finality. He immediately suffered the sense that he had just crawled inside his own coffin.

For nearly ten minutes, it felt as if they were on a highway. Soon, however, the roadway beneath the car became rough and pitted and the car slowed to a crawl. Then just as suddenly the road smoothed and their pace quickened. At one point they sped over a series of unforgiving speed bumps, which caused him to hit his head on the underside of the trunk lid. He wondered if the driver had done this on purpose.

Clement wanted to believe he was still in Paris, but after two hours of driving it was unlikely. He could be in Melun or Rambouillet or even Rouen for that matter. Anywhere. Though he was certain he was still within the borders of the French Republic.

He was rubbing the knot on his head when the car stopped again. For several seconds, he thought he heard voices but could not be certain of it. Then the car lurched forward onto a paved drive though it felt old and littered with potholes. He banged his head again when one of the back wheels dropped into an immense crater. A foul river of curses flowed from his mouth. Though his voice was muffled by the hood and the carpeted surfaces of the trunk, the driver must have heard him. Because at that very moment, unbeknownst to Clement, amidst the glow of the reflected headlights, a mischievous smile formed on his face.

Next, the vehicle proceeded slowly over a low hump and the ride became instantly smooth. The car was now on metal or concrete, perhaps. The engine grew louder, echoing against the confines of some type of enclosed space—a garage?—until suddenly the driver switched it off. Now, the only thing he could hear other than the blood pulsing through his ears was deafening silence.

23

As Clement rightly suspected, they *were* still in France. Ivry-sur-Seine lay in the Paris suburbs, along the southeastern border of the city's Thirteenth Arrondissement, a place of aging industry and a surging Asian immigrant population. Despite a recent uptick in projects aimed at revitalizing parts of the French commune, there were numerous factories, warehouses, and other buildings sitting idle. One of them, a place that had long served as a water-treatment facility but was now abandoned, lay along the Quai Henri Pourchaseé near the confluence of the River Seine and River Marne. Once a vibrant space alive with French workers and humming pumps, the aged brick and stone structure was now desolate and bare, which made it perfectly suitable for the DX's operational needs.

From the doorway of a room that had at one time been used as a laboratory, Rainey watched Tonka steer the Opel through a pair of open bay doors, past Mark Alcott and to the center of a shiny concrete floor worn smooth from decades of use. As soon as the car was inside, Alcott, wearing a balaclava and an HK MP7A1 on a single-point sling, walked the large wooden doors closed and secured them by dropping a sturdy plank into two metal elbow brackets.

Rainey muttered something to someone unseen over his shoulder then walked to the back of the sedan and waited for Tonka to pull on his own balaclava. In a coarse Russian voice, one that Clement was sure to hear, Rainey barked, "Get him out and bring him inside."

Immediately, Tonka popped the trunk and jerked Clement to his feet. He secured the man's hands behind his back with flex cuffs then turned him ninety degrees to the right. With a grunt, he nudged the diplomat between the shoulder blades, urging him forward.

His arms crossed and feet shoulder-width apart, Rainey studied the Frenchman as he shuffled by. He was trembling badly.

Good.

They ushered him into a room that smelled of chlorine and cement. The air was damp and cold as stone. He felt a strong hand on his shoulder. It forced him down onto a metal folding chair that must have been kept in a meat locker.

"Remove the hood." The order was given in French by a man with a thick Russian accent.

Clement squinted while attempting to make sense of his surroundings. The first thing he noticed was the wooden table against the wall. On it were numerous saws and knives, a pair of long-handled bolt cutters, rolls of plastic sheeting, and several heavy-duty trash bags. Beside the table stood a blue, 55-gallon, plastic drum. The shadows made the label difficult to read, but from the colorful placard above it, he was sure the drum's contents were hazardous. Unless... He suddenly realized that the drum might be empty. And that meant... The saws. The knives. The bolt cutters. They were going to chop him up and put his body inside the drum! The Russians! They were going to kill him. But *why*?!

"You've been a naughty boy, Alban." The rough, disembodied voice echoed against the cinder-block walls.

Clement twisted his head this way and that, desperate to locate the source of the unnerving wraith-like voice. "No!" he pleaded. "I've done exactly what you've asked. I swear."

"You've been holding out on us."

"I don't know what you mean! I've passed on every bit of information I could get my hands on. What more do you want?"

"Enough!" The voice boomed from within the darkness.

His eyes began to leak, his body shook in absolute terror. The kind of terror that made him forget all about the strong plastic ties that were beginning to cut into his flesh.

"You are working for someone else. For a *terrorist* organization. For *Hezbollah*!"

This time Clement didn't respond. He was confused. They already knew that he was working with Hezbollah. What could he say? Nothing made sense. His head was spinning.

"And now with your help, they have launched an attack on America!"

He jerked his head back and forth. "No! *No!!!*"

"Yes! Yes, Alban! The Americans are on to you. Do you know what that means for *us*? For *you*? Well? *Do* you?!"

He bent forward, crying like a child. "I... I... Please! Talk to Felix. He will tell you."

"Felix."

"Yes! Felix, my contact in Brussels. Surely, he will tell you—"

"Tell us what, Alban? How you betrayed our arrangement? Betrayed us for a group of bloody-thirsty degenerates?" The interrogator paused for effect then turned what little information Clement had revealed back on him. "Felix is dead. Do you hear me, Alban? Felix is dead!"

"Please. Please! What do you want?!"

"I want you to admit it, Alban. Confess your sins."

The diplomat was coming undone. He sobbed without ceasing for nearly a minute. His sobbing then gave way to heavy gasps and wet coughs that sprayed mucous into the air. Eventually, with his eyes closed, the Frenchman sat up, his head lolling back and forth with the morbid recognition of his futile circumstance. "Yes. Yes, okay? I helped them, but it's not what you think. Please! You must understand."

"I understand, Alban. I understand all too well." The man speaking materialized from the darkness, an apparition in a haze of cigarette smoke. He paced the room behind him. "You know, some of my colleagues think I should bring you back to Moscow. Give you a handsome flat on the Moskva. A thank you as it were for services rendered. Ha. Fools, all of them!"

The man stepped closer, the hard soles of his shoes grinding against the concrete. "Do you know what I say?" The man hovered over him. Clement could feel the hot breath against his ear, breath turned foul from cigarettes. "I say we kill you right here. Right now."

24

Rainey let Saul's words hang in the air for several long seconds before finally saying, "And cut!"

He flicked the lights on and watched the visage of the Frenchman transform from fear and despair to confusion and eventually utter elation. Saul remained on his mark behind Clement a moment longer, still bent forward, still drilling into the diplomat a stern, steely-eyed glare. Then, heeding the director's remark, smashed out his cigarette with the toe of his shoe and wordlessly retreated to the shadows at the back of the room.

Rainey stepped from behind a small, tri-pod-mounted video camera positioned in the far corner of the room and cleared a place on the table to sit. He hoisted himself onto it, turned toward his quarry, and crossed his arms.

"*You!* You're the man from the party. The drunkard, who..." said Clement, the hamster wheel inside his head beginning to spin. "What is this?"

"*This* is your second chance, Alban. *This* is your one shot at redemption." Rainey explained just enough to make him understand what had transpired. Obvious and therefore left unsaid was the fact that everything he had just experienced could very well have been real. Also left unsaid was the aim of their little false-flag operation: to bring him over to their side and at the same time give him a clear picture of what life might be like if he were to decline their offer.

"It's all been recorded, Alban. Your admission of spying for Russia. Your admission to aiding Hezbollah."

Tilting his head, Clement wiped his sloppy nose on his shoulder. "So, you are blackmailing me? You're as bad as they are."

"Would you prefer I beat the information out of you?"

The diplomat was silent as he considered the question then said, "You speak French very well. You have lived in France, yes?"

"Not for a long time." Rainey interlaced his hands and leaned forward, his elbows on his thighs. It was an open body posture, one that added a modicum of intimacy to their conversation. "How did it first start? How did you get mixed up in all of this?"

Clement's shoulders slumped. "Will you afford me the dignity of a cigarette?"

Rainey looked at Saul and nodded. With a small pair of wire cutters, the old spy clipped Clement free of his flex cuffs then drew a pack of Gitanes from his coat pocket, handed one to the Frenchman.

Clement placed it between his lips and continued massaging blood back into his wrists. "No light?"

"Answer my question."

Clement pulled the cigarette from his mouth and produced a heavy sigh. For several long seconds, he rolled the unlit cigarette between his thumb and index finger, studying the backs of his hands until finally with head down, he uttered his first words of allocution. "It happened in New York, ironically. I was working as an adviser to our permanent representative to the UN at the time. My star was on the rise within the diplomatic corps. I suppose that's why..." He drew his lips together, fighting off another wave of emotion.

"Why you were targeted?"

Clement nodded. "Part of my job included doing interviews with reporters and various foreign news outlets. One of them, a reporter with the *Daily News*..." He rubbed his red eyes. "She called herself Daniella. Daniella

Bozzelli. She had legitimate press credentials or at least so I thought. She also had the dark hair of a goddess, long, trim legs and big—"

"She was beautiful. I get it," interjected Rainey.

"I did a number of interviews with her. One night...it was late and perhaps I was tired or just had too much to drink...maybe it was both, because I clearly wasn't thinking straight. Anyway, we went back to her apartment and one thing led to another."

"You slept with her?"

"We were together a total of six times." He chuckled in spite of himself. "I should have known better. It was a trap right from the beginning. And I fell right into it. Apparently, she was working for Hezbollah."

"So, they recruited you? By blackmailing you, I mean."

"Yes, but the Russians, *they* approached me first. Apparently, they had me under surveillance the whole time I was in the States. They knew about Daniella—if that's even her real name. They knew everything. They blackmailed me into working for them. Threatened to tell my wife and my government about Daniella, about my involvement with a Hezbollah operative. That was when I first learned that she was working for Hezbollah. Up until then I honestly thought she was just a journalist. My family, my career... My *life* would be over." He appeared to have the sudden realization that he was complicit in the attack on America.

"Don't stop. You're doing good." Rainey flipped open a lighter and extended it toward Clement. The Frenchmen brought the cigarette to his lips again, leaned forward, letting the paper take the flame, then relaxed backward, hungrily sucking in long drags of nicotine. "What happened next?"

"I began meeting with my Russian contact, Felix. We developed a system of communication, signals, that type of thing. We met several times in New York and then later in Paris and Brussels—that's where we currently meet. I brought him whatever I could find. Sometimes he requested specific information. On a few occasions, he instructed me to advise the ambassador in ways that I can only assume were advantageous to the Kremlin's interests."

"Go on."

"Well, then along came the girl again, Daniella. This was when I was still working in New York. We met on a park bench in Central Park. Can you believe it? I was living a spy's life, like the kind you read about in a de Villiers novel." He tilted his head backward and exhaled smoke into the air. He was beginning to relax. "She gave me instructions and a keycard for a hotel room in Midtown Manhattan, kissed me on the cheek, and then disappeared. I haven't seen her since. That evening, at the hotel, I met a man."

"Your Hezbollah handler." When Clement nodded, Rainey said. "Tell me about him."

"He was older." Clement turned toward Saul. "Not nearly as old as him. Maybe late forties, early fifties. He was slender, medium height. Not handsome but not ugly either. Regular looking, if you know what I mean."

"Did he give you his name?"

"Ghulam."

"That's it? Just Ghulam?"

"Yes."

"How did he communicate with you from that day forward?"

"Through an encrypted email account. He provided the login name and password. I was only to use computer terminals in public spaces when accessing the account—hotels, hospitals, internet cafés, that type of thing. Attached to each email was a list of things they wanted as well as coded instructions for particular dead drops."

Rainey nodded. He took no notes, for he knew the camera was recording. It was also streaming a live feed via a secure link to the safe house in Bougival in addition to the XOC inside DX headquarters. "And what did you place in those dead drops?"

"At first it was blank passports. A few here, a few there. Soon they wanted a hundred. I convinced Ghulam that this was far too many passports for me to acquire in my position even through my sub-sources unless he wanted someone to start asking questions. He came back a few weeks later with a solution."

"Which was?"

"He wanted information concerning the location and/or shipments of blank passports within France."

"And did you give it to him?"

"I had to leverage some close friendships and contacts I have within the government, but yes, regrettably, I did. You may have seen news of several hijacked shipments of blank passports over the past few years. They were perpetrated upon information that I had given Ghulam. I'm sure of it."

Clement tapped the ash from his cigarette. "As time went on, there were occasions in which Ghulam gave me names, photographs, and other information, and asked me to facilitate applications for French citizenship and the issuance of authentic breeder documents. You know, birth certificates, driver's licenses, documents used to acquire legitimate passports. He would follow that up with more information needed to satisfy additional screening efforts by security services."

"Like ESTA," said Rainey. ESTA stood for Electronic System for Travel Authorization. It was a program run by US Customs and Border Protection.

The Frenchman nodded his head as the weight of his disclosures mounted. His Adam's apple bobbed up and down as he continued. "Yes. It's been a huge undertaking. And each time I unloaded a dead drop or received an email, I found that they wanted *more*."

"How did they plan to get around the electronic monitoring of the stolen passports?"

"I don't know."

"So, what you're saying is that we have a bunch of Hezbollah terrorists now with authentic French passports, heck even full-fledged French citizenship, and thus the ability to travel anywhere within Europe or the United States with essentially no questions asked."

Clement hung his head. "I haven't slept well in years."

"What else?"

"As you might expect, Ghulam is largely interested in anything concerning Israel, Saudi, too: discussions or documents on security, technology, trade, and finance. More recently, Ghulam instructed me to advise our permanent representative and our team in Brussels on—be an advocate for—some specific NGOs. The ultimate aim, as he explained it to me, was to secure grant monies and bolster credibility for the organizations."

"And?"

"So far the organizations collectively have received nearly 40 million euros in disbursements based largely on my work."

Rainey shook his head in disbelief. The EU was unwittingly funding Hezbollah. Probably bought and paid for the latest attack on US soil. And with that amount of money, doubtless more attacks were coming. At home and abroad. *Unreal.*

"When was your last contact with Ghulam?"

"The fifth of November."

"Any plans to see him in the future?"

Clement hesitated then uttered, "I'm supposed to meet with him in ten days."

"Where?"

"Brussels."

Rainey mused for a moment. "To your knowledge, does Ghulam and Hezbollah know about your involvement with the Russians?"

"I don't think so, no. What I mean is, they've never given any indication of knowing."

For the next hour, Rainey questioned Clement about every last detail—how he obtained passports despite his assignment at the EU, how he met his Hezbollah contact, signals they used, all of it—then permitted him use of the restroom, which Tonka and Alcott both monitored. The diplomat was sipping water from a bottle when Rainey turned the video camera back on and declared that court was back in session. He watched the Frenchman sit down then shifted the focus of the inquest.

"Tell me about the Russians. What have you given them?"

"Comparatively speaking, much less, I would say."

Rainey glared at him, a silent rejoinder informing the Frenchman that he need not seek refuge in the murky waters of equivocation. For there was simply no point at this stage of the interrogation. Though Rainey understood the psychology of it all, he was just not in the mood to deal with a needless interlude of rationalization.

"I've provided them passports, too, as well as information on EU economic and trade discussions. And a number of security programs."

"Does any of that concern NATO?"

Clement was silent in his shame, offering a simple nod as evidence of his treachery.

The rest was more of the same, Rainey asking probing questions and Clement responding with the guilt-riddled truth. Finally, after three and a half long hours of relentless inquiry, Rainey clicked off the camera and approached the weary Frenchman.

"I was serious when I said this is your one shot at redemption, Alban. There won't be another." He put a hand on his captive's sloped shoulder. "We own you now. You do anything outside of your normal routine and we will make our little play from earlier tonight a painful reality for you. Do you understand me?"

Clement lifted his head. "I understand."

"Cooperate with us fully and we just may be able to work something out that will solve both of our problems."

A glimmer of hope appeared in the man's eyes.

"But cross me and I will put you in a drum like that one," he pointed to it for added effect, "and will make you stay there until the acid inside melts you into gumbo. That happens and there will be nothing left of you for anyone to find. Ask me how I know."

Clement shook his head. "I will do whatever you want me to do. Believe me."

"Good. But let there be no doubt, we will be watching."

25

The trek back to Clement's apartment house on the rue Daubigny was much like the one he had endured en route to the water-treatment facility but in reverse. This included the dreaded hood and another uncomfortable spell in the trunk of the Opel sedan. This time, however, Tonka did his level best to avoid the potholes and took the speed bumps with much greater care. At the same rally point as before, the Frenchman was lifted from the rear of the car and permitted to sit in the back seat. When they arrived on his street, though he knew it not, the disabled van was no longer disabled. In fact, it was no longer anywhere near Clement's flat.

Tonka pulled to the curb and advised him that he could remove the hood. He did so, placing it in the same spot in which he had found it previously. Clement stepped out of the car and closed the door, at which point the Opel sedan pulled away, leaving him alone on the cold, vacant sidewalk. He gazed up through the misty fog to the windows of his flat and shuddered not from the brisk temperature but from an all-consuming fear.

You must carry on as usual. Be strong, Alban.

Upon entering the door of his flat, he was immediately greeted by the same beautiful woman as before. Despite the long, nighttime hours that had passed, her bourbon-brown eyes appeared alert and intelligent, her face a blank page. When she spoke this time, her tone was far less severe. Though he now knew better, she maintained her perfect French bearing so much so that he would swear she were a native of his homeland. He kept all of these thoughts to himself, however. He did not know what to say to her. In fact, he was embarrassed by how easily he had been fooled by her artifice.

"She's still resting comfortably. As you can see, she has suffered no harm."

Clement's eyes shifted to his wife, who was still asleep on the sofa. He couldn't remember ever seeing her look so peaceful. In the time that he'd been gone, the woman in his flat had tucked a pillow under her head and covered her with another blanket from the bedroom. The mystery woman now stepped past him businesslike without uttering another word. The click of the door closing behind him might well have been the hammer of a pistol falling on an empty chamber. He suddenly found himself alone and even more terrified in the silence. It was then that he fell to his knees, dropped his head in his hands, and wept with all of his body. What had he done?

———

Maddie pushed through the broad door of the apartment building and set foot onto the sidewalk. She paused long enough to adjust the headband over her ears then turned right and took up a brisk pace in the chill air. It was quiet at this time of night, even in Paris. The clicking of her boots echoed against the building facades in the narrow street. It reminded her of the rhythmic ticking of the grandfather clock in her childhood home. The clock had been in the family for years. She used to marvel at it, how the intricate pieces of tiny machinery all worked together in perfect harmony. Much like the intelligence operation they had carried out tonight.

Once around the corner, she settled into the waiting Opel sedan and pulled the door closed.

"How did it go?" asked Tonka as he eased down on the accelerator.

"Funny, I was about to ask you the same thing."

"He sang like a canary, admitted to facilitating travel and identity docs for Hezbollah. Provided intelligence to them, too, as well as the Russians. The biggest takeaway though for us is that the names he provided matched names the Agency and Bureau have already been able to tie to the attack, false as they may be."

Maddie's unfocused eyes turned toward the buildings sweeping by her window. "So, it *was* Hezbollah that hit us?"

"No doubt about it," said Tonka.

"So, what now?"

"Now, we bring the storm to their doorstep."

***

The mood at the safe house was upbeat and lively, yet the men and women within it knew their work had only just begun. The Paris operation had been a complete success, yes, but their mandate, their overall mission was to find, fix, and finish those responsible for the events in New York, LA, and Chicago not merely confirm the suspicions of Saul, Job, and a handful of analysts back home. Now they wanted names—names of those involved in every phase of the attack, the operational planners, and the man or men who had given final authority to kill Americans on American soil.

For the sake of those who lost their lives that day and the families still awash with unrelenting grief, Rainey wanted to keep his foot on the gas and stay on the offensive here in Europe. But this year—this Christmas—would be unlike any he had celebrated since he was eleven years old. This year his father was alive. And so, it was for this reason and this reason alone that Rainey was eternally thankful when Job, having just completed the post-op debrief in the living room of the safe house, ordered everyone home for the holiday.

Rainey was packing his bag in the bedroom he'd been sharing with Saul, Tonka, and Mouse when a shadow suddenly darkened the room. Glancing up, he found Maddie standing in the doorway, her arms folded across her chest.

"Good job at the Frog's place," he said. "You were great."

"Thanks. You, too. Pappy says you were really something. Especially at the hotel party," she added with a giggle.

Rainey was quiet.

"What is it? What's bothering you?"

"Nothing."

"Come on, Ray. I know you. Is it the mission? We'll get the turds responsible for the attacks. I have no doubt."

He jammed a pair of pants into his duffel bag. "It's not the mission."

"Then what? What is it?"

He hesitated, not wanting to pull back the curtain. But with Maddie it was useless. She knew him too well, and besides, she was blood. Her concern was out of love. If he didn't tell her now, she would pester him relentlessly or at a minimum tease him the way younger sisters do until he finally caved. *Maybe she should have interrogated Clement.*

"It's Kayla. She won't answer my calls," he said. "New York shook her very badly. But on top of that, I think what she suspects I do scares her. Truth be told, she's pissed that I had to run off so soon after what happened. My sense is that it reminded her of when I dropped out of school and enlisted." He stopped, looked up at her. "You can be thankful you have Wes."

Maddie stared at her big brother with eyes yellow-gold like honey.

"Anyway, it is what it is. I'm not going to let her ruin Christmas for me, especially this one." He shrugged. "Maybe it's just not meant to be. Maybe she's not the *one* after all." With that, he grabbed his bags from the bed, his muscled arms flexing under their weight, and stepped toward the door. But Maddie blocked his path.

She looked up into his eyes. "Things will work out, Ray. You're a good guy. Above all, God is good, and He is *for* you. He's got your six." She hugged him. "Have you ever considered the idea that maybe Kayla doesn't *deserve* you?"

He offered a conciliatory smile as he flicked off the light with his elbow then walked past her. Halfway down the hall, he stopped and turned back. "Thanks, sis."

Maddie's face brightened. "See you on the plane."

26

The front office of the Cabinet d'avocats Vidal Rouzet was empty but for the pretty raven-haired woman behind the reception window. Sadiq forced himself to look her in the eyes as she warmly greeted him. This was the part he hated most about coming here. The woman was attractive with a body that simply could not be hidden beneath business suits and plain knee-length skirts. He would later ask Allah to forgive him for the thoughts now racing through his mind. For Sadiq Ammar al-Hamadeh was a devout Muslim. And while he knew his Iranian intelligence and Hezbollah masters had done well to use her as window dressing on their perfectly clandestine intelligence post, he, himself, would not have chosen someone so distracting. But then again, perhaps that's why she had been hired in the first place.

"*Bonjour*, Monsieur Ghulam."

Sadiq had used the alias for so long he could scarcely recall the last time he had been called by his real name. He waved his proximity card in front of a square plastic plate on the wall next to a thick door made of blond wood, which stood next to the reception window. Nothing happened, so he swiped the card again. As he did so, the curvy woman with long eyelashes smiled at him. Hearing a click this time, he pushed the door open and stepped into a small vestibule that smelled of office paper and the receptionist's perfume.

As he had done countless times before, Sadiq padded across the room to another door. He opened it and made sure to secure it behind him. It was quiet now. He could no longer hear the busy street outside. Sadiq grinned as he made his way down the soft carpeted hallway and, without knocking, entered the well-appointed office suite he shared with the attorney for which the firm was named. Though he was a dutiful agent of Hezbollah and knew of the existence of the secure communications room, the attorney was not privy to operational matters. His job was simple: to provide a shroud of legitimacy and, truth be told, legal cover in the event their activities on French soil should become known to the French or other Western intelligence and security services. Though Sadiq was supremely confident that there was little chance of that ever happening.

The suite consisted of two private offices that faced each other. Between them was a small waiting area with potted plants and soft chairs. Through the frosted glass of the attorney's office door, Sadiq could hear the man murmuring into the phone. He was useful to the cause, but Sadiq loathed him, nevertheless.

Sadiq entered the second office, which was dedicated for his explicit use, and closed the door. For a long moment, he visually scanned the room. There were several items that he had strategically placed about that if moved would indicate someone had been inside. Satisfied the room was secure, he maneuvered to the closet door. Inside was a rod with several empty coat hangers and in the corner, an umbrella. With his phone's NFC feature activated, he held the device close to a specific location in the molding. In three seconds, the latch would reengage, so he needed to be swift. It was designed this way on purpose. Sadiq pressed into the back wall. It swung open, revealing another door, this one constructed of heavy, machined steel. Beside it was a glass plate onto which he placed his left palm. Immediately, a magnetic lock gave way, and he stepped inside a hidden room, turned, and secured both the outer and inner doors.

Right under the nose of the French DGSI, the Iranians had installed a SCIF—a sensitive compartmented information facility—in complete secrecy just two short years ago. It was one of several such rooms that Sadiq knew existed outside of Iranian embassies in Europe though he only ever utilized this one being that Paris was his base of operations.

The room wasn't large by any means. It was about the size of a small galley kitchen, long and narrow. Midway along the left wall was a computer station. He slid into the metal chair and swiveled toward the keyboard. He quickly logged on to the system, at which time he found a new cable waiting for him. Using the terminal's mouse, he clicked on it and another window opened bearing a two-sentence message.

`What is the status of our Trademark case? Our client is getting impatient.`

Despite the Iranians' promises that the comms link was completely secure, Sadiq and his Hezbollah superiors still disguised their dialogue in vague, legal language. He shifted his focus from the message text to his reflection on the screen. He saw his mouth draw into a wry smirk. They always wanted more and always needed it yesterday. But sensitive operations took time and finesse. Surely Nourani knew this.

The smirk faded from his face as he began to type.

`Our team of experts will be filing their briefs soon. I have no doubt that the case is still on schedule. We appreciate your business.`

He read over his reply several times before clicking SEND.

Sadiq sat and stroked his neatly trimmed beard while enjoying the absolute silence of the room. The past year had been a whirlwind of intense planning and coordination. The New York City operation alone had taken a huge toll on him. For several weeks now, he had endured frequent headaches and a stomach that constantly churned. He had fleeting thoughts of visiting a local mosque, where he could fraternize with fellow Muslims, perhaps discuss the news coverage of the attack on America. But no. Operational tradecraft precluded him from going anywhere near a mosque. They were surely the focus of Western intelligence agencies and fertile ground for their spies, according to Nourani. Stay clear and stay safe.

Sadiq logged off the computer and extinguished the light. As he re-secured both doors to the hidden room and exited his office, he heard the voice of the attorney on the other side of the office suite, now coarse and argumentative in his tone. For a tense moment, he imagined that the DGSI—the French internal security service—had come to arrest him. Realizing his hands were balled up into fists, he relaxed them and took a deep breath. For his job, his very life demanded that he remain focused and alert. These were dangerous times.

The attorney was still blathering away on the phone, as Sadiq slipped back into the hallway. Ignoring the festive decorations and general merriment of the impending Christian holiday outside, he headed off along the busy Paris sidewalk. His surveillance-detection route would take him nearly an hour. After that he would arrive home with no one or no thing to accompany him but his lingering feelings of loneliness and depression that only someone who had spent long periods of time in isolation could know.

The fact that there had been no news from the Saudis or the Israelis, let alone the Americans was disquieting. Something must be amiss. He had expected news of the secret meeting in the Saudi consulate to have leaked by now. How could the deaths of those attending not be all over the airwaves? A current of anger shot through him. Had their source been wrong about the meeting? How was that possible? The intelligence had been verified. As he lay in bed, his mind raced. He would need to press the source during their next meeting.

27

At the end of Harness Creek View Drive, a wooded peninsula, modest in size, jutted out into the eastern shore of Aberdeen Creek. On it stood two homes. The one on the right was owned by none other than the current head of the CIA's Directorate X, Job Jackson, while the other belonged to the Rainey family. Both were stately yet lacked ostentation, large but without pretension.

Rainey parked his black '89 Ford Bronco in the forecourt and switched off the engine. He was still suffering the effects of jet lag, but unfortunately, it was something to which he had become rather accustomed over the years. He gazed at his family home. Even now, it still felt like just that: home.

Saul climbed out the other side. "You going to take a picture?"

Rainey rolled his eyes. "No, Pappy."

"Come on, buck up. I gotta hit the head."

He could hear the revelry within as they walked to the front door, voices of Maddie and Wes—her fiancé—laughing and carrying on. He could even make out the faint sound of an old Amy Grant Christmas album playing on the stereo. *Tennessee Christmas.* He still knew the words to each song by heart. It instantly brought back fond holiday memories. He pictured his mother in the kitchen with flour on her cheek, baking batch after batch of cookies. The house all toasty and warm from logs ablaze in the fireplace.

He couldn't recall a time when an Amy Grant or Sandi Patty or Imperials Christmas album wasn't playing in the background as he and Maddie decorated the tree. He remembered the stockings hung by the chimney. Even after the news of his father's death, they had made sure to hang a stocking that bore his name from the mantel. Who knew he would now be back in their lives? Despite recent events, there was much to celebrate and be thankful for this year.

The smell of cooked ham and cinnamon greeted him as they entered.

"Ray and Pappy are here!" Maddie called over her shoulder. She hugged them both.

"Hey, sis."

Wes wasn't far behind. He meandered across the large living room, one hand in the pocket of his brown corduroy pants, the other minding a novelty glass in the shape of a moose head, which was filled halfway with eggnog. Rainey shook his hand and the two exchanged Christmas greetings.

"Where's Dad?" said Rainey, as Saul veered off toward the nearest bathroom.

"He's helping Mom in the kitchen." Then in a voice just above a whisper, Maddie said, "Any word from Kayla yet?"

Rainey's smile faded. "I've left her several messages, sent texts. She hasn't responded to any of them. I—"

His voice caught in his throat as he spied a familiar figure at the back of the house. There, gazing out the French doors that led outside onto the covered patio, was Evelina. She was wearing a long olive-drab cardigan sweater, a pair of tight blue jeans, and suede boots that left her ankles exposed. She was facing away from them, studying the dark waters of Aberdeen Creek. Or was she studying him via the reflection in the window?

"What's *she* doing here?" he whispered.

"I invited her," Maddie said with a spice of mischief in her voice. "She has no family in the area. I thought it would be nice if she joined us. No one should have to spend Christmas alone." She poked him in the ribs. "Just go talk to her. Make her feel welcome."

Rainey had no problem with someone joining them for the holiday festivities, least of all a fellow member of the DX, but with the way things were going with Kayla and now Maddie's conspiratorial tone, this felt a little too much like a setup. Guilt began to creep into his thoughts. Even with Kayla's recent chilly behavior, he knew it was likely only temporary—emotional fallout from the traumatic experience in New York. But the idea of him hanging out with another beautiful woman who was *not* Kayla Chapman on a special occasion such as Christmas made him uncomfortable. As if he were cheating on her somehow.

No. What was he even thinking? Evie didn't come here to cultivate a romance. She was here because Maddie invited her. *And* she was a co-worker. He would do his utmost to keep things professional.

Maddie must have recognized this in his eyes, because she punched him on the arm and whispered, "Hey, bro, you're not here on a date with her. And she has no illusions either. Just relax and be yourself."

"Yeah. You're right."

Maddie pointed to the packages in the bag he was carrying. "Are those for me?"

"Nope. They're all for Wes."

Wes raised his moose cup in merry approval. "Hooray!" Which was followed quickly by a comedic grunt being that Maddie had just playfully elbowed him in the stomach.

Rainey set the gifts by the tree and made his way through the great room, past the brick fireplace to the entranceway of the kitchen. He stopped just outside it when he saw his parents stealing a kiss. Neither knew he was standing there. His father was still constrained to a wheelchair, but from what his mother had recently reported to him and Maddie, he was getting healthier with each passing day. Physical therapy was obviously doing wonders for him though the doctors held no hope he would ever walk again.

Rainey studied them the way a young child spies on his parents. They looked so happy together. Minus the wheelchair, it was like old times. They could have been newlyweds. His mother now hovered over the hot ham she had just pulled from the oven. As she tended to the platter dressing, his father wheeled around her and in so doing patted her on the fanny.

"Now, Ben," his mother said, playfully scolding him.

Rainey finally announced his presence and hugged them both. His father's grip was getting stronger. The bone from the disfigured forearm though poking him in the back reminded him of the horrors his dad had endured. His being here, home again for Christmas, was truly a miracle.

When his father rolled out of the kitchen to ferry a tray of place settings to the large table in the dining room, Rainey drew close to his mother and in a low voice said, "How's he doing, Mom?"

Sarah Rainey moved a plate of freshly baked chocolate-chip cookies to an area beside the fridge and slid a dish of mashed potatoes away from the edge of the counter then rubbed her hands on her apron.

"Mom?"

"He has good days and bad. Some nights he wakes up sweating and shivering from terrible nightmares. A few nights ago, he cried out in his sleep. It was as if he were back there in that prison and they were beating him, twisting his limbs. I could scarcely bear it." Her bottom lip suddenly quivered. She steadied herself with a deep sigh. "But he never consciously talks about his ordeal, what he endured. And I don't want to push him. I know he may one day open up about what he went through. And when he does, I must be ready to listen. No matter how difficult it is. In the meantime, I pray. I pray for his health and for his soul to have peace. I pray without ceasing, Reagan."

"How are *you* doing? I know it can't be easy, something like this."

Ever the graceful wife, she smiled through a sudden swell of emotion. "It has been hard. But he is my husband, and I praise the Lord for every minute he is back in my arms. Thank God you found him when you did."

He leaned forward and kissed her on the forehead. "Dad's blessed to have you by his side. You're a good mom and a good wife. Love you."

At the sound of the wheelchair behind him, Rainey stepped back and made room for his father. "Love you, too, Dad."

The elder Rainey man patted him on the arm. "You're a good son, Ray. I'm proud of you."

Not one to show his emotions, Ray swiped a cookie from the tray by the fridge then withdrew from the kitchen and headed for Evelina. As he came near to her, she turned toward him, the light from the recessed lamps in the ceiling making her blond hair glow with angelic brilliance. She was gorgeous. There was just no other way to describe her. He suddenly had visions of her back in Paris, her stunning the crowd as Madame Appell.

Wow!

No, Ray. No.

With her left index finger, Evelina pulled a stray lock of hair from her forehead, tucked it behind her ear, and gazed up at him, her peridot eyes sparkling like the North Atlantic under a hot summer sun.

"Merry Christmas, Evie."

"Merry Christmas to you."

"Glad you could join us."

"It was very kind of you to include me in your holiday celebration. Maddie said it was your idea. So, I suppose I have you to thank."

My idea? He turned with nonchalance and spied Maddie over by the Christmas tree. She was smiling from ear to ear, giggling even. *That little stinker.*

"Normally, I'd be up in Wisconsin with my parents, but they went to Iceland for the holidays to see my brothers and their families."

"Iceland?"

"Yep. About half of my family still live there."

He must have made a face that evidenced his disbelief, because at that moment Evelina grinned with more than a hint of intrigue on her face.

"I grew up there. I thought you knew."

"Your folks aren't American?"

"My mom is. My dad's Israeli but was born and raised in Iceland, same as me."

"How'd they meet?"

"On the slopes. My mom is an executive for Ogontz Energy. At the time, she was working in the company's geothermal division, which is based in Reykjavik. As the story goes, she wanted to learn to ski, so she decided to take some lessons at a local resort. My dad just happened to be working there part-time as a ski instructor. Said he couldn't take his eyes off her. He asked her out and they quickly fell in love."

While Evelina was speaking, Rainey turned toward the kitchen and together they glimpsed his mom doting over his dad again and his dad's hand returning to her backside.

"Can you blame him for not being able to keep his hands off her? After all the years away from her? After what he went through in that dreadful place?"

They both conceded a smile.

"So your brothers live in Iceland?"

"Two of them do. The other three are spread out all over." Evelina sipped eggnog from a mug.

"Wow. Iceland. Does that mean you speak the language?"

"*Hvað finnst þér?*"

"What does that mean?"

"It means that I do," she said smiling.

"You are full of surprises, Evelina Krantz."

"*Am* I?"

He felt his cheeks reddening, thus he decided it was best to change the subject. "Come on. I think dinner is about ready."

After Job and his wife Iris arrived, everyone gathered in the dining room to enjoy the huge Christmas dinner that Sarah had prepared. After they'd filled their bellies and dispensed with the dishes, they all congregated in the living room and exchanged presents by the fireplace. Maddie had even thought to have some on hand for Evelina. In fact, she'd expertly forged one of the tags: "From Ray. Merry Christmas!" Then came the familiar—some of them embarrassing—family stories that, as always, yielded much rowdy laughter within the Rainey tribe.

As the night grew late, Rainey found himself alone outside on the covered flagstone patio at the rear of the house. At one end, a large heap of wood burned brightly inside a great stone fireplace. His eyes remained on the dancing flames even as the French doors behind him opened and closed.

"So. There you are."

Rainey was silent, the light from the fire flickering about his face. He lifted a Duke University mug filled with jet-black coffee to his lips, felt the hot liquid roll down the back of his throat and empty into his stomach.

Evelina's boots clicked on the cold, flat stone of the patio. "What are you doing out here all alone? The party's inside."

"I was thinking about Ryan Killian's wife and boys. For a long time, I was in their shoes. I know from experience that they are in misery right now."

She sat down on the outdoor sofa across from him, both hands wrapped around a mug now filled with hot tea. "I can understand how you must feel, Ray."

Rainey shifted his gaze. The firelight seemed to accentuate her beauty.

"You feel guilty. Here we are, celebrating and having fun, while Killian's family is in hell. It isn't fair, Ray. It isn't. But you are not responsible for Ryan Killian's death. They are—the people who did this. And," her voice dropped an octave, "we *are* going to get them. We're going to make them pay for what they've done." Her eyes were serious, her expression resolute.

"Oh, I have no doubt about that, it's just... I can't stop thinking about them. Mainly because I've been there, you know?"

She drew her sweater together with one hand. Still, her shoulders began to shiver as she held his eyes with her own. "I know."

He set his mug down on the wrought iron and glass table that separated them and walked to a cabinet from which he pulled a heavy woolen blanket. He draped it over her before returning to his chair and his coffee.

Together they stared into the tranquility of the flames until a loud burst of laughter that came from somewhere inside caused them to turn in unison toward the door. It was his father's laugh, full and joyful and utterly contagious. Together they smiled. It was so good to hear it ringing out again.

Evelina drew up her legs beside her on the sofa and curled up inside the bundled blanket. She brought the mug close to her mouth and blew over the hot liquid causing tendrils of steam to disappear if only for a brief spell.

"You and your family are very close."

"Yes. We are. I still can't believe my father is alive and home again."

"It's obvious that you love him very much. As you should."

After a moment's hesitation, he looked deep into his coffee mug. "I've never told this to anyone, and I know it sounds corny, but... Ever since I was a kid, he's been my hero. I'm the man I am today because of him. I've always sought to make him proud." Sensing a threat of emotion in his voice, he abruptly changed the subject. "You did a great job in Paris, Evie."

Her face lit up and not just from the firelight. "I apologize for hitting you so hard. I really smacked you good, didn't I?"

"No, no. It was perfect."

After a few minutes of awkward silence, Rainey's phone vibrated inside his pants pocket. At the sight of the notification on the screen, he leaned forward and punched in his unlock code. The text message was long, and it took him a moment to scroll to the end. After he had read it, he glanced back up at Evelina and found her studying him.

"Kayla?" she said.

Rainey nodded. "Kayla."

28

Rainey jolted awake. He threw off the blankets and sat up, trying to force the visions of a particular night in Afghanistan from his head. The screams from his fellow soldiers still haunted him. Their convoy had been traveling in Uruzgan Province when the Humvee in front of his exploded without warning. The IED lifted the vehicle up in the air several feet before it pitched over on its side. Choking on the rising smoke and dust that clouded their vision, Rainey and his teammates dismounted and raced to help their brother warfighters inside. But their efforts were in vain—the blast had ripped apart everyone inside. Then the gunfire erupted. It had been a well-planned ambush. He would never forget his first taste of combat, the look and smell of torn and burnt flesh, the loud explosions, the bullets snapping and whizzing and ricocheting all around him, the terror-stricken faces of his buddies as they fought like rabid dogs for their lives, for each other.

He got out of bed, went to the back door, and walked outside for some fresh air. But it was when he stepped back inside that an idea hit him. He hovered over the kitchen sink for several long minutes considering the ramifications then hurried to his study and closed the door. He sat down and began to make notes on a yellow legal pad. Soon it was full, and he reached for another.

As dawn broke, he called Job. It was early, yes, but Job would be up by now for sure.

"I have an idea," he said. "I know how we're going to get him."

"Come to my office, we'll talk there."

When Rainey arrived, he found the place quiet. Job's regular office staff would not arrive for another hour. The spymaster looked up the very moment he entered the office suite. The room smelled of freshly brewed coffee.

Job set his mug down and without preamble, blurted out, "So, what is this idea of yours?"

Rainey selected a K-cup from the stand on the credenza along the wall then waited for the Keurig machine to finish as Job percolated. Coffee in hand, he took a seat and explained his idea. Job sat quietly, sometimes blinking rapidly, other times staring full-on and breathing deeply. When Rainey had finished, Job asked only one question. "Who do you want?"

"Give me the rest of the day and the proper clearance to go through Agency personnel files. I'll have my team selected by then."

"Very well. I will see to it straight away. You and your team will need a place to work." Job tapped his fingers on the desk then reached for his inter-office phone. An hour later, Job accepted a call on the same phone then abruptly stood and said, "Come with me."

It wasn't until they were striding down the long sterile corridor that connected all three buildings in the DX headquarters complex—DX Main, the Hotel, and the Annex—that Job spoke again. "I think you'll find this space to be satisfactory."

"We just need someplace to plop. As long as it's quiet and secure."

The Annex was the shortest of the three DX headquarters buildings and housed everything from servers and technology labs to libraries and research rooms. Their destination, Job said, was on the ninth floor. Together they stepped off the elevator and Job immediately turned right. Rainey, having never set foot in the Annex, followed behind—a new employee being shown to his cubicle. Job stopped outside a heavy steel door. He flashed his keycard over a pad on the wall, leaned into an iris scanner, then placed his palm against a glass panel before finally pushing inside. This gave way to another hall at the end of which was another secure door. Job repeated the ritual giving Rainey time to read the placard on the wall. *S-922.*

Inside, Rainey found himself in a small lobby with sofas and chairs. It was empty and smelled of leather and freshly vacuumed carpet. On the far wall was a large reception counter, the room beyond lay dark and quiet. Job badged through a door beside the reception window and marched down a short corridor. He stopped outside the first door on his left, which had been propped open with a rubber wedge. Inside the spacious office was an L-shaped desk, numerous file cabinets, a hefty safe with a combination lock. A woman of middle age with wavy, gold-flecked hair was just now organizing her new workspace. She plucked the soft vinyl covers from a trio of adjacent computer monitors and tossed them aside. A woman's handbag and a cardboard box were parked along the end of the desk closest to the door. From the box, the woman withdrew one, two, three picture frames and several other mementos of personal significance.

She looked up as they stepped into the room. "Good morning, Chief."

Job offered a quick hello. "Janna Carlson, I'd like you to meet Reagan Rainey. This is who you'll be working with here."

"How do you do?"

Rainey stepped forward, offered her his hand. Carlson's handshake was firm, signaling confidence, her eyes alert and intelligent. "Great to meet you, Janna."

Job turned to Ray. "Janna's a staff operations officer—one of our very best. Just returned from a term overseas, in fact. She's in between assignments, or at least *was*. I know you both exceedingly well, so believe me when I say that you two are going to get along great. Now, let me show you both around the place."

The trio continued down the corridor, which emptied into a central room of maybe twenty or thirty dormant cubicles. They strode left and eventually came to a spacious planning room.

"Totally secure," said Job, pointing to a control panel on the wall inside the SCIF, which stood for sensitive compartmented information facility.

A large rectangular Cherrywood table presided in the middle of the room. Around this stood fourteen black, high-backed, leather chairs. On one of the walls hung a bank of six flat-screen monitors, beside them a pair of whiteboards and a large interactive flat panel. Numerous smaller tables, bureaus, file cabinets, and a total of six stationary chairs skirted the remaining three walls. The White House Situation Room seemed tiny compared to this, at least from what Rainey had seen on TV.

They marched on past private offices, some of them with windowed walls. Farther down the hall, Job said, were the men's and women's lavatories. Rainey gazed to his right and noted another passageway, this one probably thirty yards long.

"Down there are a few more small offices, a lounge, and a mess hall of sorts."

"This place is amazing," said Rainey.

"You don't know the half of it."

"And it's all just been sitting dormant?"

"Sad, isn't it? Well, no more."

On a sub-level far below was a secure area that would serve as the team's weapons armory/loadout room with direct access to another secure underground parking garage, Job said. There, they would find individual cage lockers for team members' gear, workbenches, shelves for everything from gun-cleaning supplies to ammo boxes, even a small, indoor firing range. In addition, the sub-level contained men's and women's locker rooms with bathrooms and showers. Not unlike those found in a professional sports arena, the spymaster continued. When they had made their way back around to the front of the office suite, Job proclaimed, "*This* will be your war room."

Rainey gazed around the suite's footprint of wood and glass and brass fixtures. "It's more than adequate, Job. In fact, it's kind of too big."

"Nonsense. I believe in giving my people the tools they need to succeed. Here, there is room to grow if it should become necessary. IT will be in shortly to get you set up on the system. Do either of you have any questions for me right now? Concerns?"

Rainey shook his head. Janna did likewise.

"Ray, if you need anything, tell Janna and she will see that you get it."

"Great."

"I apologize for running out, but I've got a meeting in ten minutes." And with that, Job was gone.

After a moment of quiet, Carlson lifted her steel-blue eyes to meet Rainey's. "Guess it's time to get to it. I look forward to working with you, Ray."

"Same here."

As Carlson retreated to her office, Rainey silently circled the suite again, poking his head into empty offices and sizing up the various smaller conference rooms that dotted the corridors. Thirty minutes later, he was behind a desk in a corner office that looked down onto Theodore Roosevelt Island, pouring through a stack of files with "Concerto for Strings in G Minor" by Vivaldi playing softly in the background. From the outset, he knew the majority of those he wanted on his team, but to round out the group, he needed to explore Langley's operations staff files. For hours, he pulled up file abstracts from the internal servers then had Janna retrieve the original hardcopy files. The two of them developed a smooth working relationship right off the bat. She was a model of efficiency and goodwill.

At sixteen minutes to midnight, he finally shut down his workstation and clicked off the lights. He had his team. It would be called Jaguar—Job had insisted it have a name, something more colorful than Special Operations Executive 77, the label it would bear in the codified DX file system. Rainey wondered if the SOE part had any significance relative to the secretive group of the same name that the British had stood up back in the 1940s.

Jaguar. I like it, he thought. Because of the animal's unique traits, the name seemed a natural fit for a team such as this.

Per his earlier instructions, Janna had already contacted each of the prospective members. They would assemble here in the morning for the team's first official briefing. Then the hunt for Qais al-Nourani and anyone else responsible for the latest terrorist attack on American soil would commence with calculated vengeance.

29

The morning light cascading through the smoked-out, ballistic office windows greeted him as he strode into Suite 922. He dropped his OD green Eberlestock Switchblade rucksack in his office chair and then, with help from Janna Carlson, readied the conference room for the inaugural Jaguar team meeting. He noted that Janna had done much of the prep work already. What time had she come in this morning?

As they finished assembling the room, Janna explained that Job had assigned her to be the team's full-time staff operations officer. Her primary responsibility would be to act as a liaison between Jaguar and various other offices and departments within the DX as well as other agencies within the Intelligence Community. In time, she would also oversee a small administrative staff within Jaguar's headquarters footprint. Her Midwestern accent reminded him of a former ODA teammate he'd served with in 3rd Group. Job was right. Janna Carlson was a smart, resourceful, and meticulous professional. The perfect person to complement Jaguar's stable of highly skilled field operatives.

She was now placing briefing packets at precise 90-degree angles in front of each chair parked around the large conference table.

"Have you been at the Agency long?"

"For the past seventeen and a half years."

"Any family?"

"A husband and two girls."

"What do they do?"

She smiled. "Gretchen—she's my oldest—is a chemist in the South Carolina State Police forensic lab. Justine's still in school. She's a junior at Georgetown and is studying to be an art therapist. She also plays tennis and cello."

"Wow. Sounds like you have some very smart and very talented young ladies."

"Thank you. Brett and I are extremely proud of them."

"And your husband? What does he do, if you don't mind my asking?"

"He teaches science at Sidwell Friends. He's been there now for just over twenty years."

Rainey noted how Janna did not ask about his family. Of course, she knew better than to ask such questions of operations staff. Yeah, Janna was going to fit in perfectly.

"So, I see you two are hitting it off." Job entered with little fanfare and headed straight for the coffee machine.

"Janna's great, Job."

"I know she is. That's why she's here." He checked his watch and drew his cup to his mouth.

Fifteen minutes later, the last members of the Jaguar team trickled in. The conference room was now full.

Rainey swiveled in his chair, swept his eyes around the table. Seated together, two peas in a pod and the closest of friends, were Evelina Krantz and his sister Maddie. He had already determined that, purely on professional grounds, Evelina would serve as the team's number two. She was a solid leader and had demonstrated a wealth of knowledge and ability in the short amount of time that he'd known her. On top of that, she was fearless and resourceful. Truth be told, he wondered why she wasn't running the team.

Billeted farther down the table were Tonka, Mouse, and Mark Alcott—all former Army Special Forces—men with whom he had served in such places as Afghanistan, Iraq, and North Africa. Sitting beside Alcott was Conrad Pietrolaj, a former F/A-18 pilot and commander of the Navy's Strike Fighter Squadron 131, who like Alcott, had made his way into the DIA before apparently being swayed to come over to the Agency's most covert element, Directorate X. Now an analyst by trade, Pietrolaj had a deep curiosity in all manner of weapons systems and, not surprisingly, aircraft. For he was considered the final authority on both topics. In his spare time, he could usually be found trolling museums or nose-deep in research at any number of libraries around the world. He also wrote for several scholarly publications within and without the American military-industrial complex. Rainey had never worked with him directly but knew him by his stellar reputation. In his late forties, Pietrolaj was witty and urbane—a blend of rare intelligence and fearless self-confidence. His reserved, casual bearing could oftentimes be confused for arrogance, which as the story goes, had made him a rich target of the backbiting bureaucrats that roamed the Pentagon's corridors of power, those who put more stock in the politics of fighting wars than in the art of winning them. Alcott had called him an egghead with nerves of steel. And thus, as Rainey sat there assessing his new teammate, he filed away the perfectly ironic moniker for the man: Macho.

Running down the left side of the table were the pipe hitters—the DX Joint Services Group's best shooters with whom he had worked on previous occasions, most recently and most notably, the operation to rescue his father from a Russian black site. Justin "Babe" Ruth, the man who was right now staring back at him with calculated precision, was a hulk of a man. He had been drafted into the Majors after college, but instead of playing baseball and making millions doing so, followed in his father's footsteps by enlisting in the Army and later being selected to the Unit.

Fig and Jazz were ribbing each other about their favorite college football teams. Ribbing was a constant in the Unit. Both men were similar in build—wiry and all lean muscle. Fig, perhaps the best all-around hand-to-hand fighter in the US military, could trace his roots through modern-day Mexico all the way back to a Spanish explorer of considerable fame. He was a devout Catholic and could be as calm as a summer breeze even in the most chaotic of circumstances.

Jazz on the other hand was nearly the exact opposite. Though he never disparaged his friends' varying degrees of faith and Christian beliefs, he did not hide the fact that he abided by a more live-and-let-live existence. He was the most foul-mouthed of anyone in the room, not because he didn't care about offending, but more so because it was how he had been brought up. Jazz's parents had both been abusive alcoholics, and to top it off, he had been the only White kid in the entire Harper High School in Southside Chicago during his youth. He hadn't hit his growth spurt until after graduation, which was a miracle in and of itself. All throughout his childhood, he had been mercilessly tormented because of his slight frame and skin color. Jazz, therefore, grew up learning how to fight—he had to just to survive. With his school and juvenile arrest record, he had no legitimate way of getting into college. The Army, therefore, had been his only way out of the ghetto and he'd smartly taken it. Even today, he could brawl with the best of them, but now preferred using his mind to decimate his enemies. Rainey had selected him to Jaguar for all these reasons and more.

Wizard and Babe, snipers both, were now quietly discussing a particular ammo load that Babe, best Rainey could hear, wanted to test out on his next trip to the range. Wizard had grown up on a farm in Alabama and told some of the funniest stories ever. He was a patient man and could sit in the same spot for hours without moving a muscle, which helped make him one of the best military snipers in the world. It was a fact he had proved not just in combat. For three years running he and Babe had won the USASOC's annual sniper competition. They were quite the lethal pair.

Then there was Darryl Mabry, aka Booster, who was also from the South. An Atlanta product, he grew up one of six kids in a single-parent home. That his mother loved him and his siblings was obvious. But as their circumstances dictated, she had never been around to keep a watchful eye on them. When not working long hours to put food on the table, the woman had been too exhausted to move. Nevertheless, like any parent, she'd wanted the best for her children, so she had taken them to church as often as she could. The sermons and the church folk certainly had had an impact on Booster's young life, but so, too, did the streets. And the streets never slept.

Booster was king when it came to stealing cars, which was how he had earned his call sign. He had only ever gotten caught once during his childhood. Not long before his seventeenth birthday, he'd stolen a Chevy Corvette then decided to let a girl, whom he'd been trying to impress, drive it. She'd responded by promptly smashing them into a parked car. The crash had been so bad that it left her pinned behind the wheel with two broken legs, a crushed pelvis, a mangled left hand, and a gash on her forehead that required thirty-nine stitches. Booster had suffered only a broken nose and bruises and could have easily run off before the cops arrived. The only reason they'd caught him was because he had refused to leave Shauntay's side in her moment of crisis. It was in his blood, you see, to never leave a friend behind. And so it was, during his mandated community service that an off-duty police officer who'd been working with the program on his own time, suggested he might be able to put his endless stores of energy to good use in the military. The Army, he'd said, would keep him off the streets and out of jail, if he weren't killed first by one of the rival gangbangers with whom he and his friends constantly feuded. The government would also pay for his college tuition, should he choose to enroll in school after serving in the military. The Army, as it turned out, ended up being the place where Booster had found himself and his calling. But it was Delta that molded him into what he was today. An elite soldier. One of his nation's best.

The others seated at the table Rainey knew nothing about aside from what he had read in their highly classified personnel files.

He finally stood. "Everyone, I want to thank you for being here on such short notice. I know you are all probably wondering why you were asked to be here. But before we dig in, let's dispense with the introductions." He went around the room, giving each attendee a moment to recite their name and draw a brief sketch of their background and expertise. As they did so, he recalled what he had come to know about them by virtue of their personnel files. Operations in which they had participated, prior assignments, their personal histories, and other biographical information.

A pretty, little redhead with invisible eyeglasses, Brigid Finn had once been one of the NSA's finest hackers until Job poached her to become one of his own. Due to her considerable expertise and eagerness to serve her country at all costs, she was oftentimes loaned out to various agencies and task forces within the US Intelligence Community. Officially, she now worked within the DX's Technical Operations Group doing all manner of things in the digital realm from cyber warfare and exploitation to signals intelligence and cryptography. She was in her mid-thirties and, based on the way she was dressed, enjoyed shopping for the latest trends, making her far from the stereotypical computer nerd. Had he not known better, Rainey would have guessed she was one of the legal hotshots from the Office of General Counsel or the Justice Department.

The man next to Brigid was James "Jimmy" Dunne. With the sleek, diminutive build of a competitive cyclist, Dunne was nothing special to look at compared to the muscled operators in the room. He had them by a good fifteen years or so, too. His neat pate of brown hair, which was quickly going to gray, gave him a priestly quality. Add to that his curious police-detective eyes and placid demeanor and it was easy to comprehend how he had become one of the Agency's most highly prized counterintelligence officers. Before 9/11, Dunne had carried a gold badge with the NYPD. Infused with anger and a burning desire to do something big for his country, he applied to the CIA the Monday after 9/11. With his experience and applicant test scores, he immediately came to the attention of the Agency's talent spotters. Now approaching legendary status, Dunne had numerous high-profile counter-intelligence operations under his belt. Some they had even written books about. The rest were shrouded in secrecy and were still reaping rewards for the Agency and the Intelligence Community at large.

Rainey selected Dunne for several reasons. Based on the man's curriculum vitae and a follow-up conversation with Job, Rainey knew that Dunne would bring a great deal of experience to the team. On top of his Agency work, Dunne had run countless sting operations as a detective in New York and was gifted at long-term surveillance. Above all, he was a thinker. He excelled at connecting the dots and considering all angles of a case. Of added benefit, Dunne could pass for a high school guidance counselor or even a dusty bookstore clerk. The guy had features such that he could blend into nearly any locale within their mission set.

Rounding out the team was Ignacio Delgado, an Argentinian by birth who had immigrated with his family to the United States midway through his sophomore year of high school. He'd grown up in the Tri-Border Area and therefore spoke fluent Arabic to complement his native Spanish tongue. His black hair, dark eyes, and naturally tan complexion were an obvious advantage for anyone considering intelligence work in the Middle East, particularly with respect to what the Jaguar team had been assembled to do—penetrate Hezbollah. Delgado's expertise was in crunching numbers. At the young age of thirty-two, he was already a tax attorney *and* a CPA. He also owned a successful financial investment firm and a fast-growing real estate company. All that on top of the fact that he worked for the Treasury Department's Office of Terrorism and Finance. That is until today.

Technically, he would remain a Treasury employee, but for all intents and purposes, he was now a permanent fixture inside the DX. It happened all the time just like that for the indispensable movers and shakers. The DX was in the business of winning. To that end, it culled the best of the best from anywhere inside America and sometimes outside, too.

"Thanks, all. I'm sure we'll get to know each other a lot more over the course of the coming weeks and months. Chief?" Rainey fell back into his chair as Job paced to the front of the room.

The spymaster gripped both sides of the lectern, which was positioned to Rainey's immediate right. "So, now that we are all acquainted, let's get to the business at hand. Ladies and gentlemen, this is the genesis of *Jaguar*, or technically speaking, Special Operations Executive Seven Seven. I have asked Ray to head it up. He will delegate assignments and responsibilities as he sees fit. And for those who think he looks a bit young for this post believe me when I say that Ray is more than qualified to run this team. You should also know that Ray personally selected each of you based on your qualifications, experience, and intangibles. Everyone in this room brings different gifts and capabilities to the table that, Lord willing, will help us quickly and efficiently administer justice to those responsible for what happened in New York City, Chicago, and LA. This is the aim of Jaguar and together you will carry out Operation End of Days."

At the mention of this, everyone in the room seemed to pay even closer attention. Just like after 9/11, everyone in the intelligence and military communities was hopeful that they might somehow be given an active role in pursuing America's enemies. This time it was not al-Qaeda they would be hunting. It was Hezbollah, hiding behind the façade of a group calling itself *Jaysh al-Naar al-Muqadasa* as Job would soon explain.

"Our mission is simple—to identify, locate, and dispatch the person or persons responsible for the attack on the homeland. We have already done some table-setting in that regard." Job opened his briefcase, pulled out a single red file, and held it up. "To start, we will focus our efforts on this man."

30

Rainey clicked the mouse wired to the laptop in front of him, which was connected to one of the large flat-screens on the wall.

"Qais Moussa al-Nourani," said Maddie, reading the screen.

Job nodded. "Based on our intel, this is the man responsible for the attack. Up to this point, Nourani—he is also known as Ishaaq Abu Ghazi and a long list of other aliases—has been a shadow, an apparition. Not much is really known about him. Truth is we have barely an idea of what he looks like. In fact, this has led some within the Intelligence Community to conclude that he doesn't exist at all. They say he's an amalgamation of a number of former senior Hezbollah commanders, a myth. The product of legends and overactive imaginations. But I assure you, he is real. As real as the dead bodies and wanton destruction in those three cities," Job said, pointing to the wall. "Historically speaking, each time we gather what we think is a fresh piece of intel on him and put assets in place to develop the situation further, we find only one thing. That he has once again managed to disappear into the ether." Job sighed. "There is still some disagreement within the Agency over this, but some of our analysts—me included—believe he is now running Hezbollah's Unit 910. The Israelis believe the same." Unit 910, also known as the External Security Organization and Islamic Jihad Organization, was the covert and extremely dangerous organ of Hezbollah responsible for carrying out terrorist operations all around the world, particularly against Israeli and Western interests. Its members received specialized training in Iran and other clandestine locations around the world.

Conrad Pietrolaj placed both forearms on the table. "What's the intel linking Nourani to the attack? Where did it come from?"

"That information is strictly compartmented, Conrad. What I *can* tell you is that it comes from a highly credible human source backed up by technical intel. Based on our source's reporting, Nourani is back in Lebanon and is intent on making trouble around the world. Lots of it. The latest Israeli operations have only fueled his burning hatred for the Jewish State. That, we are told, was his primary motive: simple revenge." Job continued. "In addition, our source has put us on to a Frenchman, who has led us to our current position. I wish I could produce more evidence of Nourani's involvement at this stage, but as we all know absolute proof rarely exists in our business. It is up to us to develop the situation."

"Do the Saudis know about Nourani?" Jimmy Dunne said thoughtfully.

Job shook his head. "As far as I can tell, no. We're going to keep this one close to the vest. At least for now." He closed his briefcase, which lay atop the conference table. "Something has been troubling me since day one. About the meeting that had been scheduled to take place in the Saudi consulate the morning of the attack."

Rainey nodded. "The Saudis canceled at the last minute."

"Exactly my point," said Job. "But the million-dollar question is *why*."

"You think they knew about the attack?" said Dunne.

"I'm not willing to go so far as to say that they *knew*, but perhaps they suspected or otherwise had cause to believe some threat was likely. Maybe they were just exercising supreme caution. Or something else altogether prompted them to postpone the meeting. The director is to be meeting with the head of Saudi Intelligence in the next day or so to discuss the matter.

"Now, getting back to Nourani."

31

There was complete silence while Rainey manipulated the mouse and navigated to the appropriate file. Soon everyone was staring at a grainy image of a skinny, teenager with angry eyes and a dusty mop of brown hair. A pair of binoculars hung from his neck, in his hands an AK-47. The background of the photograph consisted of a mangled car frame blackened by fire, the arm of an adult male grotesquely laying in the middle of the street, and in the distance, what appeared to have once been an office building that had been shelled by bombs and mortar fire. It could have been any of a hundred war-torn cities around the world. But this was not any city. This was Beirut, circa April 1984.

"We believe the boy in this photograph to be Qais Moussa al-Nourani." said Job. "By all accounts, Nourani was a scout, a watcher, a young, motivated militant from the slums of southern Beirut at the time of this photo. Though he was a few years younger, reports indicate he was a close, personal friend of Imad Mughniyeh. We heard talk of *Abu Ghazi*, Nourani's most used nom de guerre, from a number of sources in Tehran in the late eighties and early nineties, but we could never get a good bead on him. The Iranians were impressed with his zeal for spreading the revolution and from what we've been able to gather, they sequestered him away for years of specialized training in intelligence and special operations. There are reports of varying degrees of certainty that Nourani was sent to camps in Libya and Sudan. Venezuela, too. When Nourani was in his late twenties, he married into the Mughniyeh clan to further solidify his path to power both in Tehran and the Bekaa. By all accounts, he and Mughniyeh were extremely tight.

"Our best estimates put Nourani in his mid to late fifties. Frankly, little more is known about him, including his whereabouts and that of his family. Since the day we took out Mughniyeh, we have heard zip about Nourani or any reference to Abu Ghazi save for a whisper here, a slip of the tongue on an internet chat there. Nothing substantial mind you. Just a bunch of innuendo and dead ends. Clearly, he has been careful to hide well under the radar. The recent attacks, however, seem to reveal a shift in his calculus. Or that of the Iranians."

Job inclined his head toward the back of the room, indicating to Saul Baker, who up to this point had been standing quietly in the shadows, evaluating those in the room, that the floor was his. All eyes leveled on him as he made his way to the lectern. The septuagenarian's powerful arms and confident stride intimated that he was still a force to be reckoned with.

Saul gripped the podium and stared at those seated before him for several long seconds. He did not have to mention that his tenure at the Agency had been a full and lengthy one, nor did he offer any details of his curriculum vitae as it related to Operation End of Days or the DX in general. For all in Suite 922 were well acquainted with the legend of Saul "Pappy" Baker. He'd famously matched wits with the Soviets throughout most of the Cold War, stolen their secrets, and run spies everywhere from Sudan and East Germany to the very heart of the Evil Empire. He was the chief of Moscow Station when the Soviet monolith finally came tumbling down. After that, he was tasked to head up the CIA's Near East Division and focus on the rapidly expanding threat of radical Islam. He had pushed the Agency hard to rewire itself and combat the militant fundamentalists in the only language they understood: strength and assertiveness, cunning and resolve. In sum, calculated force. One of his first orders of business had been to organize a special team of warrior spies much like that of Jaguar to hunt down and kill those responsible for the abduction, torture, and murder of his friend, CIA's Chief of Station Beirut, William F. Buckley. But for reasons he could not comprehend, he'd been told to stand down, that there were other matters to work on, other cases to run, other fish to fry. And all that while, a storm had raged within him. Justice demanded that those responsible for attacks against Americans be held to account. No holds barred. Thankfully, President-elect Kendall understood this concept.

"Intelligence we've gathered over the years", he said, "indicates that as a young teenager, Nourani participated in reconnoitering the US Marine barracks in Beirut prior to the bombing in '83. We know that he was there in the dungeons of Baalbek when Hezbollah operatives tortured and killed Bill Buckley. He's believed to have been involved in the planning of several aircraft hijackings in the late eighties. Since then, Nourani has reportedly been party to countless terrorist operations around the world. He's very bad news, people. And it's now your job to stop him before more innocent lives are lost."

"Why this Army of Holy Fire nonsense," said Brigid Finn.

"To obfuscate. To hide. It seems Nourani prefers to fight from the shadows. Even after all these years, he still does not want to take responsibility for his actions," said Saul. "Nor does Iran wish to have its fingerprints anywhere near an attack on American soil. Tehran knows that if that were to ever happen, especially now that Kendall's in office, we would rain down fire and brimstone on them till there was nothing left but a smoldering pile of ash. We shall assume Iran is aware of Nourani's pursuits—Hezbollah rarely undertakes large-scale operations without Iran's backing or at least knowledge—but right now we have no evidence to prove that.

"We need to get to Nourani and put him down permanently or I'm afraid the recent attack on our soil will only be the prelude to a new widespread global campaign of terror."

Pietrolaj looked up. Until now he'd been furiously scribbling notes in the margins of his briefing packet. "It occurs to me that the best way to get to someone is not to pursue them, but to have them unwittingly come to you on their own accord."

Job smiled, stepped back to the podium. "My thought exactly, Conrad." He spoke of the operation in Paris, the conversation with the French diplomat, and the meeting that was to take place in Brussels in seven days' time.

"What are our rules of engagement?" asked Alcott.

Rainey, like most in the room, already knew the answer to that question, but it was important for the team to hear it spelled out in no uncertain terms.

Job's face turned cold, his forehead angled slightly downward. "Your only rule is to do whatever it takes to successfully accomplish the mission. In short, *win*. As efficiently and as quietly as possible. And to not get caught in the process. Rest assured, we shall not abandon our American principles in the pursuit of our goals, but we will not hamstring ourselves with unnecessary restrictions either. Clearly, we are fighting an enemy who has no regard for the sanctity of human life. An enemy who uses women and children as shields. An enemy who trains eight-year-old kids to deliver bombs to crowded streets where they blow themselves to bits. I ask you, how do you defeat an enemy such as this?" Job continued before anyone could respond. "You do not wait to be fired upon. When a legitimate threat is identified, you eliminate it. Period. You do not mount up standing armies against non-state actors. You carry out operations to seed disarray and chaos among their ranks. You send ghosts to kill them in their sleep. This will be our mission. This will be our creed.

"With respect to Operation End of Days, we are first going to inject a piece of information into Hezbollah's intelligence stream, one that they will be unable to resist. But this is something that must be done delicately. And I know just how we are going to do it."

Rainey glanced up from his notepad when Job fell silent. He now found the spymaster's and everyone else's eyes on him.

"Ray has an interesting idea, an idea that I believe has a lot of potential. As Job explained the details, Rainey reminded himself of the promise he'd made to the wife of Ryan Killian, the man who fearlessly sacrificed his life so that he could keep his.

"Through the FBI and the US Attorney's Office, we have floated this proposal to Stedman Carter, framing it as an important matter with national security implications. For his full and willing participation, he would receive special consideration at sentencing." Job mentioned nothing of a presidential pardon or a complete commutation of his pending prison sentence, though both had been suggested by the man's attorneys.

"Have you heard back yet?" said Rainey.

"I should have an answer within the hour. Until then, please feel free to scope out your new workspace. If you need something, please let me or Janna know and we'll make it happen. Thank you, everyone."

32

Exactly an hour and fifty-eight minutes had passed before CIA Director Thompson called to inform Job that Stedman Carter had agreed in full to the proposition he had put forth. Certainly, it had been longer than they had expected, nevertheless, the DX had their secret covenant, part of which included an ironclad non-disclosure agreement that would result in harsh legal ramifications should Carter, or any third parties on his behalf, choose to betray it, whether whole or in part.

In that time, Rainey and his fellow Jaguar teammates had split into groups each with specific assignments relative to their areas of expertise. Brigid and Maddie were responsible for Rainey's legend, which included everything from a rather impressive portfolio of business dealings—some above board but most well below it—to the illusion of a young man's social media footprint long abandoned. For men such as Jean-Michel Durand no longer wasted their time with such idle pursuits. Though the businesses the pair created were mere DX fronts, they had to hold up under the careful scrutiny of Hezbollah's senior leadership, Iranian intelligence, and anyone else who might go nosing into his background. All for the sake of rendering Reagan Rainey's role of international arms dealer as perfectly genuine.

Delgado and Dunne were tasked with assisting Brigid and Maddie by playing the part of a hostile intelligence service intent on penetrating his cover. What the four of them came away with was a legend that might as well have been fortified with a six-foot-thick bunker of concrete and carbon steel.

Meanwhile, the man Rainey had dubbed Macho sequestered himself away in one of the quiet offices that looked out over the Potomac. His task was to complete the draft document that would soon set Operation End of Days into motion.

Still seated at the main conference table, Evelina, Tonka, Mouse, and Alcott coordinated the security, surveillance, and countersurveillance situation for the impending meeting in Brussels, while factoring in any and all contingencies. Vehicles and equipment needed, exfil routes, fallback positions, the courses of action should there be some kind of accidental interference by the local police force or Belgian or EU security service, medical emergencies. The list went on.

The remaining team members assisted in various other capacities as needed.

"You still feel good about this?" said Job approaching him. He did not have to vocalize the fact that Stedman Carter had been one of the men responsible for Rainey's father's internment in Russia for the past twenty years, nor the fact that during that time, Rainey and his family—himself included, had believed him to be dead.

"If it were up to me, I wouldn't mind putting a bullet in his brain. But he has value to us. I think we should exploit that in light of the attack on our soil."

"Yes, but I want to know. How are you going to feel about the two of you sitting in the same room for days at a time?"

Standing with arms folded across his chest, Rainey's eyes were trained on his busy teammates. He said not a word for several long seconds. Then, slowly, he turned his head and locked his brown eyes on Job's earnest visage. "Let me ask you something. Do you think it matters one iota to Ryan Killian's wife and his two boys what I feel for Stedman Carter?" The question was rhetorical and one he knew Job would fully understand as such, though it had come out with an edge that bordered on threatening for which he did not apologize. His eyes, burning with quiet rage, returned to those within his charge. "My feelings are irrelevant, Job. Nourani needs to die. I'm on board for whatever it takes to make that happen."

The spymaster responded by placing a hand on Rainey's shoulder. In more ways than one, Rainey was the son he'd never had. Perhaps for this reason, he did not take umbrage to Rainey's sharp tone. For he, too, suffered the same exaggerated sensibility—that justice should prevail at all costs.

The work was arduous, yet six hours later, when the team reconvened in the main conference room, the countless rounds of point and counterpoint, reasoned debates, and the few impassioned arguments behind them, everyone was of one mind. Several notebook computers stood open on the table, papers and legal pads filled with scrawled notes were strewn about. Empty coffee cups dotted their workspace. Smoothing out the rough edges of their ambitious plan had taken some doing, but the bulk of it was over.

Job gave a few encouraging remarks—they had accomplished a great deal in a day's time—then dismissed them for the night. One by one they collected their personal effects and filed out of Suite 922. Maddie, Evelina, and Brigid were headed off to a late dinner and an even later movie to unwind while Mouse, Tonka, and Alcott hurried home to their families. The others, Rainey assumed, had similar plans, though they had not voiced them within earshot. Job gave him a knowing look and likewise departed for his townhouse in Georgetown.

Rainey soon found himself driving northward across Key Bridge with his window down, the cold air causing his short-cropped hair to swish and sway. The engine of his '89 Ford Bronco hummed in the background far removed from his consciousness. Earlier, he'd had to cancel dinner with Kayla. Work, he had said. It was always work. Thankfully, she'd agreed to meet him for coffee instead.

The fresh night air might have helped to recharge his yearning soul if not for the heavy burden of guilt clinging to his back like a gorilla. Soon, regret stampeded into his thoughts followed closely by its first cousin: melancholy. Perhaps seeing Kayla's smile would change all that.

He had suggested a coffee shop along Wisconsin Avenue NW. He'd heard Maddie and Wes raving about it at the Christmas party last night.

Arriving, he found the block crowded with nighttime revelers. He waited for a string of rowdy pedestrians to pass before nosing the Bronco into the lot at the back of the CVS store across the street. He waded through traffic, taking mental notes of the nearby faces on the sidewalk, in storefronts, and vehicles parked along the curb. Operational habits were hard to turn off even when on a date on your home turf. But everyone in his line of work knew that complacency could get you killed.

Inside, he surveyed the people standing behind and in front of the counter—it ran lengthwise away from him. The large seating area to the right was nearly full. The entrance to a small corridor peeked out from the back wall. A sign posted on the exposed brick nearby pointed to the restrooms and an exit. A soothing melody of violin and harpsichord flowed from the speakers in the ceiling. The song was familiar, yet the name eluded him. Bach though, if he wasn't mistaken. He decided the place had a singularly European feel and he liked it.

Kayla was waiting for him at a scarred, wooden table with a decorative bookcase that was sparsely stocked with thick tomes towering over her right shoulder. Her eyes widened at the sight of him and he responded without inhibition.

"We said nine-thirty, right?" Rainey checked the Casio Mudmaster on his wrist. It was only a quarter past the hour. "I thought *I'd* be the early one."

She grinned. "No, no. You're right. We did say nine-thirty. Call me eager."

"Eager to see *me*?" He made a goofy grin, bent down, and kissed her, before sliding into the chair across from her.

"You shaved your beard." She ran her fingers over his jawline. "Wow, your face is so smooth. I like it."

Rainey shrugged his shoulders. He did not want to encourage her. Without his beard, he felt naked. "Don't get used to it," he smiled.

The waitress came and took their order. It was café au lait for Kayla, while Rainey opted for his usual: a strong house brew, black, no sugar. When the woman was gone, Kayla said, "Nice place."

"Yeah. It's got a good vibe."

She smiled but not in her usual, toothy way. He detected restraint in her eyes. Something was bothering her. Not surprising though considering what had happened in New York.

"I'm sorry about dinner." All at once he realized that he was always apologizing to her for one thing or another. Her silence didn't help.

It took him by surprise when she reached across the small square table and grasped his right hand with both of hers. He studied her face, her eyes. Subtle lines in her forehead played hide and seek as she kneaded his muscled palm, laced her fingers in his. She stared at his hand for several long seconds, tracing lines along the corded sinews that disappeared beneath the cuff of his tan Ariat jacket. She pulled his hand against her cheek, curled her shoulder around it as her eyes fell shut. For an instant, he was back at Duke, the two of them, soccer stars both, out for a quiet date after a week full of grueling training sessions, hard-fought games, and to top it off, intense academic study.

He leaned closer, breathed in her fragrance. My, how beautiful she was. He was about to tell her so, but her mouth cracked as if to speak, so he simply smiled and waited expectantly. Instead, she said nothing, only pressed his hand more firmly against her face before slowly bringing it to her lips. It was then that the muscles around her eyes contracted as if she were suppressing a painful memory. Or...facing a difficult task. A tear rolled swiftly, surprisingly, down her cheek and dripped onto the back of his hand.

There was no need for words in this moment for he knew precisely what the evening had in store. As was often the case in times of intense emotional upheaval, Rainey's face fell flat, his affect turning stoic.

When she opened her eyes, they were watery and tinged with red. He gently took her hands in his and offered a slight, knowing grin that intimated deep understanding.

Her chin quivered. "I didn't mean for this to happen, Reagan. I didn't mean for us to start up again just for things to end up like this." She looked at the empty table between them, a divide for which it seemed with each passing second no bridge could conquer.

The lump in his throat was enormous. He forced it down with conscious thought and was about to speak when the waitress appeared with, unbeknownst to her, a poorly timed joviality. Rainey offered a meek thank you as she set down the cups in their saucers and turned back toward whence she came.

Their hands separated—strands of hope being ripped apart. Kayla continued, her body shrinking back in her chair. "I thought I could do this. I told myself I could. But... Honestly, I assumed things would be different. I wanted them to be more than anything. No one knows me like you do, Reagan. I told myself that we were perfect for each other. I've never loved anyone so strongly."

Rainey sat ramrod straight, his hands now flat and equidistant from his untouched mug, eyes fixated on the tendrils of steam rising off the surface of the hot liquid. He would offer no defense, no counter maneuvers; he would absorb whatever blows were dealt him, come what may.

"But after New York... It was just like when we were back in school. Remember? After your roommate's brother was killed overseas and you dropped out of school to join the Army. You disappeared for months, which then turned into years." She managed to subdue a sob. "I just can't live that life, Reagan, wondering what you're doing, wondering if you will ever come home. Maybe New York was a blessing in a sense. For us, I mean. Certainly, I'm not saying it was good that terrorists attacked our country, but... You know what I mean, don't you? Of course you do. You know everything." She said it in a way that bore no malice, no harsh accusation. It was simply an acknowledgment of a known fact, a simple declaration, nothing more.

Rainey remained still, his face emotionless. The thoughtful blinking of his eyes, his only response. Little did she know that he—battle-weary and broken-hearted—was in the throes of emotional retreat. It was his internal defense mechanism, one with which a thirty-one-year-old should not be so well-acquainted. *Don't show fear. Don't show weakness. No one or no thing can break you.* A warrior's mindset. A warrior's creed.

"It created a moment of clarity for us. Well, for me anyway. In the time since then, I've thought long and hard about you and me. About us. I—"

"You deserve better," he finally proclaimed with quiet resolve. "You deserve a normal life. You deserve someone who can give that to you."

Her azure eyes blinked tears, her head listed to the side, a small glimmer of appreciation that he recognized her plight. "I'm sorry, Reagan. Really, I am."

Now should have been the time for a reciprocal apology, but he said not a word. Instead, he continued to sit quietly, feeling a blitz of heavy loss, betrayal even. The vision of his future under full, frontal assault. And still, he said nothing. Deep down, he knew this was right. For Kayla to be truly happy, he must let her go, let her live the life she deserved. With desperation, he fought every instinct within him to reach out, to pull her into his arms, and never let her go.

Because of this battle raging inside him, he did not notice her stand and tighten the belt of her woolen coat. Next, she was beside him, placing her hand again on his beard-shorn face. She leaned down, tilted his chin toward her, and kissed him on the mouth, not a peck but a long kiss of finality. "Goodbye, Reagan." It might have been a rifle round through the heart.

With his eyes, he followed the sway of her hips, watched her cut through the tables and smiling patrons and disappear through the door that issued out into the street.

After a few minutes of blood-deprived numbness, he collected himself, placed a twenty-dollar note next to his still-steaming mug, and rose from the table. He took one last look at the place where Kayla had been sitting only moments ago.

Then trudged back into the night.

Alone.

33

R ainey rose to the bleating of the alarm clock, a more agonizing sound he knew not. For nearly half a minute, he sat there, perched on the edge of his bed, blankets and sheet thrown back in a heap. The plain white T-shirt he wore was pulled taut against his shoulders and arms. The Duke Soccer shorts remained twisted on his hips as he processed his surroundings. For the most fleeting of seconds, he could not for the life of him remember where he was. The night had been interminable, his dreams a kaleidoscope of augmented reality. Memories turned farcical renderings that defied the laws of physics and all semblance of reason.

As the fog of sleep cleared, he hoped and prayed that what had happened last night with Kayla was also just a horrible dream. But alas, it was all too real.

He forged into the bathroom, relieved himself then plodded downstairs and readied the coffeemaker. As he waited for it to brew, he peeled back the curtain on the windowed back door and stared across the landscape of grass and forest now blanketed with snow. Running his hands through his hair, he considered how many friends he had lost to bullets and bombs and other horrors of war, including a few tragic cases of suicide. Losing Kayla—again—was no less severe. He felt empty inside, like his heart had been carved from his chest with a rusty hunting knife.

Rainey sat down at the kitchen table. Saul had left an hour earlier according to the Post-it Note on the coffee machine. They had originally planned to drive over to the meeting location together. Apparently, Pappy was eager to get started.

After a moment more, Rainey absently turned his head to the left. He reached out and plucked a book from a shelf that also held a stack of notepads and a mug filled with an assortment of pens and markers. The leather cover of Saul's Bible was smooth and worn, its pages tinged with the hallmarks of frequent use. He opened it, paying no mind to any particular passage or verse. When he did, it fell open to a bookmarked page. His eyes caught on a verse that had been highlighted in yellow and circled several times over with blue ink. Psalm 46:10. *"Be still and know that I am God..."* This verse conjured up a memory of another. He flipped several pages more and found that it, too, had been highlighted. Psalm 57:7. *"My heart is steadfast, O God, my heart is steadfast; I will sing and give praise."*

Living faithfully to God's Word wasn't always easy; it took conscious effort. Part of him was angry that God had allowed Kayla to come back into his life only to be taken from him again. But if he was going to trust God in the good times, he certainly needed to trust Him in the rough times as well. Instead of remaining bitter and contrary, Rainey willed himself to look at the positives. God must have someone far better in store than Kayla Chapman. *"He is* for *me, not against me,"* he reminded himself. There was hope after all.

Rainey poured coffee into a mug and shuffled, barefoot, into his study. The leather chair into which he slowly sank was cool against the backs of his legs. He sat there for several minutes just thinking while he continued to sip the hot liquid. Soon the sound of a propeller plane flying somewhere overhead seeped into the room. It purred a monotonic melody until finally silence returned to him and he was once again alone with his thoughts.

Today was a big day. For him personally and for Operation End of Days.

After a breakfast of eggs and toast, Rainey showered and dressed quickly. It was only a twelve-minute drive from his farm to the place where he would meet Stedman Carter. As the Bronco's engine roared to life and exhaust clouded his rear windshield, Rainey stared through the open door of the detached garage into the storybook landscape aglow in the brilliant morning sun. He clicked on the CD player in the dash and skipped the disc to song number five, "Forgiven" by Relient K.

Coffee for the soul.

He pushed on his black wraparound shades, dropped the shifter into DRIVE, and set off, his left knee bouncing in synch with the energetic tune.

our arrangement the deal is off, and he can rot in a supermax for the rest of his days. I suspect though that he's ready to get to work."

Rainey nodded solemnly then turned toward the door.

35

Rainey entered the interrogation room, pushing a leather-backed chair on wheels. He positioned it across the table from Stedman Carter and sat down. For several seconds he said not a word, just stared straight into the face of the older man with his intense brown eyes, eyes that conveyed a familiarity with untold violence. Though his goal was Carter's unmitigated cooperation, Rainey wanted to make it clear he was not a man to be trifled with.

"I understand you now wish to make a positive contribution to society," said Rainey dryly.

Carter, a man whose net worth surpassed $27 billion, was clearly unaccustomed to being the person in the room with the least amount of power. The fact that he was in such an untenable position was born out by the meek nod he offered in response.

"Do you know who I am?" said Rainey.

"Yes."

"Then you know what it is that I do for a living?"

"I suspect."

Rainey stared at him with the eyes of a highly trained killer, as if to say: "*Don't you ever forget it.*" He could feel his heart rate tick up a notch but outwardly showed no signs of it.

"Would you like some coffee?"

"Yes, that would be nice."

An Agency support officer soon delivered two paper cups along with a third cup filled with creamers, sugar packets, and stirrers.

Rainey watched Carter empty a creamer into his cup and stir in two packets of sugar.

"Thank you," said the older man in deference.

Rainey's head dipped forward—a slight nod. "How much did they tell you?"

Carter blew across the hot liquid. "That I would be doing some consulting work of a technical nature."

"And?"

"That it had something to do with the national security of the United States."

"That's it?"

"Mmm hmm."

"I'm not here to play games, so I'll get right to it." Rainey considered his next words carefully. "I need you to teach someone how to be an arms dealer."

Carter's forehead revealed deep curiosity. "Who?"

"Me," said Rainey stone-faced.

Carter did not ask why. The intelligent man he was knew better. "How long do you have to complete your course of study?"

"Three days."

"*Three days.* That's *it*?" said Carter.

"That's it."

After the exasperation had drained from his face, he said, "Then we had better get started. Where do you want to begin?"

"How about at the beginning?"

In the next few minutes, Rainey had the shackles removed and authorized Carter to move about the room. The billionaire was afforded a whiteboard that was rolled into the room on wheels and two dry-erase markers to go with it, nothing more.

And so it went. For three straight days, Rainey sat under the careful tutelage of one of the world's most successful and ruthless arms dealers. The sessions were long and arduous. The information overwhelming. At the end of each day, Carter was ushered out of the secure interrogation chamber and into an adjacent bunk room—a cell, really, until five o'clock the next morning. He was given thirty minutes to shower and shave and then was led back to his bunk room where he was served a breakfast of eggs and toast, orange juice and hot coffee. At precisely 6:00 a.m., the sessions started anew and lasted easily until 11:00 at night. They stopped only for bathroom breaks and meals.

It came as quite a surprise that Carter was a gifted teacher. For in their brief time together, Rainey learned how to walk the walk and talk the talk. He learned how to dress, how to work a room, how to artfully negotiate the terms of a deal. There were discussions on topics ranging from trans-shipping strategies, illicit cargo routes, money laundering, and procurement techniques of some of the world's most dangerous despots, terrorist groups, and rogue regimes. For a good portion of the second half of the second day, prompted by several of Rainey's seemingly innocent questions, Carter focused on items of particular interest to Iran and Hezbollah and how their procurement agents might endeavor to do their due diligence prior to any deal being made. Rainey paid particular attention here. For it was no co-incidence that Hezbollah had been one of Stedman Carter's many clients. Now that Carter was on ice, Israel had decimated Hezbollah's weapons stores, and the smuggling routes in Syria had been erased by virtue of the rebels taking over the country, the terrorist organization would be desperate for new sources and channels to quickly and efficiently resupply their arms capability. To Rainey's mind, the black market for such materiel was a perfect place to start.

There were few topics on which Carter could not speak fluently and fewer still in which he did not have some vested interest throughout the years of his international operations. He touched on the politics of Europe and the former Soviet republics, the diamond trade in Africa, how he set up shell corporations and Red Cross accounts by which to conceal the profits of his criminal enterprise. He also delved into specific hardware. Rockets, rifles and optics, body armor and night-vision goggles. Computer chips and laser designators. Drones and crates of spare parts. And of course, ammunition, millions and millions of rounds of ammunition—7.62, 5.56, .50 cal., 9mm, and some of the less-common types that his customers sometimes demanded.

Lastly, after coming to terms with the realization that there was nothing worth withholding, Carter touched on his own network. It was not hyperbole to say that he had contacts everywhere—politicians, warlords, dirty cops, intelligence officers, and security agents who were all on the take. He had countless customs and immigration assets, too. He freely shared their names with Rainey with little thought given to the consequences. Some might even be useful down the line. Stedman Carter also knew his competition. This was a point of emphasis that he made sure to drive home. Any good businessman knows his competition after all. He also knows, even anticipates, the needs of his customers. Knowledge was leverage. And leverage was power.

All the while, Rainey kept his eyes and ears open, speaking only when he had a question or needed a specific point clarified. In the little time they had together, he tried to soak up as much knowledge as he could. Even for a man with a memory like him, it was an extremely tall order. Nearing the conclusion of the third day, his mind adrift in an ocean tide of new information and concepts, Rainey left the interrogation room to fetch some pastries and coffee. When he returned, he found Stedman Carter hunched over the table, his head in his hands.

Rainey placed the coffee and doughnuts down. "You all right?"

The older man sat back and lifted his head. His eyes were red with exhaustion. The muscles in his sixty-two-year-old face showed it, too. "For what it's worth, I'm sorry. Sorry for what I did to your father. Sorry for the pain I've surely brought upon your entire family. I... I don't expect you to ever forgive me, but I just want you to know that I *am* truly sorry." Carter looked down at his fingers; they were fidgeting in his lap. When his head drew back up, he said, "I have a great deal of respect for you in that even after all I've done to you and your family, you are still able to face me without condemnation."

Rainey was quiet as he carefully considered what to say next. Slowly, he reached his hand over the table. Though he knew it was incongruent with his faith and would later feel a burden of guilt because of it, he still couldn't quite find it in himself to utter the words *I forgive you*. At least not yet. "I don't know what the future holds for either one of us, Stedman, but I want to thank you for your cooperation. I'm not at liberty to say just how it will be put to use, but I'm grateful nonetheless."

Carter reciprocated, taking Rainey's hand as a symbolic offering of peace and forgiveness. "It's I who am grateful. Thank you for your kindness."

After Carter and the team of protective agents had pulled away from the house, Rainey and Saul climbed into the Bronco and headed home. Somewhere along the way, Rainey realized Saul was talking.

"That was good of you, Ray. He will remember the manner in which you spoke to him."

"I'm just glad it's over." Rainey stared at the road ahead of them. "So, what happens to Carter now?"

"He'll be shipped back to the jail with nothing showing in his records to indicate that he was ever gone. And he will wait. It was part of the deal. At some point when this is all over, Job and some others will make a determination regarding his cooperation and whether it was useful in the operation. If it was, then he will be given consideration at sentencing. If not, the deal will be void and he can rot in prison for the rest of his days."

Rainey nodded, his thoughts now shifting to his teammates in Paris as well as a certain French diplomat.

36

Alban Clement strolled out of the meeting room in the Quay d'Orsay, briefcase in hand. He looked at his watch and frowned. The meeting had taken longer than he had expected. Nearly seven hours of policy review. Death by PowerPoint. Some of his colleagues could talk for hours without really saying much of anything, the types of folks who sat behind desks tweaking Word documents all day long. He wondered if any of them had worked in the field a day in their lives to see if their precious policies actually made sense.

As boring and mundane as it had been, Clement knew it wasn't the meeting that had him feeling irritated. In less than six hours, he was due to meet the female intelligence officer who had been inside his apartment. He was now officially spying for three foreign governments. Well, Hezbollah wasn't exactly a government, but for all intents and purposes, it was. They essentially controlled Lebanon. What's more, whatever he passed on to Hezbollah was surely being shared with Tehran and maybe even Moscow, Pyongyang, and others, too. Years of spying on his homeland was starting to take its toll. He didn't know how much longer he could bear the weight of it all. Sooner or later, he knew he would be held to account for his traitorous activities. And that meant his family would also pay a heavy price. He was trapped with no foreseeable way out of his predicament that would not cause himself and his family pain or worse. He then remembered what the intense American man behind the camera had said about solving both of their problems. Could it be? More importantly, could he trust him?

Clement walked to his car, slipped inside, and switched on the engine. He turned the windshield defroster on full blast and fired up a cigarette as he waited for the fogged glass to clear. With his wife getting her hair done at a popular Paris salon and then going out to catch up with some of her girlfriends, he had plenty of time alone before he was to meet the attractive American spy. Part of him wanted to stop off at a local pub and drink himself to oblivion, but he wisely chose to go home, hoping to steady his nerves there.

It was just after 7:00 p.m. when he set foot on the sidewalk in front of his building. He turned the collar of his coat up and adjusted the fleece scarf at his neck. Why did tonight have to be one of the coldest nights of the year? He was only halfway down the block and already he was shivering.

Why did it have to be so cold tonight? thought Maddie as she stamped her feet on the cement sidewalk, trying to coax feeling back into her toes. She and her Jaguar colleagues were positioned along the route that Clement would take from his building to the Indian restaurant on the narrow rue de la Félicité. Their objective was to provide a blanket of countersurveillance in case one of the organizations for which the Frenchman was spying was actively monitoring his movements. Waiting just outside the entrance to the restaurant in the crook of a wall that jutted back from the street, Maddie listened to the radio traffic coming across her earpiece.

"MAPLE is on the move, turning east on Jouffroy d'Abbans." MAPLE, the Agency codename for Clement.

Maddie pictured Evelina peeking through the curtains of her room on the second floor of the Hotel Pavillon Monceau, calling out the play-by-play.

"All good so far. He's crossing the street, continuing eastbound on the north sidewalk. Passing your pos now, Victor Three." One of Rainey's rules for Jaguar, particularly with respect to their radio traffic, was that they would all be victors. Victor One, Victor Two, and so on.

It was at this time, the big man they called Tonka, who by all accounts could have been Middle Eastern or Latino, or, yes even Russian, emerged from a small store that peddled Belgian chocolates. He popped a delicate morsel the size of a golf ball into his mouth and chewed for a few precious seconds, as if lost in the sumptuous delight of the sweet delicacy, then set off in the wake of the diplomat spy.

Maddie commanded herself to be patient, her thin, black, leather gloves doing nothing to keep the raw cold from her hands.

This time the voice in her ear was male. "Left on de Tocqueville."

With the nonchalance of a professional watcher, Maddie peeked across the narrow thoroughfare and saw Ignacio Delgado, gelled black hair, leather jacket, and designer blue jeans—the visage of a lady's man if ever there was one—emerge through the glass door of the Hotel Glasgow and turn away from her. He was now headed directly for Clement and the man pursuing him.

Seconds after Delgado had disappeared around the corner onto de Tocqueville, around came Clement with Tonka in tow twenty yards behind. She heard the big man say, "These are absolutely delicious," the phrase that meant Clement was clean and was entering the Indian restaurant. Even after seeing Tonka walk into the Hotel Glasgow directly across from the location of the planned meet, Maddie waited. For it would be Delgado who would have the final say on whether or not Clement had been safely delivered to her.

One minute passed, then two.

Finally, the man from Argentina, huddled over the chalkboard menu outside Le Rouergue, gave the all-clear.

Maddie entered the restaurant, pulled off her gloves, and blew into her cupped hands as she searched the room for Clement with her eyes. He was seated, as instructed, near the back. Maddie smiled to the proprietor on her way to the diplomat's table. She took a seat with her back to the wall and issued a fond greeting in her assumed French tongue.

They ordered light fare and cups of strong Indian coffee. When the waiter was gone, Maddie withdrew a manila envelope from the inside of her coat, placed it on the table. Clement immediately secreted it inside his own with a swiftness that suggested he had done this a time or two.

"What's in it?" said the Frenchman.

"Chicken feed mostly. To Ghulam it will appear no different than the usual material you bring him," Maddie lowered her head, "just so long as you've been honest with us."

"I have. Believe me."

"You will also find a thumb drive; it's the exact make and model you have used in the past. On it are files, the topicality of which are in keeping with your previous offerings to Ghulam. There is one file among them that should be of particular interest to him. It's a copy of a highly classified white paper about illicit arms trafficking in the EU. In it, is a list of policy recommendations on how to tie up the loopholes in the laws meant to curtail such behavior and some commentary on other difficulties in bringing the problem into the light of day. There is one subtle but very specific mention of a man about whom EU investigators are growing increasingly concerned. And bits of intelligence that suggest this man is looking to expand his operations. It's a shiny thing, if you will. We are confident that Ghulam will go for it. And it's your job to make sure he does." This was the material that Conrad Pietrolaj had expertly authored.

"What's its provenance?" asked Clement. "Where did it come from? If he asks, I mean."

"As far as you are concerned, it was authored by a panel of subject matter experts that the EU security services consult with from time to time. The panelists' names are unimportant mostly because they are nowhere on any of the documents they pen. Their assessments are uniformly ascribed to the ubiquitous terms *our analysts* and/or *the panel*."

"One more question. What's the name of the arms dealer?"

Maddie looked him dead in the eyes as she uttered the name.

37

Before concluding the meeting, Maddie went over everything again, making sure that the diplomat understood his role in full. She then gave him a number to call if he should need to reach them in the event of an emergency. Calling it, Maddie stressed, would in effect sound the alarm. It was his safety net of sorts. But, she warned, if he were found to have utilized it needlessly, his future might mirror that of the boy who cried wolf.

Otherwise, Maddie explained, he was to carry on as usual. As if he had never been accosted on a Paris street, subjected to the indignity of wearing an odious hood, bundled into the trunk of a car, or suffered the menacing glare from the American with the intense brown eyes.

If for some reason they needed to reach him they would call his mobile from a number based in Belgium and would ask for a fictitious girl named Emma. There were other instructions, too, contingencies outlining prospective meeting locations and times and even a bolt-hole in the event of catastrophe. All the while Maddie spoke, her voice calm and clear and distinctly Parisian in accent, she watched his eyes. They were attentive and intelligent but contained a current of guilt that seemed to undulate beneath the surface. For this was a man who had chosen poorly in life, chosen to betray his wife, his country, and even himself. And for his sins, he was now being used once again. This time not to steal secrets but to ensnare a dangerous predator, a mastermind of terror and hate. Maddie appreciated, pitied, and reviled him all at once.

"Understand?"

"I believe so, yes," said Clement.

"Very well."

Clement leaned into the table. "But tell me. What I am doing... This will help me, yes?"

As one might expect, Maddie's reply was supportive yet non-committal and flavored with a spice of motherly admonishment. "That's entirely up to you, Alban, and how you perform. You can either make things worse for yourself or make things better. I know what I would do if I were you."

38

T he three of them sat in Rainey's study—a retired spymaster, the current head of CIA's Directorate X, and a newly christened international arms dealer by the name of Jean-Michel Durand.

It was Saul who initiated the first round of questioning while Job lounged idly in front of a bookcase, swishing the remnants of his tea around the bottom of a mug he had requisitioned from the kitchen.

"Where were you born?"

Rainey canted his head, a not-so-subtle signal to his interrogators that could only be interpreted as annoyance. For a man such as Jean-Michel Durand did not often discuss his past, to do so was to betray his cardinal policy of confidentiality. Nevertheless, as the exercise necessitated, he replied, though when he did so it was entirely in French. "France. Marseille, to be precise."

"We have friends in Marseille. In which part of the city did you live?"

"In the Third Arrondissement, a community called La Belle-de-Mai."

"I know this place well," pressed Saul in Arabic. "What street?"

"The rue Séry. We lived in an apartment on the first floor at Number Fourteen."

"Parents? French, I assume."

Rainey nodded then allowed his face to grow introspective, grim even. He had now slipped into the role completely. He was not simply reciting memorized facts and details but instead living his legend before them. If they were impressed with his performance, they failed to show it.

"My father was an engineer, good with numbers and fixing things with his hands, but without a keen sense of marketability. He toiled with his books and inventions the way old-timers do when they have already earned their pensions. He made a modest living, just enough to support my mother and me.

"Tell me about her."

"My mother? She was an artist, her specialty being gouache paintings. She also fancied herself something of a poet— '*a free spirit on a stiff breeze,*' my dad used to say—though she never managed to have anything published."

"She wasn't very good?" intoned Saul, the inquisitor.

Rainey's eyes narrowed with annoyance. "She was *controversial*. Not with her paintings or writings, but with her activism. She bucked the status quo, you might say."

"How so?"

"Always stirring up trouble with the government. She was arrested during an anti-capitalist protest in Paris in the mid-nineties and then again three months later for being in league with a group who was threatening violence upon a French government official. Spent nearly eight months in jail. Not long after her release she ran off with some fellow socialist she'd met in prison."

"Fell in love with another man, did she?"

Rainey shook his head in mock embarrassment.

"I see," said Saul.

"Dad was never the same after that. He turned to the bottle but still managed to keep us afloat financially. The two of us emigrated to Quebec when I was still just a boy."

"He wanted a fresh start?"

"His company had a job opening there. It was a chance for promotion. Dad said he could make more money, but yes, I think he just wanted to leave France behind us and start anew. We lived there a little more than a month before he was suddenly fired. He never told me the whole story. I just know that it had been due to some kind of injustice." A very real tear seeped from the corner of his left eye—drawn from the well of heartache a boy feels when he learns that his father has been taken from him. "I found him the next day when I arrived home from school. He'd hung himself." After managing to stifle any further emotional display, Rainey carried on. "As a result, I learned to look after myself. I was briefly placed in the custody of an orphanage."

"Briefly?"

It was here that Rainey evoked a glimmer of self-satisfaction. "I escaped within the week. It seems I had a knack for conducting illicit operations even as a boy. I managed on my own, rather well considering. Dabbled in narcotics for a time, selling, that is. I was good at it perhaps because of my penchant for violence. I was a solid street fighter. I had to be. During my exploits, I met a man who taught me valuable skills. In smuggling and in business more generally.

"What was his name?"

"It doesn't matter. He's dead now. As in business, I've found that it's best to eliminate one's competition."

Saul's face blanched. Perhaps it was from the cold-blooded manner with which the words tumbled from his lips.

"You killed him?"

Monsieur Durand answered with icy silence.

And so, the interrogation continued. Rainey explained how after hopping a cargo ship bound for ports unknown, he—as young Jean-Michel—had found himself in South Africa. From there, he begged, borrowed, and stole to get back to Europe. He told them how he'd visited the home of his childhood in France, why he knew not. It was just something he'd felt compelled to do. In Turkey, after earning the respect of some local street toughs, he fell in with a prominent crime syndicate and was taught how to kill like a professional and to be a ghost. This, in turn, led to an encounter with a Bulgarian oligarch, from whom he learned the profitable trade of arms trafficking. After that, Monsieur Durand traveled the world, residing for brief periods in Romania, Spain, and Algeria, under assumed names of course, while furthering his copious business pursuits. Today, he owned lavish estates on several continents, a multi-million-dollar townhouse on New York City's Upper East Side, a luxury beach house in Saint-Tropez and another in the Caymans.

"But I will always consider my home to be in the south of France. I can still smell the sea, see it sparkling in the afternoon sunshine."

"Where did you live in Algeria?"

Rainey recounted it as though it were a foregone memory tucked well into the past. "Oran. Along the Boulevard du 19 Mars." Saul's creased forehead prompted him to be more precise. "Near the Fantazia Hotel. I will tell you... Living there *did* allow me to polish my Arabic." Rainey seemed not to notice that he'd uttered these last words in the noted tongue.

"Yes. I can see that. You speak it quite well."

"I suppose some of my childhood friends in la Belle-de-Mai had something to do with my appreciation for the language. Several were immigrants from the Maghreb as well as the Mideast." He smiled as if privy to some minor conspiracy.

Acting as a senior Hezbollah official mulling over a contract, Saul questioned him now in Arabic about what he could offer the organization. The discussion lasted nearly two hours during which time Rainey did not make the slightest misstep even upon Saul's feigned provocations.

"And where does Monsieur Durand reside now, if I may ask—your primary residence, that is?"

"I'm afraid that is confidential, *mon ami*. Information like that can get someone in my business killed. Some things—things critical to my very livelihood—I will never divulge under any circumstances. The location of my home, the names of my clients. You understand. For me, discretion and secrecy are inviolable. And I take considerable precautions to keep them as such."

"How do I reach you then?"

Rainey mimed reaching into his breast pocket and withdrawing a business card, held it out for Saul.

At the conclusion of their little mock interrogation, Job marveled while Saul simply smiled and proclaimed, "He's ready."

39

R ainey was pouring through the Agency files on Hezbollah and the additional, though fragmented, intelligence on Qais Moussa al-Nourani the Israelis had sent over when Job poked his head into his office door.

"How are you making out? You need anything?"

Rainey closed a file folder and dropped it on the floor beside him atop a large stack of others. "I hate being cooped up in here when my team is out there taking care of business. I need to be out there with them. On the ground."

"Now you know how I feel," said Job. "Two more days, Ray. Just two more days."

Nodding, he selected another file from one of the piles on his desk and began reading.

"Evie said the meeting with Clement went well. I thought you'd like to know."

Rainey looked up. "Good. There's a lot riding on him. By the way, did anything come of the director's meeting with the Saudis?"

Job stepped inside the office and closed the door. "The Saudis suspect they have a leak somewhere in their intelligence apparatus. *That* is why they canceled the meeting in New York at the last minute. They did it as a kind of safety precaution."

"Lot of good it did their consul general and his staff."

"Indeed."

"So now what?" said Rainey.

"We've offered them our help, but for now they are treating it like a private affair. The crown prince, himself, is conducting the investigation. From what I hear, he's got his hands full. Keep that to yourself, okay?"

Rainey nodded and, after Job had left, returned to his reading.

The next two days were no different. All the while he was undergoing in-depth briefings with the Agency's Hezbollah experts and digesting every file the analysts could throw at him, Rainey was thinking about his teammates and wishing he were there with them.

Also nagging at him were numerous questions. Why did Nourani target the Saudi consulate? Was it truly because of the secret meeting that was to be held there? Or was it for some other reason? Why also hit the other cities if New York was the primary target? Was Nourani really the man pulling the strings? How did the Iranians factor into this? They always did in the matters of their proxies.

Something else troubled him. The fact that Hezbollah had used a honey trap to ensnare Clement was unprecedented according to the experts. If Nourani was indeed running Unit 910 like Job and the DX analysts believed, he was doing so in the manner of a professional intelligence service and all bets were off. Nourani was not acting defensively. He was playing offense. For that reason and more, he was a monumental danger to the world, especially as it concerned Western and Israeli interests and any hope for lasting peace in the Middle East.

40

BRUSSELS

Alban Clement sat listlessly in the back of the cab once again contemplating what on earth he was doing spying for Hezbollah, the Russians, and now the Americans, too. He was sure that at some point he would make a mistake that would cost him his life and maybe the lives of his wife and daughter as well. If not for their sakes, he would never have agreed to work for the Americans. But now he was counting on their vaunted CIA to be his salvation though somewhere in the back of his mind he knew it was highly probable that nothing could save him in the end.

The cab rolled over a shallow pothole gently rocking him in his seat. He needed to remain focused tonight. Everything was riding on this meeting. Everything. His instructions were clear: Get out by the bagel shop on the rue Armand Campenhout and head south for one block. Then turn around and walk at a brisk pace to the rue du Châtelain. There, he was to turn right. When he reached the avenue Louise he was to stop and stand on the street corner and wait. His handler had told him to expect a text message at some point along his route. If he received no text by five minutes after six, the meeting was off, and they would try again an hour earlier the following night.

He was slightly out of breath as he now stood watching traffic buzz past him on the avenue Louise. The time on his phone read *6:03 p.m.* He wondered if his Hezbollah handler had seen something suspicious as he slipped the phone back inside his jacket. He correctly assumed that the man had helpers, operatives doing countersurveillance. Could one of them have noticed the Americans that he knew were also lurking in the area? The American in charge had told him that they would be watching. He had also assured him that they would *protect* him. But how was that possible? He studied the faces of the people sweeping past. Any one of them could turn and shoot him dead in an instant. Or approach from the rear, stab him in the back, and leave him bleeding all over the pavement. How could the Americans really protect him?

Suddenly, he felt a jolt in his abdomen. It took him a few seconds to realize that his mobile phone was vibrating inside the deep breast pocket of his suit coat. The message was simple.

`The hotel behind you. Room 331.`

It was six o'clock sharp when Alban Clement marched past the front entrance of the hotel Le Châtelain. For several tense minutes, Maddie and the rest of her teammates thought that they had miscalculated. It had been Mark Alcott, known to his brothers- and sisters-in-arms as Shepherd, who had handed out the surveillance assignments. Thus, Jimmy Dunne and Conrad Pietrolaj were each in separate vehicles with engines idling on nearby streets—close enough to respond if need be or follow any vehicle if one should suddenly show up and whisk Clement away. Alcott, Tonka, and Mouse were out on foot with orders to stay in the immediate vicinity of Clement with only one rule: Don't get made by hostile surveillance. They each wore a simple disguise that helped them blend into the landscape. It was dangerous work, but the three of them were battle-tested professionals who knew how to do their jobs under high stress.

Tucked away out of view in two SUVs with darkly tinted windows were the guys from the DX's Joint Services Group. Fig, Babe, Jazz, Booster, and Wizard were staging in the area just in case things got spicy and their expertise as the world's premier shooters was needed. If all went well though no one would ever know they had even been in Brussels and that was perfectly fine by them.

Meanwhile, Evelina and Brigid Finn were monitoring everything and everyone from a suite inside the JAM Hotel.

"All units, Victor One Four. Stand by. MAPLE is still waiting on the text. For what it's worth, I'm still calling it. The meeting *will be* in the Châtelain."

Mark Alcott was an expert in many disciplines, but above all, he was king when it came to the disciplines of surveillance and countersurveillance. The good watchers could tail a target all day long and not get made. The great ones could divine where their target was headed and beat him to the spot. This allowed for the strategic and tactical maneuvering of personnel, so the eye was not only all-seeing but invisible to hostile counterparts. It was part science, part art, but mostly born of natural instincts and skills developed from years in the field.

When the text finally came, Evelina read it in real-time—they were still live-monitoring Clement's phone—then immediately relayed it to the team over their encrypted radio net. "One Four's right. Le Châtelain. Room Three Three One. I repeat, Room Three Three One. Over."

Clement strode through the hotel lobby and headed for the elevator, oblivious to the man and woman watching him from the hotel bar. Maddie smiled brightly at Ignacio Delgado after texting an update to the team. *Maple in elevator.*

A full minute later, a man with a thick neck and arms to match entered through the lobby doors and hit the elevator call button. He wore a gray thigh-length wool coat, black jeans, and shoes with rubber soles. Though he was trying to be casual, his dark eyes darting about betrayed the fact that he was intently searching the hotel lobby for threats or possible surveillance, or both.

Maddie giggled as if Delgado had said something funny, while at the same time, she tapped out another text message to the team. *Target has helper. Big guy...just got on the lift.*

"I saw him," said Mouse in her earpiece. "Olive-skinned male with dark hair and trimmed beard wearing a gray coat and black pants. There's also a silver Mercedes SUV parked out here that could be with him. I can see three MAMs inside and their heads are on a swivel." MAM was a military acronym for military-age male.

"Copy that," said Tonka and Alcott in quick succession. The JSG teams responded in kind. The situation out on the street was tense—a tinder box waiting for an errant spark.

41

E velina stood behind a tandem of laptops flipped open on the ho-
tel-room desk, hands pressed against its faux wood surface while Brigid
Finn looked on from the chair beside her. She closed her eyes and focused
her attention fully on the audio feed coming from Clement's adulterated cell
phone.

It was the last thing Ghulam said that had her heart beating faster. "Give
me your phone."

"Do you think he knows?" said Brigid, interrupting the silence.

"I don't know. Could be he's just being cautious." She folded her arms
beneath her breasts. "Can you turn that up a bit?"

Brigid adjusted the volume controls. "How's that?"

Evelina wordlessly nodded while continuing to stare at the speakers. Next
came a series of muffled thumps followed by nothing but a loud constant
crackle of static.

As it turned out, the sound that they heard was not static at all but
rather the bluster of the hotel shower set to full blast. Evelina deemed it
Ghulam's method of frustrating any possible electronic eavesdropping on
his and Clement's conversation. Crude but effective.

Because of this, they only had a few meager scraps of intelligible audio
at the beginning and end of the meeting featuring Ghulam's monotonic

voice. She wasn't sure it would be good enough for an adequate voiceprint. Nevertheless, they had good video footage of the man from the camera inside Clement's phone as well as from the small cameras carried by the various Jaguar team members, not to mention the hotel's CCTV system they would later access. And after a forensic team from Brussels Station was through with a careful sweep of the room, they would also have Ghulam's fingerprints and DNA. His goon's, too.

The sound of the shower being switched off thus indicated that the meeting had reached its terminus. Ghulam's voice, as he bid Clement farewell, was just above a whisper.

Evelina radioed the team. "Meeting's over. Prepare to mobilize." Now the team would shift their focus to Ghulam. Since they already had Clement's cell phone in pocket, he could be permitted to disappear on his own without them having to physically babysit him.

Maddie's text alert came next. `Helper moving thru lobby.`

"I got him," said Mouse. "He's moving westbound on the sidewalk on the north side of the street. Now he's posting up on the corner."

Another text from Maddie. `Target in lobby.`

The team remained part of the landscape as each member continued to monitor the situation. After exiting through the main lobby doors, Ghulam turned eastbound, rounded the corner onto the avenue Louise and, when he was half a block on, quickly hailed a cab.

It was something the team was prepared for. Though it wasn't easy—physical surveillance of someone on the move seldom was, especially when that someone was trained to detect and evade anyone watching him—they tracked Ghulam to the airport where they watched him board an Air France flight bound for Paris.

Evelina flashed a message to Job who in turn alerted the station chief in Paris. An Agency team there would pick up the tail on Ghulam when his flight arrived. Meanwhile, a peek at the flight's passenger manifest revealed that the man known as Ghulam was traveling on a French passport in the name of Yousef Aswad.

Their diplomat spy had done well.

42

PARIS

He eyed the chatty man seated next to him with veiled disdain. At first, Sadiq pretended not to speak the language, but that seemed not to matter. The man continued to prattle on regardless. At the midpoint of the flight, Sadiq employed the tactic of being too tired to keep his eyes open. In fact, he almost slipped into sleep once and would have, had it not been for the large man's constant wiggling and moving about.

The moment the plane came to a stop outside the gate, Sadiq leapt to his feet, grabbed his carry-on from the cabinet above him, and, despite the grumblings from other passengers, fled like an inmate granted unexpected parole.

The arrivals hall was crowded. He studied the many faces—some weary, some excited, some confused, some bored—in the non-Schengen queue line as he swept past and maneuvered to the Automatic Border Control (ABC) station. A security man eyed him curiously as he turned into the line of travelers waiting in the taxi line. For several long minutes, Sadiq pondered whether French authorities were looking for him, but when the uniformed man finally drifted down the terminal, heading in the other direction, he dismissed the idea completely.

A taxi deposited him outside a hotel near the Eiffel Tower. Forty-five minutes later, he was in the back seat of another cab heading for an address that was two blocks over from the Vidal Rouzet Law Firm.

This time when he entered, the law office was noisy with two parties engaged in a lively disagreement. The leggy, raven-haired receptionist merely smiled as if this were an everyday occurrence. He regarded her without salutation as he crossed the foyer. Vidal Rouzet and his demonstrative counterparts seemed not to notice him slip into the secure hall and then into the office suite. He soon found himself in the quiet of the soundproof SCIF where he would begin the examination of the documents he had collected from the French diplomat.

He clicked open his briefcase and retrieved the sheaf of papers from a hidden pocket inside. There were the usual economic reports and projections, an executive summary of discussions about Brexit and its continued fallout, and plans of an EU intervention in an ongoing humanitarian crisis in an African nation.

Setting the papers aside, he reached for the thumb drive Clement had passed to him. He inserted it into his computer and waited while a program developed by the Iranians scanned the contents for malware, viruses, and otherwise suspicious code. It seemed to be taking longer than usual. He was about to curse at the machine when a new window appeared indicating the scan was complete. The drive was clean.

Carefully, Sadiq sifted through the electronic files. One marked *SECRET* consisted of EU political and security positions with regard to the most recent Iranian activity in the Strait of Hormuz. Furthermore, there was information revealing that EU member nations were now strongly considering joining the Americans in a unified front to apply additional sanctions against the Islamic Republic that would doubtless cripple its economy and create extremely harsh operating conditions for its leadership.

Some of the files were chaff—insignificant fodder. As usual, Clement seemed to have just scooped up whatever he could find. Sadiq soon reached the penultimate file on the drive. It was a white paper marked *CONFIDEN-TIEL UE/EU CONFIDENTIAL*. Per EU custom, the labels of all classified documents were in French followed by English. He scanned it quickly, searching for keywords that would inform his perception of how important the information might be to his masters. Suddenly, he realized what this file represented: a blessing from Allah.

He scrolled back to the beginning of the document and this time read it much more closely. He considered that the person named in the document would need to be vetted but in the end could be a hugely valuable asset to Nourani and Unit 910, and more broadly to Hezbollah, especially in light of the loss of the American billionaire, Stedman Carter, and recent events in Lebanon and Syria. This was definitely something worth looking into. But that would be for his superiors to ultimately decide. His remit was gathering intelligence, running agents, and special operations, not procurement. Sadiq felt a wave of joy wash over him. Clement was proving to be a source worth his weight in gold.

43

The team was cloistered in a safe flat in Auderghem. As far as safe properties go, there was nothing special about it save for one thing. On the bottom floor was a game room of sorts that consisted of a dart board, a TV connected to an Xbox with limited functionality—there was no internet service to the gaming console for the sake of security—a ping-pong table, and a closet full of board games.

"That's two," said Evelina after having just spiked the ball onto Mouse's side of the table.

"Best of five. Come on, Evie."

"You would have to win three *straight*."

"Yeah, so?"

"Why don't you just admit it, Mouse? You can't beat me."

"I'm still getting warmed up." The operator shrugged his shoulders and twisted his torso from side to side.

Evelina rolled her eyes.

"I'll beat you *this* time. Count on it."

"Please. I could beat you playing left-handed."

"No way. No how."

Her eyes narrowed. "Want to bet?"

"How much?" Mouse pressed.

"Not for money."

"Then what?"

Evelina flashed a devilish grin.

When she explained the terms of the bet, Mouse only shook his head and said, "Never going to happen."

"So you agree?"

"You're on, missy."

The next game lasted only a few minutes longer than those prior. Mouse had played quite well considering his previous display of skill, or rather, the lack thereof. He'd jumped out to an early 6-1 lead. But then his luck changed. That was how long it had taken Evelina to get the feel of the paddle in her left hand. But once she had, it was game over. Mouse had only managed to score three more points throughout the remainder of the game. Perhaps she should have mentioned to him at the start that she was fully ambidextrous, but then again, he had never asked.

When Job arrived, Mouse was hiding in the bathroom with Evelina standing at the entrance of the hall suppressing her laughter. As the others crowded into the drawing room, Mouse finally emerged wearing shorts and dabbing dots of blood from his now hairless legs.

At the sight of him, Tonka just shook his head.

Mouse sheepishly looked up at everyone staring back at him.

As if on cue, Booster started singing the lyrics to Tom Petty's hit song "American Girl."

"Mouse, is there something you need to tell us?" said Maddie as more of them joined in on the singing.

"Don't ever play Evie in ping pong. Or bet against her."

"I could have told you that," Maddie replied, blinking away tears of laughter.

Curious, the former police detective Jimmy Dunne leaned forward. "How high did she make you shave?"

Mouse blushed. "*All* the way."

"Yikes," said Dunne, then promptly turned and gave Evelina a high-five. "Game, set, and match." Everyone erupted in fits of raucous laughter.

Job stood back and for the next few moments allowed the team to continue busting on Mouse. Though he rarely joined in with such juvenile behavior, Job was used to the operator hijinks by now. More importantly, he understood them. Laughter was good stress relief, and he needed his people loose and working at their optimal ability. Finally, he said, "All right, folks. Let's do this."

Without further prompting, everyone settled down and grew serious. Job briefed them on what their efforts had produced thus far. A surveillance team from Paris Station had tracked their man, Ghulam, to a law office on the rue de Vaugirard. At this very moment, they were setting up static posts around the building, which would soon include a rented flat above the shop directly across the street. Job relayed the background information that had been dug up on Ghulam, which unsurprisingly was not his real name. Incidentally, neither was Yousef Aswad.

According to the Israelis, Ghulam's true identity was Sadiq Ammar al-Hamadeh and he was full-blooded Hezbollah. The Mossad file on him also suggested he was running a cell, maybe even full-blown operations, from somewhere in Europe. Now, thanks to the newly formed Jaguar team, the two allied agencies—CIA and Mossad—knew precisely where from.

"I want you to debrief the Frenchman," Job said to Maddie. "He's already comfortable with you and you seem to have his full attention." A meeting with Clement had already been scheduled prior to his hotel rendezvous with the Hezbollah man, Sadiq al-Hamadeh. It was protocol and they needed to know precisely how things had gone and if Sadiq had made any specific requests, after all, it was the first meeting the two had had since the attack in America.

Looking on, Evelina sipped mineral water from a green bottle. "What shall we do in the meantime?"

"What we spies do best: wait, of course."

Evelina frowned. "I was afraid you were going to say that."

44

Alban Clement's office was located on the top floor at Place de Louvain 14, though at this very moment, he was nowhere near it. Having completed a surveillance-detective run the Americans had carefully laid out for him, he approached the entrance to the Hotel Brussels. The signal was simple. If the man in a red ball cap was standing outside with a newspaper folded up and tucked under his left arm, the coast was clear. If the same man tossed his newspaper in the waste bin out front, the meeting was off, and they would reconvene later that evening at an alternate location near his home.

Trying to walk at a normal pace, he glanced around the hotel entrance mentally telling himself to appear calm. At first, he did not see him, but then the couple in front of him with their tall, lanky teenage son veered into the optician's office on the right thus giving him a clear view of the sidewalk ahead. A man in a red ball cap was leaning against the building with the sole of one foot pressed against the hotel's cement veneer. His head was canted in such a way that made him seem to be devouring an article buried at the bottom of the page. For the most fleeting of seconds, Clement worried that the man did not see him approaching. And perhaps that was the point. Then all at once the man collected his paper and stuffed it under his left arm with nary a glance in his direction.

Clement did not stop until he was inside and through the lobby.

Mark Alcott grimaced as he pushed himself from the wall, bound up his broadsheet, and secured it under his arm. For the next half a minute, he stretched his neck and back. The Frenchman had already plodded through the lobby by the time the cab containing Evelina pulled to the curb and the blond warrior spy alighted from its back seat. She, with her large sunglasses and European handbag, inched upward on her toes and greeted him with a peck on the lips and an exaggerated hug. He responded by throwing his arm around her and ushering her inside as if the two of them were secret lovers and were now on the clock.

While seemingly focused on each other, they watched Clement waiting at the bank of elevators much like the rest of the team had done ever since he had left his office building. So far as they could tell, he had been clean from start to finish.

A bell chimed and the elevator door in front of him opened with a swoosh. Clement stepped into the car and thumbed the button for the seventh floor. As he waited for the door to close, he noticed the man in the red hat and the beautiful blond on his arm heading toward him. He recognized them but not until after the door had shut. It was the model, Reneé Appell, and her husband, Patrice. But surely these were not their real names. They were clearly pros, he thought. For nothing about them whatsoever was off. Even their naughty whisperings were on point. Seeing and hearing all this caused him to relax. Finally, he expelled the air from his lungs and closed his eyes. He could trust them. He was sure of it.

Clement rode the elevator alone all the while clutching his briefcase by the handle with both hands in front of him and teetering back and forth on his heels and toes. Like everyone in a lift the world round, he stared at the digital readout above the door as the number for each floor ticked by. The seventh-floor landing was clear of guests as he exited, turned left, and headed down the long corridor. The carpet beneath the smooth soles of his expensive Christian Louboutin Greggo Oxfords was slippery but quiet. He detected the fragrant scent of Champagne and strawberries as he passed Room 731 and at that moment registered the distant hum of a vacuum cleaner far behind. Glancing back toward the elevator and well beyond it, he saw an unattended cart, the kind used by hotel housekeeping, and a bright bar of sunlight jutting into the hall through a door that was propped open with a rubber wedge.

Clement approached Room 739, knocked thrice, and, with instincts borne of his triple-agent lifestyle, swiveled his head in either direction.

When the door swept inward, a large man with brown skin, short black hair, and intelligent eyes that suggested a preparedness for violence at all times, ushered him inside. Clement was immediately relieved of his briefcase and mobile phones. The items were handed through the open door of the adjoining room—the briefcase went to a middle-aged man with analytical eyes, the phones to a short, pretty redhead with invisible spectacles—before it clicked shut.

Tonka reclaimed his seat in the corner of the room while Maddie remained poised behind the hotel room desk. The window curtains—kept closed for the sake of privacy and operational security—managed to block out all but the most persistent rays of sunlight. Several had managed to knife their way into the far recesses of the room, carving bright streaks across the beds and the far wall. Legs crossed, Maddie motioned for Clement to take the empty chair in front of her and he did.

"So, Alban. How are you? Good, I hope."

"Yes. I am well."

"Tell me. How is your wife."

"Noelle?" He clearly hadn't expected *that* question. "She is good, I suppose. Busy with her shopping and womanly pursuits."

Maddie regarded him as a therapist does a patient. She listened with her eyes *and* her ears, assessed him with clinical detachment, yet showed an appropriate measure of empathy at the appropriate times. "Is everything between the two of you satisfactory?"

He did not respond. Instead, he gazed toward the shrouded window.

"Alban? Does she know about our arrangement?"

"No," he said a little too quickly. "No."

"But you are considering telling her?"

While he uttered not a word, his body spoke loudly.

"Need I remind you that no one must know you are working with us? It is simply too dangerous at this point. For you *and* your wife and daughter. You do care about their safety, do you not?"

"Of course, I do."

"Then by all means, Alban, you must continue to operate in absolute secrecy. Can you promise me that you will do so?"

He nodded sullenly.

She waited a beat before continuing, thus putting the topic firmly behind them. "You will be pleased to know that a deposit has been made into the account we have set up for you, as promised. She showed him a copy of the bank transaction receipt, then quickly placed it back in her pocket.

"Now, to the matter at hand."

While Maddie and Tonka debriefed the Frenchman on his meeting with Sadiq al-Hamadeh, Conrad Pietrolaj, Jimmy Dunne, and Brigid Finn carried out their technical duties with speed and diligence in the room next door. Finn was hunched over a laptop computer, uploading images and digital files of insignificant EU data, most of which Pietrolaj and the other DX analysts back at headquarters had cooked up to pass along to the Russians, whom Clement was to meet in another week's time. It would be more than enough to keep them at bay while the Jaguar team played with their new toy. For the time being, they needed the Russians to believe that everything was normal with their man.

Meanwhile, Finn's male peers, wearing nitrile gloves and surgical face masks to guard against inadvertently depositing their fingerprints and DNA onto the papers they were handling, placed select files containing similar useless bits of information and disinformation into the diplomat's briefcase.

Later that night, Job descended upon the team again. For Maddie and the rest of them, his visits at least broke up the boredom of being cooped up together in the safe flat for hours on end. They could only play so many board games, so many hands of gin rummy and poker, tell the same silly stories so many times without driving each other mad. Even the one about Mouse and his silky, smooth legs was beginning to age.

"What did he have to say?" said Job, referring to the Hezbollah man.

Maddie gathered her hair into a high, messy ponytail. "Clement said Ghulam asked him to keep an ear out for any discussions within the EU, France, or elsewhere regarding the attack in America. He was given instructions to immediately report anything he hears through the secure channel they have set up."

Job considered this. "They are being proactive. They want to know if we are on to them. I'll suggest to the director to have POTUS put something out that signals the FBI and IC need the assistance of the public."

"Which will mean we are stymied," added Evelina.

"Exactly. Let's give them what they want to hear. Anything else? How would you assess his demeanor?"

"He's stressed, but I think he's growing more comfortable with us," said Maddie.

"That's understandable. I've seen his type many times before." The spymaster reached for his coat. "He feels he has no control over his situation. We must keep him in a position that suggests we care for him and at the same time underscores the penalty for failing us."

"For now, I think he's there," said Maddie.

Job nodded as he buttoned his coat. "Good work, everyone. Now, I need to be going. Keep me posted. Lord willing, I will see you all in a few weeks. Stay safe and try not to get on each other's nerves too badly. One last thing: Keep Mouse from making any more bets with Evie."

Evelina and Maddie exchanged glances then joined everyone in looking at Mouse.

"Shut up," Mouse said with a guileless smile. "Just shut up."

45

At the very moment his Jaguar teammates were enduring the pangs of boredom from being cooped up in the Brussels safe flat, Rainey was hitting his stride on his European *tour de la déception*, a tour that over the course of just a few weeks had taken him to places such as Zurich, Geneva, and Luxembourg, Milan, Frankfurt, and Amsterdam. He stayed in the most exclusive hotels, ate in the best restaurants, patronized galleries containing priceless works of art, and spent untold amounts of money at some of Europe's most extravagant designer boutiques. All of it for one reason and one reason only: to draw the attention of Hezbollah and its operational mastermind.

The final leg of his tour and the culmination of his efforts was Liechtenstein. The scenic alpine principality was among the smallest nations in the world. More importantly for Rainey's sake and that of Operation End of Days, it held sway among the world's most notorious moneychangers and the shrinking warrens of secret banking, where the rich and powerful hid their money from the ever-greedy tax man, government regulators, and the world's more vigilant intelligence and security services.

Thus far, Rainey's performance as fabled arms merchant, Jean-Michel Durand, was approaching legendary status. He'd wined and dined with a Saudi prince in Zurich, broke bread with an industrialist tycoon in a castle-like mansion in Germany's Elsava Valley, and discussed the diamond

231

market with a pair of notorious brothers in a private office off the Pieter Cornelisz Hooftstraat. While attending countless private parties, Rainey had shaken the hands of government ministers, starchy bank chairmen, and a host of European power brokers. At Mosconi in Luxembourg, he had traded stories, though heavily redacted, of course, highlighting his global exploits with a mustachioed Emirati over strong cups of coffee. But for a close encounter with none other than the French billionaire Julien Battier that nearly brought the entire operation crashing down, things could not have gone better.

During bouts of shameless galivanting, Rainey had even managed to catch the eye of a world-renowned and devastatingly beautiful fashionista of Italian heritage. After agreeing to a quiet dinner with her in Milan—she had insisted—they flew via private helicopter north to her villa on the banks of Lake Como. There, from a tiered balcony, they shared a kiss with the grand, sweeping views of the lake as their backdrop. One blissful evening, during a walk along an old, cobblestone path overlooking the lake, her clutching him at the bicep, him shielding her from the stiff breeze off the water, she offered him her kingdom as well as her body. This had not been the first temptation to assault his firmly held Christian convictions. An ordinary man may have caved amidst the crushing gravitational pull toward her bed, but Rainey was no ordinary man. Somehow, whether by his effusive persuasion or by the mischievous gleam in his milk chocolate eyes—or some combination of both—he managed to demur her bedroom proposal without negative consequence. Their salacious rendezvous would have to wait, he had said. For the time being, he had pressing business affairs to attend to elsewhere on the Continent and was constrained to a murderous schedule. Truth be told, all throughout his time with the inimitable fashion mogul, his mind had retreated to his SERE training. *Survive. Evade. Resist. Escape.* As it turned out, his forbearance only drove the woman wilder for him. For no man before the eminent Jean-Michel Durand had had the self-restraint or self-confidence to parry her seductive advances. No, not one.

Rainey pushed the thoughts of the beautiful temptress out of his mind now, slipped his expensive leather loafers back on, and readied himself for another dazzling performance. In a matter of seconds, he would be touching down at Switzerland's St. Gallen-Altenrhein Airport in a private jet registered through a DX front company in Luxembourg, which was now solely owned and operated by the Dynamic Prime Solutions Corporation. As it were, DPSC, much like the man who ran it, was a dutiful fiction.

Rainey gazed out his window at a firmament of gunmetal gray and nickel, an ocean of heavy clouds that threatened to unleash a harsh snowstorm at any given moment. The jet taxied past the remnants of a recent snowfall and into a private hangar. There, having dispensed with a cursory examination from an immigration and customs official, he alighted from the plane and immediately ducked into an armored Rolls-Royce Cullinan limousine all the while being followed by a man in a dark suit with thick arms and a familiar face.

Rainey eased back into the supple leather seat and took in the full interior of the luxury vehicle. It was an exact replica of the one he and his troupe had utilized in Amsterdam. He considered whether Stedman Carter understood that his *full cooperation* with the Agency and the operation they were running extended to the pillaging of his seemingly endless bank accounts. Of course, he did, thought Rainey. Despite his personal feelings toward the man, he had to give Carter a lot of credit; he was financing the operation and thus far had put no restraint on their exorbitant spending.

Rainey turned toward the big man seated next to him—the operator known as Babe Ruth. "Last stop, bro."

"Knock 'em dead, boss."

Rainey winked. "That's the idea."

With Fig at the wheel, they shot south on the A13, tracing the western shore of the Rhine River all the way to Vaduz. Their hotel on the Mareestrasse was the most exclusive in all of Liechtenstein. And yet, exclusive as it was, nothing was satisfactory to the interminable demands of Monsieur Durand. From the very moment he'd set foot inside the hotel, the staff despised him. The room was not clean enough, the bed sheets not soft enough. The food wasn't fit for a dog, the bathroom towels not to his liking. The list went on. Even for a staff that was well accustomed to the preternatural whims of their uberwealthy clientele, there was positively no pleasing him.

Vaduz was not a large city by any stretch of the imagination. Soon word of the impossible, filthy rich guest reached the rest of its townspeople. Gert Abendschein over at the Altenbach Restaurant and Bar refused to serve the man any further after he'd sent back the veal Orloff for the third time. Seeing his fiancée's eyes preying mercilessly on Durand as he encroached on their usual seats in the symphony made Otto Perlich want to punch his lights out. But the big man with the mean face who never seemed to stray far from the Frenchman's side convinced him that to do so would only result in an appointment with a plastic surgeon. Instead, Perlich wisely chose to sulk and brood for the rest of the evening while Durand made unapologetic and unspoken advances toward his bride-to-be.

On the other hand, Durand was not entirely without fandom in Liechtenstein. Simon Lange, head of Der Prince Club, the most exclusive private club in the country, never turned his back on an opportunity to lure another rich man to his club's rolls. When news of Durand reached his ears, Lange quickly approached his myriad contacts, which extended to staff in the local hotels. Within thirty minutes, he'd found Durand and caught up to him as he marched across the lobby of the Parkhotel Sonnenhof. Lange introduced himself at once and offered Durand a complimentary one-year trial membership to the club on the spot. Maybe he could visit this afternoon, take a dip in the pool, smoke a cigar in the lounge, yes? There were other members who would surely enjoy meeting him. Durand maintained his heading and his swift pace as he issued his riposte. "I'll have my people contact you. Maybe there is some kind of tax-deductible contribution we can make to your little club. Now, if you'll excuse me."

Exactly who was Jean-Michel Durand and from where did his monstrous wealth originate? It was a question that consumed the entire city. Some guessed Durand to be a new tech giant. A snotty yuppie turned billionaire overnight. Others surmised he had acquired his wealth through a vast inheritance or a series of lucrative investments, or both. There were a few hushed voices that theorized Monsieur Durand was not the sort who made his living in a legitimate manner. Drugs, they said. The theft of priceless artifacts. One prescient soul dared to suggest that Durand was neck-deep in the trafficking of illicit arms. A merchant of war. It would show up in no report, no document or recording, that the very person to suggest such a thing was a full-fledged field operative in the Agency's bullpen of anonymous NOCs. It was just one more subtle plug in Job's carefully crafted whisper campaign. A campaign with a target audience that consisted of one man: Qais Moussa al-Nourani.

With the sun now breaking over the Alps and flooding the valley with light, the bulky limousine swept into the front parking lot of a four-story stone and glass structure along the Austrasse and disgorged Monsieur Durand outside its front doors. Valzbank AG was a private bank used by some of the world's ultra-rich to safeguard their vast portfolios and, along with a partnered law firm, manage their secretive shell company holdings. Valzbank was as old as Liechtenstein itself. As an institution, it prided itself equally on its exclusive clientele and its stout record of confidentiality. It was a true safe haven.

This was the first of several meetings Durand would have throughout the day in Vaduz. Meetings with company formation agents, bankers, lawyers, and others. One such man, a banker—and soon-to-be unwitting co-conspirator to this phase of the operation—by the name of Erik Walser, was phoned by the receptionist as Rainey waited in the sterile Valzbank foyer, his fingers impatiently tapping the marble desktop in front of her. Walser's name had surfaced six months ago in an unrelated investigation run by the US Treasury Department's Office of Intelligence and Analysis. Preliminary findings had already confirmed that Walser was providing financial support to Iran and in particular Hezbollah by funneling the organization's wealth—and some of its senior leadership's personal holdings as well—through dozens of front companies and Red Cross accounts thereby helping the group skirt government sanctions and money laundering laws. Though a principled faction within the US Intelligence Community had strongly lobbied to put an end to Walser's activities—some by legal means, some by a carefully choreographed accident or a not-so-random random act of violence, Job and a small group of others argued that it would be much more helpful to the cause, on a strategic level, to keep him in play while also closely monitoring his activities. Like Job, Rainey was now hoping, for the sake of Operation End of Days, to exploit Walser's rogue financial activities.

After several minutes, a bald man with a close-cropped gray beard and sleek, stainless steel spectacles descended an elegant staircase. With each step, his right hand clutched tightly at the polished steel railing while his left gripped a shiny metal cane. Upon his approach, he straightened his charcoal suit coat and extended a liver-spotted hand.

"Herr Durand, sorry to keep you waiting. My trick knee," he tilted his bulbous head downward. "It's been acting up again, I'm afraid."

Rainey's flawless German spilled from his lips in the dialect of a true Berliner. "Yes. Well, if you please, I would like to get started. I have a busy day ahead of me."

"But of course." Walser assessed the large man in the dark suit standing a few paces behind Durand. "Shall we all step into my office?"

At this, Rainey turned to Babe and in French ordered him to wait in the lobby. Babe nodded then walked over to the receptionist's desk, where he stood at parade rest, his eyes taking on a rather cold affect that translated into any language meant: "Mess with me or my boss and I will hurt you."

Walser's office was warm, doubtless to keep the thin-skinned older man from shivering in the alpine cold of Vaduz. The wall behind his massive mahogany desk was nothing but windows. A plush, leather sofa stretched along the left side of the room at the end of which was a door that Rainey assumed led to a private washroom. He nonchalantly checked the rest of his surroundings and found a wall of bookshelves and office-variety knick-knacks that wrapped around the room to his right. A globe upon a heavy cedar pedestal. A brass clock—no, it was gold—that incidentally was a minute too slow. Above the sofa, ensconced in an ornate, gilded frame, hung an oil painting that depicted armies of rough men with clashed swords and charging warhorses—some rearing back, others trampling maimed and lifeless bodies beneath their thundering hooves—set against a background of an all-encompassing fire that raged white and red and orange. A small, brass plaque beneath the wall-lighted canvas read in decorative Arabic font, *The End of Days*. Rainey had never heard of the painting or the artist whose name was scribbled wildly in the bottom corner in a dark, earthy pigment. Was this where Job had gotten the name for the operation or was it simply a coincidence of monumental proportion?

"It's magnificent, isn't it?"

"Indeed," said Rainey without the slightest hint of irony.

"It was a gift from a client."

"I see."

"Please. Have a seat. You indicated on the phone that you had a rather delicate matter to discuss."

Rainey sat down and crossed his legs. He assumed a facial expression that bespoke the fact that he was a man who was accustomed to getting what he wanted. "That's precisely right, Herr Walser. To get right to the point, I would like to open an account in your bank."

"Surely your lawyers are more than capable of making such arrangements. Perhaps—"

"My lawyers are busy with other matters," he snapped. "I prefer to handle this personally and with utmost discretion."

"Oh, perhaps I should have mentioned that I, myself, am not taking on any additional clients at the moment but allow me to refer you to one of my associates. They are more than qualified to address your—"

"No, no. You don't understand." Rainey smiled. "I want *you* to handle this new account." His tone was unequivocal, his words non-negotiable.

For a moment Walser gazed back at him as if trying to decipher the subtext of the man seated before him. "I must ask, why *me?*"

"Let's just say that I have heard good things about you, Herr Walser, about the manner in which you service your clients' accounts. Specifically, how your sensitivity for discretion and confidentiality are paramount. It is such a bank and such a man that I am seeking."

Walser's eyes narrowed as his chin sunk into his bleached-white shirt collar. "Liechtenstein is no longer a place to hide one's money, Herr Durand. I suggest you look elsewhere if that is what you are getting at."

"Herr Walser, you seem like a reasonably intelligent man—a man of the world. I assure you whatever business I intend to transact with this bank will be perfectly legitimate."

"So you say," said the banker, a wary, if not accusatorial, look about his face.

Rainey grinned. They had reached the point where both men knew full well the other's intentions. Though there was nothing yet revealed but innuendo. Walser was being careful, covering his flanks *and* his backside. "Whatever proof you need, I can and will produce."

The banker hesitated at the veiled meaning. Whatever Durand's dirty business entailed, he would provide ample cover, an impenetrable shroud of legitimacy. It was at this moment, that Rainey knew they had him.

"And yet you are seeking a pseudonym account."

Rainey's intense brown eyes yielded nothing. He sat calmly, fingers interlaced in his lap, legs crossed, and forehead angled slightly downward, assuming an icy gaze that could very easily be interpreted as the foreshadowing of peril. A flash of lighting on the distant horizon.

Walser's forehead creased almost imperceptibly. A microexpression. He was thinking. After a few beats, Rainey sensed a crack in his armor. Greed does that to a man. "Suppose I *were* to take you on as a client. Just how much business should I expect to handle?"

"Roughly four hundred million euros per annum."

Rainey detected the slightest widening of Walser's eyes, yet the man did well in his attempt to conceal his surprise. Surely, his illicit business dealings demanded caution and great care.

"We do have an initial deposit requirement in order to open the type of account you are seeking," said Walser licking his lips.

"How does twenty-five million sound?"

"I would prefer it be broken down into smaller increments. If I might make a suggestion, Herr Durand, let's begin with a balance of five hundred thousand euros."

"That'll be fine," said Rainey as if the amount were mere pocket change.

At Walser's request, Rainey handed him his false French passport, then hefted a black, hard-shell attaché case onto his lap, rotated the barrels of the combination locks, and clicked it open. From a pocket just inside the lid, Rainey produced the necessary documents pertaining to his DX-fronted businesses as well as signed letters and affidavits from two law firms in Europe. Both were long-established and very legitimate firms. Both were also very close friends of the Central Intelligence Agency's Directorate X.

Using an elegant, black Montegrappa Venetia fountain pen with a gold-plated nib he had pulled from the inside of his suit coat, Rainey signed a series of documents ablaze with Valzbank AG letterhead in a bold, sweeping flourish. It was the signature of a powerful man, of someone who was used to acquiring things with the stroke of a pen.

The words came forth if only by rote. "We will need to do a bit of due diligence on our part. For the sake of appearances. You understand."

"Of course, Herr Walser. I wouldn't have it any other way. I trust you will be thorough and enterprising in executing your duties." With an executive smile, Rainey had laid down the gauntlet and in the same fell swoop dangled a carrot.

The banker now spoke with an air of servitude. "I would only need the deposit at this point, sir."

"Ah yes, the deposit. Is cash acceptable?"

"Quite."

Via an intercom on his desk, Walser summoned his assistant into the room, who silently appeared and swept up the documents. As she scurried away, Rainey's mobile bleated inside his suit coat. After a studious show of examining the screen, Rainey looked up and said, "You'll have to excuse me, I need to take this. Is there someplace private inside the building that I may do so?"

Walser, now amiable and eager to please, directed him to a small conference room down the corridor. "Take as much time as you need."

"*Dankeschön.*"

Upon his return to the banker's office fifteen minutes later, Durand and Walser shook hands thus consummating a very lucrative and beneficial relationship for not just the two of them but quite possibly for a terrorist organization as well.

Walser stood in his office, leering through the closed window blinds of his private washroom. With two scissored fingers he held the thin slats open and watched Durand's limo usher him away from the building. He waited until he could see no further trace of it then informed his assistant that he would be stepping out of the office for about an hour.

He drove south on the Austrasse till he reached the traffic circle. There, he turned right onto the Kirshstrasse then left onto Gerberweg. After thirty minutes of watching for and maneuvering to expose surveillance the way he'd been taught, he drove back the way he had come. Retracing his route back to the Austrasse, this time he headed north. Soon he pulled into the car park in front of a concrete and cedar wood building adjacent to which stood an apothecary on one side and a small bookstore on the other. Looking both ways as he exited his vehicle, he hustled beneath a large atrium and into an attorney's office. Walser had known the man for years. Together they had closed many business deals though most had never seen the light of day.

Using his own key, he pushed into a quiet little room at the midpoint of a dim corridor. Here, he would have exclusive and secure internet access that would be cloaked as legitimate and privileged legal business. Twelve minutes and thirty-seven seconds later, he was finished. His encrypted email had been received at a similar law office in Istanbul. Though he knew it not, from there the message would in turn be forwarded to another law office in Beirut, where the contents would be copied to a thumb drive and then hand-delivered to a courier. Each person along the way could not possibly know what the message entailed because only the two endpoints in the communication stream had the encryption keys to decode the messages between them thus securing any critical information from interception. Operational security was paramount.

46

The thirty-five-year-old courier, carrying no cell phone or other electronic device save for the secure thumb drive he had been handed at a café in the city center, traveled by black motorcar to a shopping district in the north of the city then switched to a small gray minivan, grimy from trips into the dusty regions of Lebanon where Hezbollah still maintained numerous training camps despite Israel's recent attempts to bomb the organization into oblivion. He switched vehicles again near the Saint George Hospital University Medical Center and still once more outside an electronics repair shop in the suburb of Ghobeiry. In the back room of an art studio specializing in ceramics two doors down from the Bank of Beirut on El Imam El Khomeini, he wordlessly passed the thumb drive to a bearded older gentleman of about fifty, who was outfitted in a faded brown tunic and worn leather sandals that revealed jagged, yellow toenails.

The usual ninety-minute drive took a laborious four and a half hours due to Nourani's stringent security requirements. After the last of five vehicle switches, the bearded porcelain artist, who also happened to be one of Nourani's most trusted spiritual advisors, trekked up a narrow, winding dirt footpath through a small copse of cedars. The trail ended outside an iron gate that looked like it could have been standing there since the time this region was called Aram.

A man heavily clad with a vest full of ammo and an AK-203 strapped to his chest waved the cleric inside then peered militantly into the woods that skirted the compound. Soon the thumb drive found its way to Jawdat Shukri, one of Nourani's trusted lieutenants. Shukri, in turn, handed it unceremoniously to another man in the compound, this one a skinny little fellow who had a rather impressive background in technical matters thanks to his government-funded education in London and additional training in Iran. The IT man stuck the thumb drive into a standalone machine and in a matter of minutes printed out the decrypted message. Next, using an old-school, book-size tape recorder, he transferred the digital audio file on the thumb drive to a cassette tape. These items were in turn placed inside a manila envelope and handed back to Shukri, who walked them via an underground passageway to Nourani's fortified residence hall.

Qais Moussa al-Nourani looked up from his lunch of labne, olives, manakeesh, and shish taouk as Jawdat Shukri entered his lair with a jubilant twinkle in his eye. He leaned back in his upholstered, wooden chair, which creaked beneath him, as he finished chewing. "You have good news."

"I do." Shukri held out the envelope. "It's from the banker in Vaduz."

Nourani set down his fork and with his powerful hands folded back the flap of the envelope and removed its contents. He placed the cassette tape on the table next to a half-empty bottle of Dr. Pepper—he was addicted to the stuff—as he read studiously from the sheets of white computer paper. For a moment, his dark eyes narrowed, and his lips contracted as if he were taking a drag from an invisible cigarette.

```
New client: Jean-Michel Durand. French
national. Suspected arms dealer. Ex-
```

```
tremely  wealthy.  Primary  business
holding: Dynamic Prime Solutions Cor-
poration. See attached copy of French
passport. Based  on  surreptitiously
recorded phone conversation, Durand
will  be  in  London  next  week  for  arms
fair.
```

"It seems the banker has taken on an interesting new client," said Shukri to Nourani's thoughtful silence. He set a small boom box stereo on the table and opened the cassette-tape door with the push of a button.

Nourani handed the cassette to his lieutenant. "Play the tape."

The recording began with a click, which could have been the sound of a door closing, followed by what were obviously several muted footsteps. Then a male voice in a harsh tone.

"What is it? I'm busy!"

"There is a complication with the African's shipment. It is stuck in port."

"Why? What's the problem?"

"Our inside man wants more money. He says if he doesn't get another million, he's going to have it seized by his government."

"Listen to me. Listen! I have already given him plenty of money for his trouble. You tell him that if he does anything to further delay that shipment, heads are going to roll, and his *will be the first. Followed closely by his wife's and kids'. There is no place I cannot find him."*

"Okay. I'll tell him."

"If he balks any further, send a team to deal with him. I promised the African he will have his armaments by the end of next week and I keep my promises. Do you hear me?"

"Loud and clear, boss."

"I'll be at the Canary Riverside Plaza Hotel all next week. I have several important meetings and some other business to attend to, therefore I may not be available for calls. If you run into any other problems, leave a message, and I'll get back to you as soon as I can. But, Aleksy, I don't want any more problems. I pay you exceedingly well to prevent problems. Understand?"

"Yes, sir."

The voices had been entirely in French. The first and loudest was clearly Durand's. He had a commanding presence if only on the phone. Nourani knew the type. He was a man who prided himself on being in control of himself and those with whom he did business at all times. The second voice was weaker, likely only picked up because of the strategic positioning of the tiny, covert microphones within the banker's conference room. It belonged to a man. Like Durand, he too spoke French but with a strange accent. It sounded as if it could be Czech, Russian, or Ukrainian, Romanian even. Too hard to tell based on the volume of the audio and the shortness of the conversation.

Nourani hit REWIND and played the tape again. When it was through, he clicked the cassette player off and stared into space, making mental notes from the recording. Durand had a temper but apparently did well to hide it for Walser had made no mention that Durand was either distracted or displayed any signs of distress following the private phone call. The Frenchman was also unafraid to wield violence, or the threat thereof, as a means to an end. In light of recent intelligence from their source inside the European Union, Nourani had to concur with Walser's suspicion: Durand's business was surely illegal and clearly included the trafficking of arms. Durand would be staying at the Canary Riverside Plaza Hotel in London next week. It was common knowledge that the Defence & Security Equipment International expo was taking place there within the same time frame. It was a huge event that brought government officials, security professionals, defense contractors, arms manufacturers, and other like-minded industry people together. Like he did every year, Nourani had already put the word out to his procurement people to be on the lookout for potential agents to recruit or ingenious technology plans to steal. Or both. There would surely be similar opportunities for a man like Jean-Michel Durand.

"Have the banker transfer twenty thousand euros out of our numbered account for services rendered."

"Yes, sir."

After Shukri had left the room, Nourani listened to the audio recording again. Jean-Michel Durand. It was the same name mentioned in the intel they had acquired from their source inside the EU. Two independent sources. Perhaps, it was true—Durand was looking to expand his operations. Though he wanted to believe that the intelligence was genuine, Qais Moussa al-Nourani was the careful sort. Born out of extensive training and personal experience, his default setting was that of skepticism. It had kept him alive on more than one occasion, even during the recent Israeli campaign. Nourani also had a keen eye for a Zionist deception. So, in the interest of operational prudence, he decided to dispatch Sadiq to see what he might learn about Durand first. If there was anything untoward or potentially dangerous lurking about him or his business dealings, Sadiq would surely flush it out. On the flip side, if Durand was, in fact, the man he presented himself to be, a relationship with him may be well worth cultivating.

Praise be to Allah.

47

BRUSSELS

Less than forty-eight hours later, the virtual bell above the virtual front door to Dynamic Prime Solutions—Jean-Michel Durand's virtual umbrella corporation—jingled to life. Brigid Finn, the diminutive redhead with the big brain and rimless spectacles, immediately sounded the alarm by flashing a secure message to the operations center within the bowels of DX headquarters. Something, nay someone, was nibbling at the bait. Now to find out just who that someone was.

Brigid went to work and before long had traced the interloper to a popular commercially available virtual private network (VPN) service hosted by a server farm in Switzerland. The service was well known for its impenetrable encryption. Without the encryption keys, breaking through the security of the network would be nearly impossible. Thankfully, this particular VPN service had already been penetrated by the NSA via a human source within the company. From there, following the digital trail was easy. It led to more servers spread across Eastern Europe but finally settled on an internet connection in Lebanon, more specifically, the war-torn city of Beirut.

"Can you penetrate the user's machine?" said Maddie, leaning over Brigid's shoulder. Maddie was the only other person in the room who seemed to have any sense of what the former NSA whiz was doing.

Brigid's forehead scrunched up as she furiously typed on her laptop. "Give me a sec." But after three minutes more, she sat up straight, stretched her neck and back, then with an audible sigh proclaimed that there was nothing more of any consequence to exploit. For now, the trail had reached a dead end. Though in which neighborhood it did so was a clue in and of itself.

Beirut meant Hezbollah.

And Hezbollah meant Nourani.

48

While one of his trusted Unit 910 brothers carried out an in-depth background investigation on Durand from the safety and security of an office five stories beneath an apartment building in northwest Beirut, Sadiq al-Hamadeh was en route to London to put physical eyes on the man. He had already activated a number of his surveillance operatives to assist in that regard.

The Eurostar was crowded but thankfully his seatmate was a twentysomething man who was more interested in leering at women on his phone via a mobile dating app and liking things on TikTok than engaging him in conversation. Nevertheless, Sadiq wore wireless earbuds—a universal symbol among travelers that one wished to be left alone. He now gazed through his reflection in the window at the lights snapping past in the dark abyss of the Channel Tunnel while considering the target of the surveillance operation. The information thus far obtained on Durand ran through his mind in much the same manner.

He considered the picture of the man in the photocopied French passport. Durand had a pair of intense, dark eyes not unlike his own. His rugged features were softened only by his hairstyle—one that had been trendy several years ago. The intelligence given to him by his superiors was limited, thus the need to do some eyes-on surveillance. However, a Google search had already produced some preliminary insights. Durand was the owner of several companies all of which seemed to operate under the umbrella of the Dynamic Prime Solutions Corporation, or DPSC, as it was known in the industry. There were several oblique mentions of the company in a series of online periodicals, the earliest dating back seven years. Only one of them seemed to have anything negative to say. Though veiled in subtlety and obscure industry language, it included a reference to underground arms markets. None of the publications touched directly on Durand's background. Though there was a subtle intimation in one of them of a murky, troubled past.

Sadiq turned back toward the passenger compartment at which time a middle-aged woman with wide blue eyes seated across the aisle smiled at him. A fire of rage kindled within him, yet he revealed it not. How could Western men live like this with women openly engaging in such vile behavior? Though he wanted to grab her by the hair and draw a knife across her throat, he forced a smile that seemed as natural as a blade in his hand.

49

As word from the remaining team members in Brussels traveled back and forth to DX headquarters, Rainey was mapping out potential surveillance detection runs throughout the city. The Defence & Security Equipment International expo was being held at the ExCel London convention center, a mammoth structure situated on the northern quay of the Royal Victoria Dock. Soon Hezbollah operatives would doubtless be activated to monitor his every move. In fact, he was counting on it. Unlike most occasions in which an intelligence officer might want to make sure he was *black*, before, say, meeting an agent or emptying a dead drop, Rainey wanted to make sure he *would* be under surveillance. It was the only way his plan would work.

He memorized chokepoints, areas where he could perform natural reverses and other countersurveillance techniques in order to draw out any watchers, then, when the time was right, lead them down the primrose path right into an ambush. His planning was meticulous. It had to be.

Rainey rubbed his tired eyes. He wanted nothing more right now than to crawl into his executive suite's king-size bed and fade into a deep slumber. Fig and Babe were already fast asleep in the suite next door. He could hear the latter's riotous snoring through the wall.

Turning back toward the secure laptop on the desk, he resumed his prep work. After another hour, he shut down the computer and drifted over to the large floor-to-ceiling window. Placing his fingertips against the glass, he looked out over the moonlit River Thames. Rainey recalled the conversation he had had in his study with Job and Saul after his fast apprenticeship under the tutelage of Stedman Carter, the eminent international arms dealer.

"They are going to surveil you. Then, when they are satisfied you are who you say you are, they will make their approach. You must carry on the Durand charade at all times. You must be him even when you are alone soaking in the tub of your hotel."

"Soaking in the tub?"

"You know what I mean. Assume you are being watched at all times. And possibly not just by Hezbollah. Remember, the Russians know about Clement's involvement with Hezbollah. For now, they are an X factor in our little operation. We must not forget about them."

That was the moment Rainey had presented another idea: Why not approach one of the ailing defense contractors in Europe and make a purchase offer? It would be a little tenuous, *but*, he had argued, if they could pull it off, it would solidify Durand's stature as a man of means and industry and also go a long way to dispel any suspicions held by Hezbollah's senior leadership concerning future business relations with him. But Job had deemed it too risky, and the idea was scuttled with no further debate.

On his back now, staring at the ceiling, he prayed for sleep to come quickly. His mind soon rested again on the face of Ryan Killian's wife as she wept over her husband's lifeless form. The images of her helpless pleading played over and over in his head until he was lost to sleep, a place where his nightmares could begin anew.

In the morning, he rose and went through a quick regimen of pushups, dips, squat thrusts, and arm curls, using the heavy table chairs as makeshift dumbbells. Not being able to stay active gnawed at him. Before long, Fig and

Babe were knocking on his door. The three of them shared a room-service breakfast that consisted of eggs, bacon, toast, and black coffee. When they were finished, they again discussed the plan for the week to the point that each knew every facet inside and out.

Sunday came and went with each of them following the same routine as before save for the two occasions when Rainey checked in via secure link with the other Jaguar team members holed up in a safe house in Bromley. As the night grew late, a message now flashed on his mobile. It came from Evelina.

ROYAL is here in London. And he has helpers. Stay loose & be safe.

ROYAL was the cryptonym they had chosen for Sadiq.

He tapped out a quick response then placed the phone on the nightstand and forced himself to sleep.

I have helpers, too.

50

The first day of the expo was a blur of activity. With a laminated badge dangling from his neck—for Dynamic Prime Solutions Corporation was indeed a player in the military-industrial complex, if not for real, at least in the grand fiction of Operation End of Days—Jean-Michel Durand mingled amongst the numerous guests and exhibitions, focusing the bulk of his attention on meet-and-greets. The expo was partitioned into various zones and hubs. On Tuesday, he negotiated the Land and Aerospace Zones. On Wednesday, he moved on to the Security and Joint Zones. He would reserve the whole final day of the expo for a deep dive into the Naval Zone.

Monsieur Durand sat for conferences and seminars. He even learned a thing or two along the way. In the evenings, he held several meetings at nearby hotels—all of them staged—with fellow Jaguar team members in disguises that would make the best makeup artists in Hollywood proud. Monday night's dinner meeting showcased Jimmy Dunne as a socially awkward systems design engineer from a well-known American firm who specialized in high-tech armaments. Dunne donned a department-store suit, an Oxford shirt that refused to stay tucked due to the false belly he wore beneath it, which easily added forty pounds to his otherwise trim frame, and a wide necktie.

The next evening, Monsieur Durand shared his company with a man who even upon close inspection did not resemble Conrad Pietrolaj. The false teeth and gum-line inserts added width to his face and the glued-on eyebrows and hairpiece lowered his forehead considerably, giving him a perpetual scowl. The part Pietrolaj played was that of a cash-strapped director of research and development at a Norwegian arms manufacturing company.

Then there was Booster. His role and costume in this little play by all accounts took the cake. Wearing the uniform of a general—ribbons and all—from the Central African Armed Forces, he was a conspicuous figure within the expo. The streaks of gray that had been brushed into what little hair he had on his nearly shaved head made him appear fifteen years older. The fake scar on his left cheekbone denoted a man with battlefield experience while his ramrod posture perfectly communicated military officialdom. On consecutive nights, Booster could be seen in four-thousand-dollar suits, dining with the mysterious Jean-Michel Durand then later slipping into the hotel room of a dolled-up woman precisely the same height and build as Brigid Finn with flowing hair black as ebony before lumbering back to his own hotel suite in the early morning hours.

Of course, most of the acquaintances Monsieur Durand made throughout the week were not of the fictitious variety. Among the legitimate contacts he had managed to forge were Major General Ingmar Forslund, commander of the Swedish air force; Caroline Harris, director of defense research and engineering for advanced capabilities with the US Department of Defense; TAGR Applied Intelligence, Inc.'s head of data platform, Sanjoy Naidu; Colonel Arjen de Boer, who bore the title, program officer robotics and autonomous systems for the Royal Netherlands Army; director of engineering at GlobeCom, Heike Brugger; and a youthful and exuberant Director, Cyber Defence and Chief Information Security Officer Liam Davey of the United Kingdom's Ministry of Defence. The list went on. Rainey wondered how many of these were intelligence officers and/or clandestine agents of foreign governments. Certainly, the expo was fertile ground for intelligence services on the prowl for potential recruits. Especially after hours when the attendees stampeded into the London streets in search of cocktails and other vices, including those things that might place them in a precarious situation and therefore ripe for a pitch.

Not one of the authentic attendees had any idea they were helping an American warrior spy assemble his curriculum vitae so that he might attract the attention of a terrorist organization in search of an arms dealer. To the unsuspecting, Durand channeling the role of military supply-chain expert seemed perfectly plausible. Many of them exchanged a handshake and a business card without a moment's hesitation.

As far as surveillance, the first three days of the expo had gone by without the slightest hint of coverage. It was why Rainey had saved his best series of chokepoints for the fourth day. Any coverage team by then would doubtless be tired from following him around London all week, to cafes and hotel restaurants, to parks and riverbank benches. If they had noted anything it was that Jean-Michel Durand seemed to relish the idea of conducting his business right under the noses of the British security services. Logic and experience indicated that now was the time when anyone watching him might be apt to make a mistake or at least let their guard down a bit. In fact, Rainey was counting on it. For his plan to work, he needed to draw them out.

So it was, on the fourth and final night of the expo, that Fig—Monsieur Durand's dutiful driver—pulled to the curb in front of the Murray Grove Post Office. He waited long enough for Rainey to climb out and head north on Cropley Street before pulling away and disappearing into the evening traffic.

The collar of his woolen overcoat pulled high, Rainey took a circuitous route west to an alehouse aptly named, The Wenlock Arms. He found a seat near the window and ordered a pint. He made several furtive glances at his wristwatch then at the allotted time, without ever touching his beer, he dropped a ten-pound note on the table and exited the tavern. To any pavement artists surveilling him, it would appear as though he were waiting to meet someone.

Rainey stepped out into the cold air, hesitating long enough to pull his black leather gloves back on and yank up his collar. He checked his watch once again then turned north. He skirted along the western edge of Shepherdess Walk Park, past a lady and her yipping little dog and a man in coveralls sprinkling salt on the sidewalk. When he reached the northwestern corner of the park, he veered right, onto a snow-dusted pathway, and forged eastward. He ducked through a narrow passageway that led beneath a row of homes and bore him out onto Shepherdess Walk. Here, he stopped and listened intently. They were faint, but the echo of hurried footsteps scuffing across the park behind him was clear.

Inwardly, he grinned. *That's right. Don't lose me.*

Rainey hooked a left and pressed on across the footbridge to the north with the ice-cold ribbon of Regent's Canal stretching in either direction beneath him.

Sadiq was a pro when it came to street surveillance. It was a tricky and exhausting proposition to follow a target for a week with only a seven-man team and three vehicles at your disposal, yet with Allah's beneficence and eternal guidance he was confident they had pulled it off without being detected. This was nothing really. He had once tailed an Israeli spy for three weeks as the man met with his Lebanese agent in Asunción, Paraguay. And he had done so with two less men than he had here in London. When they were through, both the Israeli pig and the evil traitor were dead, and he and his team had disappeared into the ether without leaving so much as a trace of their existence.

There wasn't much that Sadiq hadn't seen thus far in his career, which is why he didn't fully understand what the target was doing now. From the information Nourani had sent him, Sadiq knew Durand to be smart, wealthy, and powerful—he'd seen it with his own two eyes all week long. The man had many contacts and seemed to be quite adept at making new ones rather quickly. He had witnessed Durand hob-knobbing at the expo during the day then conducting clandestine business meetings after hours, all having to do with things that were probably very illegal if he had to venture an educated guess. In Durand, he saw intelligence, guile, and decisiveness, and, based on the conversation he'd overheard via the bug his team had planted in the Frenchman's hotel suite early in the week, ruthlessness. They had captured Durand in a moment of fury ordering someone to be killed in a most gruesome manner and left sprawled out in the street in order to send a message to his competition.

Why then was Jean-Michel Durand out walking alone late at night in such a place as this? Was he suspicious of surveillance or just being cautious? The more Sadiq and his team followed him, the more he began to think that Durand was working his way toward meeting someone. He was *getting black* as they say in the trade. Making sure he was free of surveillance. He had seen better—and worse—from professional spies, but all in all, Durand's techniques and aptitude for the street were not bad for an international arms dealer.

He radioed Waleed and instructed him to back off a bit. The target was on the towpath, they could parallel him on the street above; he wasn't going anywhere. Sadiq had to remind his team only once during the week that they were just doing basic surveillance to see what Durand was up to in London and to determine if he was the man he seemed to be, and thus someone with whom their masters in southern Lebanon might consider doing business.

———

Rainey passed through the old redbrick archway beneath Wharf Road. There was a rumble of traffic above him as he peered along the far side of the canal for silhouettes among the shadows. Then silence. He waited a beat then ascended the brick-walled stairs to his right and darted into another pub, this one called The Narrowboat. He huddled close to the doorway, standing in a position that allowed him to watch the stairs and the street for movement. Upon seeing none in fifteen minutes' time, he exited the pub, retraced his steps down to the towpath, and continued in a westerly direction.

———

Sadiq keyed his radio. "Unit Three? Anything from your position?"

"No. Still inside the pub," said Bahat from the south side of the Wharf Road bridge. "Do you want me to go in after him?"

"Negative."

"Wait. I see him. He just came back outside. And… He's going back down to the canal."

"Which way is he headed?" said Sadiq in his native Arabic.

Bahat slowly peered over the brick wall. "West. I repeat. Target is headed west."

"Very good. Now stay put. Let me know if he resurfaces."

Bahat leaned into the wall. "Yes, sir. I will."

"Unit Four, start working your way to Colebrooke Row."

Waleed's voice came through his earpiece. "Copy that. Moving now."

Sadiq accelerated down Frome Street, crossed over to Burgh, and pulled against the curb just shy of Danbury. He immediately killed his headlights and turned to the man seated next to him—Uthman was his name. "Get down to the towpath and see what Durand is up to. If I'm right, he is meeting someone down there. See if you can snap a photo of whomever it is but only if you can do so safely. Now, go. And by all means, be careful."

Uthman dismounted and hurried toward the Danbury Street bridge. He wore a tracksuit, earbuds, and an iPhone strapped around his bicep. It was not uncommon to see runners moving about the city even at this late hour. The towpath was no different. It was why he had chosen such a wardrobe tonight. For the sake of making a fast change, as was often necessary on a surveillance operation, he kept a second running jacket in the boot of Sadiq's Volkswagen Golf along with a pair of orange New Balance sneakers that were drastically different in appearance than the green and silver ones with which he now pounded the pavement.

The second-born son of an English woman and her Lebanese businessman husband, Uthman was well acquainted with European customs. Two more things made Uthman extremely valuable as a member of Sadiq's surveillance team: one, he could speak the refined English of the educated elites—he had spent the bulk of his youth here in the city, even graduated from Kings College London with a degree in medicine before his Hezbollah recruitment; and two, he bore the White English facial features of his mother. All this and his genuine British passport meant that he could blend into any European city with zero difficulty. To top it off, he was a man who could think on his feet.

He now stood at the top of the ramp that led down to the towpath, hands pressed against the adjacent brick wall, ostensibly stretching his calves. After a minute or so, out of the corner of his right eye, he caught Durand walking, still westbound but now with a cell phone to his ear.

"Target is passing Danbury, still westbound," he whispered into his mic.

Sadiq's voice came back in his earbuds. "Copy."

Uthman forced himself to wait another twenty seconds in order to give the target some distance before setting off down the ramp in a light jog. When he reached the end of it, he slowed to a walk, pulling each leg up to stretch his quads between alternating steps. The towpath here was damp from an earlier snow shower that had quickly melted into the pavement. And dark. The ambient light from the city beyond the treetops created an annoying glare in the eyes. What resulted was a long dark shadow disjointed at various points due to the intermittent lamppost or the flush of light leaking through the pulled curtains of the houseboats moored along the canal.

Rolling his neck back and forth, he observed the target just now ducking under the redbrick archway in the distance ahead. Durand was suddenly out of sight as the bridge and the curve in the canal created a natural gap in his surveillance. Uthman walked softly to the archway, placed his hand against its rough, cold surface, and crouched down, but it was no use. He still couldn't see around the bend. And the path was narrow—there was no way he could maneuver to get a better view without falling into the canal.

Uthman quickly glanced back to the east, along the still, dark water of the canal and the path along its left flank. There was no one in sight. He decided to ease forward and follow Durand. As he cut around the blind corner, his eyes again found the target now some thirty meters farther down the towpath, cell phone still pressed to his ear.

In a flash, a pair of large hands lashed out, grabbed him off his feet, and swung him sideways into the brick wall. Before he knew what was happening, one of the powerful hands clamped down around his throat while the other smacked the earbuds from his ears.

If the man still walking along the canal would have stopped and turned, Uthman would have seen that despite being dressed in identical clothing and shoes as his target, the man was not Durand. For Jean-Michel Durand was now standing before him, his eyes dark and full of restrained fury.

51

Reagan Rainey stepped closer to the man as Babe stripped a semi-automatic pistol from his fanny pack and tossed it into the canal and did likewise to the cell phone strapped to his arm. The splash of the items caused ripples to radiate across the otherwise calm water. The surveillance man mounted a fruitless struggle while Babe also removed a small handheld radio from his waistband attached to which was a wired microphone. Babe tossed the items to the ground while continuing to hold the man's throat in his vice-like grip.

Rainey studied the man, the thick eyebrows, deep-set brown eyes, the pained grimace revealing rows of bad teeth as he tried in vain to draw in fresh oxygen. The man threw a string of impotent punches at Babe's midsection and tried to claw for the big man's eyes, all the while more desperation and urgency filled his senses. His resistance only caused Babe to pin him to the wall with more force. The big guy was well-known in the special operations world for his natural brute strength. This scrawny, little surveillance man was no match for him.

As the man labored to breathe, Rainey stepped closer and spoke calmly and directly in French-accented English, an edge of violence in his tone. "Why are you following me?"

Babe loosened his grip on the man's neck so that he could offer a response, which came out a pained hiss. "What?"

Babe looked over at Rainey, who nodded. Babe smiled then punched the interloper hard in the ribs, which probably cracked more than a couple.

"I'm going to ask you again and this time think *carefully* before you answer. Why are you and your friends following me?"

Again, Babe allowed the man to fill his lungs with enough oxygen to respond, which caused him to wheeze as pain from his broken ribs coursed through him. "I don't...know...what...you are...talking...about." The man's English was very good, with the type of accent you'd hear out of the mouth of a BBC news anchor.

Rainey took a deep breath as he picked up the man's radio. "Kill him quickly then toss him into the canal."

Babe wrapped his hands around the man's throat and began to squeeze. Uthman protested with a gurgled grunt. Rainey stared at him for a few seconds then calmly stretched out his hand—the universal signal for stop.

"Last chance, my friend."

"Yes! Yes. We are...following...you. I admit it." The man gasped for air.

"I know that. My question is *why*?" pressed Rainey, still glaring at him.

His voice was raspy now. "To see...if you...might be...worthy...of working...with us."

"Who is *us*?"

The man hesitated. "I'm not...at liberty...to say."

"Very well." Rainey looked at Babe, nodded.

Once Rainey, Babe, and Ignacio Delgado were safely in the back seat of the SUV and Fig was maneuvering them away from the area, Rainey keyed up the radio they had taken off the man in the tracksuit.

Again, he spoke in French-accented English. "Hello?" When no response immediately came, he repeated the greeting but this time with more agitation in his tone.

After a few seconds of silence came a man's voice. His English, too, was accented. "Who is this?"

"I could ask you the same question," said Rainey. "Are you the one in charge of the men following me?"

"What do you want?"

"I will take that as an affirmative response."

"Your man said something interesting before he was...put down."

"What are you saying?"

"I am saying I would like to propose a meeting. For tomorrow night."

"Where? When?"

"You will find the precise answers to those questions in the pocket of your friend's jacket, assuming you find *him*."

There was never a more pregnant silence.

"Come alone and come unarmed. I will be watching." Rainey clicked off the radio and tossed it out the window.

It was Waleed who finally found him. Uthman was propped up in a seated position supported by the corner of the brick wall that ran the length of the towpath. As it turned out, he was only unconscious, snoring softly like a drunkard who had drifted off to sleep after a long night of drinking. When Sadiq arrived, he ignored Uthman entirely save for the pockets of his tracksuit jacket. He rooted through them hurriedly. When he found what he was looking for, he stood and jammed it into his pants pocket without examining it, then ordered everyone to disappear as quietly and efficiently as possible. Go in separate directions, use utmost caution. Everyone would be out of the country by morning. Everyone minus Uthman, of course.

When the others were out of sight, Sadiq drew his Eickhorn Bellator TAC G10 German Tactical Knife from the Kydex scabbard he kept in a horizontal carry position at the small of his back and plunged it into Uthman's heart. Using the dead man's pant leg, he wiped the blood from the blade and secured it back in its sheath. The man's death would be chalked up to a robbery gone bad and doubtless be counted among the other unsolved murders that accumulate in London each year.

Uthman had been a good soldier for a long time. But if there was one thing Sadiq and his masters in Lebanon could not stomach, it was failure.

The subsequent surveillance detection run to Southampton took him three hours. There, Sadiq took a bus north to Calmore then boarded a southbound train to Cosham. He walked for thirty minutes more, constantly checking mirrors and windows for a tail. Certain he was free of coverage, Sadiq hailed a taxi to Portsmouth and bought a ticket for the ferry to Cherbourg.

He was exhausted. His mind spun as he considered what had happened in London. Durand had led them into a trap. He had *made* them. But when? Sadiq and his people were well-trained. Somehow one of them must have made a mistake, a small blunder that tipped Durand off to the surveillance on him. The man was good. That much could be said of him.

The motel in Valognes was dingy and dark. If not for the fact that he was operational, Sadiq would have never set foot in a place like this. Once in his room, he locked the door, walked to the bed, and sat down. The mattress was spongy, its covering smelled of body fluids and stale alcohol. Finally, he reached inside his jacket pocket and removed the item he had found on Uthman. It was a leaflet for the Heritage Trail at Tower Hamlets Cemetery Park. Inside the fold was an illustrated map, on which Durand had delineated various points of interest along the trail. Marker five was circled with the time of 11:45 p.m. scribbled in the margin. He examined the rest of the tri-fold pamphlet and found nothing of note.

Sadiq let a long breath flow from his lungs as he sized up the man in the small mirror above the particle-board dresser across from him. He studied the man's dark eyes, the hard features of his face, the wrinkles in his forehead. This was a decision for Nourani.

He tapped a text message into his secure mobile phone and waited for a reply.

52

In the moments after Sadiq and the others had found their comrade along the canal, they executed a series of maneuvers that stripped themselves of any possible surveillance. What resulted was the Jaguar team losing the eye on Sadiq. Even Mark Alcott could not maintain coverage without jeopardizing his safety. Thus, Sadiq and his men disappeared into the ether. There had been some rather heated discussions between Job and the director back at CIA headquarters in Langley about carrying on with Rainey's proposed meeting. Headquarters was growing increasingly cautious about Operation End of Days. Primarily, they didn't want a flap with their international partners, which was keenly possible in that the Jaguar team was now operating on British soil without the knowledge or permission of His Majesty's Government. Moreover, in light of what had occurred last night along the banks of Regent's Canal, some thought it much too dangerous to continue on. In the end, though, Job prevailed.

The meeting was on.

———

The site of the proposed meeting was by a round, metal trail marker—marker five, to be precise—on the Heritage Trail inside the Tower Hamlets Cemetery Park. At this time of night, the historic, wooded park in the

East End of London was a dark, desolate place. Rainey imagined the grim, macabre setting looked very much the same as it had in Jack the Ripper's time. Incidentally, Whitechapel, where the Ripper had done most of his killing, was only a stone's throw away.

Rainey stood next to a moss-covered headstone, at a spot in the center of the park where four paths converged. He reached out and touched it with his bare hand. It was much too dark to read the name on the stone, but from the feel of its weather-worn surface, he figured it had been here for a hundred years or more. The big shadowy figure standing next to him studied the darkness in the opposite direction. Together, they had 360-degree coverage of the meeting location.

"You think he'll show?" whispered Babe without taking his eyes off his area of responsibility.

His pupils wide, Rainey stared into the blackness. A slight breeze stirred, allowing tiny pinpricks of city light to filter through the trees. "To be honest, I'm not sure. I'd say the chances are eighty/twenty he does not."

The rest of the Jaguar team were spread out all over the park with orders to watch for and report any signs of Sadiq or his cohorts. So far, there had not been a peep from anyone save for Mouse. Ten minutes previous, while crouched amidst the dead vines and scrub brush near the Bear Monument, he'd thought he heard someone approaching, which he promptly reported over the secure radio net. It turned out to be just a noisy little raccoon out on the prowl.

At fifteen minutes past the time of the meeting, there was still no indication that Sadiq was going to show. It was the same story at thirty minutes on and again at forty-five, yet they held their positions in the chilly darkness. As 1:00 a.m. approached, Rainey saw a raccoon scurrying through the forest, completely unaware of his presence. He absently wondered if it was the same one Mouse had seen earlier.

By 1:15, it was quite obvious that no one was coming. Five minutes later he gave the order to terminate, and they quickly broke down their posts and slipped out of the park unseen. To everyone but Rainey, it meant that the operation may be over, Sadiq and his Hezbollah masters had been scared off. They would go elsewhere for their illegal arms; Jean-Michel Durand was too dangerous, too unpredictable. Or perhaps too suspicious. And yet for some reason, Rainey held to his gut instinct: Hezbollah was not finished with Monsieur Durand. They *would* come. But the approach would be on their terms. He just had to stay ready for when it came.

53

The safe house in Bromley lay along Mavelstone Road beyond a wooden fence and a tall hedge. Due west was a cricket club of notable acclaim, to the east a distinguished academy school for girls. A sturdy wooden gate painted bright white separated the driveway from the street. Ivy climbed high up the left side of the white brick building and over the pickle-green door. Several of its strands were expeditiously forging onward across the rest of the home's facade.

As it turned out, Rainey and his Jaguar teammates didn't need to wait long for the approach from Hezbollah, though it was a careful and furtive one, all things considered. Thirty-six hours after they'd been stood up by Sadiq in the cemetery park in London, a curious email landed in Monsieur Durand's private inbox. Only one person on the planet was privy to the existence of this particular Dynamic Prime Solutions-registered email account: Erik Walser, the Hezbollah banker in Vaduz. Clearly, he had shared it with his masters in Lebanon.

On Rainey's orders, Brigid forwarded the email via secure link to DX headquarters in Arlington. A response came back from Job a short time later with a message to proceed.

Rainey now scrutinized the decrypted message with Evelina seated next to him, their shoulders touching, behind a desk in the nicely appointed office on the second floor of the safe house. He could feel the heat of her body as he read the email for the twelfth time; interestingly, it had been composed entirely in French.

```
To: JMD@dpsc1.com
From: wa435900@kvr-secure.com
Subject: Request for Product Catalog

Greetings, Monsieur Durand. My name
is William. I have heard good things
about your company. Would you kindly
provide a product catalog of DPSC's
current offerings and services. Re-
quests for quotes to follow upon re-
ceipt of your catalog.

Thank you.


Respectfully,


William Asada
KVR Group
Radnička cesta 39
4 KAT
10000, Zagreb, Croatia
```

"What do you think?" said Rainey.

Evelina squinted into the screen. "The email is cordial and direct and intimates a future business relationship. The fact that it is written in French means that the email was sent by someone who has some amount of knowledge of Jean-Michel Durand. The mention of a product catalog reveals he is aware of Durand's industry." The antique wooden chair in which she sat creaked as she leaned backward. "The sender is also exercising a healthy measure of discretion. This *Mr. Asada* is not playing his hand quite yet. Bottom line: Someone is interested in taking the next step with you."

Rainey turned toward her, which caused her to respond in kind. Evelina's endless sea-green eyes met his. She blushed ever so slightly and there was a brief and somewhat awkward pause between them over her choice of words.

"Hezbollah, Ray. Hezboll*ah* is interested in taking the next step with you. Durand, I mean. Not *you*." A bead of perspiration glistened along her hairline.

It was the first time he had ever seen her flustered. Rainey finally let her off the hook by dryly stating, "That's what I thought." He smiled, satisfied in his ability to bait her. It was immature, sure, but sometimes the operator in him just couldn't help himself.

Evelina looped a strand of her blond hair behind her ear and smirked at his clumsy attempt at humor. It was operator stuff, of course. They were always making jokes. In truth, she liked him, liked all of her Jaguar teammates, in fact. She and Maddie were already the best of friends—they had met several months ago while working on an unrelated operation—but there was just something about Reagan. The thing that tickled her most about him was his mischievous smile, the way it complemented his dry wit and calm, confident bearing. The fact that he was intelligent, ruggedly handsome, and had eyes of melted chocolate didn't hurt either. She wasn't exactly sure what was happening between them, but whatever it was she liked it.

She offered to fetch them both a cup of hot tea then stood for a moment inside the doorway, silently watching him from behind. He cut quite the profile there in the glow of the afternoon sun, its rays streaming through the louvered windows and lashing across his features. He reminded her of a footballer in his prime, which was not entirely off the mark. Maddie had told her once that Reagan had been something of a phenom during his university days. He still had the build of a star athlete. Yet his arms were thicker than a footballer's, his shoulders, too. She noticed his triceps flexing and bulging as he adjusted his frame in the desk chair. They might as well have been shaped with a carpenter's chisel. And his hands. His hands were sun-tanned and powerful, those of someone familiar with physical labor and accustomed to spending long hours outdoors. The temporary operational tattoos on his arms and the webbing of the back of his left hand only added to his mystique. Whether Reagan Rainey or Jean-Michel Durand, he was a dangerous man and fully looked the part. She suddenly realized he was gazing up at her. She did not turn away.

"Did you say something?" he offered with a guileless smile.

She managed to salvage her embarrassment by quickly saying, "Cream, sugar?"

"A pinch of sugar. No cream."

When she returned with the tea and her senses, they set about crafting a response to Mr. Asada. Rainey had half of it written inside five minutes. In thirty minutes more, after careful inspection by Pietrolaj's discerning eye, they settled on their final draft. Rainey then had Brigid run it by Job back in Arlington. He messaged back his approval almost immediately with one simple rider: `Give it another six hours then send the reply. After all, Durand is a busy man.`

54

Their message landed in the secure servers of KVR Group, a conglomerate of companies based in Zagreb, Croatia and entirely under the control of Hezbollah, where it remained until a representative of KVR Holding Company—a full-fledged Hezbollah operative—forwarded it onward the next morning via secure channel to a non-descript law office in Beirut. Like Herr Walser's message from Liechtenstein, the email was printed out and couriered to Jawdat Shukri, who read it without emotion then walked it down the corridor of the hardened underground bunker to Nourani. The operational leader of Hezbollah's Unit 910 studied it intensely for several minutes. He offered no comment, made no facial expression that might betray his inner thoughts. Finally, after a moment of additional deliberation, he removed his reading glasses and passed the printed email back to his lieutenant.

"I want to speak with Turaj."

"Yes, sir. I will summon him at once."

Three and a half hours later, a man of medium height with a trimmed gray-white beard and bald head appeared before him. Except for a pair of inscrutable black eyes, the man's face bore no remarkable features and could reasonably be described as docile. His sixty-some-odd-year frame was healthy, his posture confident yet reserved. He wore plain black, single-pleat-ed slacks, and a crisp white dress shirt sans necktie, which aided in his portrayal of casual professionalism. Though he could have easily passed for an academic, an engineer, or even a mid-level statesman, Turaj Mahfouz was none of those things. For he was the head of Hezbollah's procurement efforts. What's more, he was the author of the email that had been sent to Jean-Michel Durand.

Nourani held out the paper containing the Durand email. "What do you make of the Frenchman's response?"

Mahfouz appraised the email again thoughtfully while Shukri eyed him with borderline contempt. Clearly, Durand had forwarded Mahfouz's orig-inal email to someone named AJ, probably an administrative staff person. The contents of the original email were at the bottom of the page. Mahfouz focused on the reply, reading each word again carefully, all the while ignoring Nourani's penetrating gaze.

```
To: wa435900@kvr-secure.com
From: AJJ@dpsc1.com
Subject: Re: Request for Product
Catalog


Mr. Asada,


I am not sure who you are or how you
have come to know of our company. In
any case, we are a private enterprise
and conduct our business with utmost
discretion. Therefore, at this time we
cannot offer more information, e.g.,
```

a product catalog, without knowing more about you and KVR. If you wish to learn more about, as you say, our "current offerings and services," please consider making an appointment with one of our representatives so they can assist you further. For your convenience, I have included the contact information for our sales team. Team members are standing by 24/7/365 and will be happy to direct you to the appropriate regional sales representative to schedule an appointment.

Good day and best wishes.

Annika "AJ" Johansen
Dynamic Prime Solutions Corporation

Mahfouz looked up with thoughtful concern. "I think we need to be cautious."

"Jawdat thinks we should proceed."

Mahfouz pondered Nourani's play. The commander of Unit 910 was notorious for pitting his subordinates against one another. "Though what we've heard about Durand thus far has been positive and may well have great potential for the cause, it would only be prudent to learn *more* about him before we jump into bed with him. It could well be a Zionist plot. We all have seen firsthand what happens when we act injudiciously."

"Please," said Shukri, shaking his head. "Forgive me, sir. But I believe Turaj is being obtuse and un*duly* cautious. In my humble assessment, Durand is a gift to us. In the absence of the American Stedman Carter's business and the recent loss of our weapons stockpiles, I strongly feel that the Frenchman should be pursued diligently. All due respect, Tehran would agree, sir. Durand clearly has good connections. And he has already demonstrated to us his facility for calculation and operational security. The fact that he detected Sadiq's surveillance team shows that he is highly capable. I see that as a sign of good things to come."

"Capable of what?" said Mahfouz in a calm, nonthreatening manner. "We know nothing of his actual industry, his business dealings, clientele past or present, or what he can offer us. In truth, we don't know much about *him*, which is why I would advise having someone meet with him or his sales representative to have a very direct and candid conversation. Only then will we be able to begin a proper vetting of the man."

Nourani stroked his beard, his calculating eyes shifting back and forth between Mahfouz and Shukri. Finally, they settled on his procurement chief. "I agree with you, Turaj. So, go. Meet with him. See what he has to say."

"*Me*? I'm a procurement specialist, sir. I'm not a field agent. I'm used to emails and faxes."

Nourani offered a slight grin. "Don't worry, Turaj. You will be fine. No one is better suited to conduct such a meeting. You're the expert. You know the materiel we are interested in acquiring as much as anyone in this room. What's more, it is Allah's will that you go."

Mahfouz finally bowed his head. "Then Inshallah, I will go."

55

BROMLEY, UK

Huddled in the safe house in Mavelstone Road, the Jaguar team labored to pass the time as they waited for a response to the email that had been sent to William Asada of KVR Group at 39 Workers' Road, 4th Floor in Zagreb, Croatia.

Tonka stirred logs in the fireplace as Mouse, looking on, tugged at a large strip of beef jerky with his teeth. Fig and Babe, Monsieur Durand's security detail, were engaged in a spirited exercise regimen in the basement. Sounds of their workout playlist, clanging barbells, and lively operator trash-talking were muted, only slightly, by the thick wooden floorboards.

Meanwhile, Conrad Pietrolaj, in consultation with Job and some analysts back in Arlington via satellite link, was putting the finishing touches on the digital portfolio that would serve as Durand's product catalog. It had been Pietrolaj's idea early on to do so. After all, Durand was an arms dealer. He must have some way of showcasing his wares to prospective buyers. In the time since the team had met in Suite 922, with Pietrolaj's urging and specific instructions, Job had tasked a group of DX analysts to do just that. Now, it was nearly complete.

Incidentally, the bulk of the items listed in the catalog were those that the FBI had seized from Stedman Carter-owned properties at home and abroad. About twenty percent of the haul was currently collecting dust in a secure warehouse at Marine Corps Base Quantico. The remainder was under tight security at various points around the globe, where it would stay until the FBI and its international partners could figure out what to do with it all. It was not hyperbole to say that Carter's inventory could equip the armed forces of a medium-size country.

Come morning, tired of being cooped up, Rainey pulled on his parka and made for the door. Passing Evelina, who was seated at the dining room table behind her open laptop computer, he said, "I'm going for a walk. Care to join me?"

"Sure. I was just about finished with my report anyway." Evelina tapped out a few more keystrokes and clicked her laptop shut. "I'll get my coat."

Once outside, they turned right, keeping to the sidewalk, which followed the gentle downward slope of the road. The neighborhood was quiet and inviting with attractive wooded lots and homes that offered seclusion without being misanthropic. What would be a leafy preserve in springtime and summer, now stood cold and barren as if winter had strangled the life right out of her.

"I will never get used to the waiting," said Evelina. She wore a beige, knee-length Box-Quilt Down Puffer Coat, black leggings, and a hunter-green knitted headband with a tiny hole at the back through which her blond ponytail bobbed as she walked.

"Like Pappy always says: 'Spying is waiting.'"

"John le Carré, too. *The Russia House.*"

Rainey offered a knowing smile. "Wonder who said it first." Several paces later, in a conspiratorial tone, he added, "I hate it, too."

She grinned, eyes sparkling like emeralds in the morning sunlight. "Why exactly do they call him Pappy?"

Hands shoved into his coat pockets, Rainey studied the landscape while pondering the question. Finally, he said, "I'm not really sure, but it suits him.

Don't you think? Truth be told, I'm pretty sure he likes it. For me personally, he's kind of like the grandfather I never had."

Evelina glanced at him introspectively. "Maddie told me your grandfather—your father's father, that is, Patrick Rainey—was some kind of war hero."

A goldcrest leapt from the branch of a fern spilling over the brick wall beside them. Rainey's eyes continued scanning with practiced subtlety. "He was a sergeant major in the Army, served in a special unit called the MACV-SOG. He was killed during the Vietnam War when my father was just a boy." It wasn't until they had hooked left onto Hill Brow that Rainey spoke again, his breath visible with each word. "I never knew him obviously, but some of the old-timers have told me stories about him. He was *special*, they always say. A warrior's warrior. And a true patriot."

"Like you," Evelina offered with sincerity. Several seconds passed. "Is that why you joined the military?"

Rainey shrugged. He eschewed talking about himself. It always made him uncomfortable to do so. Perhaps it was due to his years of clandestine work in special operations and now with the CIA. Or maybe it was just his nature. Whatever the reason, he deflected the question. "So how did *you* wind up in this business?"

"I suppose it began with *my* grandfather." Evelina told him the story of how, in 1941, after word spread of the first wave of killings perpetrated by Hitler's *Einsatzgruppen*, her grandfather's parents and grandparents had fled with him and his older sister east from Ukraine into Russia where relatives lived. "They thought they had reached safety in Pochep, but in the spring of 1942, they were arrested by a Nazi patrol. Somehow my great-great aunt and uncle managed to escape with my grandfather—he was only seven at the time. The rest of the family was murdered...there in Pochep." She was quiet for a moment, as was Rainey. "In August 1952, fearing Stalin's growing anti-Semitism, my great-great aunt and uncle left the USSR for good, taking my grandfather with them. They arrived in Israel in early October of that year."

The more she talked the more Rainey detected the slightest hint of an accent. He quickly reminded himself of her Icelandic heritage. She was no longer guarded or thinking of the consequences of telling her story, her *real* story, much as it was in direct conflict with the nature of being a spy. He felt himself being drawn to her as if by a strong magnetic force. He spoke not a word, recognizing that she would continue when she was good and ready.

"My grandfather was a smart man, attended Hebrew University of Jerusalem, graduating at the top of his class. After school, he joined the IDF and was quickly recruited by Aman, Israeli military intelligence. His first overseas posting was in Copenhagen. There, he met my grandmother—she was a medical student at the time. They fell in love and briefly lived in Denmark. They moved back to Israel after my grandfather's term in Copenhagen was up. About a year or so later, they picked up again and moved to Iceland due to my grandfather's work. He was posted to Reykjavík, from which he ran counterintelligence operations across the whole of Scandinavia. His job was to hunt spies that threatened the security of NATO on behalf of Israel."

"I couldn't help noticing that you spoke of your grandfather in the past tense. Is he...?"

Evelina nodded reflectively. "Lung cancer. He'll be gone five years this April."

"I'm sorry."

"Thanks. He had a good, long life. A happy life. I miss him though. He told the best stories."

They walked contemplatively for half a block more before Rainey finally said, "You still haven't answered my question."

"I'm getting to it," she said with feigned admonishment. "All the way through school, I thought I would be a professional football player. I thought that's what I wanted."

"Wait. You played soccer, too?"

"We call it football in Iceland."

"Of course. Were you any good?"

She smiled as if withholding a great secret. "I was on the U-17 and U-19 national teams. You can look it up if you wish."

Rainey felt himself being drawn to her even more now. "So, you weren't just *good*. You were *exceptional*." He returned her smile. "What changed your mind about playing?"

"Around the beginning of my last year of high school, I started thinking about serving in the IDF. My father had done so after all."

"Your dad was in the IDF?"

"Mmm hmm. Unit 8200, in fact."

"So, he's a tech guy?"

"Yep. Has his own computer firm now. Does cybersecurity, web design, that type of thing. Anyway, my desire to serve grew stronger and stronger. I realized I needed to do my duty to protect my family's homeland. *If not me, then who?* I would always ask myself.

"So, after school, I flew to Israel and joined. I served two years in military intelligence: the Nachshol Reconnaissance Company. It's a select, all-female unit." She gazed into the distance as if recalling a fond memory. "I would do it again, too, in a heartbeat. I loved working with those girls. We had some real tough firecrackers in that unit."

"You gave up soccer then?"

"For something far better. In any case, after returning to Iceland, I tore my knee up in a training session. Rehab was rigorous and I made a full recovery, but I had lost my window to play professionally. Which in the big picture of life was fine by me. I still love the game, but I now see that I would have never been truly happy playing professional football. There are so many other things far more important to me.

"So, I got my degree in the States during which time I was apparently being watched by Job and his people. He approached me with an invitation to work for the DX upon graduation, and I jumped on it."

Rainey shook his head in wonder. "I said it once before, Evie. You are full of surprises." Just then his phone buzzed inside his pocket. It was a text message from Maddie. Tapping out a reply, he said to Evelina, "It's Asada. He wants to meet. In Oslo."

56

By the time they had returned, the house was considerably less noisy, perhaps because Job had already ordered Alcott and some of the others to fly to Norway, where they would begin advance work—liaising with Oslo Station, renting cars, scouting hotels, mapping out SDRs, infil and exfil routes—in preparation of the meeting with William Asada of KVR Group, Zagreb, Croatia. The DX analysts back in Arlington had correctly assessed him to be a high-ranking Hezbollah official and KVR Group an obvious Hezbollah front.

Those who remained were now packing their things. They would deploy forward to Olso, too, and like their teammates who preceded them would take separate flights to the city. Rainey's route to the Norwegian capital took him through Stockholm. When he arrived at Oslo Airport, he found a bored-faced man who looked to be of Hispanic or perhaps Middle Eastern descent—Angel Figueroa—waiting for him outside the terminal in a dark blue Audi Q7.

Fig drove in a manner that would expose any surveillance on their tail. When they were sure they were clean, Fig delivered Rainey, a carry-on bag and a small suitcase in either hand, to the front entrance of the Hotel Bristol then promptly pulled away.

At check-in, Rainey mentioned with a German accent—in order to match his false German passport—that he was an author and wished not to be disturbed during his lodging. He was facing a tight deadline and needed absolute peace and quiet. The clerk made a note in the computer, nodded, and wished him a good stay in Oslo.

When Rainey reached his room, he secured the door and immediately messaged the others. He would supervise the operation from here. Monsieur Durand would not be attending the meeting with Asada. Instead, Conrad Pietrolaj, acting as Durand's European sales representative, would do the honors.

———

At the precise moment Rainey was standing at the front desk at the Hotel Bristol, Job Jackson was checking in with Peer Holberg, head of the counterintelligence unit within Norway's *Politiets Sikkerhetstjeneste*, or PST, an agency comparable to America's FBI and Britain's MI5. Attributable to several high-profile successes, thanks in part to the CIA's Directorate X and Job in particular, Holberg was a man on the rise in his country's Police Security Service. He was also a personal friend of the DX chief.

Holberg's house was a red wooden number on Borgenveien. A plow truck had recently come through the narrow single-lane street. High mounds of snow transformed the road into a kind of deep trench with labyrinthine paths shooting this way and that to the various homes and streets throughout the neighborhood. Zane, Job's bodyguard, pulled the black GMC Yukon into the small car park in front of Holberg's house. Job alighted from the back of the vehicle and hurried to the front door. He knocked and then turned to watch Zane reverse the SUV and disappear back into the snow-packed maze. The security man would remain close by should he be needed.

Holberg led Job from the foyer past the open-hearth stone fireplace and into his den. Before the men were seated, Holberg's wife Vilde appeared with a welcoming smile. She hugged the American and offered to bring both men coffee and cakes.

"How are the little ones?" Peer and Vilde had two boys, Magnus, seven, who looked very much like his father, and, Olav, two years his junior, who had the blond hair and glacial blue eyes of his mother. Both were developing interests in cross-country skiing after their parents, said Holberg. They also both liked to wrestle. Job recalled the last time he was in town. The boys were thumping around so loudly upstairs that he thought they were going to bring down the whole house.

"They are getting bigger by the second," added Vilde with her world-class smile. "There is scarcely a time when they are *not* eating. We have trouble keeping the cupboards stocked. Between Peer and the boys, I find myself running to the market nearly every day."

After some more small talk, Holberg glanced at Vilde who knowingly excused herself from the room. He closed the door of the den and gazed at his American friend. "So, what is it that has brought you to Oslo this time? You said on the phone that it was a matter of some urgency."

"A member of Hezbollah is coming here for a meeting. We'd like you to help us watch him while he's on your turf." Job probed the chocolate treats in the dish on the end table beside him. Finding one he liked, he stripped off the foil and popped it into his mouth.

Holberg's head tilted a few degrees to the left. He was a savvy veteran intelligence officer and was good at connecting dots. "Would this have anything to do with the attack in America?"

Job answered with silence.

"Do you expect there to be trouble *here*?"

"We are meeting with someone. That's it. We have no intelligence to suggest that there is anything planned that involves Norway or its citizens."

"Then why bring him here?" said Holberg.

"Because I know I can trust you and your service." Job made no mention of the balance sheet that represented their cooperative past. In fairness, it was getting pretty one-sided. And Holberg knew it. Most recently, Job had helped root out a Russian spy and a three-person team of illegals who had been operating in Oslo. It was an operation for which Holberg received a lot of credit within the realm of clandestine agencies, and a quick promotion to boot.

"Who is he?"

"We only know him by the name he's been using in his communications: William Asada. It's almost certainly an alias as is the business from which he purports to be working." Job told him about KVR Group. Analysts back at DX headquarters had learned that KVR had several subsidiaries throughout Europe. "We assume he won't be traveling alone." Job produced several photos of Sadiq Ammar al-Hamadeh and the members of his team as they followed Rainey around London. He mentioned that one of them had been found dead after Rainey, posing as Monsieur Jean-Michel Durand, had confronted him.

"Durand, the *arms* dealer? We've heard whispers recently about him from some of our liaison officers in Europe. He's one of yours?"

Job smiled. "One of our best and brightest."

"Where is the meeting to occur?"

"The Hotel Continental."

"When?"

"Thursday. Three o'clock."

"And the topicality of the meeting?"

"Asada is coming here to discuss the nature of Durand's business, perhaps foster a relationship."

"Which is?" said Holberg knowingly.

"Weapons. Armaments. Military technology. You name it. You are correct to assume that this has to do with the attack in America, Peer, because it does."

The PST man nodded. "Then we will do whatever we can to help."

"Thank you, my friend. And please, not a word about Durand's true identity to anyone. The operation depends on it."

"I understand completely."

———

Following his meeting with Peer Holberg, Job slipped into the American Embassy and fully briefed the Oslo station chief, then, after a bit of dry cleaning to be sure he was free of surveillance, he popped into the Hotel Bristol and went directly to Room 41. There, he found Rainey and Conrad Pietrolaj studying the DPSC digital product catalog and going over contingencies concerning the Asada meeting.

"PST is on board. They are going to alert us the moment Asada clears passport control. Assuming he is flying on that name," Job said.

Rainey patted Pietrolaj on the back. "Great. Macho, here, is all set."

57

The next day, William Asada arrived on Lufthansa Flight 110 direct from Zagreb. According to the PST watchers, he cleared passport control at precisely 1732 hours and made a somewhat zigzagged route through the flowing current of fellow travelers. He had clearly never been to this airport before as evidenced by the way he searched out the signage. Though he knew it not, his photo was snapped a total of 37 times as he marched through the arrivals hall and later stood in the queue to board the train to the city center. Video footage, recorded by Holberg's people and beamed via secure link directly to Rainey's laptop computer in Room 41 in the Hotel Bristol, revealed a man of medium height and build in his early to mid-sixties. He wore a charcoal-colored fedora, coal-black, single-pleated slacks, and an open-necked white dress shirt. A heavy woolen overcoat was slung over his bent left arm. With his right arm extended backward, he towed a suitcase on wheels as he walked. He could have been a physics professor or one who sells insurance door-to-door.

Rainey studied several of the still images taken by the PST surveillance teams. One in particular showed Asada after having just removed his hat to dab his brow with a handkerchief. Switching camera feeds, Rainey watched Asada disappear through the door of the train bound for the city center. Several seconds passed and another man slipped into the carriage—Mark Alcott, a carry-on bag looped over his shoulder, a map of Norway in his hand.

He had been loitering inside the duty-free shop as Asada paraded past. Now as the doors of the train closed behind him, Rainey fired a secure text alert to his Jaguar teammates that included a clear photo of their target's face. Then another to the operations center in the bowels of DX headquarters, which, in turn, was shared with Israel's Mossad and Britain's MI6. The Israelis responded first and did so with some amount of urgency. The man in the photo—William Asada of KVR Group, Zagreb, Croatia—was none other than Turaj Mahfouz, head of Hezbollah's procurement department.

Rainey read the news then glanced up at Job and Pietrolaj. "We've hooked a big one, fellas."

"That was the plan," said Job with a mirthless smile. "The trick now is not letting him get away."

Mahfouz exited the train and walked toward the street in search of a taxi. For someone accustomed to the mild temperatures of Lebanon, the cold was excruciating. He shivered beneath his woolen overcoat until he finally caught the attention of a man driving a small BMW SUV with *Oslo Taxi* in large block letters on the side. He waited as the driver made a U-turn and negotiated the vehicle to the curb. By then all the feeling in his face and toes had vanished. He could scarcely move his lips when the man asked him for his destination. "The Thon Hotel Vika Atrium," he said, though due to the frozen muscles in his face, he wasn't sure it had come out right, so he said it again, this time louder and more pronounced.

After check-in, Mahfouz stowed his things in his colorful, fifth-floor room and wandered down to the street. Five minutes later, on the recommendation of the woman behind the hotel's front desk, he was walking into the Lofoten Fiskerestaurant. No, he did not have a reservation, he told the slight Nordic blond who greeted him. Thankfully, he did not have to wait long to be seated. His table was set against a wall of windows that offered an agreeable view of the harbor. As he gazed toward the boats docked outside the window, a handsome couple passed behind him and sat down—the man with his back to him, the woman seated across the table. Refocusing his eyes, Mahfouz caught their reflection in the window. For several long seconds, he fretted that they might be intelligence officers and were on to him, knew he was Hezbollah and why he was in Norway. But his anxiety melted away the moment the woman's face lit up with laughter—the dark-haired man with whom she was dining must have said something funny. In Russian, if he was not mistaken. She was far too beautiful to be a spy anyway, he told himself.

Relax, Turaj. Breathe.

Maddie and one of Holberg's men, who it turned out spoke Russian, too, watched him order wine and dine on lobster then indulge in something that looked very much like chocolate cake. At no time during their vigil did Turaj Mahfouz, aka William Asada, speak to or signal anyone—though a signal could be anything, thus this point was very hard to be sure of—or even check his phone for messages, emails, or missed calls. For all intents and purposes, it seemed that Mahfouz was alone in Oslo and that there was no place in the world he would rather be.

Their surveillance that night turned up nothing. The same was true the next day. At the appointed time, they watched him enter the Hotel Continental and disappear behind an elevator door.

58

The operational recording would later document that the knock on the door came precisely at 3:00 p.m. and that it was administered just as prescribed in the previous email correspondence. Pietrolaj rose from the desk chair and padded to the door, contented by the fact that the room was wired for audio and video, the feed streaming live to Room 41 in the Hotel Bristol a few blocks away. For the sake of Pietrolaj's safety and the operation's overall security, a contingent of Jaguar team shooters was deployed across the hall and ready for anything. Another consisting of PST officers was farther down the corridor. But no one would make a move unless Rainey gave the order or they heard the unmistakable sound of gunfire.

Pietrolaj spoke first. "Mr. Asada. Welcome. I'm Aleksy. Please come in." It had been Pietrolaj's idea to speak in an accent from his family's native Poland in order to further obfuscate his American affiliation.

On the monitor, Rainey saw the man outside the door walk toward the camera and shake Pietrolaj's hand.

"Thank you for agreeing to meet with me."

"By all means. I trust your travels were uneventful," said Pietrolaj, which translated in the parlance of underworld operatives meant: You weren't followed?

Mahfouz understood immediately. "Yes, thank you. The trip was a pleasant one. No issues."

"Can I offer you a drink?"

"No, thank you."

Pietrolaj poured himself a scotch from a service tray on the dresser and motioned toward a table in the center of the room. Mahfouz shed his woolen coat and draped it over an empty chair then took a seat across from the DX man. With legs crossed and hands folded in his lap, Mahfouz focused his attention on the face of the Dynamic Prime Solutions Corporation's European sales representative.

"So. You are interested in DPSC?"

"That depends."

"You'll have to forgive me, I don't understand."

Mahfouz's face was expressionless.

Pietrolaj sipped his drink. Mahfouz would not be drawn out easily. "You are certainly not government."

"No."

"Then who?" said Pietrolaj.

Mahfouz offered a glimmer of a smile. "I work for someone who might be interested in the services you provide."

"And what services might they be?" said Pietrolaj taking a leisurely sip. He was prepared for this careful dance.

"Come now, Mr...?"

"Nowak. But please, call me Aleksy."

"Come now, Mr. Nowak. If we are being honest with each other... I know that you deal in arms."

Pietrolaj's eyes narrowed as if he were considering something of utmost importance. Mahfouz was going to be a tough negotiator. "As you say, if we are being honest with each other, for whom exactly is it that you work?"

"An organization based in the Middle East."

"The Middle East. That's not very specific."

"Lebanon," said Mahfouz without enthusiasm.

"Hezbollah?"

Mahfouz did not deny it. "There are people in my organization who would like to know more about you and your specific offerings before any business arrangements can be formalized."

"The feeling is mutual, I'm sure."

Mahfouz began to bounce his knee. "Your boss, Durand, I have it on good authority that he is looking to expand his portfolio. The people I represent might be willing to help in that regard. We would like to know if he is someone with whom we can do business. But, as it stands right now, we have no idea if what he has to offer would be of any benefit to us."

"Just what exactly are you seeking?"

"That depends on what Monsieur Durand has to offer."

Now we get to it, thought Pietrolaj, smiling. "You requested a product catalog." He held up a thumb drive. "Please, feel free to peruse it now if you wish—you may use my laptop over there—or you can take it with you. The drive, not the laptop," he said with a grin. "The drive is locked, therefore, you will need the unlock code in order to read the files contained thereon.

"I should add that if there is something in particular your organization desires, something that you don't see in our product catalog, please don't hesitate to say so. We have a number of methods and resources at our disposal, and if the price is right, we can see about making the appropriate accommodations to locate what you are in the market for."

Mahfouz slipped the drive into his pocket.

"For security reasons, I must ask that you not write down the code or save it to any electronic device. The code begins with '77jVX&.' The remaining digits you will find match the ISBN number for this book." Pietrolaj slid a book about Scandinavian architecture across the table and told Mahfouz where he could find the ISBN. "Be careful though. If you enter the wrong code three times in a row, the drive will execute a command and wipe itself clean. Thus, everything will be lost."

The Hezbollah man studied the glossy book cover for a few seconds then nodded. "And if I wish to send you an RFQ for a particular item, how do I reach you directly?" RFQ stood for *request for quote*.

Pietrolaj handed him a business card. It was all very professional. "Send an email to me at this address—it's totally secure. All RFQs will ultimately be passed along to my boss."

"Durand."

Pietrolaj nodded. "He will personally review the list of any items in which you are interested. Assuming an agreement on a price can be realized, he will proceed from there. Generally, he meets with buyers—especially any first-time clients—before a contract is finalized. At that time, he will discuss payment options and any additional concerns, for example, if you would have any specific transshipping requirements, et cetera."

Rainey focused on the screen of the laptop with an intense gaze with Job doing likewise over his shoulder. Together they scrutinized Mahfouz's every word, every facial expression. They were embarking on a dangerous phase of the operation. They were exposing themselves to the likes of Hezbollah. There was no turning back now. Every move had to be calculated with utmost precision. One false step and the whole operation could come crashing down, not to mention get people hurt.

"Tell the teams already in place to stand fast. The others I want to back out of the area," said Job. "I don't want him getting spooked now that we have made contact. Let him run."

Rainey typed the message into his secure mobile phone and alerted the teams accordingly.

They watched Pietrolaj and the Hezbollah man stand and shake hands. The meeting was over, their big fish had taken the bait. Now it was time to sit back and wait. And prepare to reel him in.

59

After a series of cab rides, circuitous walks, and more cab rides all heading in divergent routes to throw off any possible surveillance, though he had seen and felt no coverage since landing in Oslo, Mahfouz returned to his hotel room and gathered a leather satchel containing his notebook computer then set off again eager to see what was on the thumb drive. He walked in a northerly direction toward the Royal Palace, a busy public area that was popular with tourists and locals alike. His mind was still focused on the meeting with Aleksy Nowak, the thumb drive, and avoiding surveillance, otherwise he might have noticed that the wet, unplowed snow on the Palace Park grounds was beginning to soak through his leather brogues. He stood for a moment by a park bench—it, too, was covered in snow and thus he did not sit down—and took stock of his surroundings. From here, through the scattered, barren trees, he had a clear line of sight in all directions. He then realized that his heart was pounding inside his chest. He was not a field operative, he again told himself. Yet some part of him was exhilarated. He was in a foreign country and had complete autonomy over his actions.

Mahfouz adjusted the strap of the satchel on his shoulder and began to relax a little. He wished his wife, Jabira, could be here to see this. The snowy park views in the fading sunlight were magnificent. Strangely, it reminded him of Moscow—he had been there once for a conference—save here in

Oslo there were no onion domes, shuttered relics of the Soviet era, FSB officers lurking on street corners, or gray faces lost in their hopelessness. Here, people appeared genuinely *happy*. There was an enthusiasm in the air that was difficult to put into words.

The Kaffebrenneriet at 18 Universitetsgata was alive with customers when he entered and stamped the remnants of snow from his soggy shoes. The intoxicating allure of fresh-baked pastries struck him instantly. He had to have one. The walk through the park had chilled him to the bone, so in addition to a *konelbolle*—a large gooey, cinnamon bun—he ordered a piping hot cup of coffee, in this case, a strong Kenya blend.

He paid the young blond behind the counter then searched out a seat at one of the tables around the corner and in the back. With his back against the wall and more importantly, the laptop screen facing away from any curious onlookers, he fired up the computer and, once it had booted, pushed the thumb drive into one of the USB ports. He clicked on the icon for the drive after it appeared on the screen, and immediately a dialog box popped open with a blinking cursor. It was here where he needed to input the unlock code. Slowly, he entered the first few characters *77jVX&* then reached into his satchel and pulled out the book that the DPSC man had given him. He set it next to the laptop as if he might later do some reading. He took a bite of his *konelbolle* and washed it down with a sip of his coffee, glancing up as he did so to take in the faces that were coming and going. Just as Nowak had instructed, he typed in the rest of the unlock code from the ISBN number on the book's back cover and with his middle finger tapped ENTER.

Nothing happened.

Mahfouz quizzically stared at the screen for several seconds until the empty dialog box reappeared again with the same blinking cursor. Apparently, he had typed in the wrong code. A quick charge of adrenaline shot through him as he remembered Nowak's warning about entering the wrong code too many times in a row. Again, he set out to enter the code, this time proceeding much more deliberately. *Success!* Several seconds later, he was staring at a directory that listed the contents of the drive in a series of categories: Small Arms; Light Weapons; Heavy Weapons; Ammunition & Explosives; Optics; Communications; Radar & Targeting; Aerial Platforms & Weapons; Naval Platforms & Weapons; Miscellaneous Equipment & Services.

Within each category, there were drop-down boxes containing sub-categories and headings. Some files had photographs attached, others merely had descriptions of products. Mahfouz could scarcely believe what he was looking at. Just who on earth was this Jean-Michel Durand? He had to be someone who was very well connected not just to the black-market arms trade, but to the military-industrial complexes of governments. Mahfouz brought the *konelbolle* to his mouth again and realized his hand was shaking. What would a relationship with a man like Durand mean for Hezbollah, for Lebanon, for the Middle East, and the world in general?

After thirty minutes more of perusing the DPSC product catalog, Mahfouz shut down the laptop and stowed it in his satchel. The thumb drive he would carry in his breast pocket. For the sake of appearances, he lingered another twenty minutes, pretending to skim through the book as he finished his coffee. Finally, he dropped it into his satchel, glanced at his watch, and did some quick calculus in his head. Then stood and headed out into the cold Norwegian air.

60

BRUSSELS

Alban Clement switched on the engine of his car. He huffed several breaths of warm air into his cupped hands, attempting to fend off the bone-chilling cold of the morning. As the seat heater began to penetrate his thin dress slacks, he eased out of his parking space and headed off for another busy day at his EU office. When he reached the sharp turn onto the rue Paul Wemaere, he glanced back at the side of the Velo-Boxx, a lockable, metal storage shed for bicycles. The downward line drawn at a 45-degree angle from left to right in white chalk was plain as day. It was a prearranged signal from his Russian handler that meant he wished to meet outside of their regular schedule. It was old school, but effective. The same could be said of Felix.

For several minutes, he began to panic. *They knew.* Knew he was spying for the Americans. Knew that he had betrayed them. Clement shifted his grip on the steering wheel and forced himself to behave as normal. They could be watching him. In fact, he was sure that they were.

Midway through his workday, for it had taken him most of the morning to calm his nerves, he stole away to Bel Panino, a sandwich shop around the corner from his office building. He ordered the Salade Caprese and a San Pellegrino to go, then, as his food was being prepared, headed for the restroom. Inside, he affixed a piece of tan masking tape to the back of the toilet tank, flushed, and after running the tap, returned to the dining area, where he collected his food and walked back to his office. According to the beautiful American intelligence officer—the one who spoke flawless French and had the killer legs, if he ever needed to get urgent word to them outside of their planned meeting schedule, he was to use this signal to communicate. As he understood it, each day someone—probably a CIA case officer from the American embassy in Brussels, but never the same person two days in a row—would mosey into the quaint, little restaurant for lunch or dinner. At some point during their patronage, they would assuredly have to use the unisex bathroom at which time they would check the designated location for the four-centimeter-long piece of tape.

Having to remember all the signals and communication methods was beginning to weigh on him. He wished he could take it all back. His infidelity. The lying. The spying on his country. None of it was worth the situation he now faced. He was stuck being a triple agent whether he liked it or not. Who knew what the Hezbollah monsters or the Russian gangster spies would do to him if his relationship with the Americans were to ever be discovered? It would certainly not be pleasant. The Americans were his best chance at redemption, the man with the intense brown eyes had said so. He was just praying that they would not break their word. His life and the lives of his wife and daughter were in the balance.

The Parc de Woluwe was only a short drive from his flat. In the summertime, evenings in the park would normally be brimming with all kinds of people doing all kinds of things. But now, at six o'clock on a brisk February night, it was quiet and desolate and cold. While the trees cast long, dark shadows that cut across the earthen paths, the rolling hillocks and frozen ponds were awash in a hazy, silvery glow brought on by a full moon, which was still visible despite a patchwork of clouds gathering overhead.

Wearing a woolen overcoat, blue jeans, and comfortable walking shoes, Clement strode onward to the spot where the meeting would take place. He had timed his pace so that he would arrive just within the prescribed fifteen-minute window. As the rules went, if either of them failed to show, they would try again the following night only an hour later.

As Clement drew near to the park bench, the designated meeting location, he slowed and took in his surroundings. His story for being out here if questioned was simple: He was out for a bit of exercise. The same might have been said of the sixty-some-year-old man now ambling toward him with the little Griffon by his side.

Felix's iron-colored hair was disheveled, his cheeks rosy from exertion in the chill air. He switched the leash to his right hand and reached into the pocket of his thick topcoat. With a flourish, he dropped several pea-size objects to the ground and watched the brown-haired mongrel with the round head and Chewbacca-like face gobble them up.

The Russian was the first to sit. He did so with a mild grunt. Clement looked out across the frozen pond then down the far recesses of the path to the point where it disappeared into a grove of trees. Felix smoothed his hair and said something in the direction of his little sidekick who by now was sniffing the ground where the ducks had congregated earlier in the day and left behind evidence of their grazing in the form of tiny tubules.

Clement eased onto the other end of the bench, pulled out a handkerchief, and dabbed at his nose.

"We are two people out for a stroll, both of whom needed to sit for a spell. I for the sake of my knees, you because of a sore hamstring." Having dispensed with establishing a cover story for their winding up on the same bench in the same park, the Russian, leaning side to side, pulled at the bottom of his coat, flattening it beneath his hindquarters. "We'll meet again in a month at Fallon Stadium."

Clement mentally filed away the date and time and other specifics as the Russian leaned forward and patted the dog on the head.

A light snow began to fall. "I won't keep you long," he finally said. Felix had the air of a man who could be downright charming but was someone you most assuredly did not want to cross.

Clement was silent, unsure what to say.

Eyes still focused on the little dog, the Russian continued. "The last batch of information you provided contained something that my superiors and I are interested in learning more about."

"Which is?" Clement's hands were freezing though he had them jammed into his pockets. He wondered if his lips were quivering.

Felix turned his dead, gray-blue eyes upon him and held them there as if sizing up his agent for behavioral indicators. Signs of deception. Signs of fear or maybe something else. "Durand. Jean-Michel Durand. We want to know more about him. The Russian subtly placed a tightly folded piece of paper on the bench then tossed a few more bits of kibble to the ground.

Clement with equal acuity palmed the paper in his frozen hand and immediately pushed it into his coat pocket.

"We want to know what intelligence the EU has on him. We have other sources looking into him as well, but you are rather well-placed to look a little deeper."

"Anything else?"

"If there is anything you can learn about his involvement with a company called Tomovco, or a Bulgarian by the name of Stefan Tomov, we would be very interested to know this."

Clement inclined his head toward the heavens, the billions of snowflakes gracefully descending. He blinked several away. "Who is Stefan Tomov?"

"He owns an arms manufacturing firm outside Sofia."

"Tomovco?"

The Russian answered with a single nod. "Let's just say that we are concerned that this Frenchman, Durand, may be thinking of climbing into bed with Tomov."

"I understand."

"There is a chance your Bulgarian counterparts in the EU may have more information with regard to Durand's intentions. Or members of this *panel* that wrote about Durand. If you happen to stumble across the name of one or more of these members, it would be quite helpful to us as well."

The snowfall had sugared the heads and shoulders of both men. The dog, too, had a crystalline streak of white going down his back. The little thing was now shivering to death.

"My service has authorized another disbursement into your account. Depending on the information you bring to our next meeting, I may consider advocating for an increase in our arrangement."

"That would be splendid. I will do my utmost."

"See that you do. But be careful not to arouse suspicion. We wouldn't want to lose you."

The Russian stood, indicating the meeting was over. Clement watched as he moved away from him, the little dog scrambling back and forth to either side of the snow-covered path as it tested the length of its leash.

Clement considered for a moment that that was him—a little dog on a leash, being fed kibble and dragged to cold, dark meetings with dangerous intelligence officers against his will. Before he could begin feeling too sorry for himself, he rose and continued on. He had to finish his evening constitutional. If for no other reason than for the sake of his cover. One never knew who was watching.

61

ARLINGTON, VIRGINIA

Rainey sat in the conference room of Suite 922, silently staring back at Job as the spymaster delivered the news. The others were there, too, at least the ones who were not still abroad.

"Our station chief said it was received at the embassy the day after Conrad met with Mahfouz." Job tapped an arrow key on the laptop in front of him and the image on one of the large flat-screens affixed to the wall changed. "As you can see, it was postmarked the same day Mahfouz flew out of Oslo."

"You're saying that Mah*fouz* sent this?" said Mouse.

"Who else could it be?" replied Evelina from the other end of the table.

All the while, Rainey offered not a word. He was deep in thought even as he read the letter again from the blown-up photo now on the screen.

To whom it concerns,

This message serves to inform you that Hezbollah has been in contact with a man by the name of Jean-Michel Durand. Durand is affiliated with Dynamic Prime Solutions Corporation, a company that is involved in the trafficking of illicit arms, to what extent globally is not known for sure. What is known is that in recent weeks Durand has taken a keen interest in expanding his clientele. This very week, a senior official from Hezbollah met with a DPSC representative in Europe. Hezbollah is seriously considering a relationship with Durand for the sake of their procurement needs. Please exercise utmost discretion with this letter and the information contained herein. The author urges that it be promptly forwarded to the proper authorities to do with as they see fit.

The letter was unsigned and there was no return address on the envelope.

Evelina's voice pulled him back from his reverie. "What do you make of it, Ray?"

Studiously, he answered her. "It isn't an offer of service. It's essentially a warning. A tip."

"Why?" said Rebecca Swalgin, head of CIA counterintelligence. Job had requested her presence. She was one of only a handful of people from Langley's top floor who knew of Jaguar and Operation End of Days. "Why would Mahfouz provide such a warning about Durand?"

"Maybe it's a trap. Some kind of provocation."

"No, Mouse, I don't think so," said Rainey.

Pietrolaj held his chin in his left hand. "The letter was typed...on a computer, not handwritten. Where did he print it?"

"Maybe he brought it with him," suggested Evelina, to which Rainey nodded.

"But *why*? That's the question we need to answer." said Job.

Rainey looked at the spymaster and offered the hint of a smile. "There's only one way to find out."

What resulted next was a debate of some magnitude. On one side were Rainey, Evelina, Pietrolaj, and Janna Carlson. The other consisted of Job and Swalgin. The rest of those present, some still hovering over half-finished bottles of water or cups of coffee and plates of sandwiches and fresh fruit, were content to be spectators.

It all started with Rainey. "I would like to take a run at him."

"Mahfouz?!" said Job with incredulity.

Rainey nodded with a nonchalance that belied the gravity of his suggestion.

"Out of the question. If we lose him, it'll jeopardize the entire operation."

"I believe I can turn him."

"Based on what? The *letter*? No!" It was an emphatic no. The kind that would end an argument between any normal boss and employee.

In this case, however, Rainey plowed on, as he was wont to do when he fully believed in a particular course of action. "Job, the objective all along has been to pique Hezbollah's interest and then look for an opening through which to penetrate their senior leadership so we can target Nourani. I'll grant you that the opportunity has come to us rather unexpectedly, and yes, we're still early on in the operation, nevertheless, here it is. And I think we should take it."

"You're talking about the head of their procurement network."

"Yes."

"It's impossible. He's a true believer. Can't be done."

"I'm telling you that I think it can."

"We don't know what his motivations are. We don't know *him*."

Rainey sat in silence with his fingers interlaced on the table—a lawyer who has rested his case. He glanced around the room. Clearly, he had won everyone over to his side. Everyone save for Job. But it was only a matter of time. The foundation of his argument was built on solid rock. Deep down he knew Job was only being cautious out of concern for his safety. He was like a son to the man.

It was about this time, as the tide was beginning to turn in Rainey's favor, that the phone on the table rang. All watched as Job lifted the handset and held it to his ear. His eyes moved from the leather-bound legal pad in from of him to the faces of his gathered warrior spies.

"Send her in," said the spymaster.

A moment later, a fresh-faced page from the XOC—the DX's operations center—entered the room with a folder bearing the requisite seals and stamps of highly classified material. In this case, it contained a new batch of cables from abroad. She handed it to Job, who accepted it with a thank you and a nod, then turned on her heel and took her leave.

The DX chief pulled the thin stack of papers from the folder and for several long moments studied them. Finally, he looked up at the group. "It's Maddie's report from her meeting with Clement." The meeting had been a deviation from their planned meeting schedule, which meant that what Job was about to say was important. They waited in anticipation. "The Russians are on to Durand. They've tasked Clement with finding out more about him, his business and such."

"That doesn't surprise me," said Pietrolaj. "We included some chicken feed about Durand in the files we provided Clement to give to the Russians. Just enough to make them curious."

"Well, it worked." Job stared at the cable thoughtfully then finally looked up. "They also want to know about Durand's involvement with Stefan Tomov and his company, Tomovco."

Rainey leaned forward in his chair. "Tomov. I met him at the expo in London. We only talked briefly."

"Who is he?" asked Carlson.

It was Pietrolaj who responded first. "He's Bulgarian. His company, Tomovco, manufactures arms, ammunition, all kinds of military equipment. One of Tomovco's notable clients is the Ukrainian government. He also has a hold on several substantial markets in Africa."

"And therein lies the Kremlin's interest," said Job before turning to Rainey. "The Russians must be keeping a close eye on Tomov. What exactly did you two discuss at the expo?"

"As I recall, he mentioned that he was looking for a suitable partner, if not someone to outright *buy* his company. I told him that it sounded like an interesting proposition. I said I would be open to meeting with him sometime in the future to discuss the matter in more detail."

"This changes things."

Job was a brilliant spymaster and Rainey had a ton of respect for him both professionally and personally, but he did have a weak spot, at least from Rainey's perspective. He could sometimes be too cautious, too deliberate in his thinking. For Rainey and those like him, planning was admirable and yes, abundantly necessary, but there needed to be room for operating on the fly. Adapting to changing situations. Flexing. With each passing day in the DX, Rainey was feeling more and more comfortable. He was born for this type of work. No longer did he feel the weight of military bureaucracy, the dog chain of command structure. He had long ago lost count of the carefully planned and coordinated missions that minutes from launch were canceled for no apparent reason at all. Now he had a say. Now he had juice. And he was going to use it.

"This is good, Job." He explained what he meant and thus what he had in mind in light of the new developments. The responses now from his Jaguar colleagues were varied, from mouths agape, to snickers, to stern, graveside faces. Hearkening back to the briefing when Jaguar was first introduced, Rainey smiled. "'You carry out operations to seed disarray and chaos among their ranks. You send ghosts to kill them in their sleep. This will be our mission. This will be our creed.' Those are *your* words, Job. Words I happen to agree with by the way."

The DX chief drew in a breath, let it out. "This all falls apart unless you can turn Mahfouz."

"Have faith, Job. Have faith."

62

ARLINGTON, VIRGINIA – WASHINGTON, DC

T he Metro car smelled of popcorn and beer. It could be worse, thought Rainey. The man standing behind him coughed and wheezed as the train car jostled on its rails. Several times, Evelina was jerked backward into him. They had taken the Blue Line from Rosslyn on account of Rainey's recommendation for dinner. He was starving—they both were—and he was eager for a good burger.

At the Farragut West Station, they disgorged with a river of people, everyone heading for the stairs while another frenzied current flowed past in the opposite direction. The air was cold as they made their way up to street level. Rainey thrust his hands into his coat pockets and instinctively scanned the faces sweeping by. Halfway across 18th Street, he felt a gentle tug. It was Evelina looping her arm into the crook of his. At first, he didn't know what to say or do, the sensation was foreign and quite unexpected. She offered an understanding smile as he gazed down on her radiant features, the shimmering green eyes, blond hair set aglow by the brilliant afternoon sunlight. For a fleeting moment, he envisioned an angel. *His* angel. And thus, he did not resist her advance as she battled to stay warm.

They fell into a natural rhythm as they pressed onward, their bodies moving in perfect synchronicity. Part of him wanted to smile, another told himself not to read anything into it. They were friends, colleagues. Nothing more.

The Blackfinn Ameripub was busy as usual, but it didn't take them long to be shown to a table. They ordered beverages while Evelina was still struggling to warm her hands.

"I figured you'd be used to the cold."

"I'm from Iceland, not Greenland." When the waitress had gone, she leaned forward. "You really think you can turn him?"

"I watched him in Oslo. I looked into his eyes, albeit through a monitor. What's more, I sense something behind the words of his letter. A yearning. I believe in my gut that it can be done."

They did not engage in any further discussions about Mahfouz or the operation until after they had eaten and were on their way back to Lynn Street. And even then, they kept their voices low and their words vague.

"How do you intend to do it? To approach him, I mean?"

"With a man like him, I believe it's best to be direct. No games. No hidden agendas. In other words, the approach needs to be simple and uncomplicated."

As they returned to the Annex and boarded the elevator for the ninth floor, he felt her eyes on him. And when he turned toward her, she did not look away. "What?"

"Nothing," she said with a faint blush.

Upon entering Suite 922, they found Job in Rainey's office pow-wowing with Saul Baker. Job's back was to the door. The movement of his hands indicated that Job was doing the talking, while Saul appeared the stoic listener.

Pietrolaj emerged from his own office and jerked his chin toward the two men speaking in camera. "They're discussing your idea about approaching Mahfouz. From what I could hear, Job wants Saul to make the pitch. He thinks compartmentalizing the Durand part of the operation is crucial. That way even if Mahfouz rebuffs our approach," Pietrolaj adjusted his glasses,

"Durand will still be in play. Also, Saul is closer in age to Mahfouz, which might increase the odds that he goes for it."

Rainey considered the logic of this. It was sound. In fact, it was a great idea. If the attempt to bring Mahfouz into the fold should fail, it would not harm the Durand angle being used to penetrate Hezbollah. Plus, having a man of Saul's age and experience doing the pitch might help convince Mahfouz that they were not only taking the matter seriously but that his case would be handled with an appropriate level of professionalism and care. Grigory Kapustin had basically said as much in Greece.

Soon Job paced out of the office with Saul in tow, at which time Rainey patted the old-timer on the shoulder. "Just can't stay away from it can you, Pappy?"

"Some of you need more supervision than others," said Saul with a wink as they headed off for the main conference room. "I'm not trying to step on your toes, Ray, but I think it makes sense to keep the Durand side of the operation clear of any inkling of Agency affiliation for as long as possible."

"I wholeheartedly agree."

Job claimed a chair on the opposite side of the conference table. "I'm authorizing the operation to move forward on your concept under two conditions. Saul makes the pitch, and he does it in Norway, but *not* in Oslo."

"Okay."

"We've already got Holberg's people read in to what's going on, for the most part, that is. And Mahfouz will hopefully feel comfortable going back there. Plus, Saul—"

"I said okay. I'm agreeing with you."

"Oh," said Job. "So you are. Well okay then. Let's make it happen."

63

Over the course of the ensuing weeks, a series of emails shot back and forth from a secure server in Croatia to its counterpart in a clandestine DX field office in London. The nature of the conversation was businesslike with only enough detail provided by either party as was necessary to effectively communicate their positions. Hezbollah, care of William Asada of KVR Group Zagreb, Croatia, was asking for price quotes on a number of Durand's products, which for security reasons were only referred to by their corresponding number codes found in the product catalog on the thumb drive that had been given to Asada—that is, Turaj Mahfouz—in Oslo. There were additional questions, too. For example, how many of XYZ were available for purchase at one time? Were there additional handling and transshipment fees that needed to be taken into account? How were shipments secured while en route to their destinations? Did DPSC guarantee delivery within a certain timeframe?

Rather than communicate via the digital realm—Durand's company prided itself on its security, after all—Pietrolaj, acting as the amiable DPSC sales rep. Aleksy Nowak, suggested another meeting so all of Hezbollah's questions could be answered clearly and efficiently. Once again, he and Asada would meet in Norway, but this time instead of Oslo, it would be Bergen.

And so, with Saul en route to Norway to coax Mahfouz into spying for the Agency, Rainey headed for Athens, where hopefully by week's end he would be wrapping up negotiations for a strategic deal of monumental importance. Another operational expense with Stedman Carter's money.

In his role as Jean-Michel Durand, Rainey had already contacted Stefan Tomov and arranged to meet him in Athens in two days' time.

———

Grigory Kapustin had been putting the finishing touches on an ops plan for his boss back at Moscow Center when an urgent cable came for him. A special guest would be arriving from headquarters in a matter of hours, it said. He was to meet the man at eight o'clock at the northwestern corner of the Temple of Hephaestus, the best-preserved ancient temple in all of Greece. There were no other details.

Kapustin was squinting down the darkened path that circled the temple when the headquarters man appeared from behind one of the large, marble columns. How long had he been there?

"I was beginning to think you weren't going to show," said the apparition as he stepped over the steel cable put in place to keep tourists from treading all over the ancient ruin.

"You wouldn't want me arriving with a hostile intelligence service's surveillance team in tow would you?"

Valery Chernikov lowered his forehead, an obvious sign that he didn't care for the tone of the Athens *rezident*. "I want you to listen carefully because there isn't much time. What do you know about Jean-Michel Durand?"

"Wealthy Frenchman. Been bouncing around Europe lately. I've also heard some whisperings about him dabbling in the arms trade."

"He does a bit more than dabble, I'm afraid. He's the reason I'm here. We have reliable intelligence that strongly suggests he is planning to meet Stefan Tomov here in Athens tomorrow night."

With that, Kapustin knew instantly why Chernikov was here. It was no secret to anyone in Russian Intelligence, specifically anyone working out of a Europe-based *rezidentura* that Stefan Tomov was quietly searching for someone with deep pockets on whom he could foist his ailing arms factories. Kapustin also knew that Tomov was currently the target of a carefully orchestrated operation to sink the man's business for good. So far, he had been an obstinate old goat and rebuffed all of the Kremlin's not-so-subtle maneuvers to take the company off his hands. The SVR—Russia's foreign intelligence service—at the behest of the Tsar would soon be moving on to more drastic measures. Sinking the man, himself, in a body of water after outfitting him with a pair of custom-made cement shoes, for example. Or dispensing a vial of a Novichok agent in his tea, for another.

"I want you to monitor the meeting. Get a team briefed and ready to go. We must know the precise details of their discussion. When it is over, you will report directly to me. Do you understand?"

Kapustin nodded. "I understand."

"They are meeting tomorrow night at nine o'clock at Tudor Hall."

"I'll have people in place by six."

"See that you do. And Grisha. No foul-ups. The president, himself, has taken a special interest in this case. You know what that means."

Chernikov need not have uttered those last five words. For if Boris Voronin had any interest in a case, it meant that there could be no mistakes. Unless, of course, one wanted a bullet to be fired into the back of one's skull.

———

Rainey stepped from the rear, passenger-side door of the armored Range Rover—an Agency support staff member, posing as an employee of the Dynamic Prime Solutions Corporation, had rented it for him to use—and marched through the entrance with his bodyguard in tow. Tudor Hall was an up-scale restaurant on the seventh floor of the King George Hotel. Even at this late hour, the place was brimming with a particular class of people: the refined, dignified, and, above all, rich.

The reservation was for nine o'clock. It was fifteen minutes till when Stefan Tomov arrived. At the sight of the eminent Monsieur Durand, Tomov's face brightened with recognition. Tomov shook his hand vigorously with a sad, almost desperate glint in his eyes. They spoke of the weather and the beauty of the Greek city until the waiter brought them their drinks. Then the negotiation for Tomov's life ambition commenced.

"As I recall from our conversation in London, you are looking for someone to shoulder the burden of your company's considerable *debt*," said Rainey.

Tomov offered a polite, though it could have been painful, smile. "Not quite. I am not looking for a lender or even a partner."

"A buyer then."

"Yes," he said in little more than a whisper. "I built my company from the ground up, battled fluctuations in the markets, and stiff-necked regulators and competitors alike, but I'm afraid I can no longer endure with my current financial position. And I am certainly not getting any younger. I just don't have the will or the time to revive her on my own even with a considerable cash injection. The bottom line is that I want to enjoy whatever time I have left with my family. The grandchildren are growing faster with each passing day."

Rainey did not give life to the rumors swirling around in some intelligence and even a few of the more serious journalistic circles concerning the Kremlin's disdain for Tomov. Word was that Tomov had been personally threatened on several occasions with the unequivocal message being to curtail his business dealings with the Ukrainian government and end his pursuit of several lucrative African contracts. Based on assessments from Pietrolaj and some other DX analysts, this was the real reason Tomov was hot to sell his arms manufacturing company. Not because he wanted to sit on the beach somewhere sipping Mai Tais with his wife or entertaining the grandkids from the side of a pool.

"Have you brought the documents that I requested on the phone?"

"Yes." Tomov popped the latches on his briefcase and passed a stack of several bound documents across the table, which Rainey accepted after dabbing his mouth with his thick cloth napkin. He spirited them away into his own black aluminum attaché case and lifted his flute of Champagne to his lips. "I will review them over the next few days. Meanwhile, I would love for you to join me on my boat tomorrow. And I won't take no for an answer. It will give us a chance to hold further discussions in a more private venue."

"That is very kind of you. I accept."

They decided on a time to meet, at which point Rainey provided the name of his yacht—though there was no need, simply saying "the big one" would have been sufficient—and instructions on how to find it. However, truth be told, this little bit of information wasn't meant for Tomov, but for the ears of the Russian intelligence officers who were studiously monitoring the meeting. He knew so because Grigory Kapustin was not just their man in Athens, he was literally in the dining room sitting five tables over with a blond-haired woman in a pearl necklace and a black dress that left nothing to the imagination. Kapustin had sent word to his handler in Athens Station as soon as Chernikov had taken leave of him. If he was surprised to see Reagan Rainey in the role of Jean-Michel Durand he did not reveal it.

By his estimation, Rainey figured there were at least six SVR watchers in the room not including Kapustin and his attractive dinner date, but probably more. It was assumed that the Russians had Tomov's phone under constant electronic surveillance. The objective here in Athens was to pull the

Russians into the operation, confirm their worst fears, and string them along until the moment was right. It was all about deniability. For the DX, the Agency, and the whole United States government. Not because the Americans weren't justified in taking out Qais al-Nourani. Indeed, they were. But because it made more strategic sense to kill Nourani and have another adversary take the blame. This had not been Rainey's vision from the start, but when an enemy hands you a gift, you take it. The plan was certainly not without risk, but if the DX could pull this off, the operation would go down in history as one of legend.

———

Rainey sat in his hotel room behind the glow of his laptop screen. The sun had not yet broken over the horizon. He poured over the watch reports from last night's surveillance operation. At 0303 hours, from various posts around and within the marina, a Mark Alcott-led team of talented DX surveillance artists observed eight men and a woman emerge from two large SUVs and quietly approach the yacht as the darkened water of Flisvos Marina licked at its hull. The woman seemed to be in charge. One of the men remained on the dock, smoking cigarettes—a lookout—while the others, carrying suitcases, boarded the vessel. The reports indicated that the interlopers first made sure the yacht was empty then immediately got to work planting miniature cameras and covert microphones in the salons and staterooms, sun decks and galleys, even the bridge and bathrooms. Attached to the reports were video clips and photographs of the clandestine technical operation carried out by the Russians.

His performance later today would have to be a good one, but so far, they were off to a great start.

64

BERGEN, NORWAY

Turaj Mahfouz arrived at Bergen Airport in much the same manner he had done so in Oslo previously, though this time when he flagged down a Norges Taxi at the cab stand, it was driven by one of Peer Holberg's men. Instead of driving Mahfouz to his hotel, the man pulled into a nearby parking garage where a team of waiting PST operatives calmly opened his door and asked him to step from the vehicle. Mahfouz, confused and disoriented, was immediately ushered into a waiting Mercedes SUV with heavily tinted windows and a powerful engine. He offered only minor protests all of which were readily ignored by the PST men. Despite all this, Mahfouz was only moderately frightened. This was Bergen after all, not Beirut.

They drove east on the 580 then swung northward on the 556. He felt the roadway sloping downward and soon realized why. The tunnel into which the vehicle plunged was long and winding. For a few nervous moments, he had a suffocating sense of the walls pressing in on him made all the more severe by the sturdy men seated on either side of him. When they finally emerged into the sunlight, they were just south of Bergen's city center. If they were nearing their destination, none of the grim-faced men in the vehicle made any such indication. Indeed, not one of them had said a word since they'd pulled away from the parking garage.

As they wound around the public library on their right, Mahfouz examined the faces of those standing in line outside its heavy wooden doors. They all shared a sense of... What was it? *Enthusiasm.* Yes, that's it. He'd seen the same thing in Oslo. What was it about the people of Norway? He considered how they compared to the citizens of Lebanon, Beirut, in particular—the city of his birth. Here, they seemed hopeful, energetic, and forward-looking. Beirut on the other hand was a city of war and despair and anachronisms. But it hadn't always been that way. He remembered a time from his youth, when his grandfather, walking with him along the Corniche, once called it the Paris of the Middle East.

Mahfouz glanced upward to the gray, brick wall above the sidewalk, which had been freshly cleared of snow. A vertical banner advertised that a reading and book signing was to take place today at 1:00 p.m.—according to the clock on the dash, that was only fifteen minutes from now—with Norwegian crime fiction author, Jo Nesbø. Mahfouz had never heard of him. Sadly, much of the world was still foreign to him.

His attention was next drawn to the colorful houses that spotted the rising hillside before them. They appeared as Lego blocks that had been glued onto a sheet of snow-white felt and draped over a chair—a children's diorama. *The view from up there must be stunning.*

Soon they were above the Lego houses, zigging and zagging and climbing higher into the seven mountains that surrounded Bergen, until finally, they left the road altogether. Unfazed by the treacherous conditions, the driver shifted the vehicle into four-wheel drive and pressed onward. They continued up a steep, snowclad lane for what seemed like a mile, maybe two. Rather suddenly a pretty, red *hytte* with white window casings came into view. Smoke from its chimney slithered into the azure sky. As they drew nearer and then jostled past it, Mahfouz looked farther ahead and observed a larger version built in the same style and color scheme. However, this one was not just a simple cabin in the woods but a great mountain house.

A man appeared on the front porch as the SUV lurched to a stop. Sucking on a cigarette, he peered almost nonchalantly at the wilderness that stretched beyond Mahfouz's vantage point. The man wore an unzipped parka over a green and tan and white flannel shirt, khaki pants with pockets on the legs, and brown hiking boots. The vibrant old-timer did not bother to avert his gaze from the beautiful landscape as the men from the vehicle escorted him toward the front door of the house. Surely the man was expecting him.

The sharp crack of an axe splitting wood caused him to jolt involuntarily. Mahfouz had not seen him, because of the small stand of pine trees that had blocked his view until now. A lean, muscular man just shy of six feet with striking blue eyes and a wad of chewing tobacco tucked into his bottom lip, jerked his chin to the right as he spat. In a fluid motion, he hefted the axe and brought it down again with an ominous thwack. Another man—he was wiry and shorter than the one swinging the axe—stood in the sun-cast shadows along the corner of the house. He chuckled and barked something Mahfouz couldn't quite make out. It must have been some kind of insult because the next swing came down with considerably more force. It was here that Mahfouz felt the first pinch of fear. *Who are these people? What am I doing here?*

Inside, the house felt warm and cozy, but far from cramped. He was shown to a great room with a ceiling of exposed timbers and a large stone hearth ablaze with a crackling fire. A clay pottery crock of decorative ferns and dried purple heather looked down from the wooden mantle, bookended by two black-iron lanterns that housed thick, unlit cream-colored candles.

A large man, with brown skin and eyes that were nearly black, sat at the far end of a sofa. Mahfouz guessed him to be a few inches over six feet and easily 240 pounds. His heritage could be Middle Eastern, Mexican, or even Italian, thought Mahfouz. It was too hard to tell. The big man gestured for him to sit down. Mahfouz turned once toward the door then eased into the opposite end of the sofa.

The moment he sat down, a woman with blond hair and athletic curves delivered a tray of coffee and tea and small plates of apple cake. Mahfouz silently watched her set the tray on the low table in front of him. She did not say a word, did not even look at him. One of the men who had brought him here was now standing at the edge of the room; he followed the woman with his eyes as she retraced her steps and disappeared from view.

The axe fell again outside, though it did not sound nearly as threatening through the dense wall. Mahfouz leaned back on the sofa, folded his hands in his lap, and waited.

———

Saul Baker burned the last of his cigarette down to its filter then blew a cloud of smoke into the cold Norwegian air before waving it away with his hand. He hated that he had taken up smoking again; it was such a dirty, rotten habit. But his operational tendencies and thought processes had all come rushing back to him the moment Job asked him to pitch the Hezbollah procurement chief. Unfortunately, along with them came the smoking. For some reason, it helped him focus, while at the same time, steadied his nerves.

He waited on the porch as Peer Holberg, having successfully delivered Mahfouz to the mountain house, approached.

"How was he on the way up?" said Saul.

"Fine. Quiet as a church mouse."

"You think he knows what this is about?"

"I suspect he does," said Holberg.

Saul nodded and shook the PST man's hand. "Thanks for your help. Tell your people I said so."

"I will. See you tomorrow afternoon."

Saul waited until the PST men had driven out of sight then entered the house. He hung his parka on the back of a wooden farm chair. Evelina paced from the kitchen and took a seat at a rustic table on which was a chessboard with pieces moved about, some were off to the side, casualties of their game, which had been interrupted by Mahfouz's arrival.

Saul gazed at her expectantly to which she responded, "He's all yours."

His boots squeaked against the wooden planks as he made his way into the sitting room. "I apologize for the inconvenience and for all this cloak-and-dagger business. It's a necessary precaution, I'm afraid." Saul eased into a leather wing-back chair opposite the coffee table.

Mahfouz remained silent. His eyes, calm and betraying nothing, moved from Saul to Tonka then back to Saul.

"My name is Paul Staffieri," said Saul. It was an operational pseudonym. "I work for the United States Government." Mahfouz clearly got the message: He was CIA.

"William Asada."

"Come now, Mr. Mahfouz, let's be candid, shall we?"

He hesitated then said, "Very well."

"Can I offer you some coffee or tea? Some apple cake, perhaps? It's quite good."

"Coffee, please. Two sugars."

Saul leaned forward and poured coffee from the thermal carafe, dropped in two cubes of sugar, and stirred while Mahfouz looked on. "Do you know why you are here?"

"It's about my letter." Mahfouz accepted the cup from Saul, drew in a careful sip. If he were apprehensive about meeting with someone from the CIA let alone an American, he did not show it. The fact that he was taking ownership of the letter this early on was a great sign. Earth-shattering, in fact.

"Indeed, it is."

"I should first tell you that I have someone waiting for me in Oslo. My absence will be noticed."

Saul tipped his cup toward his lips and let the liquid roll down his gullet. "Yes. We know. Rest assured that we've taken a few measures to safeguard your standing with Mr. Nowak."

"You know about him?"

"He's one of Jean-Michel Durand's faithful minions. Right about now, he's experiencing some inconvenience of his own. It seems his flight from Copenhagen has been delayed due to *mechanical* problems." Saul grinned. "On top of that, he will find that his hotel reservation has been lost when he arrives. I suspect he will try to contact you about his troubles in the next few hours."

Mahfouz blinked, sipped at his coffee again.

"Which brings us back to your letter."

"Yes."

"Well, Turaj... May I call you Turaj?"

Mahfouz nodded.

"I've come a long way to ask you this, Turaj: What is it exactly that you hope to accomplish? What are your *intentions*?" This was the moment that would telegraph how the remaining conversation would go. Either Mahfouz would open himself up for the pitch or he would plead ignorance and clam up, thus making it a wasted trip for Saul and the others.

Mahfouz set his cup down on the table, cut himself a generous piece of the apple cake, and levered it onto a plate, then, lifting a fork from the tray, took a small bite.

"How is it?" said Saul.

"Marvelous. Just marvelous."

Saul was patient, allowing Mahfouz to finish several more bites as he surely considered this monumental decision. The transcript of their recorded conversation would later note the awkward pause was due to Mahfouz's chewing—a credit to Peer Holberg's wife. After all, she was the one responsible for the world-class apple cake.

He washed the cake down with another sip of coffee after which he brought a napkin to his mouth and dabbed it with a mannerly flourish. Mahfouz quickly became solemn, introspective. Serious. The muffled voices of Mouse and Jazz trash-talking outside bled into the silence. Then came the crack of the axe. Then another. And another.

The hidden microphones could not have picked it up any more clearly. "My intentions are simple," he said. "I want peace. *Last*ing peace for my family and for Lebanon."

Adrenaline leaked into his bloodstream, but Saul had been there too many times, seen too many promising sources on the river's edge, looking down at the raging current beneath them only to watch them step back, turn, and walk away, never to be heard from again. He needed Mahfouz to take the leap. To jump across to the other side and into the protective arms of the Central Intelligence Agency. It was not without its share of risk. In truth, the consequences would be deadly should he put a foot wrong.

Saul would need to guide him across. To hold his eyes with his own so Mahfouz would not look down into the abyss.

65

So, by informing us about Durand, you are hoping that we will disrupt any prospective relationship he might forge with your organization, one that would doubtless bring sophisticated weapons and armaments into the Bekaa Valley, to Iran, and its other proxies."

"And—"

"Spare your life, of course," said Saul, intimating at Israel's recent and merciless campaign to eliminate Hezbollah's leadership structure.

"We understand each other perfectly."

Saul interlaced his fingers as he contemplated this all in a matter of seconds. Hinging forward slightly in his chair, he made his pitch in all its subtle glory. "The question I have for you, Turaj, is just how far are you willing to go to see that to fruition?" Seeing no outward reaction, he pressed on. "We would like for you to work with us."

"You want me to *spy* for you."

"As you say, we understand each other perfectly."

Their discussion lasted into the late afternoon. The shadows grew long on the hardwood planks of the sitting-room floor. Saul proposed that they stretch their legs and get a bit of fresh air. The two men, one a former intelligence officer thrust back into action, the other the chief of Hezbollah's procurement efforts, crunched through a layer of fresh snow that had fallen on the footpath during the previous hour. Tonka, armed with a suppressed Sig Sauer MCX-Rattler LT on a short sling under his open parka, trailed seven yards behind them scanning the landscape with combat-ready eyes. Evelina and Mouse protected their flanks in similar fashion though they remained well out of sight. Meanwhile, Jazz stayed behind to safeguard the house.

The path wound up through the woods, cut across a normally grassy opening but for the newly fallen snow, and eventually deposited them on a boulder-strewn patch of earth not far from the mountaintop. The view from here was nothing short of breathtaking. To their left, the city of Bergen, outlined by its harbors and coves, was radiant in the splendor of the setting sun. Saul's gaze shifted to the sun-fired mountains above and beyond the city then farther right to a cruise ship headed off for ports unknown. The magnificent view swept over shadowy land masses and stretched far out into the shimmering waters of the North Sea.

A harsh wind soon clawed at their faces, forcing them to tuck their chins into their parkas and squint. Yet nothing could diminish the majesty of this moment. For Mahfouz, it was the view. For Saul Baker, it was the prospect of landing the unlikeliest of sources within Hezbollah's senior leadership.

"I took walks like this with my grandfather when I was a boy. We traveled the hills of Lebanon, all over in fact." Mahfouz turned toward the rocky escarpment. "This place reminds me of a mountain I used to hike with him called Jabal al Baruk. We went on so many adventures he and I."

"Forgive me, Turaj, but why did you *really* send the letter? Why come to us *now* after all these years? Is it because of Israel's targeting campaign of your organization's officials? Is it because of the recent attack in my country?"

Mahfouz turned back toward the setting sun, his face taking on an orange glow in the process. "I've never told anyone this, but when I was a boy, there was a family that lived nearby. They were Jewish. A man and his wife. They had a son—Lemuel was his name. He was my friend. We played on the beach together nearly every day. We caught fish. We swam in the ocean. We built sandcastles and collected seashells. We did all kinds of things together. Neither of us knew the other's heritage. Neither of us cared. We were just kids enjoying each other's company.

"I want the same for my grandkids. I want them to enjoy life. Have friends. Not Lebanese friends or Jewish friends, but just *friends*. The wars, fighting, corruption, and disharmony have gone on long enough. They have ruined countless lives, destroyed cities, vanquished hope for future generations. I say enough is enough."

Saul could scarcely believe his ears.

"I will work with you and your organization,"—even now Mahfouz made no mention of the CIA—"but not for the purpose of betraying my country. I will work with you in order to save it."

Back inside the mountain house, Saul and Mahfouz reclined in front of the fireplace, sipping on hot tea and trying to warm their chilled limbs. Over another batch of apple cake, they developed a meeting schedule, communication methods, signals in case of emergency or in the event of the need for an unplanned meeting. It was decided that the next time they would meet would be in Zagreb in just over a month's time.

Mahfouz had his shoes off now, flexing his stocking feet in the warmth of the fire. "What is it that you want exactly, Paul?" he finally said.

Saul did not hesitate. "We want Nourani."

"The attacks in those cities."

"Yes."

The flames flickered against Mahfouz's eyes. They appeared suddenly tired and sad. "I didn't know what he was planning. There was talk of something big, but I'm afraid that's all I was privy to. Nourani keeps everything very compartmented. Had I known..." His face turned dark. "Had I known I would have come forward sooner. I fear for what may happen to my homeland now."

"We only want to destroy those who planned and participated in the attacks. The Lebanese people are not our enemy. The important thing to remember here, Turaj, is that you are doing something *now*. And for that we are grateful.

"Let me ask you... Any guess as to why the attack in New York was different from those in the other cities? I mean, why the truck bomb and why storm the Saudi consulate?"

The Hezbollah man shook his head slowly. "I'm afraid I haven't a clue."

When Nowak's email finally popped into Mahfouz's inbox, it bore a tone of both exhaustion and earnest apology. His flight had been forced to divert to Gothenburg. There'd been no available flights to Olso from there, so he had decided to rent a car, but it broke down on the E6 five miles north of Kungälv. On top of that, he had just arrived in Oslo and learned that the hotel had lost his reservation. It was the trip from hell. Nowak asked if they could reschedule their meeting for next week. Mahfouz looked to Saul who nodded his assent.

"You set the terms now though," said Saul. "Ask him to meet you in Beirut."

Head angled toward the screen of his mobile phone, Mahfouz tapped out the message, but before hitting SEND, allowed Saul a chance to review it.

"Tell him he will receive instructions for the time and location of the meeting when he lands at Rafic-Hariri. For security reasons."

Mahfouz added the extra line of text to his email and, after Saul gave final approval, fired the message off into the ether. A response came within minutes.

Okay. I appreciate your understanding. Thank you.

The next day, as Saul and Mahfouz were eating lunch, an SUV pulled up outside. The sound of a car door closing preceded footsteps—a woman's—on the wooden decking. Standing by a window near the entrance, Evelina peered outside then opened the door. She greeted Maddie and showed her to the table where the guest of honor was indulging in a *smørbrød*, an open-faced sandwich, topped with pickled herring and dill. Maddie handed a manila envelope to Saul and helped herself to a *krumkake* from a serving plate at the end of the farm-style dining table.

As Mahfouz continued chewing, Saul donned a pair of blue nitrile gloves and worked the clasp of the envelope.

"What is that?" asked the Hezbollah man.

"*This* is for your protection. To prove, should the need arise, that yesterday and today you were nowhere near Bergen."

By the quizzical expression on Mahfouz's face, it was obvious that he didn't understand.

Saul reached over and grabbed a clean plate from the counter behind him, then emptied the contents of the envelope onto it. He went through the articles one by one, handing them to Mahfouz as he did so. "Hotel invoice. Restaurant and café receipts. You like the *konelbolle*," said Saul dryly as he continued. "Ticket for the Fram Museum. The exhibit about the Antarctic pioneers you found especially interesting."

"I get it now."

"If anyone asks you about the meeting, be truthful. Durand's man didn't show. But you rescheduled it for next week in Beirut. This time he comes to *you* if he wants to sell his wares."

Mahfouz nodded. "I like it."

"You mentioned Jawdat," said Saul.

"Yes. Jawdat Shukri. He is Nourani's right-hand man. He has been pushing the connection with Durand from the beginning. I initially advised that we should be cautious, but now perhaps—"

"No," said Saul. "Now more than ever I want you to caution Nourani about hitching his wagon to Durand."

Mahfouz cocked his head. The expression was lost on him.

"What I mean is that I want you to be the voice of suspicion, restraint. You'll have to trust me on this."

"I'm trusting you on everything, Paul. My life is in your hands. Very well. I will do it."

Saul nodded. "Have a *krumkake*."

———

Evelina typed up the report of the meeting with Mahfouz for Job and shot it back to headquarters via the secure link. With Saul snoozing in a recliner and the male operators outside throwing knives and tomahawks into a tree stump, she and Maddie now dominated the sitting room.

"I'm worried about Ray," said Evelina. She didn't know why she had said it, but then again, yes, she did. In the past few months, she had begun to have feelings for him. It was the strangest thing.

Maddie glanced up from the fireplace, their shadows dancing on the walls around them. "He's a big boy."

"I know that, but if the Russians find out who he is..."

"He knows what he's doing, Evie. I think it's brilliant." Maddie continued to stare at her. "What's going on?"

"What do you mean?"

"I mean, it isn't like you to worry."

Evelina shifted her focus to the fire in the hearth and held her silence.

"You *like* him."

"Stop it. No. I... I'm just concerned about him. He doesn't know the Russians like I do." It was a stupid thing to say. Of course he knew what they were capable of. Ray and Maddie's father was living proof. "What I mean is that—"

"It's okay if you like him, Evie. I think it's sweet." For several moments, neither of them said a word. In their silence, the sound of the fire roaring and crackling dominated the room. Maddie finally looked over at her again. "You know he and Kayla are no longer an item. Just sayin'."

Evelina felt her face burning up and it wasn't because of the fire. "Can we just drop this?"

Maddie's smile was full of mischief. "Drop what?"

66

The Heesen Monaco Wolf superyacht was currently the largest vessel berthed in Flisvos Marina. It had once belonged to a Saudi prince, that is until the man's eye caught something much bigger—a mega yacht in the 400-foot range. In any case, the DX had promptly acquired it through one of their front companies during an operation in the south of France a few years back. Thus, making this in a round-about sort of way the only Saudi contribution to Operation End of Days.

Now registered as a private yacht in the Cayman Islands, *Midnight Song* had every luxury a man such as Jean-Michel Durand might need from the grand, sweeping salons to a master suite built for a king, or a Saudi prince as it were, making it a compelling place for two arms dealers to hold a private meeting.

"Do you have children?" said Tomov.

Rainey shook his head. "Maybe someday when I have time."

"Is there a significant other, at least?"

Rainey considered the last time he'd seen Kayla Chapman. "No."

"Perhaps it is none of my business, Jean-Michel, but there is more to life than work."

He looked at him sternly. "You're right. It's none of your business."

Tomov withdrew into the supple sofa. "I apologize. I did not mean to offend."

Ignoring the comment, Rainey poured Tomov a drink as the yacht listed back and forth in the steady, tranquil rhythm of a metronome set to 4/4 time. "As you might expect, I've done a lot of digging into your company as part of my due diligence. I must say that I've heard some unpleasant things about Russian *interference*"—it was a careful mischaracterization—"in your business dealings. What can you tell me about this?"

Tomov looked deep into his glass. "There is a certain Kremlin-backed oligarch that would like to see me dead." It was blunt and honest and entirely unexpected, at least without further probing on Rainey's part. "Not only do the contracts I have with the Ukrainian government threaten Russia's recent activities in Crimea, but also their broader interests in the emerging NATO states. In addition, I have the edge on a number of African markets that this oligarch would love to have for himself."

"Who is he?"

"Gennady Luzhkov."

Rainey had heard of him. The story was that Luzhkov had made his fortune in oil and compounded it with metals, only recently adding a media empire and a major telecom company to his vast holdings. It was also no secret that Gennady Luzhkov was one of the Russian president's closest friends.

"Have the Russians approached you with an offer?"

"I will not sell to those filthy maggots," Tomov barked before launching into a tirade in his native language. "I would rather die a poor man," he concluded.

Rainey did not point out the obvious fact that Tomov may do just that. Die, that is, at the hands of those very maggots. Pacing the salon in deep thought, he said, "What kind of security do you have, Stefan?"

"Ah!" Tomov waved his hand dismissively.

"What I am suggesting is that someone—this Luzhkov, in particular—may have sinister designs to prevent our deal from going through, assuming that I am still interested in purchasing your company after I've had a chance to fully review your books. It might be wise to consider a personal security team. If you'd like, I could even provide some assistance in that area. My people are very good." Rainey made no mention of the four sheep-dipped Navy SEALs that made up the yacht's crew, nor did he point out that Fig and Babe, his own personal security detail—and he, himself—were among the world's best combat shooters.

"That's very thoughtful of you, but I will be fine. I can look after myself."

"Very well, but please be careful. Gennady Luzhkov is a dangerous man. You could be making a very expensive wager. You may wish to reconsider, if not for your own sake, then for that of your family's."

"Thank you. I'll give it some thought."

Rainey had heard that Tomov was a stubborn, old goat. But stubborn and stupid were two different things. And yet one could be both. He would push him on this again before they went their separate ways. "Let us move on, shall we? What do you wish to discuss next?"

"Yes, let's. I should like to mention the matter of an export license."

Rainey held up his hand. "That should not be a problem. I am prepared to pay the appropriate bribes."

Tomov smiled. "You seem to know Bulgaria."

"As I alluded before, I take great pride in doing my homework. And my people are the best at what they do."

The two talked for hours, after which Rainey, peering through the cabin windows as Tomov plodded from the marina toward his waiting SUV, considered his next move.

Inside the cramped quarters of the surveillance van, Valery Chernikov cut an uncomfortable, displeased profile. The Russian intelligence officer cupped his hands over the headphones he wore and pressed them to his ears while at the same time, his eyes followed the Frenchman across the screen of his notebook computer.

Durand's commanding French accent bled into his brain. *"I would need to tour your plant—the one in Sofia—as part of my due diligence."*

"Certainly. Is there a time next week that is suitable?"

"No, no. I'm all booked up. How about this? I will be in touch after I've had a chance to consult my schedule. Meanwhile, my attorneys and I will review the papers you've supplied. If everything is in order, and I like what I see, I see no reason that we won't be able to have an offer for you by then. After the tour, that is."

"That would be splendid."

Chernikov stared intently at the video feed, watched the Bulgarian lift his glass and nod in agreement. "Durand is really pushing for this deal." The headphones ruffled his hair as he yanked them from his head. "He is going to be trouble," said Chernikov, before turning toward one of his muscular subordinates packed inside the van behind him. "We may have to do something."

67

The very moment Tomov was safely motoring away from the marina, Rainey began issuing curt orders to the crew aboard *Midnight Song*, strictly for the benefit of those listening. He was insufferable, anyone would think.

Over the intercom, he summoned his driver from the bowels of the yacht. Less than a minute later, Fig trotted ashore to retrieve his master's SUV.

Rainey with Babe, Durand's dutiful bodyguard, in tow stormed down the gangplank and made for the vehicle, its dual tailpipes issuing small puffs of exhaust into the marina air. The scent of the Aegean was strong but soon the aroma of supple leather overtook it. Babe ducked into the cabin after him and pulled the door shut. And with that, they were off.

Fig drove furtively for a while then began delicately engaging in maneuvers designed to free themselves of pursuers both seen and unseen. Thirty-some odd minutes later, after making a quick turn into a cramped alley behind a tattoo parlor, Rainey slipped out of the vehicle, which then sped on without him. He would link back up with his teammates later.

Sure that he was free of any surveillance coverage, Rainey entered the back door of a small business, waited a few beats then exited through the front. He walked to the appointed parking garage and popped behind the wheel of a small sedan rented earlier by a member of Athens Station. The key fob had been left in a cell phone-size Faraday bag and duct-taped above the left front wheel. He switched on the engine then immediately dialed Job from his secure mobile phone.

Rainey explained how the meeting had gone and voiced his concern for Tomov's safety. "I want a security team on him, ASAP. No vis. As in people who can blend in and not be noticed. Even by Tomov. Based on how our discussion went, I have a feeling the Russians are going to move on him quickly."

"Yes, I agree." After a brief pause, his voice came back on the line. "There are a number of private security groups we've utilized in the past. For small jobs just like this."

"Great. Tomov is flying back to Sofia in the morning."

"What time is his flight?"

"Zero eight hundred."

"Okay," said Job. Rainey could tell he was scribbling on his notepad. "Let me make some calls. I'll check back with you in a few."

Rainey sat there for close to twenty minutes before his phone buzzed in the palm of his hand. "Yes?"

"A five-man team is en route from London. They will be in Sofia by oh four hundred. Alcott and his people can keep an eye on him until then."

"Perfect. Thanks."

68

A dark-haired man in a security uniform with rings under his eyes approached him in the concourse. "You will come with me."

Conrad Pietrolaj had expected something like this, nevertheless, he felt a sudden dampness beneath his arms and a bead of sweat that slowly trickled between his shoulder blades. This was Beirut, a place where anything could happen.

The Hezbollah man led him to a room at which point another man in urban camo, bigger than the first and not lacking for muscle, relieved him of his mobile phone then took his suitcase and tore into its every nook and cranny. His laptop was removed and placed on a table.

Then it was his turn.

They strip-searched him and without apology did the same kind of thorough survey of his body. Once satisfied he was not secreting any kind of tracking device, they allowed him to dress and ushered him through another door at the back of the room. A short hall in turn bore them out to a secure entry/exit point. A sedan was waiting, its engine already running.

With prompting, Pietrolaj ducked into the back seat, where he found a man with a film of sweat on his forehead smoking a cigarette. The door closed with a thud and the car immediately shot forward.

A few seconds passed before the man next to him spoke. "Mr. Asada is waiting for you. Forgive us for the security precautions. These are dangerous times."

"Indeed, they are."

Their route was circuitous. After the second vehicle change, he was asked to wear a hood. Then came two more vehicle changes. Precautions, he was told again.

He finally emerged into what seemed to be a small, ill-lit warehouse at which time the hood was removed. The space was empty but for several pallets in one corner—foodstuffs according to the packaging. The man in charge fired up another cigarette as they waited beside the sedan just the two of them for what or for whom he wasn't sure. Then four armed men stepped from a room and assembled themselves in a half circle. They did not look friendly.

In time, a garage door clattered upward and a Land Rover with heavily tinted windows roared inside. Not until the door was fully closed did the occupants exit the vehicle. First out was an athletic-looking man in a khaki shirt and faded blue jeans. Strapped around his torso was a short-barreled Colt M4 carbine. *Wonder where he got that?* thought Pietrolaj.

Mahfouz was next. He stretched out his arm and the two of them shook hands. "Mr. Nowak. Welcome to Lebanon."

"Thank you."

As the last person rose from the far side of the vehicle, Pietrolaj thought for a second that he might lose control of his bowels. Jawdat Shukri, Hezbollah Unit 910's second in command walked around the back end of the SUV and sized him up with intelligent suspicion.

Mahfouz, hands clasped in front, made the introductions. "Mr. Aleksy Nowak, I'd like you to meet Jawdat Shukri." They shook hands. "Mr. Shukri—"

"You will be dealing directly with me from now on," the deputy commander said.

Pietrolaj suspected something like this might happen. Mahfouz had reported to Saul in Bergen that Shukri was angling to take credit for the budding relationship with Durand and the prospective materiel he could bring to Hezbollah. And just as Saul had suggested, this created an interesting opportunity for the DX and the Agency at large. An opportunity to exploit and in turn use to protect their source.

Shukri turned to one of the armed men. "Please escort Mr. Asada back to his office."

Mahfouz seemed confused about the unfolding dynamic but did not object. Pietrolaj looked on as Mahfouz somewhat vacantly climbed into the back seat of the SUV that had just minutes ago transported him here. The vehicle's engine roared back to life and then he was gone.

"Come with me," said Shukri as he led him into a room with fluorescent lights hanging from the ceiling. "Sit down. Would you like some coffee or tea?"

"Tea, thank you."

A man of far lesser rank scurried off and soon came back with a tray of tea. When they were alone, the Hezbollah man continued. "I want you to forget about Mr. Asada. As I said before, from this moment on you will deal directly with me."

Pietrolaj ventured a sip of the tea and suddenly his throat was on fire. His eyes bulged and a tear soon trickled down his cheek. It must have been quite the spectacle, because Shukri laughed aloud as he returned his cup to the table, nearly spilling it in the process. Pietrolaj recovered after several moments. A sheepish smile formed on his lips, but inside he was ecstatic. The intelligence Mahfouz had provided thus far was bearing out right before his very eyes. The procurement chief had said Shukri would angle his way into the picture so as to elevate his status with Nourani.

"Very well," Pietrolaj coughed. "You have viewed our *catalog*? Yes?"

"I have. It is quite comprehensive. I'm curious, however. Why haven't we heard of Monsieur Durand and his company before?" Shukri gulped his tea like he was impervious to the scalding liquid.

"He prefers to keep a low profile. Only recently has he decided it necessary to step from the shadows, so to speak. It's part of his plan to generate a broader customer base. Speaking of which, we hope we can add you to our list of satisfied clients."

"Yes." Shukri eyed him like a tiger stalking its prey.

Pietrolaj would have to be careful with him. His life depended on it.

"I wonder. DPSC must have remarkable connections to offer such a diverse listing of products. What kind of access does your employer have? What I mean is, does he source his products privately or through governments?"

Pietrolaj evoked a knowing visage and smiled. "Both. In fact, we are in discussions to purchase a large arms manufacturing firm in Europe. It stands to be very lucrative for us, and extremely beneficial to our customers. I'm not at liberty to go into specifics but we have sources in some rather large companies with whom several Western governments have extensive contracts. Part of our business involves acquiring information and design plans with regard to cutting-edge technology and weaponry. Right now, we are actively looking for places in which to manufacture them for ourselves, so we can in turn sell them to organizations such as yours."

The gleam in Shukri's eye told Pietrolaj everything he needed to know: He was buying it.

Their conversation soon turned to specific armaments, price points, and logistics. Here, Pietrolaj navigated the conversation with great care in much the way a magician performs a trick—simple sleight of hand, misdirection—leaving Shukri with a lasting impression of Jean-Michel Durand's industrious capability, client care, and, most importantly, his discretion.

Pietrolaj quoted a number. "Keep in mind, this is just a ballpark figure. Our final price will be contingent on any bribes we might have to pay relative to your shipping needs. There is a variety of options in that regard. But we can get into that later."

"And method of payment?"

"We accept cash, of course. Half up front, the other half on delivery. But as you probably know, cash can be tricky, because it brings with it a good deal of risk. It will need to be washed, et cetera. We *are* flexible, but I will tell you that we prefer a trade-related method of payment."

"Go on."

"Once all the details are worked out, a company of your choosing will receive a back-dated invoice for something like *farm equipment* or *consultancy*. You get the idea. You will then wire the money to an account that we specify. Both ends of the transaction will be protected with legitimacy."

"Is there a way in which we can see the products—a sampling perhaps—before we commit to a purchase?"

"Absolutely. In fact, we recommend that you do."

"One more thing. Before we agree to anything this significant and costly, we will want to meet Monsieur Durand."

Pietrolaj almost smiled. "That can be arranged. In fact, my employer's standard operating procedure is to meet first-time clients personally prior to any agreements being formalized."

69

SOFIA, BULGARIA

Rainey walked to the window of the third-floor flat. It was just across the street from the Bolyarka Tavern. Through parted blinds, he peered down on the street and wondered if Jawdat Shukri was really going to show.

Yesterday, he had toured the main Tomovco manufacturing plant and its offices, which culminated in the meeting he had held earlier this morning. During that meeting, he and a team of DX-fronted lawyers and financial advisers signed off on the purchase of Tomovco Ltd. Durand's Dynamic Prime Solutions Corporation—the CIA, in point of fact—was now the owner of a legitimate Bulgarian arms company. The deal would solidify Durand's status in the minds of Hezbollah and prove to them that he was indeed a force to be reckoned with. But there were also some pressing and very real concerns, namely that Durand was now a huge target. The Russians would be actively looking for him. This was made all the more real considering that no less than three attempts on Tomov's life had been made and thwarted in the days prior to the sale of his company to DPSC, all thanks to the team of ex-SAS men now guarding him around the clock. If Tomov didn't already know that Jean-Michel Durand was involved in saving his life, he had to at least suspect as much.

Rainey wondered how much longer he, himself, could play this game, how much longer he could string along the Russians, let alone Nourani, and Hezbollah.

For as long as it takes, he thought. *For as long as it takes.*

A persistent gnat buzzed around Pietrolaj's head as he maintained a careful vigil from the park bench at the edge of the Lake with the Lillies in the Borisova Gradina. He swatted it away with his ball cap for the fifth or sixth time and again took in the fragrant springtime aroma. Still weighing on his mind was his last conversation with Jawdat Shukri. It had taken place via an encrypted text messaging platform they had agreed to use. Pietrolaj had arranged a meeting with Durand and a little *show-and-tell*, he called it, in Bulgaria. Durand was already there on business and the opportunity seemed ideal for the two sides to finally come together.

News of the meeting had soon gotten back to the DX by way of Mahfouz, which proved to Job and the Jaguar team that they could trust the procurement chief's reporting. As far as sources went, he was turning out to be a gold mine.

The engine noise from a commercial airliner that had just taken off from Sofia International drew his attention skyward. As a former pilot, Pietrolaj considered what the man or woman inside the cockpit was doing right now as the plane steadily rose overhead, banked slightly, and headed for central Europe.

Three and a half minutes later, a middle-aged man with an expensive camera around his neck appeared and took up an odd position beside him. He snapped a few photos of the lilies and began absently adjusting the settings of the device. "Beautiful aren't they, the buds in springtime?"

Pietolaj eyed him warily. "Yes. Very. First time in Bulgaria?"

"In Bulgaria, no. In springtime, yes."

"Well then, may I suggest the Skaklya Waterfall."

The photographer turned and stared at him apparently satisfied with his bona fides. "Take that path," he said, pointing. "Follow it to the road. When you get there, sit down at the bus stop and remove your hat with your left hand. There, you will receive further instructions."

At the bus stop, Pietrolaj gazed down the sidewalk in either direction. A few people were jogging. A woman pushed a baby stroller. A man in a suit carrying a briefcase was headed directly for him, but then veered around him and continued on.

Pietrolaj took a seat at the far end of the bench inside the covered plexiglass structure. He removed his hat with his left hand and squinted toward the left. In a matter of twenty seconds, a white Mercedes Benz GLS 550 lurched to the curb, and a man with a grim disposition, wearing a light-weight sport jacket and no tie, alighted from the front-passenger seat. He quickly opened the back door and hovered in place with one hand on the door handle, the other beneath his open jacket, channeling a taller, more menacing version of Napoleon Bonaparte. His eyes were in constant movement.

"Mr. Nowak. Please, get inside."

Pietrolaj hooked the cap back on his head and paced to the SUV, ducked inside. The cabin plunged into darkness with the closing of his door. Eyes still adjusting, he gazed around the cabin.

"Hello again, Mr. Nowak."

"Good day."

"May I ask where it is that we are going?" said Jawdat Shukri.

"A small warehouse. It's not far."

Pietrolaj directed them onto Mihai Eminescu Boulevard past a series of homely Soviet-style apartment buildings. As they approached a traffic light, he instructed the driver to take the left, which bore them down a leafy two-lane street. The National Museum of Military History soon glided by their left flank, rather ironically, thought Pietrolaj. Here, the street took on the look and feel of a university campus, then just as quickly the collegial imagery melted away. A highway passed beneath them along with several sets of brush-choked railroad tracks.

"We're getting close," proclaimed Pietrolaj. Several more minutes and a few turns later, the SUV nosed into a trash-strewn street. "Go all the way to the end." Head tilted downward, Pietrolaj tapped a text message into his phone, indicating that they had arrived.

Soon a rusty gate came into view. It was thrown open the moment the SUV approached. A man in coveralls waved them through, then, in a slight jog, closed the gate.

The warehouse was in a run-down, industrial part of town not far from Sofia Central Station and the city's airport. Somewhere nearby someone was grinding metal. The smell of it coupled with diesel fuel lingered in the air.

Once safely inside the warehouse yard, a large man with a tricked-out AK-12 slung over his muscled torso emerged from a metal door and walked toward them. Pietrolaj greeted him warmly and engaged in small talk while Shukri and his coterie managed their way out of the back of the SUV. No one would ever believe that Justin Ruth, otherwise known as Babe, had once long ago been a top MLB prospect. The former slugger turned special operator had been perfectly cast as Monsieur Jean-Michel Durand's personal body-guard. If not for his physical stature—he was an imposing six-foot-four-inch figure of pure power—then for the mean visage he now exuded.

With Babe leading the charge, they stampeded down a dimly lit corridor to a door that led into a secure section of the warehouse. Another man armed with a Brugger & Thomet MP9—Fig, as it were—stood guard here.

"Your men can wait here in the hall," said Pietrolaj without artifice.

Surprisingly, Shukri did not object. Rather, he turned and uttered something in rapid Arabic to his lead bodyguard. The man offered a disapproving glare before finally acquiescing.

The room was barren but for a sturdy metal table on which were a series of wooden crates. The mysterious Jean-Michel Durand stood next to them in an eight-thousand-dollar suit, looking like a million bucks. And so it was that Reagan Rainey made his Hezbollah debut. Only later would he call it the role of a lifetime.

Pietrolaj handled the introductions.

"It is very nice to finally meet you," gushed the Hezbollah man.

"The sentiment is mutual, Monsieur Shukri." Rainey's French was flawless, a credit to his childhood abroad. He held out his hand but kept his feet planted on the ground. It was a subtle way of saying that Hezbollah needed him more than he needed Hezbollah. After all, he did not want to seem overeager. "Aleksy has been filling me in on your organization's interest in my company and how I might be able to sufficiently accommodate your business pursuits."

"Yes."

"He also tells me that you wish to see firsthand a sample of one of the products you are interested in purchasing."

"That's correct."

And with that Rainey turned to Pietrolaj and nodded. "Open the box."

Pietrolaj picked up the crowbar from the table and with it stepped to the first crate, pried each side of its lid upward. With each exertion came a terrible screeching sound that echoed throughout the room. And all the while Pietrolaj was laboring with the box, Rainey was watching Shukri. The man's eyes were wide with anticipation. Soon Pietrolaj placed the crowbar down on the table, hefted the lid off the crate, and leaned it against the wall.

"Remember, this is merely a sample," intoned Rainey cryptically.

"Yes, yes."

At Rainey's prompting, Pietrolaj clawed back a layer of straw and foam, revealing a short, metal tube with varying sections of black and shiny silver.

Rainey stretched out his hand, a merchant showcasing his wares. "Please, have a look."

The senior Hezbollah official strode forward and leaned over the box. Shukri's jaw dropped slightly then he smiled in obvious wonder.

"You will see that it is in fact genuine. Thus the American markings. What's particularly noteworthy is that the FGM-148F is the latest generation of this type of missile."

"How did you—"

"I never discuss my sources, monsieur. You understand. But rest assured, they are impeccable." Rainey offered a curt smile that was very French and very compelling.

"What about launchers?" pressed Shukri.

"What about them?"

"Do you have any here for me to view?"

Rainey considered this, if for no other reason than to let Shukri flounder in suspense. Then he looked at Pietrolaj and motioned for him to open the next crate.

Shukri's reaction at seeing the LW CLU, the Javelin's Lightweight Command Launch Unit, was even more jocular. Incidentally, it had nearly taken an act of God for the DX to obtain this inert missile and its fully functioning launcher from the US Army base in Novo Selo in time for the meeting.

"Each weapon system comes complete with training materials."

"*Incredible.*"

"So, do we have a deal?" From the intelligence Mahfouz had provided, Rainey knew that only Nourani could authorize an expense such as this.

"I will have to check with my superior and get back to you."

"Very well. When can I expect you to be in touch? These things don't exactly collect dust on the shelf, you know. The demand is quite significant."

"How many do you have for sale?"

Rainey offered a sporting smile. "How many are you in the market to purchase?"

70

Rainey shared a late dinner with Stefan Tomov the following evening at the Panorama Restaurant in the Hotel Marinela. The two men had much to celebrate. Shortly after they had finished an appetizer of kati-no meze, Rainey's phone vibrated inside his suit coat. While he examined the phone's screen, Tomov reached for the wine bottle and began pouring himself another glass. According to the caller ID, the call emanated from a private number. This, coupled with the fact that he was expecting contact from Shukri factored heavily in his decision to answer it.

Erect in his chair, a vision of wealth and privilege, Rainey plainly stated, "*Oui?*"

The voice of Jawdat Shukri was collegial and upbeat. "Monsieur Durand, this is your friend from KVR. We met yesterday." Shukri was using the front group as he surely did not trust the security of a telephone conversation.

"Yes. How are you, my friend?" Rainey covered the microphone with his palm and whispered to the Bulgarian, "I must take this."

Tomov issued a jovial smile and raised his glass in approval.

Rainey removed his hand and asked Shukri to hold, please. With a formal flourish, he excused himself from the table, dabbed his mouth with the cloth napkin, and stepped into the corridor outside the restaurant. In the quiet of a dormant conference room, he eased into a padded chair and lifted the phone once again to his ear. "I apologize for that. I am in the middle of dinner and wanted to be sure we could speak freely."

"It is I then that should apologize, monsieur."

"No need. Now, what can I do for you?" prompted Rainey.

The smile almost came through the phone. "My superior would like to speak with you."

Superior meant none other than Qais Moussa al-Nourani. "Excellent. I should like that very much." Rainey had mentioned in a rather off-handed manner to Shukri during his warehouse show-and-tell that he would need to remain in Bulgaria for the next few weeks to tend to important business. He had numerous meetings that dealt with a recent business transaction. Though he had withheld the name of the company from their discussion it wasn't long before the local media picked up the story that the Jean-Michel Durand-owned Dynamic Prime Solutions Corporation had purchased Tomovco, which then in short order made its way into international headlines.

Rainey could hear the phone changing hands. "Congratulations," said a new voice—it was Nourani's. "I understand you have made a recent acquisition, a Bulgarian manufacturing firm."

"Tomovco. Yes. Thank you, it was a bargain really."

Nourani's tone bore the tang of suspicion and a willingness for accommodation at the same time. "I would very much like for the two of us to finally meet."

"As would I."

"A friend has permitted me the use of his lake house. It is private and very secure. May I suggest we make each other's acquaintance there?"

"Yes, that would be splendid."

After some bouncing back and forth—both had busy schedules, they finally agreed to meet on Wednesday.

"Now, if you will kindly indulge me one last thing. I'm afraid my security requires it. My subordinate is sending you a message now."

Rainey's operational phone—the phone that Jean-Michel Durand carried—chimed with an incoming message on the secure text messaging app through which he and Jawdat Shukri had agreed to communicate. He pulled the phone from his ear and perused the message then returned to the call with Nourani. "Yes, I understand. One can never be too cautious when it comes to one's security. That will be fine."

"Thank you," said Nourani. "I will see you Wednesday."

"I'm looking forward to it." In more ways than one, thought Rainey as he disconnected the call.

71

Mahfouz waited until Jabira was asleep before retrieving his phone from the nightstand and slipping out of the bedroom. Barefoot, he padded into the bathroom, clicked the door shut quietly, and sat down on the closed lid of the toilet. Studiously, he swept his finger across the screen and navigated to what appeared a simple calculator app. He typed in the appropriate three-step mathematical calculation and hit the button that bore the square root symbol. Then, he tapped out a predetermined combination of buttons which brought up an entirely new screen on his phone—a covert and heavily encrypted messaging application that one of the female CIA officers had installed on his phone while at the mountain house in Bergen.

Mahfouz entered the 6-digit passcode at the prompt and hit ENTER. From that point forward, the application appeared like any other standard text messaging app. He collected his thoughts, giving careful consideration to each word he would type, then watched as the characters he selected appeared on the screen. Upon its conclusion, he read the entire message again and, satisfied, touched the SUBMIT button. The message immediately transformed into an indiscernible mess of encrypted text, which in turn gave birth to a green check mark that disappeared after three seconds. With no other messages to draft or read, he tapped the command to close the app. The display immediately returned him to the phone's home screen.

Before stuffing the device into his pocket, he made sure its Bluetooth feature was turned on. He quickly found a pair of loafers, donned a light jacket, and ambled to the door.

Outside, the night air was thick. A breeze washing in from the ocean brought with it a faint odor of fish. He set off toward the bookshop just north of the Martyrs' Cemetery. If anyone bothered to ask, he would tell them that he was simply out for a stroll. It helped him sleep, which happened to be true as a matter of fact. Somewhere along his pre-planned route, according to the man he knew as Paul Staffieri, he would pass by a covert, digital receiver—a type of modern short-range agent communications, or SRAC, device—that would connect to his mobile via an electronic handshake. When the handshake was complete, the phone would vibrate, and any messages he had for the Agency and they him would be immediately transferred. At the same time, the Agency's hidden communications device would burst a data packet to a satellite in geosynchronous orbit high overhead. The entire process took about 1.3 seconds, Staffieri had said, and thus made it an effective method of communication for spies in denied areas as it involved no face-to-face meetings, hidden communications equipment that could be easily discovered in a security sweep, or unusual cellular traffic coming from his phone, and thereby minimized risk of detection. It was assumed that Iran and other hostile intelligence services were monitoring the cellular networks inside Lebanon. This technique would protect him and his spying for the CIA.

In tonight's case though, Mahfouz already knew no messages were waiting for him. If there were, he would have previously received an email message in his spam folder from a European company touting a limited-time 70%-off deal for a certain male reproductive product in the subject line.

Jabira was still fast asleep when he returned. He considered for several seconds as he slipped back into bed what she would think if she were privy to what he was doing. She would be proud, he concluded. He was doing this for Lebanon. For his family. For peace.

———

Mahfouz's encrypted message landed in the XOC back in Arlington, Virginia a blink after the hidden device in Beirut had detected the Bluetooth signal from the Hezbollah procurement chief's phone. It was then flashed to Job, who was still abroad in the field. At that very moment, the DX spymaster was in Rome checking in on staff stationed there pursuant to an unrelated operation. Alerted about the urgent message, he made his way to the station's SCIF, where he immediately reviewed Mahfouz's first electronic missive.

BONNET making trip to Bulgaria on Wednesday, 15 March, for meeting with JUNIPER. Location: a lake house near Dospat. No more details known at present. Will advise if learn more. End.

At the cottage in Bergen, code names had been assigned to Durand (JUNIPER) and Nourani (BONNET) for the purposes of Mahfouz's reporting. For the sake of operational security, however, they had not enlightened Mahfouz, nor would they, to the fact that Durand and the Central Intelligence Agency were one in the same. The intelligence he provided in his first communication with them was reassuring on two accounts. First, it further proved his credibility as well as his access to Hezbollah's senior leadership. Second, it meant Rainey's meeting with Jawdat Shukri had been a resounding success in terms of selling the fiction of Durand to Nourani. Hezbollah, and thereby Iran, had bought the deception.

Immediately upon reading Mahfouz's message, Job picked up the secure phone and began setting things in motion for what was to come.

The Russian embassy in Sofia was located at 28 Dragan Tsankov Boule-vard along the eastern fringe of the forested Borisova Gradina. Inside a secure conference room therein, Valery Chernikov leaned over a desk, listening intently to the recording emanating from the sophisticated audio equipment in front of him. An hour ago, the head technical officer from the *rezidentura* notified him about a peculiar telephone call that had been made to the mobile phone of one Jean-Michel Durand. It turned out to be a rather for-tuitous byproduct of their near-constant monitoring of Stefan Tomov. For through their technical surveillance of the Bulgarian arms dealer, they had captured Durand's phone number and, in turn, installed a powerful software product on his device, something akin to the Israeli-designed Pegasus. This resulted in unfettered access to the Frenchman's calls, texts, and emails.

The recent sale of Tomovco, Ltd. had shifted the operation rather signif-icantly. Stefan Tomov, the original target, had never been one to surround himself with a security presence until only recently, that is. Though the three recent failed attempts to kill him angered Chernikov to no end, he shelved any plans for a fourth attempt. They knew where he was, and besides, Tomov was no longer in their way. Jean-Michel Durand on the other hand was now the primary threat and he was always well-protected. This, however, might just be their chance to eliminate him and thus, the infernal Tomovco matter, once and for all.

Chernikov listened to the recording again while reading through a print-out of the text message Durand had received on his compromised phone. The text consisted of a set of instructions and the location of a rally point in Dospat. Chernikov folded the paper into a square then summoned one of his subordinates to the conference room without haste. When the man arrived, he handed him the slip of paper. "Gather the teams. There isn't much time."

72

ASVESTOCHORI, GREECE – DOSPAT, BULGARIA

As it turned out, the Russians weren't the only ones listening in on the Durand phone call. The DX, too, had a similar recording of the call between Rainey and Nourani. Upon learning the specific meeting place in Dospat where Rainey would link up with Nourani's people, Job immediately dispatched the remaining members of the Jaguar team to the area. Based on what the analysts back in Arlington were telling him, the lake house was undoubtedly somewhere along the southwestern shore of the Dospat Reservoir. The terrain made it difficult to access as it was mountainous and heavily wooded, or in the words of Qais Nourani, "private and very secure."

For the sake of operational security, they arrived on separate flights from all over Europe. After passing through the city of Thessaloniki, they converged at the safe house in Asvestochori, which became a forward command post of sorts, a way station for the members of Special Operations Executive 77, a/k/a Jaguar, to link up before they each set off for points due north.

It was here where Maddie, Tonka, Mouse, Jazz, Booster, and Wizard crammed themselves and their gear into two minivans driven by Mark Alcott and Jimmy Dunne and set off for the mountains outside of Dospat. Day had become night by the time they reached their staging area. Alcott pulled off the road into a gravel track that led to a small clearing within the anonymous pine forest that blanketed the entire region. Here, he switched off the engine and turned toward Tonka, who was seated in the front seat next to him.

"I sure wish I could go with you guys. I miss the action."

Tonka's lips moved beneath his NODs. "I hear you, brother. But you know as well as I do that your job is just as important as ours."

Alcott sighed and fingered the button that opened the electric, rear cargo door. "Be safe, all."

The operators climbed out, shouldered their gear, and disappeared into the dark woods. At a similar location nearby, Dunne's carload of shooters was doing the same thing. Having deposited their respective teams, he and Alcott would drive into town and monitor radio traffic with their primary responsibilities being to keep a watchful eye for suspicious characters and to be in a state of constant readiness in case a speedy exfil was necessary.

Half a mile into the wooded terrain, the team led by Tonka set up a small camp. The big, former Delta medic stripped off his ruck and, with Jazz's help, began piecing together the various parts of the drone stored within. Fully assembled it was the length of a large coffee table. Tonka carried it a few paces away from everyone and with several running steps heaved it into the air. A tiny, whisper-quiet motor took over from there. The drone rose steadily until it was invisible against the night sky.

With the others providing security, Tonka returned to where Jazz stood. In the latter man's hands was an electronic instrument that much resembled a tablet computer although beefier and ruggedized to protect it from the weather and war. Jazz's head was angled downward, pressed against a cone-like hood that shrouded the digital screen so its light would not illuminate half the mountainside and expose their position. A laptop computer was set up on a small stand beside him beneath opaque camouflage netting. Atop a telescopic tripod next to that was a small satellite dish, which pointed toward the heavens.

With Tonka and Maddie looking on, Jazz first flew the drone over the mountains then took it out over the water. The drone's ISR feed revealed an unremarkable coastline along the southwestern lip of the Dospat Reservoir. For nearly fifteen minutes, the screen of the laptop exhibited nothing more than varying shades of black and gray. As the drone swept back and forth over the landscape, shapes and colors changed. Several structures soon came into view, some large, some small. But only one of them stood out from the others. It was more compound than lake house and it was aflame with lights.

"Take a pass around this one," said Tonka pointing at the screen of the laptop.

Jazz guided the drone over the well-lit lake house then flew wide concentric circles around the property on which it sat. The drone's thermal sensors picked up the heat signatures of several figures along the outskirts which, on the screen, shone like white apparitions.

"Security force?" Maddie said.

Tonka nodded. "That's it. That's our target house."

73

Rainey had left his operational phone with a support staff officer from Sofia Station who had been given the all-important task of living the legend of Jean-Michel Durand in the digital space at least for the next day or so. The man had been given only one commandment: no calls, only texts and emails. That way the charade would not be exposed by voice recognition software the Russians or anyone else might be employing in their technical exploitation of the Durand's phone. It was safely assumed, after all, that the phone was indeed compromised at this point.

The support staffer had been armed with a list of ready-made emails to send at predetermined times. To Aleksy Nowak. To AJ, the fictitious office staff member at DPSC headquarters, who in reality was Janna Carlson, the Jaguar team's staff operations officer dutifully holding down the fort inside Suite 922. The support staffer would also shoot emails to a handful of business contacts that Durand had made at the expo in London. To further facilitate this deception, anytime the young support staffer used Durand's device, he'd wear a Hollywood-type mask made of synthetic materials that had been expertly crafted by the science and tech gurus at Langley. Rainey needed to be in two places at the same time, thus, the stand-in needed to look identical to Durand, too—the phone was compromised, after all, and that certainly would include the device's cameras.

All this, while Rainey, wearing his own masterful disguise, slipped away to the airport, where, using a false passport, he boarded a commercial flight to Naples then another to Thessaloniki. Once there, another support staffer, this one a woman from Athens Station—Rainey had met her briefly during his and Saul Baker's little rendezvous with Grigory Kapustin—collected him and whisked him to the safe house in Asvestochori, where Job was awaiting his arrival.

"We've found the lake house." Job pointed to it on a topographical map, which was spread out on the dining room table. On a laptop next to it, Brigid Finn had a digital version pulled up. Flashing blue dots marked the location of each member of the Jaguar team. A number of them were spread out in the town of Dospat. Others were congregated on a wooded hillside overlooking a large central structure, which was encircled by buildings of lesser size on the southwestern shore of the reservoir. A grassy knoll ran from the three-story main house down to a small, man-made, sandy beach and a modest boat dock.

"What's the security situation?" Rainey asked.

"Armed guards are spread out all over. There are overwatch positions here, here, and here. There is a roving patrol, too. We've counted a total of twelve men thus far and that's just on the exterior."

"Is Nourani there?"

"We haven't been able to confirm that yet. Though the security posture would certainly suggest an HVI is currently inhabiting the property." HVI stood for *high-value individual*.

Rainey nodded, his eyes still fastened to the screen. "I'll do it."

"Ray, I'm not asking you to go through with the—"

"We need to verify he's there. If he is, it's the perfect time to take him out."

Job did not debate the point, but everyone knew what was at stake if Rainey were to be discovered. "Very well," he said. "We need a code word such that when you utter it, we will know he is present."

The word came to him immediately. "*Divine.*"

"Okay. Now, I only want you to ID him. After the meeting is over, you, Fig, and Babe will leave—I repeat, you *will* leave—and then we will look for our opportunity to dispatch him."

"There is one thing I have been meaning to ask you," said Rainey.

"What is it?"

"When Nourani is dead, it will be assumed that either we or the Israelis are responsible."

"Without a doubt. What are you getting at?"

"We need to protect Mahfouz," said Rainey. "I have an idea that will do just that as well as throw Hezbollah's and maybe even Iran's leadership into chaos. But we need to move quickly." Rainey shared his idea.

Job stood there, silently taking it all in before he finally spoke. "I like it."

Rainey cracked a smile. "I thought you might."

"In truth, I was conjuring up something similar. Great minds think alike." Job winked then padded over to his laptop computer and began issuing orders via the secure feed to his staff back at headquarters.

The door creaked open, and Rainey turned toward the man just now entering. "Pappy. What are *you* doing here?"

"I'm *every*where, young buck." Saul Baker bellied up to the table. "I've heard from our Russian friend. Apparently, you are quite the hot topic in the cable traffic coming into and out of their European *rezidenturas*. Not *you*, mind you, but Durand. I know I don't have to tell you to be careful, but I'll do it anyway. The Russians would like nothing more than to kill the new owner of Tomovco, Limited. The purchase of that company right under their noses was akin to pantsing them in the town square and having it broadcast on primetime TV. The Kremlin is in a rage."

Rainey considered this, but nothing could distract him from his mission: killing Qais Nourani and anyone else involved in the attack on America soil.

After the briefing, Rainey changed into shorts and running shoes—he needed to get away for a bit, to think and to pray. There were two places where he did his best thinking: in the blacksmith shop on his Northern Virginia farm while pounding on red-hot metal; and during strenuous, long-distance runs in the wilderness. Since he was nowhere near his forge, Rainey took to the mountains rising out of Asvestochori.

He soon found himself treading in a steady rhythm up a long gradual slope with a forest of cypress and pines pressing in on either side of him. As he rounded the next corner, he glimpsed a castle-type structure perched on the wooded mountaintop like a giant bird's nest. He soon heard singing. It grew louder as he drew closer. By the time he finally reached the turn-off for the Holy Monastery of St. Timios Prodromos of Serres, the singing had stopped, the earth now filled with a consolable silence but for the breeze gently jostling the trees.

He followed the narrow, gravel drive to an iron gate. It stood open, an outstretched hand welcoming him inside. He proceeded onward through it, his pace now a slow walk. His heart rate was racing steadily back to normal, his breathing returning to a relaxed state. A large stone complex rose up before him. It looked to have been built 500 years ago, probably more. A few tourists wandered about, their smartphones out, pointed this way and that. He was about to turn and head back toward the road when an old woman cloaked in a black, hooded robe appeared. A nun, he thought.

She invited him to come inside, first in Greek, but after noticing the look of incomprehension on his face, repeated her proposal in English. She slowly bowed her head when Rainey, smiling, accepted.

They entered through a heavy wooden door with a thick, wrought-iron ring for a handle. He quietly followed her down a dark corridor that smelled of incense and earth. It bore them into a chamber of wood-paneled walls and dusty, blood-red candles that were set about in various places. The only light came from the sun as it seeped in through the narrow stained-glass window on his left. A worn Bible lay open on a hand-carved table next to a sturdy chair with wings and aged upholstery. She offered him the chair on the opposite side of the table then withdrew back into the corridor, pulling the door closed behind her. Rainey searched the room with his eyes as he waited, politely trying not to sweat on the old furnishings. The paintings and prints on the wall told the story of the life of Christ and various other significant events detailed in the Bible. In one, the Son of God lay in a manger—the only source of light in the picture—while Mary and Joseph and three shepherds looked on in awesome wonder. The shepherd nearest the Christ Child appeared as though he were offering a prayer of thanksgiving. Rainey had seen the painting before. He was struggling to remember the painter's name when the old nun re-entered the room. She came bearing a tray with coffee and cake.

"Thank you, Sister," he said, accepting the small plate of sweets.

"Actually, it's Mother." The woman's eyes fell closed as she bowed her head. "What brings you to Greece, my child? You are quite obviously not a local."

"Business. I was just out for a run and noticed the," he was searching for the right word, "church. It's very beautiful."

The nun smiled graciously. "This is a monastery."

"Sorry."

"Some people would say we are all running. Some of us are running *to* something, and some are running *from* something. Which is it for you?" Her English was very good. It had only the slightest bit of an accent—a German accent.

Rainey wasn't quite sure how to answer. "The paintings are lovely."

"Thank you, but you failed to answer my question." She paused before adding, "I've made you uncomfortable. Forgive me." She stood and walked across the room to a desk as old as the paintings. "Would you believe me if I said that I knew you were coming?"

You're a nun, why wouldn't I believe you? Rainey took another bite of his cake and shrugged his shoulders.

"You are conflicted. Between your faith and something you did or must do. I don't know which. I want you to know that forgiveness is real, my child. And confession is good for the soul."

Rainey reached for his coffee cup. He let the hot liquid wash down his throat. Then before the nun could utter another word, he said, "I'm going to kill someone."

The nun was suddenly in want of words. She paced back to the chair and eased her diminutive frame down into it. "I see."

"I've upset you."

"The suggestion of killing someone is rather upsetting. Is there any way of talking you out of it?"

"No. It must be done." Rainey gazed at the wall. Set within a decorative wooden frame—probably hand-carved like the furniture, he thought—was a reproduction of Michelangelo's *David and Goliath*. "All I will say is that there are times when killing is righteous."

"And you consider yourself to be the purveyor of righteousness?"

Rainey took a sip of coffee and looked her dead in the eyes. "I take no pleasure in it, believe me. But it is a task that must be done. And someone has to do it." A pause. "Are you familiar with chapter thirteen, verse four in the book of Romans?"

If the nun was surprised by his reference to Scripture, she didn't show it. "I am. And you think you are God's minister, His avenger sent to execute wrath on those who do evil?"

Rainey cradled his cup in his hands and was silent.

"You think that by acknowledging this verse you are somehow absolved of your sins, your intention to commit murder?"

He shook his head. "I didn't say that, but there is a stark difference between a murderer and a killer."

"Which is?"

"One kills to take life. And one kills to save it."

"And you are the latter then?"

"I'm certainly not the former. But you would agree that sometimes there are actions so heinous, so evil, that by engaging in them, one gives up his right to live?" At her lack of response, Rainey finished his coffee and placed the cup back on the tray as though he were putting the matter firmly beyond the limits of further discussion. "So, how is it that a woman of German heritage finds herself here in a Greek monastery?" It was an educated guess, but still a stab in the dark, nonetheless. One he hoped would turn the conversation in a new direction.

There was a bit of shock in her eyes, but she recovered quickly and grinned albeit nervously. "You are the first one to notice." She drew in a long breath and sighed as if she were finally relieved to have the opportunity to confide in someone. She twisted her body and looked toward the door then turned back to face him. "I *was* born in Germany, just as you say, outside Berlin. We fled the country when I was still just a girl." She seemed to be content to let it go at that, but Rainey's expression nudged her on. She looked down at her hands. They were folded tightly in her lap because they had begun to tremble. "My father did things, you see. In the war."

"Which war?"

"The only one that mattered for Germany."

He thus knew she was referring to the Second World War.

"We were on the run for years, for what I did not know until much later in life. When I was ten, we joined the ratlines. We lived among a small community of fellow Germans in Argentina for almost ten years. Until one day my father suddenly decided to move us back to the Continent. He never said why, or at least never told us kids. We settled briefly in Italy before finally making our way here to Greece. We lived in the port area of Athens, called

Piraeus. We were only to speak Spanish. Never German. Though I suppose my English still betrays my German heritage."

"Your father was a Nazi."

She began to cry but maintained her composure as she continued. "He was SS. I learned the truth about him when I was twenty-six years old. I learned things about him, things he did to those poor Jews. Things I can never forget no matter how hard I try." Her frail, liver-spotted hands twisted and turned in her lap now. "He was posted to Auschwitz, you see. He was Mengele's understudy. His protégé."

"What happened? Did they come for him?"

"No. They never did. So far as I can tell, no one has ever been able to figure out what became of him. He was one of those that got away."

"So, what happened then? Did he live out his years here in Greece?"

She shrunk into her chair and for a moment, Rainey thought she may have fallen asleep but for the subtle shaking of her head.

"What then?"

She cried again now, the tears streaking her face. When the wave passed, she swallowed and confessed, "I shot him."

Rainey was quiet at first then gently said, "I think I see now why you are here."

"My mother had been dead for two years. My brother and sister had moved away to begin their lives. I was home alone one day, going through old photographs and... I had always been curious about why we had moved to South America. I suppose in truth I always knew deep down in my soul.

"So, I went into his study and began in earnest sifting through his private papers, his personal effects, you know. In the back of his closet, hidden under some bags of old clothing, I found a small lockbox. I don't know why, but I pried it open. Inside, I found some old war medals and a typed letter from an Argentine intelligence official offering safe haven to him as well as some other correspondence from Himmler. Items that confirmed my father was *Schutzstaffel*. I also found something else."

"What?"

"His Walther. I immediately wondered how many innocent people he had killed with it. I took it in my hands, loaded it. I was beyond rage." There was pleading in her eyes. "I felt an unbearable burden of guilt. How was it that my father could still walk the earth, go about his business as if nothing had ever happened, knowing full well what he had done? He was a cold-blooded murderer in the truest sense.

"Anyhow, the next day, I arrived in Thessaloniki. It was there that I met a woman who offered me a new life. A different life. A life free from the dirty deeds of my father. And from what I had done to him. A life dedicated to God."

Rainey noticed how she had managed to skip over the most significant details from that day, but he dared not point it out. Clearly, they were still traumatic for her to revisit even now after all these years.

They sat in silence for several long minutes. Rainey wondered why he was here. Perhaps God had led him here for a reason.

"I understand what you must do, child. But be careful. Do not let the fires of wrath consume you. Do not become like the monsters you hunt." Somehow she knew, thought Rainey. "Tend to your soul. Let love into your life. For love conquers all."

When Rainey looked at her, he noticed that she was staring at a painting of Jesus on the cross. "Indeed," he said. "Indeed."

An unspoken bond had formed between them. After another moment of silence, he said, "Well, I must be going. Thank you for the hospitality and for your confidence."

The old woman smiled. "Be safe, my child. I will be praying for you."

Rainey took her tiny, frail hands in his and kissed them. "And I, you."

74

SOFIA – DOSPAT – ASVESTOCHORI

O nce back on Bulgarian soil, Rainey hired a taxi to drive him from the airport toward the city center. A few blocks south of his hotel, the luxurious Sofia Hotel Balkan, he barked at the driver in German-accented English to let him out at the corner. He headed away from the hotel until he was sure no one was following him, then switched course and forged into the stately building by way of a rear entrance. Seeing him enter the suite, the support staff man from Sofia Station—Ted Pharr was his name—promptly handed back the Durand phone and took his leave. Such was the anonymous and oftentimes dull work of an intelligence officer.

The following day, Rainey donned a smart gray suit, silver Battistoni shirt, and an electric-blue necktie before heading downstairs. He took his breakfast with a purposefully garish flare in the hotel restaurant. And when the waiter appeared and asked Monsieur Durand, in the quite rhetorical sense, how he was doing this morning, Rainey uttered something to the effect that he was feeling *much* better today. This would explain to any eavesdroppers, digital or otherwise, why he and his mobile phone had been cloistered away in his room for the past day or so.

Rainey entered his armored SUV at precisely 11:00 a.m. Ninety minutes later, with Fig behind the wheel and Babe seated next to him in the back seat, they were gliding past the Shell station and over the Maritsa River at the south end of Pazardzhik. Next came the mountain villages of Radilovo, Peshtera, and Batak. From there it was an endless panorama of verdant pine forests and brilliant blue skies and not much else for miles and miles.

They stopped to stretch their legs soon after passing a sign that indicated they had entered Smoljan Province. Here, they also checked their weapons one last time—only Fig and Babe were armed—while Rainey sent a cryptic message to Pietrolaj to denote the fact that they were fifteen minutes out from the town of Dospat. An equally cryptic reply came twenty seconds later, causing his phone to pulse. Rainey read the screen. The message was clear: The team was in place, ready, and waiting.

It was just after 2:00 p.m. when they rolled past a pull-off overlooking the sunbathed lake. The weather this week in Bulgaria had been unusually warm for this time of year. As a result, several vehicles were crowded into the small lot, families seated at picnic tables. A man wearing short pants and a backward cap stood behind a tripod-mounted camera that was pointed toward the water. His legs were white as ivory.

Fig pulled into the petrol station on the outskirts of town and topped off the tank. It was one less thing to worry about if they needed to hightail it out of the area. Rainey glanced to his left toward a group of boisterous young men playing soccer inside a rectangle of chain-link fence. Memories of his youth came flooding back to him. But just as quickly he pushed them from his mind. He was no longer Reagan Rainey. He was Jean-Michel Durand.

The motel lot next to the fruit and vegetable store was nearly empty when Fig nosed the SUV into it. He circled around so they were facing the road and shifted the gear lever into PARK.

The time was 2:17 p.m.

Ten minutes and thirteen seconds later, a black Land Rover entered the lot and pulled in behind them. A Middle-Eastern-looking man with sharp, angular features in a lightweight jacket alighted and approached Fig's window.

He glared into the dark glass, struggling to see inside. Finally, still squinting, the man motioned for Fig to roll down the window.

After Fig had lowered the glass, the man said, "Durand?"

"*Oui*," said Fig, covering the pistol he was right now pointing at the man with the left side of his jacket.

The man placed his hands on the sill and leaned into the opening, causing Fig to adjust his aim upward. With penetrating black eyes, the man peered deep inside the vehicle. Apparently satisfied, he withdrew, straightened at the waist, and said to Fig, "You follow."

Fig nodded, then, as the man climbed back inside his vehicle, shifted the SUV into gear and waited for the Rover to nose forward and pass.

The two vehicles turned left out of the parking lot and headed south toward the edge of town. Just as they rounded a bend and continued down the steep slope, another Land Rover emerged from a side street and pulled in behind them.

The three-vehicle convoy glided across a narrow bridge. Beneath them, a large green pipe shot up the valley floor toward the looming dam that held back the waters of the Dospat Reservoir. The road abruptly turned left and led them away from the reservoir and civilization, wound upward into a dense forest of evergreens, where it bent back on itself several times like a coiled snake. Based on the position of the sun, Rainey deduced that they were now headed back toward the southern edge of the lake, where Job and the others had assessed Nourani's friend's lake house stood.

For the sake of anyone listening by virtue of his compromised phone, Rainey grumbled about the circuitous route. "I just hope this isn't a waste of time." He glared out the window as they swept past the dam on their right, a small villa-style hotel their left. Then there was nothing but forest. It reminded him of a place in the Canadian wilderness outside Montreal where he had once endeavored to save a kidnapped scientist and nearly paid for it with his life.

Rocky outcroppings now framed the road as they curled farther up the rising gradient. Runoff from the snowmelt had turned some patches of the road into a mud-caked mess. Fig navigated through the obstacles while Rainey gazed out his window in quiet contemplation. Momentary glimpses of the sun-reflected reservoir shone between the trees. Soon a gate came into view. The trio of vehicles passed through it without slowing. The private lane curved gently to the right and pitched downward through a thick canopy of pines. Here, the pavement leveled off for a bit then dropped again.

With the lake house still out of view, the lead car drew to a stop and a man materialized seemingly out of nowhere. He was armed with a submachine gun and gazed upon them with unmasked suspicion. Rainey recognized him immediately. He had been one of the men in Jawdat Shukri's entourage during the show-and-tell in Sofia. The man walked to Fig's door, smiled, and through the open window, directed his words toward Rainey seated in back, "Your men can wait here." He seemed to be relishing the reciprocal arrangement. "Boss's orders."

"That'll be fine," said Rainey with a polite smile. He murmured something to Fig and Babe before alighting from the vehicle. Outside in the clear mountain air, he buttoned his suitcoat, adjusted the cuffs of his expensive shirt then followed the security man to the lead vehicle. Someone inside opened the rear door from within and an unseen voice asked him to come aboard. He did so without complaint or so much as a look over his shoulder. No sooner was he seated than the armed man who had ushered him to the vehicle, prompted him to slide to the middle seat. He did so at which time the security man climbed in after him and yanked the door closed with a thud.

Outwardly Rainey appeared relaxed and perfectly at ease. He watched with an air of nonchalance as two ATVs ridden by men with long guns emerged from a nearby trail, parked and the men dismounted.

The SUV maneuvered forward enough so that the trailing vehicle could squeeze past Fig and Babe, then together both vehicles shot down the wooded lane out of sight.

75

Dospat, Bulgaria

Rainey casually sized up the men inside the vehicle as they cruised at speed through the dense Bulgarian forest. He noticed their eyes, the way they scanned the landscape. He also took stock of the manner in which they held their weapons. These were not rented security guards. These men were well-trained and no doubt combat-tested.

Soon the wooded canopy gave way to a small clearing on which the sun shone brightly. They continued across it then disappeared back into the woods once again. The lane then began to slope downward toward the water. Finally, they drew to a stop outside a large house. The exterior was all windows and stone and red cedar. Low fieldstone walls stretched around the structure and disappeared around the far side. The house was not unlike many he had seen on the coast of Maine. It possessed a grand, rustic beauty.

As he exited the vehicle, Rainey detected the fragrant scent of pine and grilled meat. In between the haunting screams of a honey buzzard, he could hear the water not more than a hundred yards away lapping at the shoreline. A small boat was buzzing across the lake in the distant background.

They led him across a paved forecourt, up a set of steps made of stone, and inside the home's main entrance. He was shown to a spacious sitting room with a great stone fireplace. Black lantern-style pendant lights hung from timbers high above. Rainey walked to the far wall—it was nothing but glass.

The view it gave of the sun-sparkled water, the lush forest, and sapphire-blue sky was breathtaking.

A familiar voice wandered into the room. A confident baritone. Rainey immediately recognized it as the same voice he had heard on the phone previously. But this time the man was speaking Arabic with a distinctly Lebanese flavor. As Rainey turned toward the sound, the leader of Hezbollah's Unit 910 descended the three steps that separated the large sitting room from the corridor beyond, which incidentally gave the room a noticeable nest-like feel.

"Monsieur Durand, I am Qais al-Nourani. So nice to finally make your acquaintance." Despite the slight Lebanese accent, the man's French was flawless. Hezbollah's external operations commander extended his right hand.

"*Oui*. I have been looking forward to this." Nourani's hand was dry and strong and calloused. How many innocent lives had he taken with those hands? Rainey had to fight the strong urge to kill him right then and there. But of course that would be suicide. There were armed men all around. And he carried no gun.

"Yes. I as well," said Nourani. "Thank you for agreeing to meet with me on such short notice."

"Believe me. It is my pleasure. This area of Bulgaria is beautiful. The view on the drive in was divine."

Job circled behind Brigid Finn, his attention fully tuned to the monitor showing the drone feed as the sound from Rainey's adulterated phone came across the speakers. Initially, there had been a few moments of static, but now the audio was crystal clear.

"This area of Bulgaria is beautiful. The view on the drive in was divine."

"There's the code word," said Job. He stopped pacing the room as he pressed the push-to-talk button connected to his headset mic. "Victor Four, this is TOC. Do you read? Over."

Tonka's voice was clear and calm as if he were casually ordering dinner in a restaurant and not preparing to launch an assault on one of the world's most dangerous and well-protected terrorists. "TOC, Victor Four. Roger. You're five by five. Over."

"Victor Four, we are a go. Initiate DIVINE protocol. I repeat. Initiate DIVINE protocol. How copy?"

"Good copy, TOC. That's a big Rog. Initiate DIVINE."

"Godspeed, all. TOC out."

"I've heard good things about you," Nourani said with a mirthless smile.

Rainey replied with silence and assumed the disposition of someone who enjoyed his privacy. He followed Nourani's lead and sat. The man was apparently not a pious Muslim, for he summoned an aide to bring them spirits at once. Rainey declined the alcohol and instead opted for tonic water with a lime.

They soon fell into a discussion about the politics of Europe—the continued fallout from Brexit, the status of the EU, and so on.

"My people tell me you are looking to expand your operations."

So now we get to it.

Rainey lowered his forehead. "My people tell me you are looking to fortify yours."

Nourani smiled. His eyes diverted to another man, who had just now entered the room. Sadiq Ammar al-Hamadeh eased into a chair equidistant from both men and when offered a drink by his master held up a hand. Sadiq did not consume alcohol.

"Monsieur Durand, I believe you know my associate."

Rainey raised his glass, and with a twinkle of mischief in his eye, said, "We haven't been formally introduced."

Sadiq was not amused. Save for a flash of pure hatred, his face remained emotionless.

"No hard feelings?" said Rainey.

Nourani assessed his man who chose to remain silent at the subtle provocation. "Apparently, he is still upset over how you compromised his team in London. He'll get over it.

"Now, to the matter of your industry. We, that is my organization, should like to arrange for the immediate purchase of ten Javelin launchers and 50 missiles. Here is a list of some other items that we would like to acquire."

Rainey examined the paper studiously, at one point pulling his expensive fountain pen and a slim notepad from his suit coat and doing some quick math. Afterward, he folded the paper and squirreled everything away in his breast pocket. He held Nourani's intense gaze for a few beats, ostensibly thinking, then quoted his price.

"Twenty-eight and a half million euros is a lot of money."

"It is indeed."

Nourani considered this. "This includes shipping charges?"

"No. That would be on top of the twenty-eight point five. The exact amount would depend on where and how you want the items to be shipped. I could offer assistance in this matter if you wish. For an additional fee."

"You are not cheap, my friend."

"*Oui, monsieur*. But in this business, you get what you pay for. I specialize in quality products. If you want third-rate Chinese knockoffs that explode when they are fired or fail to fire at all, then I suggest you go to one of my competitors. What I provide is top-of-the-market quality merchandise." Rainey sipped his drink.

"How would you suggest these items be shipped? Security is of utmost concern to us." He did not have to mention the recent Israeli operations: the exploding pagers and radios, the bombing of Hezbollah headquarters and weapons depots.

Rainey crossed his legs. "For these items, I would prefer to ship through Dubai. The freight would be labeled as something like farm equipment. It would be placed on a ship there and delivered to the port of Beirut. Or for an additional cost, it could be flown instead. In either case, I have a number of companies at my disposal through which to make the shipment appear one hundred percent legitimate. And I *guarantee* delivery. Once the cargo reaches Beirut, my job is done. At that time, you will pay me the balance of the purchase price."

"Speaking of payment, how does that work with your company?"

"I'm glad you asked. Prior to shipping the merchandise, I will have one of my companies send an invoice to Mr. Asada of KVR Group for the first half of the payment. Upon receipt of the order, he shall receive a second invoice. He will be given instructions regarding how and where to wire the money. Or if you would prefer, we can arrange for another method of payment. I am quite fond of diamonds." Rainey grinned.

"Your operation seems very professional."

"As I said, you get what you pay for."

Fig and Babe were still parked along the wooded lane at the far reach of the property. The pair of Hezbollah security men hovering around the Polaris Ranger 570 ATVs they had arrived on had apparently been tasked with babysitting them. Fig tried making small talk early on, but the grim-faced men weren't interested in fraternizing. Perhaps they didn't speak English. Since then, the two Jaguar men sat in their SUV, listening for radio traffic via the small earpieces each of them wore. Each, too, carried a key fob remote in their left pants pocket with which they could click responses back to Job in the TOC without the need of uttering a word. This allowed them to remain covert in their monitoring of what was going on with all Jaguar elements while outwardly appearing to be nothing more than Durand's bored bodyguards. A third button on the key fob would activate a VOX feature turning their earpieces into voice-activated radios.

At the mention of the code word DIVINE, Fig made eye contact with Babe in the rearview mirror. Together, they listened intently as Job and Tonka communicated back and forth.

Then it was their turn.

"Victor Six and Seven, this is TOC. Do you read? Over."

Babe clicked an affirmative response.

"TOC copies. We have initiated the DIVINE protocol. I repeat. We've initiated DIVINE protocol. How copy?"

Babe clicked again. As soon as Rainey was off the X and had returned to the vehicle, the three of them would make a hasty retreat from the area while Tonka and the others would move on Nourani. Assuming all went according to plan, that is.

"TOC copies. Over."

76

Evelina and Ignacio Delgado were sipping coffee beneath a salmon-colored umbrella at an outdoor café along Route 37, Dospat's main thoroughfare. To anyone paying attention, they would appear as an attractive couple lazily touring European out-of-the-way places while on holiday. Their job, however, was to monitor the activity in town—look for signs of countersurveillance or anything else of concern to the operation. If all went well, the two of them would simply disappear as inconspicuously as they had arrived. If there were complications, however, they would act as an additional transport option for the operators upon exfil.

Delgado nudged her leg with the toe of his shoe. "Not liking the look of *this*."

Evelina casually pulled her hair up into a ponytail. As she did so she looked left and noticed the four vehicles approaching swiftly from the north. She finished tying up her hair and bounced her foot on her crossed legs. Now, holding her phone up to seemingly take a photo of Delgado across the table, she pretended to tease him into a pose. As he made a goofy face in response, she hit record, focusing her phone's video camera on the vehicles racing by. When they were out of sight, she keyed her radio.

Though her tone was calm, her message was urgent. "All, this is Victor Two. I think we've got trouble. Four black SUVs with blacked-out windows just sped through town. They are traveling in tight formation. TOC, I'm sending video now."

"Roger, Two. TOC copies."

Jimmy Dunne was next on the air. "Victor One Three copies. I see them. The vehicles are following the road south past the dam. Looks like they're headed for the target location."

"TOC copies."

Brigid Finn guided the drone's camera toward the dam at the southeast end of the reservoir and made several adjustments to its settings while Job hinged at the waist beside her, trying to get a better look at the video file Evelina had just sent.

"All Victor elements, this is TOC," Job said. "Four black SUVs are moving toward the target. Believed to be a hostile force. Execute now. I repeat. Execute. Execute. Execute. Please acknowledge, over."

Fig and Babe clicked a response. Tonka and his team of shooters on the hillside acknowledged the radio transmission as well. The rest of the Jaguar team responded in kind.

Fig leaned his arm out the window and waved over one of the security men who had taken refuge in the shade of a large tree. "You mind if I get out for a smoke?" He made a hand gesture that mimed his question.

The man shrugged.

Fig swung his door open and stepped onto the weather-worn pavement, variously coated with caramel-colored pine needles. For a moment, he stretched his back and legs as if sore from the long journey, then patted his pants pockets in search of his cigarettes. Finding them, he tapped one out, but before he extracted it from the pack, held it out to his contemporary. The man swiveled his head back and forth then walked over to accept it. Suddenly, his eyes widened, neck muscles tensed, and his right arm began to move instinctively toward the weapon strapped around his torso in the split-second before Fig's viperlike hand snapped into his windpipe. The blow stunned him long enough for Fig to drive his fixed blade into his abdomen then the side of his neck just above the clavicle.

Everything happened so quickly that the other Hezbollah man failed to notice Babe exit the far side of the vehicle, circle around it, and approach him from behind. As the gunman ran to attack Fig, the big operator stepped forward and caught him around the neck with his right arm. Babe locked his right hand onto his left bicep and cinched up his grip. It was vice-like. Unbreakable. Next, he drove his right shoulder against the man's temple while squeezing firmly with his other arm. Then using nothing more than leverage, he torqued his upper body to the left. It all happened in a matter of seconds. The sound of the man's neck breaking was like that of someone crunching a hard pretzel in a coat pocket. Babe hefted the lifeless form over his shoulder and walked into the woods, where he dropped the dead man behind a fallen tree.

When he returned, Fig was in a kneeling position, wiping the blood from his knife on the dead man's pant leg. Together they carried the body into the woods and placed it next to the other.

Both men activated the VOX feature on their earpieces and rapidly exchanged their small sub-guns for their more substantial kit, which until now had been hidden in a special compartment under the back seat. This included tricked-out HK416 A5s with suppressed 11-inch barrels, chest rigs with extra magazines, and other gear. They also donned tactical gloves and battle belts on which they each carried a Sig Sauer M17 pistol with a Romeo-M17 red-dot optic and more ammo.

"TOC, Victor Six," said Babe. "Sitrep, over."

"Six, the convoy is thirty seconds out."

"Roger that."

The drone high overhead continued beaming live video via satellite link to the DX operations center in Arlington, Virginia as well as to the safe house in Asvestochori. There, Brigid Finn sat behind a bank of laptop computers with Job Jackson hovering over her like a bird of prey. Together they watched the heat signatures of Fig and Babe dispatching the Hezbollah security men and kitting up. Tonka and the other operators were already moving stealthily through the forest toward the lake house while Wizard, outfitted in a ghillie suit, would provide overwatch from a position with a good vantage point of the property. He would eliminate any threats to the team from afar.

Tonka threw up a hand signal to Mouse, Booster, and Jazz. Each of them in their camo face paint and tactical kit, halted and settled into a combat crouch. They peered through the trees while keeping their rifles up and ready to fire. They could just make out the sound of engines revving and tires chirping from somewhere within the wooded hill country.

Tonka keyed up his radio and ordered his men to prepare to engage. This might be one heck of a gun battle. He didn't have to tell everyone that Rainey was still inside the lake house. They were professionals after all, but the stakes had just gone way up.

Fig and Babe both secreted themselves in the woods near their vehicle. Soon they heard the full-throated growl of an engine and then the commotion of four large SUVs racing down the lane. Fig caught the face of the driver through the windshield of the lead vehicle as it flashed by. The eyes, cheekbones, and skin were decidedly Slavic. The last vehicle in the convoy stopped briefly and two men—the first one also had Slavic features, the other dark hair and olive skin—deployed. It then sped down the lane after the others. The duo moved tactically toward the empty vehicle and checked it for occupants. It was then that one of the men must have seen the blood trail and gazed toward the place in the woods where the dead Hezbollah men lay.

From behind a large rock, Fig whispered to Babe, "I got the one on the left."

"Roger that. On my mark. In three, two, one."

Then in a thunderous chorus, the entire mountainside erupted in gunfire.

77

R ainey was not wearing an earpiece. He'd thought it too risky to do so in that if it were discovered in a search of his person it would tip off Nourani to his intentions and therefore spoil the kill operation. Consequently, he knew nothing of the vehicle convoy racing down the lane toward the lake house. And thus his alarm when Hezbollah security men began shouting wildly in Arabic. His eyes were locked with Nourani's in the precise moment that the first shots rang out. If the terror mastermind suspected Rainey was in any way responsible, he was not given the time to reveal it, for his security minders sprinted into the room and whisked him away with great urgency. Sadiq on the other hand remained behind. As automatic gunfire chattered outside, he rose from the chair and drew a sidearm from beneath his untucked flannel shirt. "I knew you were not to be trusted."

Rainey erupted without a hint of contrived dramatic effect. "I am not responsible for this, you idiot! What have you people—"

Rounds suddenly shredded the walls, throwing up dust and bits of debris all around them. Both men threw themselves to the floor. Sadiq spun his head rapidly searching for the origin of the shooting. But Rainey's eyes were still locked on the man stretched out on the Brazilian hardwood before him, the man who had correctly deduced that he was either there to kill Nourani or had led those intent on doing so to their target. In those next chaotic seconds, as bursts of gunfire ripped across the room in seemingly all directions, Rainey understood exactly what was happening. The Russians had come for him. Not for Reagan Rainey, but for Jean-Michel Durand. Pappy had said as much. *The Kremlin was in a rage.*

His mind was moving rapidly now. The operation could still be salvaged, though it would have to be delayed. Rainey considered several things in quick succession. Mahfouz needed to be warned. They would have to let Nourani go, at least for the time being. Most importantly, Jean-Michel Durand must now be dead, and the world would need to know it. But first, Rainey had to survive the immediate situation.

Rainey reached for the familiar metal loop of his karambit. It snapped open as he yanked it from his waistband. Sadiq must have caught the movement in his peripheral vision. Still pressed against the floor, the terrorist extended the gun toward Rainey's face, but Rainey anticipated this. With his left hand, he clamped down on the gun's action, careful to direct the muzzle away at the same time. In that very instant, the pistol spit a round, but because the slide was obstructed when fired, the gun jammed. It didn't matter in any case, because when Rainey lashed out with the karambit, he eviscerated the tendons connected to the flexor muscles in Sadiq's wrist leaving the man unable to grip a pencil much less maintain and fire a pistol. In a flash, Rainey easily disarmed him, cleared the stoppage by rote, and turned the gun back on him. The gun kicked twice in his hand. What resulted were two dime-size holes in the bridge of Sadiq's nose and a Rorschach pattern of blood and brain matter on the sofa beyond.

Window glass sprinkled the room. More gunfire rattled from beyond the house walls. He heard men shouting in Russian. Rainey crawled across the floor and peeked through a hole in the wall created by a burst of 7.62mm rounds. The interlopers were now being fired upon from the woods and they were being decimated. It was clear that Nourani and his security handlers had already fled. This allowed Tonka and the others to focus their efforts entirely on the mystery gunmen. During a brief break in the gunfight, Rainey thought he heard in the distance a motorboat being thrust into action.

The gun battle raged for several minutes more then there was arrant silence. He waited until he saw Tonka, Mouse, and the others descending onto the property with tactical precision. Suddenly, but not for the first time, he felt immense pride in his men. They had saved his hide yet again.

Eleven assaulters in various positions were scattered over the compound. Each one lay dead. One man, mortally wounded after being riddled with bullets, was writhing in agony in the center of the forecourt. In a panic, he was struggling to comprehend the fact that his intestines had spilled from his abdomen. As Fig and Babe came screaming down the lane in the SUV, Mouse stepped to the doomed man, adjusted the muzzle of his carbine, and sent a single round into his forehead thus freeing the man from his abject misery.

Rainey gazed toward the reservoir below. Its mirrored surface still shimmering between the forest trees added a strangely serene effect to the gunsmoke wafting across the landscape. The pungent odor of rent bowels, coppery tang of shed blood, and burnt gunpowder brought him back to his senses. Tonka was already on the radio with Job when he joined his teammates in the forecourt. Rainey pounded fists with each of them as he waited for Tonka to clear the radio net. Once briefed, Rainey issued orders. The SSE—sensitive site exploitation—would need to be quick. Bulgarian authorities were doubtless already en route to their location.

Hurriedly, the team snapped photos of the dead men's faces, rifled through their pockets. None carried identification. *Big surprise.* They searched the four SUVs of the Russian covert assault force. In the lead vehicle, Wizard found a secure handheld radio with Cyrillic markings. He clicked it off and stowed it in a pocket on the leg of his pants.

Twenty minutes later, Jazz emerged with Sadiq's cell phone and a laptop computer that had been left in a bedroom Nourani had apparently been using as an office. It was on this laptop that DX analysts, a week from now, would find files outlining plots to strike locations in Tel Aviv, DC, Riyadh, and six other major metropolitan areas. From the phone of Sadiq al-Hamadeh they would uncover an intricate cell of Hezbollah operatives and facilitators scattered across France and other European nations. Raids in twelve cities would follow leading to numerous arrests, and on two occasions, shootouts in which a total of thirty-two hardened Hezbollah terrorists would be killed. Each raid in turn would lead to three more. It was an avalanche of intelligence collection. The analysts in Langley and Arlington and a number of other allied intelligence services would be busy for months, years even.

The photos they had taken of the dead Russians would later provide incontrovertible proof of precisely who was behind the surprise assault on the Bulgarian lake house.

The operators now assembled in the lane as the other team members who had been previously positioned around Dospat descended upon them in various vehicles for the choreographed exfil.

"Pack it up, people. We gotta roll," said Tonka before turning toward Rainey whose attention was again focused on the sun-sparkling water of the reservoir that continued peeking between the jostling pine branches. "You good, Bronc?"

"Yeah, I'm good. Let's get the heck out of here."

78

MARGARITA ISLAND, VENEZUELA

Within forty-eight hours of the team's return home from the mountains of southern Bulgaria, the incident made international headlines. Various news outlets were now reporting that a large gunfight had broken out on a grand patch of land situated on the shore of the Dospat Reservoir in southern Bulgaria. Among the dead was a Frenchman by the name of Jean-Michel Durand, a mysterious man, who, according to anonymous sources within the Bulgarian government and elsewhere, had been an illicit arms dealer of international renown. More digging uncovered the fact that his company had only recently acquired the Bulgarian arms manufacturer Tomovco, Ltd. From there it didn't take long for several of the more scrupulous journalists to draw a connection to a certain Russian oligarch who had been rumored for some time to have been gunning for Stefan Tomov, the previous owner of the arms manufacturing firm. Requests for interviews with Tomov went unanswered though it soon became known that he had been the target of several recent failed assassination attempts himself.

In a highly sensitive and clandestine coordination with Bulgarian authorities, and working with President Kendall's explicit approval, Job orchestrated everything like the gifted spymaster he was. The confirmed death of the fictitious Jean-Michel Durand along with a genuine autopsy report that had been created out of whole cloth. The production of indisputable evidence of Russian involvement in the fiasco. For the protection of their Hezbollah source, Job arranged for $1.2 million—another consensual though unknowing contribution from Stedman Carter to the operation—to be deposited into a private and very secret Cypriot bank account held by Jawdat Shukri. Shortly thereafter, with Job's orchestration, the US Treasury Department froze the account due to Shukri's designation as a terrorist. After a little digging by Hezbollah and Iranian investigators, the money would appear to have come from the French DGSE. This all came thanks to the DX analysts' tedious vivisection of Valzbank AG and Erik Walser's secret financial activities.

For their part, the Bulgarians would very quietly receive an expedited and discounted deal on the sixteen new F-16 fighter jets they had been wanting to purchase from the United States along with promises for future bargains on military hardware.

In the ensuing days, Job provided additional information through his trusted media surrogates that would further propel the international intrigue to new heights. It seemed that just days before the dreadful incident in Dospat, a Russian intelligence official named Valery Chernikov had arrived in Sofia. And within mere hours after it, he was seen leaving his embassy and boarding a flight to Moscow. The implication was clear. The Russians were behind the slaying of the Frenchman, Durand. What soon followed was a fast but thorough—and seemingly overt—investigation by Bulgarian authorities which led in turn to the immediate expulsion of Russian diplomats from Sofia and elsewhere as news and outrage spread to other European capitals.

The French were still fuzzy on the details, but Job had provided them with just enough information to cause their declarations of "no comment" to the international media to appear insincere and lacking in candor. When Patrice Bechard, the French DGSI director, finally put the screws to Job Jackson and the CIA's Paris chief of station about what in the world was actually going on, Job informed him about their misguided diplomat, Alban Clement. But by then, Clement and his family had already disappeared. Rumor had it that the Russians had been responsible for that, too. Flying them to Moscow and setting them up with new names and a flat overlooking the Moskva River. But the truth was much simpler in fact. The real story was that Clement and his wife had boarded a private flight in Brussels and were flown to a small airfield outside Frederick, Maryland, where they were then whisked away by members of a US Marshals Service WITSEC team. Clement's daughter had had a similar experience although her disappearance had been administered by rail.

Meanwhile, word came from Turaj Mahfouz through the established covert communication channel regarding the status of Qais Moussa al-Nourani. The operational mastermind of Hezbollah was back in Beirut. The episode in Bulgaria had shaken him badly, but based on the news reports flooding the airwaves, he, Shukri, and the rest of the Hezbollah leadership were buying the story about Durand being the intended target all along. Nevertheless, Nourani had since beefed up the manpower around him and added additional security protocols within the organization.

So, it came as a bit of a surprise when Mahfouz told them Nourani had scheduled another trip abroad so soon after the ordeal in Dospat. This one, as far as Mahfouz could tell, had nothing to do with the procurement of weapons, or any other business relating to the organization. Apparently, Nourani had a mistress who needed tending to. Though Mahfouz did not know exactly how Nourani would be traveling, he did know the date of embarkation, Nourani's destination, and the length of time he planned to be there.

Which is why Reagan Rainey was now gliding through the warm tropical waters off the northeastern coast of Venezuela near a place called Margarita Island. At twenty-four feet below the surface of the water, he looked down at the RNAV screen on the STIDD Diver Propulsion Device, or DPD, in which he lay prone. The ocean water ran smoothly over his dive mask and hooded head, the latest-version Draeger rebreather system strapped to his back, all the way down to the ends of his flippers fluttering as if in slow motion behind him. After another five minutes, he disengaged the autopilot and steered the underwater vehicle along the contours of the sea floor, paying special attention to his instrument panel in order to avoid the rocky outcroppings. It was a moonless night, thus the normally crystal-clear water was black as ink, making it all the more critical to keep his eyes fastened to the RNAV.

At a depth of ten feet, he dismounted, letting the specially modified Maxim Defense SDX-510 with an integrated suppressor and Aimpoint CompM5 red dot strapped to his torso dangle freely. He anchored the DPD to the sea bottom then from a utility rail that ran the length of the starboard side of the vessel, he unclipped a waterproof gear bag and slung it over his shoulder before setting off toward shore. When the water was shallow enough, he poked the top of his head through its surface so that only his eyes were showing. With waves lapping against him, he continued moving forward, quietly bringing the carbine up to meet his shoulder. The sound of water running off him and his gear as he emerged from the sea was drowned out by the crashing tide. Though the technology he wore on his wrist made it unnecessary, he made a mental note of a landmark in front of him to visually mark his landing spot then tactically maneuvered to a crag within the rocky shoreline where he peeled off his mask, rebreather, and dry suit and donned a pair of black Danner Fullbore mids.

His face, smeared with black and gray camo paint, was already slick with sweat from the humid, tropical air. He quickly wiped the dampness from his hair then reached into the gear bag and pulled out his bump helmet, attached to which was a set of NODs (night observation devices). He slipped on the helmet, adjusted the already connected Peltor headset, and rocked the NODs down in front of his eyes, clicking them on by rote. Next, Rainey unclamped a hard plastic container and removed his AN/PRC-148 JEM encrypted multiband radio, slipped it inside a pocket beside the three magazine pouches on his chest rig. He plugged it and his headset into the Invisio PTT unit affixed to the MOLLE strap on the left side of his chest rig, right next to his heart, where he liked it. Whether it was an operation-specific chest rig like this one or full battle kit, Rainey was a creature of habit when it came to his gear setup.

Now, under his four-tube, alien-looking NODs, he scanned up and down the coastline and quietly powered on his radio. "Swordfish, Victor One. The hurricane has landed. How do you read? Over."

"Victor One, you are Lima Charlie and we see you on station. Godspeed. Over."

"Roger. Out."

The voice in his ears was that of Petty Officer Second Class Gage Terasi, a SEAL Team 8 operator from Naval Special Warfare Group 2. Right now, Terasi occupied the bridge of *Midnight Song*, the super yacht that Rainey and the Jaguar team had used in Athens. Terasi and the rest of his four-man fire team along with some of Rainey's Jaguar teammates were parked just over twelve miles off the coast, watching him via an ISR feed from a stealth drone flying high overhead. If all went well, Rainey would be rejoining them soon. Then Terasi and his SEAL buddies could recommence with their relentless jabs about why *they* should have been out here and not him. Singleton mission or not, he wasn't even Navy. The fact that a former Army D-boy had gotten the nod for this op over them would rub them raw for weeks, months even, and Rainey would make sure it did. But at the end of the day, they were all one team—elite special operators, American warriors—and would die for each other if need be.

Rainey stowed the dive mask, dry suit, and rebreather behind some rocks then checked the digital readout on the armband device affixed to his left wrist. The target location was a little over a half mile away just over the rocky cliff face then a short walk down a slight grade into the small gathering of homes known as Punta Cazonera. Technical surveillance put Nourani in a modest house that stood on the rising hillside directly behind a large mansion owned by a high-ranking Venezuelan army general. But for an older man and woman who tended to its daily maintenance, the mansion was unoccupied and dormant.

Job and Directorate X had watched Nourani for three days after picking up his voiceprint during an electronic sweep of the island. Nourani taking meals. Nourani and his mistress standing ankle-deep in the afternoon tide. Nourani making phone calls and making love. As a result, they knew about the continuous flow of ten armed guards patrolling the area not counting Nourani's fierce four-man retinue of personal bodyguards. The biggest unknown was the mistress. Would she fight? Would she scream? Each night after their sexual exertions, she would bed down with Nourani until morning. Rainey did not wish to harm her and, if possible, would avoid doing so. But if the necessity arose, he would not hesitate for an instant.

With the digital armband device, Rainey could see the ISR feed, thus by virtue of their heat signatures, he could assess exactly where the patrols and Nourani's bodyguards were in real-time.

Silently, he ascended the cliff. It was a less-than-90-degree climb with plenty of footholds and crevices for his gloved hands. However, the darkness and added weight of his gear ramped up the danger. If he fell from up here, he'd likely break his back or a leg. Nearing the top, he paused to catch his breath and let the blood return fully to his limbs before pressing onward.

The first one to die was a man of Venezuelan birth, a local security forces man. Like the others on his team, he had been tasked by the nation's dictator to guard Nourani while he was in country. Smoking a cigarette, the man walked the ridgeline in jungle camo with his AK-103 slung tight against his chest. The subsonic .300 BLK round struck him just below the left eye, making a mess of the back of his head on the way out. Rainey ground out the lit cigarette with the toe of his boot as he moved past the lifeless form sprawled on the rocky path, which soon gave way to patches of wild grass and scrubland.

Rainey kept low as he crested the peak of the beachy ridge then made his way down the escarpment. According to his armband, the next closest human being was nearly a thousand feet to the east—another patrol looking for boats or low-flying helicopters or drones perhaps. Rainey's quiet stroll down the hillside was therefore uneventful. Reaching the edge of the scrub brush, he stopped and knelt. For close to fifteen minutes, he studied the community of homes spread out before him. Lamplight still burned in the windows of a few of them. Minus the dormant mansion, none were close enough to the target house to be worrisome. Aside from the distant swoosh of tides flowing in and out on the beach beyond the homes, he heard only the wind and the intermittent barking of a dog.

He leaned his head back and, looking beneath his NODs, checked the display of his armband again. A white splotch—another guard on patrol—paced into the bushes not more than fifty yards away. Rainey could see the heat signature of urine streaming from the man's waistline and splashing on the ground. He eyed the man through his rifle's optic, concentrated on his breathing for a second, then dropped him where he stood. There was a hushed jostling sound as the man fell face-first into the urine-caked dirt.

Then silence.

The sliding door at the back of the target house stood halfway open. Thin, white linen curtains fluttered in the sea breeze. A large man was perched in a chair on the landing just outside the door with his back to him. According to the armband readout, Nourani's other three personal bodyguards were huddled around a TV at the front of the house. They were probably watching a soccer match based on the rise and fall of crowd noise escaping through the walls.

A ghost who had come to exact vengeance on the man who'd orchestrated the recent attack on America, Rainey crept from cover and drew closer to the bodyguard at the back of the house.

With the suppressor, the subsonic rounds he carried were insanely quiet, but they lacked accuracy and punching power outside of about seventy-five yards or so. Therefore, he needed to get closer.

When he was within fifty yards, Rainey stopped. The muzzle from the shouldered weapon rose not even a little bit as the bullet whispered into the man's left ear. Those watching the ISR feed on the yacht and back in the XOC in Arlington saw a spray of white lava burst from the right side of the bodyguard's head before it dropped sharply downward. There it remained as if the man had suddenly nodded off to sleep never to awake again.

Rainey stalked onto the property and when he reached the corner of the house, stopped once again to watch and listen. As far as he could tell, he was still undetected.

"Victor One, Swordfish. Target and the girl are on the bed."

Rainey clicked his PTT button twice in response. He could now hear sounds of lovemaking.

Ugh.

If tonight were anything like the previous nights they had watched them, their coupling would soon come to a crashing conclusion after which the young twentysomething would retreat to the bathroom for a long, hot shower. And Nourani would collapse on the bed and imbibe his first of several alcoholic beverages.

That's when Rainey would make his move.

But as Rainey would soon learn tonight was nothing like those other nights.

79

Target is getting up. He's walking toward the terrace."

Rainey didn't bother to respond to Gage Terasi, the Navy SEAL in his ear. There was no time. He heard the strike of a match, saw its glow within the dark void of the open door. Next, he smelled the secondhand smoke escaping into the night air. He quietly lowered his carbine, let it hang from the sling around his frame, flipped up his NODs, and, with his right hand, slowly drew the black Toor Knives Valor fixed blade from the Kydex sheath on his chest rig.

Nourani stood just inside the door, his bare toes visible on the other side of the threshold. A cigarette pinched between thumb and index finger, flashed upward in an arc. Nourani's face and the rest of his naked body were still veiled in darkness just inside the doorway. A red glow blossomed within the void, as the terrorist took a long drag from the cigarette. After several tense seconds, the terrorist's left hand emerged, gripped the edge of the door, and pushed it the rest of the way open. Another cloud of secondhand smoke wafted through the opening, this time followed by the terrorist himself.

Wait for him, thought Rainey. *Just a few more steps.*

Nude and self-satisfied, Nourani stepped fully onto the terrace and rotated his head toward the bodyguard slumped in the chair. Alarm all at once shot through his body. It was in that very instant that a strong hand clamped over his mouth, and simultaneously something long and sharp pierced him from behind. Nourani let out a grunt, jerked his head from side to side. For a brief second, he observed what at first registered as the tip of a spear jutting from his sternum. Then his brain made sense of it. The sharp metal object was not a spear but a knife, and it was slick with dark, inky blood. *His* blood.

He attempted to shake free, but whoever was on the other end of the blade only rammed it into him with more force, the hand vice-locked on his face squeezed tighter. Nourani groaned in agony. He lurched, swung an elbow backward, clawed helplessly for the man's head behind his own. But his attacker dodged the frantic swipes as if he'd done this a thousand times before, tilted him backward, and at the same time torqued the blade violently upward so that Nourani was now off balance. His bare feet scraped the surface of the stone terrace but could find no purchase.

As blood pumped from his mortal wound, Nourani attempted to squirm. But in his weakening state, his head merely rolled to the left and to the right. Over his shoulder, he glimpsed what simply could not be. *Horror*. There, beneath special night-vision eye gear and black-and-gray camouflage face paint was the arms dealer, Jean-Michel Durand.

For he was not dead but alive.

Rainey withdrew the blade and this time thrust it downward on a forty-five-degree angle through the side of Nourani's exposed neck just above the collarbone. He levered its tip forward, severing the man's windpipe and major blood vessels. As he lowered Nourani to the ground, he whispered into his ear, "For God and country, scumbag."

Nourani's blood-drenched face was a rictus of shock and doom. He knew. Knew that Durand was not dead. Knew he'd been betrayed. Knew that the Americans had bested him.

Knew he was a dead man.

Rainey stood up, carefully scanning the terrain that surrounded the terrace as he wiped the blood from his knife on the fluttering curtain next to him. The radio suddenly came alive in his ear. "Victor One, Swordfish. Someone is coming toward your pos. From the front of the house."

One of the guards must have heard something, or maybe he was just doing a routine check.

Rainey slipped inside the bedroom and immediately heard the lilting voice of Nourani's mistress spilling from the bathroom. She was singing in the shower, oblivious to the fact that her secret lover was dead on the terrace.

He killed the dim lamp by the bed and pulled down his NODs as he moved across the room, posted himself in the doorway. As soon as the bodyguard came into view, Rainey smoked him with two rounds to the chest. The sound of the suppressed weapon and that of the large man falling to the floor drew the attention of the others in the living room. One of them called out something in rapid Spanish.

In a matter of seconds, Rainey was on them firing whisper-quiet controlled bursts into their chests and heads before they could raise their weapons or radio for reinforcements. Gunsmoke mixed with bits of dust and aerosolized blood and brain matter hung in the air while the soccer game on the big screen played on. The TV's colorful, crisp display provided an undulating glow that flickered and flashed and bounced about the room.

Game over, turdballs.

Rainey left everything as is, retraced his steps through the bedroom, across the terrace, and back down the rocky cliff. He pushed his kit into the waterproof bag and squeezed back into the dry suit then pulled on his dive mask and made a few quick adjustments to the rebreather. Once ready for the long ride back to the yacht, he submerged himself beneath the surface of the water and disappeared.

80

Nourani's naked, blood-caked corpse was discovered along with the bodies of the others the following morning when a servant came to deliver the Hezbollah man's breakfast. By then Rainey had already returned to *Midnight Song*, which, too, had long since vanished. There was no sign of the mistress either. The woman surely must have realized that she would somehow suffer the blame for the ghostly massacre, which seemed to have struck the Margarita Island home like a biblical plague.

It didn't take long for the hot-fire news of Nourani's assassination to rage through Hezbollah's offices, military bases, and secret training camps in Lebanon, Syria, and Iran. Its newly christened secretary-general was livid. So, too, were Tehran and its terrorist conscripts the world over. Though who was responsible was not entirely a mystery, *how* it happened was an altogether different matter. An operation like this could have been carried out by only a handful of people. At the top of that list were the Israelis, the Americans, and the British. Strangely, not one of them was saying a word beyond the typical vanilla responses. When asked point blank by an oppositional reporter who prided himself on putting less-than-thoughtful questions to White House officials in the Press Briefing Room, the president's new fresh-faced press secretary blithely stated that the world was a better place because of Nourani's death, though she artfully refrained from mentioning him by name, choosing instead to refer to the Hezbollah mastermind as one of the world's biggest monsters of terror. In the weeks and months that followed, her words would become one of the most repeated chyrons in cable news history as media outlets relentlessly dug for the true circumstances that led to Nourani's return to prominence and ultimate demise. In the meantime, all that existed in the public domain were wild speculation and exaggerated rumors.

For the president's part, he was utterly silent. So, too, were the premiers of Israel and Great Britain. Even the Saudis seemed to be keeping quiet. For those in the Agency and the tight-lipped ranks of special operators who were accustomed to their politicians running to the cameras and grandstanding after a celebrated American operation, President Kendall was a breath of fresh air.

Rainey took in his surroundings as he waited on the doorstep. The neighborhood was leafy and tranquil, not unlike the one outside Annapolis where he had grown up. The sound of a lawn tractor droned from a yard somewhere out of view. He tilted his head back and took in the aroma of freshly cut grass, honeysuckle, and lilac. High above, a silver-white jet silently drew a chalky white line across a canvas of pure blue sky. Briefly, he wondered about the people aboard it. Who were they? Where were they headed?

When the door swung open, he turned back toward the house. On the other side of the threshold, he found a much different Lacey Killian than the one he had encountered in New York City in December. Her hair was neatly done, her clothes were classy and fashionable and not marred by the grime of war. She stepped back and welcomed him inside. After showing him into the living room, she made a gracious offering of coffee or tea. Coffee, he said.

He gazed about the room as he waited in silence. Countless sympathy cards were stacked on one of the shelves of a large white bookcase. Potted flowers—some of them were beginning to wilt—and other colorful mementos from Ryan Killian's funeral and memorial services were still scattered about the room. Inside a glass case on the mantelpiece was a folded American flag bookended by wood-framed photographs. On one side was a portrait of her husband in his dress blues, the other a candid picture of him smiling broadly at a family gathering.

"He was always the life of the party," said Lacey, returning to the room. "His antics kept everyone in stitches."

A beautifully framed tribute hung from the fireplace above the flag. Rainey studied it as Lacey related how it had been given to her as a commemoration of Ryan's life of service to the Upper Darby Township Police Department and the surrounding communities. At its center were his badge and handcuffs, surrounded by which were an official department photo and two citations, one signed by the governors of Pennsylvania and New York, the other by the president of the United States of America.

"He was a patriotic man who would literally give anyone the shirt off his back." She stared at the photo of her late husband, the one with him smiling.

Rainey had been here before. Not the Killian home, of course, but the place where freedom's rent came due. It was the aftermath of a hero's final act. The space where family and friends, co-workers and brothers- and sisters-in-arms mourned the loss of their loved one. He hated this place with every fiber of his being. He had been here far too many times in his life already.

They sat down. "I won't stay long. I just came by to offer my condolences to you and the family. And to give you this." He held out his hand. Inside was a worn piece of embroidered fabric. "I will never forget what Ryan did for me."

Lacey grinned through the painful memory evident in her eyes.

"I made you a promise in New York. Do you remember?"

She nodded as she accepted the departmental patch.

"That's from one of his uniforms—a friend procured it from one of Ryan's fellow officers. I hope you don't mind. I carried it with me when I..."

He gathered himself. "Suffice it to say that I've kept my promise. The person responsible for what happened in New York, for what happened to Ryan, won't hurt anyone else ever again. I can't go into any further detail, but I wanted you to know that."

Lacey's arms curled inward. She drew the patch into her balled-up hands and pressed it against her chest. She closed her eyes, bowed her head as if she were right then and there offering a silent prayer of thanksgiving. When she looked back up her eyes were red, her face streaked with tears. Finally, she rose and walked to the dining room table from which she retrieved a box of tissues.

As etiquette dictated, Rainey also stood and followed her to the edge of the room. He waited as she staunched a fresh flow of tears. Outwardly, Rainey was stoic. His jaw muscles flexed as he willed himself not to cry. When Lacey moved toward him and hugged him, he couldn't help but respond in kind. "I pray this will give you and your family some measure of comfort."

She withdrew and again dabbed her eyes. "It will. Thank you."

Rainey noted a family portrait on the wall above the sideboard. "How are the boys doing?"

"Caedmon's only three, so I don't think he fully understands yet." Outside the French doors, the little boy was playing with Matchbox cars in the grass. His car and truck noises carried easily through the glass. "I'm more concerned about Carson. Outwardly, it doesn't seem like anything is bothering him, but I know he is hurting. He and his father were very close. I think he's trying to hide his true feelings."

Rainey knew instantly what she meant. He could relate perhaps more than anyone.

He followed Lacey's eyes through the back door. Carson was in the treehouse, which had been constructed in a massive oak tree in a far corner of the yard. Legs dangling from the platform, his arms were folded over one of the wooden deck rails, his chin resting atop them. He was facing away from the house, toward the setting sun, and seemed to be thinking or daydreaming or both. Every now and then he would swing his feet.

"Ryan and Carson built that treehouse together. Carson's spent a lot of time in it since..." She sniffled. "I worry about him. He loved his daddy very much. Ryan was a wonderful father." With a tissue, she again dabbed at the corners of her eyes.

"Do the boys have other men in their lives?"

"They have lots of uncles and my father is over almost every day, but it's just not the same as having a father, especially one like Ryan. He was so invested in their lives."

Rainey grinded his teeth, fighting back a swell of emotion then confided, "I lost my father at a young age, too." Hearing himself say the words brought another wave, so he paused, collected himself all the while focusing on the 11-year-old in the treehouse. He couldn't be sure, but it seemed like Carson was talking to himself out there. "Do you mind if I speak with him?"

She shook her head and walked off as a flood of tears washed down her face.

Rainey patted the head of the younger brother, knelt briefly, and commented on a few of the trucks that were piled high with grass clippings. The boy smiled and poured a tiny dump-truck load of dirt on the toe of his shoe. Rainey laughed, which caused the boy to laugh, too. His smile was like that of his father. He took his leave when the boy turned back to his trucks and began with the engine noises again.

Reaching the bottom of the tree, Rainey gripped several of the wooden slats screwed into the bark. They were solid and held his full weight without creaking as he climbed. He poked his head through the opening in the floor and rapped his knuckles against it. "Permission to come aboard?"

"Who are you?" said the boy.

"My name is Ray." Not knowing how else to describe himself, he said, "I was a friend of your father's."

"I guess you can come up."

Rainey negotiated his way into the treehouse and sat down. "This is a *great* fort."

"My dad and I built it." There was a slight rasp to his voice.

"You did a wonderful job. It's solid as a rock."

They sat in silence for some time just looking off into the distance. The sun began to dip below the horizon, creating a spectacular show of color and texture.

"You want to know something?"

Carson looked at him and shrugged his shoulders.

"I lost my dad when I was about your age. It's hard, isn't it? *Very* hard."

The boy turned and stared at the iridescent sky.

"You know what I could never understand? It was why God allowed it to happen. I mean, it wasn't fair. My dad was a good man, treated me and my sister better than anyone. He loved my mom, worked hard at his job. He was a kind man. Why did he have to die? Why couldn't it be someone else? Someone bad?"

Carson was now looking at him again.

"I struggled with that for a long time. I still do."

"Why does He? Why did God let the bad men hurt Daddy?"

"I don't have all the answers, Carson. Be suspicious of anyone who tells you they do. But I guess I finally came to realize that maybe God allows bad things to happen to good people so that we and others will be drawn to Him. So that people, who might not otherwise think of God or seek God, will turn to Him and draw closer to Him and His Word. Of course, this doesn't mean losing a loved one, like your dad, is any less painful. It still sucks, believe me." Carson nodded. "But I promise you, it *will* get better. That pain right here in your chest"—Rainey reached out and patted him—"will get better with time." He saw the bead of a tear in the corner of the boy's eye but made no mention of it. "Nothing I say will bring your dad back, but one thing that no one can ever take away from you is the memories. Hold on to them. Visit them often. Laugh. Cry. Yeah, I know, I don't like crying either. But it's okay to cry now and then. Allow the memory of your father to drive you to be a better man. Also, and this is huge... Take care of your mom and little brother. You're the man of the house now. That's a lot of responsibility. Can you promise me you'll do your best to protect and comfort them? And be on your best behavior?"

Carson nodded. "I promise."

"Work hard at everything you do. And show those who love you just how much you care about them. Doing this will make your dad proud." He offered his hand and the boy shook it. "Oh, and one more thing."

The boy stared up at him expectantly.

"If you ever need someone to talk to you can always call me." He handed him a challenge coin and a business card. The coin held the emblem of the Greenbriar Foundation, the card, too, along with his email address and the number for his direct line.

Carson looked at each, rubbed his thumb over the embossed logo and 3-D text arching around the circumference of the coin.

"It was nice meeting you, Carson. Stay strong, buddy."

Back inside the house, he handed Lacey a card as well after jotting down his personal cell phone number on the back. "If you need anything, anything at all, I'm just a phone call or text away."

"Thank you, Mr. Rainey."

"*Ray.*"

"Thanks, Ray."

81

R ainey padded into his study, where Saul was reading by lamplight. He pulled a devotional off the shelf and fell into the leather chair in front of the fireplace, which was aglow with lambent flame.

"Do you mind?" he said, picking up a remote from the small round table beside him.

"Not at all. I was just about to hit the sack anyway."

Rainey clicked on the stereo and Schumann's "Kinderszenen, Op. 15: No. 7, Träumerei" instantly filled the room. Book in hand, he stared at the fire crackling inside the hearth for nearly a minute then flipped to the business card he used for a bookmark and began reading. Unfortunately, the words on the page were soon lost to memories of past exploits, including Operation End of Days, as well as friends he'd lost to war and suicide. There were far too many in both categories.

In the morning, Rainey awoke early, did some light housecleaning, and prepared to receive his Jaguar teammates and their families. It had been Maddie's idea for everyone to get together outside of work. Soon they were pulling up in the drive, kids tumbling out of SUVs and minivans. His heart lightened as Mouse's three girls, each of them with long, yellow-gold hair, alighted from a big Suburban and took in their pastoral surroundings. The youngest—she was two—clung to a baby doll as she followed her mother and sisters to the front door. Mouse hefted a cooler, atop which teetered a picnic basket, from the back of the vehicle then trailed behind in their wake.

He had to admit, it was refreshing to see all of his teammates—old and new—together for the first time outside of the grim-faced reality that was their daily existence. These were people, human beings, after all, not machines. And they had wives, husbands, sons, and daughters, who in their own right were heroes, too. They sacrificed daily in their support of America's warrior spies. It brought joy to his heart to see them, to hear them laugh and play, to embrace them.

Before long Jazz and Wizard commandeered the grill. Throughout the afternoon, they kept the burgers, brats, steaks, and hotdogs coming. And the operators especially, along with the older boys, kept making them disappear.

Soon Janna Carlson produced a box of board games, and several groups of adults and kids gathered around tables. Others tossed a football for a spell until they eventually rallied enough people to play volleyball in the yard. In the shade by the tree line, Booster and Conrad Pietrolaj pitched horseshoes. The man they called Macho had just clanged home a ringer on top of Booster's, judging from the sound of their reveling.

Seated on the patio, Brigid and Maddie were chatting about an upcoming white-hat hacker contest in Las Vegas. Job and his people were already looking at a few prospective attendees as possible recruits.

Standing nearby, each of them cradling a drink, Wes Ruehle (Maddie's fiancé), Jimmy Dunne, and Ignacio Delgado were discussing the intense political battle lines being drawn between the elites entrenched in DC, their cronies in Big Media and Silicon Valley, and the rest of the country.

A few hours in, Tonka's boys sheepishly appeared before their mother. They'd been off on a little expedition from the looks of them. One of them was covered in mud from head to toe, the other sopping wet. Tonka's wife just shook her head. "We can't take you boys anywhere," she said to much laughter.

Ben and Sarah Rainey, Job and Iris Jackson as well as Saul Baker were still huddled around one of the folding tables that had been erected for an outdoor eating space. Ben was smiling broadly as Tonka and his wife labored to clean up the energetic young boys.

Meanwhile, Rainey was sprawled backward in a camping chair with one foot up on one of the large watermelon-size rocks that formed the fire pit, his right arm hooked over the back of the chair. In his left hand, he held an empty bottle of pineapple-coconut juice that he now drummed against his knee in no particular rhythm.

Evelina relaxed into the chair next to him. "I love your place, Ray."

"It's good to see people enjoying it."

"You know, your family is really something. I was talking with your father earlier. He's such an amazing man. And your mom... She's incredible. What a classy lady."

Rainey smiled. "I agree." He turned toward her, saw her staring at the building that housed his blacksmith shop.

"What's in there?"

He told her.

"Maddie mentioned that you had a knack for that kind of thing. Mind showing me?"

The sunlight danced in her eyes. They were oceans of varying shades of green. Like waters of the deep, they held untold secrets of treasure and plundering, mystery and adventure.

"I know what you're doing by the way."

"What?"

Rainey just shook his head.

They walked to the blacksmith shop. Inside, he clicked on the light. What at first he thought would be a simple guided tour, soon, with Evelina's shameless prodding, turned into something of a drawn-out show-and-tell. She wanted to know how the forge worked, at what temperature the firepot needed to be to adequately heat the iron, what each tool was used for, and what types of things he had made thus far. The conversation then turned to projects he was planning. Rainey told her about a fixed-blade knife he intended to make and the materials that would be used from start to completion.

Finally, she asked with sincerity if she could give it a try. Rainey smiled and easily gave in. He handed her an apron and some thick gloves and kindled a flame in the forge. When the level of heat was right and with Rainey's careful instruction, Evelina pulled a metal rod from the fire. The far end was bright red. Rainey guided her to the anvil, then hovered over her as he described the proper technique of hammering. Before long, she had given the rod a proper tapered end. It now took on the appearance of a thin, medieval pike.

At last, Evelina thrust the rod into a bucket of cold water and a sudden burst of steam erupted into the air. Rainey freed her of the rod and handed her a clean, blue paper towel, which she used to dab the beads of sweat from her forehead. He paced to a wooden upright beam affixed to which was a large iron hook. He pulled down a blackened rag from it and wiped the wetness from the rod. When it was clean and dry, he held it up in a beam of setting sun that was right now shooting across the room through one of the building's leaded windows. He twisted the rod between his fingers, scrutinizing the craftsmanship.

Evelina looked on in silence, eyes wide with exhilaration.

Finally, with nary a show of humor, he handed it to her and proclaimed, "Looks like you get the point."

ACKNOWLEDGMENTS

Thank you to **Almighty God**. For without You, and the redeeming work of **Your Son**, **Jesus Christ**, there would be nothing worth writing about. May You be glorified in all that I say and do and write.

To my wonderful wife, **Jill**. Thank you for loving me and for supporting me from the very first moment I set out on this crazy writing journey. I love you!

Claire and **Jackson**, I am extremely proud of you both! Congratulations on all of your accomplishments, including your recent graduations! Watching you grow and mature into fine human beings has brought your mom and me so much joy. I can't wait to see what God has in store. Thank you for your love and support...as well as your patience during my bouts of write-life frustration. You mean the world to me.

Thank you as well to the rest of **my family**. I'm truly blessed to have such encouraging, God-fearing people in my life.

One special person who I've been blessed to have met early in my writing career is author **Jan Thompson**. I often think of her as my literary guardian angel. She's such a constant source of joy, encouragement, wisdom, and guidance. Always friendly. Always quick to offer a kind piece of advice or lend a helping hand. Thank you, Jan, for all you have done for me and so many other authors out there as well. You exhibit what it truly means to be a Christ-follower.

Beth Murray and **Debbie Jamieson** were gracious in reading early versions of the manuscript. Both offered valuable feedback, for which I am especially grateful. However, since I do all of the editing of my books, I therefore take full ownership of any mistakes, typos, etc., that readers may find.

The following are dear author friends who have been steadfast supporters of me and my writing over the years. Allow me to offer a special, heartfelt thank you to **Eric Bishop, Luana Ehrlich, John Galt Robinson, Steven Wilson, Ryan Steck, Brian Andrews & Jeffrey Wilson**. If you haven't already, please check out their incredible books. Thanks also to Eric Bishop for the recon work in NYC. Hopefully, you're not on a list somewhere now.

The writing community is such a friendly place. I've made so many wonderful friends since I first laid pen to paper. What's truly remarkable is when other authors agree to provide blurbs for your book. The following folks were extremely gracious in doing so for *Agency at War*: **Jack Stewart, Steve Urszenyi, Colleen Coble, Bob Hamer**, as well as my friends **Ryan Steck, aka the Real Book Spy**, and the killer writing duo **Andrews & Wilson**. I greatly respect each of these authors and highly recommend their books. Go grab some now. You'll be happy that you did.

Several folks aided me in my research of various aspects of the story. Thank you to **Peer Sandberg**, my Norwegian friend and fellow brother in blue. Perhaps I'll get to visit you in *your* office someday. **Fred Burton**, I appreciate not only your insights on Hezbollah but also your comments on embassy life and what it's like to be an intelligence officer in denied areas. **Steve Adelmann** of Citizen Arms graciously offered his considerable, experience-based knowledge about gear and firearms. I'd love to hit the range sometime with you, Steve. You've doubtless forgotten more than I'll ever know when it comes to trigger-pulling. **Scott Swanson** provided valuable details on money-laundering techniques that bad actors commonly utilize. What a fascinating subject.

And to that small cadre of folks who wish to remain nameless. I thank you from the bottom of my heart for your contributions to this book.

Thank you to **America's real warrior spies**—the real "ghosts." I know you're out there, working in the shadows for peace, for good, and for our national security objectives. Intelligence is a tough and oftentimes dirty business. Your sacrifice and commitment to America and its citizens are critical for our free society to remain so. You will never be forgotten. At least not by me.

Likewise, to **everyone serving in uniform**, from the newest cadets and privates to those at the highest levels of our military, to the pilots, the special operators, the medics, logistics specialists, mechanics, and everyone in between, who strap in and strap on and head downrange to combat the worst of humanity all around the globe, you inspire me. The same goes for those on the law-enforcement side of the house, **my brothers and sisters in blue** at the local, state, and federal levels. My family and I offer you our deepest gratitude.

I also want to give a big shoutout to the brave pundits and podcasters, reporters and journalists, everyone who fearlessly dares to speak and seek truth and proudly stands firm for America's founding principles and traditional values. Even when it's not popular to do so. Tacitus is credited with the saying: "In valor, there is hope." This simple but powerful statement is well-known to the police and military communities. But the same could be said of the brave men and women on the battlefields in the war of information. Remain steadfast. Fight on. And never give up. The noble cause of freedom requires it.

I consulted numerous books and articles during the research phase of this book. Perhaps I'll reveal some in future Reader Intel Bulletins (my email newsletter). If you have questions about something you've read, please don't hesitate to reach out. I love to engage with readers.

On occasion, I took dramatic license to move the story along, protect real tactics, techniques, and procedures, or, frankly, just because I felt like it. This book is fiction, after all.

If you enjoyed *Agency at War*, I encourage you to check out my other novels. Please consider leaving a review—even if it's just a few words—on Amazon, Goodreads, and anywhere you buy books. Reviews are crucial for authors to survive in our modern world, which is crowded with millions and millions of books. Share the love on social media, too. In addition, I strongly and humbly urge you to tell a friend or family member about my books. Word of mouth is perhaps the best way for authors to reach new readers.

Whether you're a reader, the host of a podcast, a book club member, or someone who just wants to talk books, please don't hesitate to reach out or connect with me on social media. Of course, you can always find me through my website at **DonyJayBooks.com**. I love hearing from readers and fellow book addicts!

Lastly, to **my wonderful readers**, thank you! I consider each of you a friend and appreciate you more than you know. Until we meet again...

God bless!
DJ

ABOUT THE AUTHOR

DONY JAY attended Penn State University and York College of Pennsylvania. He holds a BS degree in criminal justice. Dony is a police detective with over 22 years of law-enforcement experience. He has served on a US Marshals Fugitive Task Force and is currently a member of a county-wide Child Abduction Response Team (CART) and his department's forensic unit. When he's not reading or writing, Dony loves spending time with his family, staying fit, and cheering on the Philadelphia Eagles. Above all, he's a follower of Jesus Christ. He resides in south-central Pennsylvania.

To learn more about the author, go to **DonyJayBooks.com**. He invites you to sign up for his email newsletter—Dony Jay's Reader Intel Bulletin—to stay up to date with the latest news. And don't forget to follow Dony on social media.

www.ingramcontent.com/pod-product-compliance
Lightning Source LLC
Chambersburg PA
CBHW030333120726
47901CB00007B/1777